I0590211

This is a work of fiction. Names, characters, places, and incidences are either the product of the author's imagination or are used fictitiously, and any resemblance to actual persons living or dead, business establishments, events, or locales, is entirely coincidental.

Cover Art—Beautiful Book Covers by Ivy

Developmental Edits—Rachel Throp and Susan Marie Graham

Copywrite/line Edits—Jessica McKeldon

ISBN 979-8-9925456-0-9 (ebook)

ISBN 979-8-9925456-1-6 (paperback)

*To Kara*
*For being a beautiful force of nature.*

# ALSO BY A. GORDON

## WRITING AS ALEX GORDON

Wicked Wish

Wildest Wish

# CRIMSON JEWEL

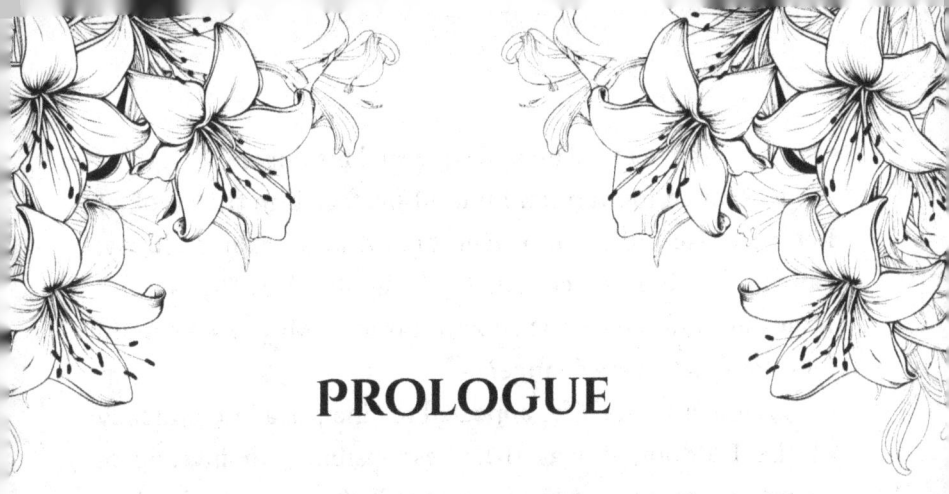

# PROLOGUE

S inai stared at her son Raiden with a heavy heart. His eyes flashed like liquid silver as he laughed at his cousin Loch's—more than likely—filthy joke. Except for the color of their eyes, they could've physically passed as twins. Personality-wise, they were exceptionally different.

Loch was studious, serious, and responsible at the ripe old age of thirteen and a half. Raiden, six months his junior, followed his instincts, was primal, and had trouble with authority.

Sinai pressed her hand to her lips, hiding her smile. Most of *those* characteristics had come from her side of the family. So, as they said, karma was a bitch. But despite Raiden's rebellious streak—which she secretly admired—she couldn't have been prouder of her only son, or her nephew.

"Are you ready?" her husband, Eyal, asked. He stepped behind her and set his hand on her shoulder. Even after twenty years of marriage, a wave of electricity traveled over her body, sending shivers up her spine.

"No." She reached up and squeezed his fingers.

He leaned forward and buried his face into the crook of her neck. He pulled in a deep breath and exhaled slowly, causing her long black hair to tickle her skin. "Sylvia and Issac have offered to track down this lead. Maybe we should let *them* search for a change?"

As much as the offer appealed to Sinai, as a lord and lady of the Fiefdom, it was their responsibility to investigate reports pertaining to the prophecy if the lead was in their jurisdiction. She cocked her head, giving the idea pause. She was tired of leaving Raiden behind to be cared for by her sister, Sylvia. While she knew no harm would come to him, her sister was a selfish woman bearing no maternal instincts. Though, in the Fiefdom, every child was cherished, and Loch was no different. Sinai might have not birthed him, but she loved him just the same. When she and Eyal were home, Loch often lived with them. The two boys were inseparable.

"You know we can't. Besides, something about this information seems different. My gut tells me we are close to finding her. I can't in good conscience leave this in Sylvia's hands."

Over the last thousand years, the prophecy pertaining to their salvation had been widely interpreted. But Sinai didn't take the words of the bygone queen as literally as some of the other giants in the realm. *The Crimson Jewel it will take for Obsidian the gate to break.* She believed the Crimson Jewel was a person, not an actual stone. If giants wanted to survive, they needed to find the savior promised to them. Their existence depended on it.

"You're probably right," Eyal grumbled.

"Darling, I'm always right." She chuckled, tugging

gently on his earlobe. "Loch, Raiden, come give us hugs. We have to leave," she hollered over their laughter.

Raiden zipped in front of Loch and buried himself in her arms. At a hair under seven feet tall, he was nearly as big as she was, though his limbs were long and gangly. In a few years, when he filled out, he was bound to be devastatingly handsome. They both were.

She sniffed away her pooling tears. "You be good. You hear me?" She hugged him tighter.

He nodded into her shoulder. "Bring me back something good," he said.

"What would you boys like?" She traded Raiden's embrace for Loch's.

Loch looked at her with wide, aqua eyes. "Oh, Auntie, I'm desperate to read more fantasy books. Something about giants would be entertaining. Humans get so little about us right."

Raiden groaned as he jabbed his cousin with an elbow. "A knife. Or a sword. Or a crossbow."

Eyal simultaneously messed up their dark hair. "We'll do our best, boys."

"Thanks," they said in unison before they raced off to find trouble.

Sinai didn't worry about them—much. Loch's good sense kept them from venturing too close to danger, and Raiden's strength and courage kept them safe when they strayed.

Sinai walked over to Arnold, her beloved pegasus, tied to the paddock fence. He snorted and tossed his head impatiently, ready to take to the skies.

Navarre, her black dire wolf and constant shadow, sat on

his haunches as he let out a sorrowful howl, fearing he'd be left behind.

"Do you think we should take him or leave him with the kids?" she asked.

"They'll be fine, dearest. Let's take him with." Eyal patted the wolf's side heavily.

She leaned over, looking the massive beast in the eyes. "Okay, you can go, but you can't accompany us to Earth. You have to stay behind with Arnold."

Navarre barked in agreement and twirled with excitement. He danced on his paws as he waited for Eyal to strap the riding basket under Arnold's belly. Arnold's tail twitched as he stamped a hoof. He was only a few years old and still getting used to the contraption. Once it was secured, Navarre jumped inside the basket and laid down.

Sinai stroked the midnight feathers on Arnold's wings to calm him before she climbed onto the saddle. Eyal mounted his pegasus and nodded when he was ready. Once they were in the air, she turned and waved to the boys.

If she'd only known it was to be their final goodbye.

It took Eyal and Sinai less than a day to arrive at the portal that would lead them to Earth.

After they landed in a small valley surrounded by a ring of snowcapped mountains, Navarre hopped out of the riding basket and immediately marked the nearest tree. Sinai unsaddled Arnold and pressed a kiss to his nose before she pushed him away and slapped him on his rump. He ran toward the meadow, kicking up his feet. Their loyal pets would hang around the vicinity until they returned from their mission.

She patted the knife at her waist and adjusted the blade in the scabbard strapped to her back. Though dressed in contemporary clothing—black tactical gear and combat boots—modern weapons, such as guns and tasers, were useless to giants. They could pull the trigger, but for some mysterious reason, the weapons wouldn't fire. She'd assumed it was the magic in their blood that negated their ability to use them.

And while giants were almost invincible in the Fiefdom, even bullets didn't harm them so long as they were within its protective veil, Earth was a different story. They were still stronger and faster than humans, but the moment they set foot upon the soil, they became vulnerable. Modern weapons didn't work *for* giants—but on earth, they worked *on* them.

Trying to abate the building apprehension, she rubbed along her sternum as she walked toward the portal. She stopped in front of the shimmering hole in the ground and peered inside the dark interior. The gateway was a stairwell carved from black obsidian with ten-foot walls and deep treads. The Fiefdom relied on this stone for its magic, though if the prophecy didn't come to pass soon, it wouldn't matter how much magic the stone held. Extinction was in their near future. For the last one thousand years, their population had steadily dwindled. In the last decade, no child had been born.

Eyal walked up next to her and grabbed her hand before they stepped down into the stairwell, breaking through the electrical barrier securing their world. It didn't affect giants, but a human would instantly die from the voltage.

Side by side, they bounded down the stairs two at a time.

Last week, their scouts had informed them that there was a faction of humans living in a bunker near Girdwood,

Alaska. Not unusual. The curious part was, as far as they could gather, in the last two years, no one there had died of natural causes, only accidents. Considering the turmoil and violence Earth and her people experienced daily, that, in itself, was strange. Then there were the rumors of a redheaded girl around the age of twelve that the remaining military seemed particularly interested in.

Sinai felt in her bones—this girl—she was the key. *The Crimson Jewel.*

As Sinai and Eyal came to the end of the stairwell, they paused for a moment.

"You ready?" Eyal asked.

She heaved out a long breath between puffed cheeks and nodded reluctantly.

She set foot onto the soft, moss-covered ground and waited for her husband to follow.

The scent of human sweat and raw onions tickled her nose a second before a bolt of electricity threw her twenty feet backward. She landed in a mud puddle with a splash, her body twitching with the voltage.

The last thing she saw before she succumbed to the darkness was the hazy outline of humans wielding an array of weapons.

———

LATER, when Sinai awoke, she was lying on a green cot behind a set of iron bars. Eyal was across the cell on his own cot. She sat up with a groan. One hand darted to her waist, the other between her shoulders to find her weapons missing. She checked the pocket inside her boot and growled when she came up empty-handed. Whoever had put them there had confiscated all her gear.

She rose on trembling legs and shook Eyal's shoulder violently. "Wake up," Sinai hissed. She held onto the concrete wall to maintain her balance.

Eyal groaned as he rolled over to vomit off the side of the cot. "What happened?" He wiped his mouth with the back of his hand. "That tasted like thornberries."

Her eyes widened. An electric shock would take a giant down momentarily, but a dose of thornberries would incapacitate them for hours. "We've been double-crossed," she said, not quite believing it. But if he tasted thornberries, then it was the logical explanation. The toxic plant only grew in the Fiefdom.

"It seems so." His face said everything his voice didn't.

Sinai was thankful he'd left it at that. He didn't care for her sister Sylvia. Over the years, he'd questioned her motives on various issues. He believed Sylvia wanted Loch to be the First-Born son, not Raiden. Sinai had always defended her sister, trusting she wasn't evil.

"Hello," a feminine voice said from outside the cell.

Sinai jumped toward the bars, Eyal seconds behind her. He growled low in his throat.

"Please, I'm not here to hurt you." The woman held up pale, freckled hands.

"Let us go," Eyal demanded. He curled his fingers around the bars, his knuckles whitening with pressure. Normal steel would bend under his strength.

"If only I could," the woman sighed. "Though I'm not behind bars, I'm as much of a prisoner as you are."

"I doubt that," Sinai said.

The woman tucked a long strand of wild, red hair behind

7

her ear. "You might be surprised," she whispered under her breath.

"Where are we?" Eyal asked.

"You're on Elmendorf Air Force Base in Anchorage, Alaska."

"What do you want with us?" Sinai slid next to Eyal and set a hand on his shoulder.

The woman clasped her chest. "Me? Nothing. If I had my choice, I'd let you go." Her eyes darted to the corner of the room.

Sinai spotted a small red light coming from a tiny black box near the ceiling.

"But them? I'm a geneticist and they want me to study you. They want to see if your pure blood will help them create a line of humans with your strength that are resistant to disease and death. More than likely, they want to build an army."

Sinai's eyes narrowed. "So you know what we are then?"

"Yes, of course. A few months ago, two others—one a woman who resembled you—" she pointed to Sinai, "—came here. I don't know what they wanted or why they were here. Seeing as I'm a prisoner, the commander doesn't tell me much, but they did tell me to prepare my lab for your arrival."

Sinai gritted her teeth. Sylvia and her husband, Issac, had taken a holiday trip to the capital about three months ago. She wondered if they'd come here instead. Had they fed the scouts false information to lure her and Eyal to Earth? Her sister didn't believe in the prophecy, but Sinai did. Taking account of all the evidence, it seemed Sinai was mistaken. Sylvia *was* evil and this was her perfect execution of bait and wait.

And now, not only would it cost them their lives, but it might cost Raiden his as well.

She squeezed her eyes shut and pressed the pads of her fingers over her lids as anger bloomed behind her ribs. They'd lied about where they were going and what they'd been doing—and she knew the reason why, even if she didn't want to admit it. If she and Eyal were eliminated, their titles of lord and lady would pass to Sylvia and Issac. Then they would have the power to usurp Raiden's inheritance and declare Loch the First-Born son. If the prophecy came to pass, then Loch had a chance at being crowned king.

Not that Sinai thought Loch was a bad choice—she had often mused he was more fit for lordship than Raiden. But by proxy, Sylvia would be named the queen regent if Loch was not yet of age. And if he was, she would still be the queen mother. Even though Sylvia wasn't overly fond of humans, she would have no qualms about marrying her son off to one if it meant she could wield more power.

Nausea sloshed in the pit of Sinai's stomach. *Her son. Her baby.* She could only hope Sylvia would demote him and not have him murdered. Lord help her sister if Sinai got out of this alive.

The redheaded woman pulled a small knife out of her pocket, unfolded it, and pricked her finger. A small amount of blood welled at the tip. She stepped up to the bars and stuck her hand inside the cage.

"Awfully trusting, aren't you?" A wicked smile curled Sinai's lips. Though she wasn't as strong here on Earth as she was in the Fiefdom, tearing off the woman's limb with her bare hands wouldn't be a problem.

The woman quirked a brow over her rich-brown eyes but didn't answer. "Taste it."

Deciding against violence, Sinai licked the blood from the woman's finger. Her breath hitched in surprise at the familiar taste. A small amount of giant blood ran in the woman's veins.

The woman turned her head sideways, away from the blinking red light. She whispered so softly a human wouldn't be able to pick up what she said. "If you want to escape, you're going to have to trust me and my husband. I need you to be at your strongest for my plan to work." She stepped back, her voice going to a normal volume again. "My name's Scarlet, and that's my husband, Angus." She canted her head toward the back of the room, where a tall man with broad shoulders stepped out of the shadows. A black curl fell over a set of very blue eyes as he nodded his head in greeting. "We're the Walkers."

# CHAPTER
# ONE

During those rare moments when someone, or something, wasn't trying to kill me, my subconscious *still* tried coaxing me into false security. *Relax. Everything will be fine.* But I'd been fooled before.

I scanned the tree line along the riverbank and cocked an ear toward the sky as I listened for predators—in particular, the On-Grids. After the fall of the modern world, a militia took over the old military base in Anchorage, Alaska —Joint Base Elmendorf-Richardson, better known as JBER. Once a day—everyday—they sent out a scouting party in either a helicopter or a prop plane. For some unknown reason, they hounded our every move. It was difficult enough trying to survive in this post-apocalyptic nightmare without them hunting us.

When I didn't see or hear anything, I sat on a log perched above the fishing hole to keep watch. A beam of sunlight reflected on my brother's copper hair as he pulled off his hat to adjust the fit.

"Kevin, you better hurry and put that thing back on

before the neon glow sends out an SOS to the wrong people," my best friend, Tee, said.

As a man of few words, he reached over and messed up Tee's hair, the colorful beads at the ends of her dark braids clicking together.

Sid, my dog, curled around my feet. His pointed ears twitched as he listened too. He was solid black and twice the size of a normal shepherd—and had twice the intelligence of most humans—so our best guess was that he was a German Shepherd-wolf mix.

A few years ago, I'd found him caught in an old, rusted trap while I was out hunting. Normally, I would've done the humane thing and put him out of his misery, but instead of growling at me like a normal predator, he'd wagged his tail and whined, as if excited that help had finally arrived. Despite my training, I couldn't let him die. Something about the way he'd looked at me had penetrated my frosty heart. It was love at first sight. When I'd arrived back at our bunker carrying a seventy-pound puppy, Kevin had nearly lost his mind. I convinced him that if the dog lived, I would train him to guard our camp. Eventually, he'd agreed that my plan held merit.

Just as I reached down to pat the top of Sid's head, Tee squealed, and we both jumped.

"Ohhhhh! I got the first fish!"

The silver skin of a salmon flashed under the glacial-blue waters where Bird Creek met the Turnagain Arm of the Cook Inlet.

I hurried down the bank and grabbed the stun stick sitting next to the cooler. Tee reeled the fish out of the water while Kevin slid the net under her catch so it didn't get away. He reached for the stun stick, and I slapped it into his palm. With one hard whack to the head, the fish was dead, though it continued twitching.

"Yeah!" Tee clapped. "You owe me, Bea!" She pointed my direction.

Earlier, we'd made a bet as to who would catch the first fish. I was much more excited for her to win because she didn't get to go fishing often.

All thirty-seven of us who had clustered together for survival had assigned jobs. I provided meat. Tee and a few others prepared our food for the long winter. Rarely did we get a break, but this year was proving to be more abundant, so this morning, Kevin had suggested that the three of us go together. Four, if you counted Sid. And we did.

"I'll go grab the other cooler," Kevin said.

"No. I got it." I took off toward the parking lot before he could argue.

Our parents had disappeared twelve years ago after going to work and never returning. I was ten at the time, and Kevin was eighteen. He'd spent most of his life looking after me—and then everyone else who subsequently joined our motley group. He never relaxed, so when the opportunity presented itself for me to make his life easier, I took it.

Sid dashed ahead, down the crumbling stairs, and waited for me at the bottom. Just as I opened the back of the Jeep Wrangler, my ears honed in on the faint sound of rotor blades.

Sid barked, confirming the threat.

"Go!" Kevin yelled from above.

"I'll meet you at home!" I shouted.

Sid jumped in the back, and I slammed the tailgate before running to the driver's side and hopping behind the wheel. The tires spun, kicking up dust, as I raced out of the dilapidated parking lot.

I had no fear for Tee. Kevin was the king of badasses and would have her safely home in our underground bunker in no time. But erring on the side of caution, I turned onto the Seward Highway going in the opposite direction of home.

Tee, Kevin, and Sid were my everything, and I wasn't about to lose them. Kevin was going to kill me but I'd deal with him later.

I gripped the steering wheel with one hand, and the gear shift with the other. The off-road tires slipped and the transmission whined as it struggled over the broken highway. Years of earthquakes, landslides, and volcanoes had left the pavement rugged.

My eyes darted to the rearview mirror and my heart mule-kicked before landing in my throat. The black helicopter, with its nose tilted downward, had finally spotted me. I wasn't sure if the On-Grids were searching for me specifically, at least not this time. Though, because I often seemed to be their target, I yanked the baseball cap off my head and let my blood-red tresses fly. My hair was so bright, the man on the moon had to shield his eyes from the glow.

Kevin was literally going to kill me.

I dodged the chopper for a few more miles until the pavement disappeared, leaving a canyon too wide for the Jeep to navigate.

As we stopped, Sid launched out of the open top and waited for me next to the vehicle. The *thwap, thwap, thwap* of the rotor blades grew louder.

Quickly, I threw the keys under the floor mat and tossed my rucksack over my shoulders. I adjusted the 9mm sitting on one hip and the machete in its scabbard on the other.

My heart pinched as I tapped the mud-covered hood before whispering a silent goodbye to the 4x4. My dad had promised to teach me how to drive her one day, but the task had fallen to Kevin. He'd wasted no time putting me behind the wheel. I was ten when he'd said, "Ruby Rose, I wish this could wait, but with the way things are going, you might need this skill sooner rather than later." Unfortunately, he'd been right.

Concealed under the thick canopy of trees, I motioned for Sid to lead the way. He, like the rest of us, understood hand signals.

My worn hiking boots slipped over the crumbling asphalt, slick with moss, as I scrambled to keep up with Sid. Twenty feet ahead, he veered off the road into the northernmost tip of the Alaskan Pacific rainforest. Tiny shards of sunlight peppered between the branches of the spruce trees and birch, but never found their way to the forest floor.

"What are you doing?" I hissed.

He barked, sharply penetrating the humid air.

I thrust my finger in front of my lips to shush him. He knew better than to make noise. While the people chasing us were bad, the things lurking in the wilderness were worse.

He barked again.

My nostrils flared as I shook my head fiercely. He was going to get us killed.

When I stepped off the road, his ruckus ceased. "What are you doing?" I whispered through clenched teeth.

He jumped over a rotted log and peered back at me, the whiskers above his golden eyes twitching.

A wildlife trail was a gamble. While it made passage

easier, you never knew what might be lurking around the bend.

Grumbling, I thought about pulling my gun from its holster, but decided not to because it wouldn't do much good. After the downfall of civilization, only the strong and prepared survived. That applied to animals as well. Here in the land of the midnight sun, the bears, wolves, lynx, and moose were bigger and badder and smarter than ever before. Humans were once at the top of the food chain—now, our ranking was debatable.

Instead, I unsheathed my blade and swiped at the massive fiddlehead ferns. Their fibrous stalks sliced easily under my sharpened blade and toppled to the ground. The plants were also bigger, and some, like the cow parsnip, were badder. On a sunny day, one sting from its thorns could kill a person.

For added protection, I yanked the sleeves of my rain jacket down and pulled up the hood. A river of sweat poured down my back, soaking into the waistband of my cargos.

Our summers, though short, had become almost tropical after the climate change disaster. The environmental destruction progressed slowly in the beginning, then like a boulder rolling downhill, picked up speed.

First, the West Coast all but disappeared when it collapsed into the ocean after the giant quake. And what didn't go was washed away by a monstrous tsunami. In the plains and most of the South, temperatures plummeted and then skyrocketed, withering the land into a vast desert. The Midwest was now a swirling pot of calderas and burgeoning volcanoes, running the length of the continental divide.

In Girdwood, Alaska, the earth still shook—quite violently at times—the volcanoes still erupted, and the snow still fell, but I wasn't sure anywhere else in the world was safer.

In front of me, Sid stopped short and lifted his nose into the air. Shiny black hackles rose all the way to the tip of his tail. The overpowering scent of rotten fish oil and ripe urine surpassed the smell of damp earth and lush greenery. Dread coiled, waiting to spring as I stood motionless.

Deep inside the quiet forest, a branch snapped, echoing eerily and shattering my hopes that the bear had passed through a while ago.

Adrenaline spiked, sending pain to my fingers and toes. I gripped the machete tighter, and we bolted, ducking and dodging ferns, devil's club, and tree limbs. They slapped me across the face, leaving stinging welts behind. As my ankle rolled over an exposed root, I faltered. My free hand caught me on the muddy ground, but I managed to stay mostly upright and keep going.

Behind me, a roar thundered so powerfully that it reverberated inside my ribcage. The hairs on the back of my neck and arms prickled. Exertion cramped my muscles, but terror propelled me forward. And though I was faster and stronger than anyone else I knew, even I couldn't outrun a bear for long. But fleeing was the only logical choice. There was no standing your ground with these bears. Shooting them made them angry. Playing dead entertained them.

Somewhere up ahead, hidden from my view, Sid yelped. My heart froze. Only when he started barking again, did it resume beating. I could only assume he was making noise so I could locate him.

With my arms pumping, I almost shot past him—right past the strange staircase hidden in the middle of the forest.

It was a wonder. A black behemoth. Like finding a lost

altar in the middle of an uninhabited jungle. Massive obsidian steps with matching stone walls ran in a straight line upward, cutting through the underbrush. It went up and up and up until it disappeared into the fluffy white clouds.

A split second *WTF* flashed in my brain, but with the bear hot on my heels, I didn't have time to contemplate the oddity.

I slid to a stop and dashed inside the entrance. An electric shock zapped my skin. I flinched violently but scrambled up the stairs until my legs collapsed, and I fell next to Sid. I spun around to see if the bear would follow, but kept moving, scooting upward on my butt one step at a time, putting more distance between us. A hundred-yard head start wasn't sufficient for a creature that dangerous. I tried holding my breath to stay quiet, but my lungs scorched, begging for oxygen.

A huge shadow of an Alaskan brown bear, measuring six feet tall at the hump of his shoulders, paused in front of the staircase. Tiny slivers of light dappled his russet fur. His nostrils flexed and flared, searching for our scent. He huffed and chattered his teeth like he was trying to taste the air—trying to taste *us*. His ears twitched and his beady eyes drifted past as if we were invisible—as if he couldn't hear, see, or smell us. A frustrated bellow tore from his mouth and drool flung from his six-inch yellow canines.

I slapped my hands over my ears to muffle the noise.

After a long few seconds, he shook his enormous skull, then padded away silently.

My head sagged, and I breathed a sigh of relief before turning around to check on Sid. He rested on his haunches one step above mine, exhausted from the run. I scratched behind his ears. His tongue lagged while his sides heaved. I slipped off my pack to pour him a splash of water and took a sip myself. As he drank, I slid my machete into its case and tied my rain jacket around my waist.

Then I turned my attention to the strange staircase. I briefly questioned whether I'd been stung by the thorn of a cow parsnip plant. Its toxins not only hurt like a mother but were hallucinatory. I rubbed my eyes. Perhaps I was high? Maybe dead? Was this the stairway to heaven?

The polished obsidian slabs, so shiny and glasslike they looked wet, were three times the depth of a normal step. They reached toward the sky, beyond the towering canopy of trees, past the wispy white clouds, until they disappeared. The volcanic stone, prevalent in Alaska, flanked the entire stairwell but didn't enclose the ceiling. I laid my palm on the surface, expecting it to be hot under the direct sunlight, but it was as cold as ice.

I was confused, and though I felt physically fine, was I? I touched my forehead—no fever, and I wasn't clammy either. No funny taste in my mouth, and besides the strange staircase, no weird visions. All motor functions intact.

I wanted to investigate the enigma further, but my need to see if Kevin and Tee were safe overrode my curiosity. I'd bring them back later—they weren't going to believe me unless they witnessed this thing themselves.

Not one to let a mystery go unsolved, I sighed. But we'd lost enough friends and family out here that I didn't want Kevin and Tee to worry.

Sid barked again.

"What?" I snapped. My patience was waning. I was tired and hungry and sweaty.

He bounded further up the stairs, his nails clicking on the smooth surface.

"No!" I slapped my arms against my sides.

He responded with a single bark. And people said animals didn't talk back. Obviously, Sid had missed the memo.

"We need to go!"

Sid ignored me as he continued upward. It wasn't like him to disobey, so I assumed he knew something I didn't. Maybe the bear was loitering?

There was no way I was leaving him behind, so I followed. Sid was family. Plus, Kev was probably back at our bunker by now, safe and cozy. He wouldn't come looking for me because we were bound by a promise not to. Well, he'd wait a few days before he started his search.

As we ascended, I expected the air to get heavy and damp, like when you hiked a mountain into the clouds. But instead, it got lighter and sweeter, like clean sheets hung on a clothes line. About a quarter of a mile into the climb, we discovered a door off to the side of the staircase made of the same black stone and carved with foreign symbols. Sid stopped and waited as I traced my fingers over the ciphers before pushing, but the door didn't budge. I pushed harder and then slapped it for good measure. Nothing. I hopped up a few more steps and patted Sid on his ribs.

"Haven't you had enough? It's gonna take at least a day to reach the top." It was a never-ending journey. I certainly wasn't going to make it today. My legs had already filed a complaint with the boss.

He sat down a few feet above, facing me, and barked. His tail wagged rapidly, dusting over the surface.

"You're not welcome here, human," a deep voice said from behind me.

My nerve endings flared, and I muffled a scream. Instinctively, I reached for my gun.

"That's not going to help you here, human."

I spun around, locking eyes with the coldest set of irises I'd ever witnessed—the color of menacing thunderclouds.

He stood three treads away with his hands draping loosely at his sides. His hair was short, almost military style, and dark. I assumed he was near my age, somewhere in his early twenties. I'd seen pictures of handsome men in my mom's old magazines, but never to this extent. Gorgeous didn't cover it. Flawless. Ethereal. Angelic. Even as he glared at me with those cold steel eyes.

He stepped up another rung. And then another. I estimated each riser to be a foot high, and I was six feet tall, so that made him around seven feet. I gripped my firearm tighter, but I didn't pull it from the holster. Yet.

His gray eyes darted to my weapon before meeting my gaze. A dark brow quirked in a dare. "Feeling lucky, *human*?"

What was with this guy calling me human like it was an insult? He looked human too—two eyes, two ears, a nose, a mouth, and ten fingers. Yup, he appeared human down to his utility pants and the white T-shirt that pulled tightly across his chest and abs, leaving little to this girl's imagination. *No judgment.* We had slim pickings when it came to eligible men.

He joined me on my step, invading my personal bubble, and scowled. A vibration in the air tickled my bare skin. I wanted to swat the sensation away like a mosquito.

"I'm going to ask you this only once. How did you get in here?" he snarled.

I saw no reason to lie. It wasn't like we'd broke down a door or knocked out a window. "We were being chased by a bear." I gave him a once-over. He wasn't a threat, just some overgrown dude with an attitude. I spent my days competing with crafty predators to provide food for my friends and family. This guy was nothing.

His eyes narrowed, intensifying the lines between his brows. "You're not supposed to be here," he said, almost as if I was bothering him.

I shrugged. "I don't know what to tell you, pal. Sid got in. I followed. I figured it was safer in here than out there."

He threw his head back and laughed, covering his mouth with a hand. The sound was as cold as his eyes. "Don't be so sure about that."

"Well, let us go by—" I glanced down the stairs past him, "—and we'll leave. No harm, no foul." I raised my left hand as a white flag.

He crossed his arms, bulging muscles straining against the sleeves. "You're not going anywhere, *human*."

# CHAPTER
# TWO

I snapped my head toward Sid and glared. *This* was a bad idea. We should've turned around and gone home after the bear left.

Even though the guy was blocking my way, I wasn't intimidated. I was used to dealing with mutant predators, and he was human. A weaponless one at that. Plus, my instincts weren't screaming at me to run, and Sid wasn't growling. Nevertheless, I was going home because what scared me was trying to get back to the bunker after dusk. Bears. Lynx. And especially the wolves. I shivered. Even the moose could be problematic.

"Get out of my way." I met the guy's cranky scowl with one of my own as I stepped to the side. The staircase was wide enough to accommodate both of us.

He spread out his arms and touched the walls with the palms of his hands, cocking his head as if saying, *I dare you.*

"I said—get out of my way."

An ugly snarl lifted the corner of his lip and exposed

what looked like a fang. "No." His tone was absolute and deadly serious.

My breath hitched. My pulse double timed, the hair on my neck bristled, and those instincts finally kicked in. I'd misjudged him—he was a predator. He checked enough of the boxes—he had fangs, and he wasn't going to let me go home. I'd killed for less.

Sid, instead of barking and growling like he normally would for a threat, whined.

"Heel." I snapped my fingers, and he took his position next to my leg.

A breeze carrying the faint scent of peppermint cooled the clammy layer of sweat beading on my forehead. My heartbeat echoed inside my skull, muting all other noise. I retreated a step.

I'd give him one more chance to voluntarily stand down. My hand hovered over the holster.

He blinked lazily, his deep-set eyes shadowed by his thick lashes.

"Move. Now," I demanded. This time, I pulled the gun from my holster and held the weapon steady. "Don't make me do this." I had been taught early in life never to point a gun at someone if you weren't willing to use it.

A tight-lipped chuckle rumbled in his throat as he shook his head.

*Did he just laugh at me?*

Without any more hesitation, I pulled the trigger. The shot boomed, then echoed inside the stairwell.

He slapped his hand to his chest, but when he pulled it away there was no blood, only a single hole in his T-shirt. "Ouch," he said, sounding more amused than hurt.

I was having trouble registering his bizarre reaction, but

before I could shoot him again, he ripped the gun from my hand and tossed it carelessly over the side of the stone barrier. He was so fast I didn't see him move. *At all.*

"What!?" I glanced after my favorite weapon, then back at him. I tried swallowing but my throat was desert dry.

"Don't be stupid. That toy won't help you where we're going," I heard him say over the ringing in my ears.

With Sid next to me, I retreated up another step, never taking my eyes off the guy. I stared at his chest. He should've been bleeding. I couldn't have missed at that distance. Not possible. I didn't miss at any distance. Besides, there was a hole in his T-shirt. Maybe he wore Kevlar? At the least, he should've been knocked backward. Most people would've tumbled down the staircase and ended up in a heap at the bottom. I questioned my original assessment of him being human.

"And where exactly are we going?" My voice betrayed me by shaking.

"Home." He casually slipped his hands into his pockets as if I hadn't just shot him.

"Good. Let's go," I shouted the order to Sid as I tried dodging past.

Again, he moved superhuman fast. I smacked into the middle of his chest, falling backward and bouncing onto my butt. My tailbone zinged, though I held back the profanity trolling through my head.

Studying him, I could see the similarities to a famous comic book superhero—dark hair, light eyes, and wide shoulders. Throw a set of thick-framed glasses on his face and bingo—hottest reporter ever.

"My home, not yours," he grumbled. He held out a hand, offering to help me up.

*How chivalrous.* I ignored him and stayed on the frigid stone.

"Now. I don't have all day." He snapped his fingers when he realized I wasn't going to take his hand. "Don't make me carry you," he said in a tone that suggested I was pathetic.

I frowned—that's exactly what I'd been thinking. I should make him carry me and put those obscene muscles to good use, but I wasn't ready to humiliate myself yet. An internal smile bloomed behind my schooled expression. He had to sleep sometime, and I still had my machete tucked under the rain jacket tied at my waist.

---

FOR HOURS WE CLIMBED. Sweat ran between my boobs, pooled in the small of my back, and dripped further down, giving me a serious case of swamp ass, as Kevin would call it.

I glanced over my shoulder, contemplating trying my luck again. I wasn't worried about Kevin and Tee. I knew they were safe. What worried me was Kevin organizing a search party when I didn't show up at home by tomorrow morning. He would head straight for JBER, the home of the On-Grids—the place our parents made us promise to never, not ever, no matter the circumstances go near. For me, Kevin would ignore their warning.

"Don't even think about it. You won't make it ten feet," the guy said.

He was right. I needed some rest. My legs, already screaming after running from a bear, trembled uncontrollably. I'd stumbled more than once.

This time when I dropped, I didn't get back up.

My head lolled between my shoulders and debris

stabbed my knees and palms. "That's it. I can't go any further. You're going to have to drag me the rest of the way," I panted.

"Don't think I won't, *human*."

"Enough with the *human* already." I slapped the step and instantly regretted it as pain shot up my forearm. "I got it. I'm human. Congratulations for noticing. Would you like a gold star?" I'd lost my *give-a-shits* a few hours ago.

The color of his eyes swirled. "Fine. We'll stop for the night."

My rucksack slipped from my weary shoulders, and I leaned against the wall. The icy cold soothed my back.

"Not out here," he said.

I looked around but didn't state the obvious, though I was certain my expression conveyed my internal sarcasm. For miles in either direction was a staircase. I sniffed and rubbed under my nose.

He walked up a few steps to a small landing and placed his hand against the wall, saying something in a language I'd never heard. As he spoke, the hairs on my arms lifted like his words held magic. But magic didn't exist. Truthfully, I wasn't sure if I was hallucinating or not. Maybe I had been stung by a cow parsnip. And if I was tripping, would I even realize it?

Miraculously, a door appeared in the obsidian stone, right in front of him. He slid it aside and waved for me to go in first. Sid dashed inside.

Reluctantly, I stood and dragged my bag up the steps. I hesitated in front of the entrance to peer through the opening. The black interior absorbed the sunlight as if it were forbidden from passing over the threshold.

"If I wanted to kill you, I would've done it already and

tossed your body over the side for the scavengers to eat." I turned and caught his polite smile, though it didn't reach his eyes.

A chill ran down my spine like someone walking over my future grave.

I stepped into the cave-like room and the temperature plummeted. As my vision adjusted to the dark, a couple of benches and two worn sleeping cots appeared around a blackened firepit.

He followed me inside and started to close the door.

Pretending to freak out, I yelled, "No! Please! I'm claustrophobic. If you shut that, I'm going to have a full-fledged panic attack." I forced my breathing fast and shallow because I didn't want him to think I was lying. I wasn't claustrophobic. I lived in an underground bunker. And I didn't suffer from anxiety, but he didn't know that.

I bit down hard on the side of my lip. "Please," I whispered in my best damsel-in-distress voice. Though in reality, I was more of a damsel-causing-the-distress kind of girl.

He grunted but didn't shut the door as he whisked past me and grabbed an armload of wood from the back of the cave. He squatted down and arranged some logs in the fire pit, stuffing tinder under the teepee formation. With a flint and a puff of gentle air, the flames roared to life. The wood snapped and popped, sending glowing ashes drifting into the air.

Finished, he sat down on the bench closest to the exit, leaving the other one free. Sid, after having explored the tributaries of the cave sufficiently, jumped on one of the cots, curled in a tight ball, and fell asleep.

I was a bit concerned about the way my dog was handling our predicament. His instincts were usually spot-on. It was part of the reason I wasn't particularly afraid of the guy, just more concerned about getting home.

My captor dug through his backpack and offered me some dried jerky.

I shook my head and sat down on the oversized bench.

"Suit yourself." As he ripped off a large bite, his fangs glinted in the firelight.

"What *are* you?" I hugged my legs to my chest.

"What do you think I am?" An unfriendly smile lifted one corner of his lips.

*Demon? Elf? Supervillain?* My list was growing. I'd now moved on to vampires, though I was questioning the whole sunlight thing.

He stopped chewing and swallowed. "What, no guesses?"

I shrugged. None that I was willing to voice.

"Fee, Fie, Foe, Fum, I smell the blood of an Englishman. Be he alive or be he dead, I'll grind his bones to make my bread."

"What?"

My voice must've lacked the necessary awe because he scoffed. "Oh, come on. You've never heard that poem?"

"Of course I have." My mom used to read *Jack and the Beanstalk* to me all the time. "Seriously? Are you trying to say you're a *giant*? You're . . . kind of small." I gave him a once-over. And insanely hot. I didn't remember *that* part of the story—or had my mom accidentally left it out? I didn't believe in giants any more than I believed in vampires or Santa Claus.

Or magic staircases in the middle of the forest . . .

He stood up. His shadow rose on the cave wall, long and distorted behind the dancing flames, looking very much like the giant he claimed to be. "You think I'm small?" He tapped his muscular chest twice and then held his hands out in a question. "You think *this* is small to a ten-year-old boy?"

"Well, I guess if you're trying to intimidate a *child*, I suppose not." Though between the massive width of his shoulders, his height, and his pointy teeth, perhaps he *was* a bit frightening.

He ripped off another large bite of jerky and chewed slowly as he sat back down.

*Wait? Did he say* . . . My eyes darted toward the dried meat he held in his hand, then uneasily to the fire.

He tossed his head back and roared with glee. My stomach clenched.

"I'm not going to eat you. We quit doing that years ago. Well, at least most of us stopped." He held the jerky out and waved it around. "It's chicken."

I wasn't sure. I'd heard rumors that humans tasted like chicken. Cannibals called the plump meat above the thumb the drumstick.

Sid, predictably awake in the presence of meat, jumped off the cot and promptly sat in front of the dude, drool dripping on the dirt floor. He pawed at his leg, begging for a bite. I didn't blame him. It broke my heart to see his ribs under his skin. I always shared my food with him, but it was never enough. I'd grown used to the constant gnawing inside my belly and the gauntness under my cheekbones.

He stroked Sid's head and handed him a piece of the mystery meat. "You remind me of Navarre, my mom's dire wolf."

Sid, always the gentleman, took it politely despite his hunger.

"*Ladyhawke*? Is he named after the wolf in the movie?" I said before I could catch myself.

The guy's eyes flashed to mine and his expression held a sort of awe. "Yeah. I love that movie."

"Me too." For a second, comradery brewed.

As if to build on it, he offered me the other half of the meat. When I declined, he gave the rest to Sid.

"You scared to eat it?" he asked.

*Maybe.* "No. I have my own food." Digging through my pack, I pulled out an expired energy bar. I ripped open the brittle packaging and shoved a bite into my mouth. It tasted like dirt and went down the wrong pipe. A cough racked my chest.

He handed me a glass bottle. "Take a drink."

I shook my head. Tears ran freely while my lungs gasped for breath. He patted me on the back, his hands hot even through my shirt.

"It's just water." He took a swig and then jiggled it in front of my face. He stood there and waited for me to drink.

I relented. The cool liquid soothed my throat.

Once my coughing fit passed, he screwed the lid back on and set it next to me then unrolled a sleeping bag, placed it on his cot, and sat down. "My name's Jack, by the way."

"No fucking way," I gasped.

He laughed again, for real this time. Humor softened the hard edges of his face, making him more handsome, if possible. "You're right. No fucking way. It's Raiden."

I almost laughed too—it seemed as if he had a sense of humor—and I would have, if he wasn't holding me hostage.

"And yours is?"

I cleared my throat. "Bea," I said, sticking with my nickname. I didn't like the name Ruby. Everyone had to

31

comment about my name matching my hair, like I wasn't aware. "So, do you have a problem with all humans or is it just me?" He'd lost the attitude fairly quickly, so I had a feeling *I* was the issue.

He laid down and clasped his hands behind his head. "So far, just you."

"Why?"

"Because I had a mission," he mumbled, "and you messed it up. Now I have to drag you all the way home. Who knows how long it will take me to get back here? By then, my lead might be cold."

Good to know he didn't hate all of us. Just me.

"How is all this possible? I don't understand." Curiosity was winning the war against fear. Plus, I'd realized, I wasn't hallucinating, and whether I wanted to believe it or not, the situation was real. Giants *did* exist. It left me wondering what else was out there.

"Don't worry about it." He turned over, facing away, effectively ending our conversation.

*Don't worry about it? Whatever.* I wasn't going to be here long enough *to* worry about it.

Sid cuddled behind my knees as I laid down on the cot. There was plenty of room for both of us to sleep comfortably, but I didn't plan on sleeping. I was going home. Tonight.

My mother's voice resonated inside my head—*patience is a virtue.*

Although she'd been gone a long time, I still remembered most of what she'd taught me. Even as a child, she'd treated me as if I were an adult. I wasn't sure if she had done it on purpose, or if that was just who she was—or is—because I didn't have irrefutable proof that my parents were

32

dead, and though it was unlikely they were alive, I didn't want to give up hope.

Thankfully, I still had Kevin. Though we had different fathers, my dad adopted him when our parents got married, we looked a lot alike. Both of us were tall with hazel eyes that adjusted their hue with our moods and a head full of curly red hair. Mine was blood red—hence my name, Ruby —and Kevin's was more copper. Over the years, he'd taught me the important things in life—how to shoot, hunt, fish, fight, and forge. I certainly wouldn't have survived this inhospitable world without him.

I had been so young when our parents disappeared. My mom, a geneticist, and my dad, a construction contractor, went to work at JBER and never returned. The place was now a prison where people lived in a cage behind an electric fence with armed guards.

Similar to the one I was currently in.

I waited until Raiden's breathing evened out. Then I waited hours longer, until the flames died into glowing embers. Around four-ish in the morning, I quietly slipped on my rucksack and motioned for Sid to follow.

My pulse raced between my ears, making it hard to hear anything else as I tiptoed past the sleeping giant.

"You're an early riser."

I screamed, high-pitched and girly. I was positive he'd been sleeping. "You can't kidnap me like this." I stomped my feet into the dirt. A cloud of dust puffed ghostlike in the beams of moonlight shining through the entrance.

"*Kidnap* you? That's what you're calling this?" He swung his legs over the side of his cot and scratched his fingers through his short hair.

"Yes. Because that's what it is. Kidnapping."

"Not the way I see it. I caught you trespassing in our Fiefdom. Now I'm taking you in for questioning." He rubbed his hand over his chin, the rough stubble sounding like sandpaper.

"Who are you?" I said.

"I'm what you humans call the law—and you, little lady, broke it."

CHAPTER

# THREE

S weat burned my eyes and I could taste the salt beading on my upper lip. Using my hands on my knees for leverage, I made the final push to the top of the obsidian staircase and moved past the exit out into the open. A shock zapped my skin, like I'd touched an electrical fence. I jumped. "Ouch! Mother—" Would've been nice if Raiden had warned me. *Jerk.*

Once outside, I leaned against the edge of the shiny black stone, afraid that if I sat on the ground, I wouldn't be able to get back up.

Beyond was a vast meadow surrounded by jagged snow-capped mountains. Long, blueish grass wafted under the continuous breeze, and the scent of wildflowers perfumed the air. Light-pink clouds traveled swiftly across the periwinkle sky, giving me the uncomfortable sensation of vertigo. The colors shined brighter and more intensely here, and the shapes were crisper, as if in high definition. It seemed bigger here, or maybe it was because, for the last twelve years, I'd been hiding amongst the cover of the trees and living underground.

Raiden came out of the stairway holding a bag, a massive saddle, and an equally large bridle—where he got them from, I had no idea. He stopped what he was doing and stared at me. Bright gold rays reflected blue off his hair and turned his eyes a lighter shade of gray.

I glared. "What?" I didn't like people staring.

Ignoring my attitude, he put his fingers in his mouth and whistled sharply. A minute later, the ground shuddered beneath me as a monstrous black horse with feathery wings galloped through the meadow and slid to a stop, clumps of dirt and grass spraying Raiden's pants. I had to give him credit—I would've ducked for cover.

Sid's hackles rose, but he didn't bark. I rubbed my eyes, convinced I was hallucinating again. I was adept at keeping calm—my survival counted on it—but this was getting ridiculous.

"Hey, boy." The horse whinnied and tossed his head as Raiden scratched between its ears. "You ready to go home, big guy?"

The horse nudged him hard enough that he stumbled backward. He chuckled at the brute force, then tossed the saddle on the beast's back and adjusted the cinch. "Bea, you'll ride with me. Sid, you're going in the basket, okay?"

Sid barked as his tail beat against my thigh.

Raiden opened the bag and took out some stout material. He unfolded it time and time again until it was a basket sack. He clipped two straps to rings on either side of the front cinch, repeated the process with two more straps connected to the back cinch, and then ratcheted the basket until it was hanging below the creature's belly.

"Don't you dare get in there!" I pointed at Sid. I looked over my shoulder at the entrance to the stairway. My fingers tingled in anticipation of our mad dash to freedom.

Instead, Sid ignored me and scrambled over the side of the basket. I inhaled sharply from shock—Sid always behaved—and fear—because I couldn't leave my dog. I wouldn't.

"Your turn," Raiden said, wearing a half-smirk that implied he'd won.

Panic fluttered in the hollow of my throat, and I planted my feet. I'd had enough of his little adventure. "Nope. Not getting on that horse. No way. Not going to do it." I couldn't let him fly me away from the entrance of the staircase. If he did, I'd never find it again. Kevin and Tee would think I'd died—or worse, been taken by the On-Grids. There was no way I was going to disappear because I was an idiot who got kidnapped by Mr. Stranger Danger. Kevin was probably organizing a search party despite our promise not to. I needed to get home before someone lost their life looking for me.

"He's not a horse. He's a pegasus."

I backed up a few paces. "Sure it is. Still not going."

Sid barked from inside the basket. *Why was my dog so keen on going with this guy?* What a traitor. My feelings were hurt.

"You either do this willingly, or I'll make you do it. Your choice." Raiden rubbed the back of his neck as if saying my decision didn't matter to him one way or another.

My chin trembled while tears stung the corners of my eyes. Sometimes anger made me cry.

I stepped forward, arms raised and fists balled, ready to throw down. I wasn't leaving, and neither was Sid.

Raiden reached right past my defenses and touched my forehead as I said, "You son of a—"

Tiny spots of light flared before blackness descended.

---

I SNUGGLED into the warmth encircling my body as if cuddled in a heated blanket, groggy with contentment. I deeply inhaled the scent of crisp air, leather, and . . . horse? My eyes slowly fluttered open, awakening from a dream—or a nightmare, as the events came back to me.

Directly ahead, the horse's black mane tangled in the wind, and on either side of us, its wings held steady as they soared along the currents. At the sight of lush valleys and winding muddy rivers 100 feet below, every muscle seized.

*WTF?*

My stomach dropped and slung back to my throat like a slingshot. A set of arms tightened their grip to keep me from falling.

"Welcome back, Sleeping Beauty," Raiden whispered in my ear.

The close contact seemed intimate and made me uncomfortable, but I was too scared of heights to scoot away. Instead, I gritted my teeth and practiced—*if you don't have anything nice to say, don't say anything at all.* A tidbit of wisdom passed on from my mother. She'd liked to remind me that if my actions didn't get me in trouble, my attitude surely would.

"Have a nice nap?"

I ground them harder and patted the side of my waist, searching for my machete. Not that I would've used it up

38

here, but having it next to me was a safety measure of sorts. It was gone.

His laughter rumbled over my back.

"You knocked me out," I hissed.

"Naw, I just zapped you with a little extra."

"What's that supposed to mean? You're like a *wizard*?" I said with as much acerbity as I could fit into a single word.

"Don't be ridiculous. We giants have an affinity for electricity, and we can use it if we need to. Think of what I did to you like dragging your feet over the carpet and touching a light socket. Only more."

"I hate you," I grumbled. So much for being nice. Okay—perhaps *hate* was too strong a word.

"Awww, thank you. You're cute when you're angry, like a toy poodle."

My breath hitched at the slight.

"No, more like a Chihuahua," he goaded.

My shoulders stiffened.

He wrapped his arms tighter around me—probably to irritate me further. "You know the kind of dog that thinks they're dangerous, but really, they should run? Yeah, that's what you remind me of."

Nope. I was sure of it. I hated him. But there was nothing to do about it presently. I didn't want to tumble to my death, so I stewed in silence, dampening my fear with anger. Surviving in post-apocalyptic Alaska had hardened me in a violent way. Apex predators, natural disasters, and starvation would do that to a person. By the age of twelve, my emotions had been well within my control. Because reacting out of fear was the surest way to die.

For the next few hours, I kept my mouth shut as we coasted through valleys, alongside mountain ranges tipped with bright snow. I wanted to enjoy the beauty, but the anxiety resting on my sternum distracted me.

My thoughts bounced in my head. How was I going to get back to the staircase now? I didn't even know where I was. Frustration brewed, then turned to guilt and disappointment. How had I been so stupid in the first place? I should've known better. I should've gone home immediately after the bear had left.

The urge to punch something itched under my skin. Usually, Kevin and I would take to the ring when we needed to burn off some steam. The only other person brave enough to battle me was Frank because he was a judo master. But with no other options present, I took a deep breath through my nose and exhaled out my mouth to the count of ten. I'd learned that from Frank also. Besides Kevin and Tee, Frank was the only other person in our motley group with whom I spent time. After my parents had disappeared, and then we'd lost a few friends, I'd sealed off my heart. Because the more people you loved, the more you had to lose.

I yipped when the pegasus took a sharp turn and drifted toward the tallest peak. It was flat, like the top had been cleanly sliced off. As we got closer, a modern city made of glass, concrete, and metal came into view. Afternoon sunlight bounced off the smooth surfaces, blinding me in a blaze of gold.

I forcefully gripped Raiden's arms as we landed in a slow lope on a granite courtyard. Pizza pan-sized hooves clipped sharply on the stone before finally coming to a stop.

Raiden slid off and offered to help me down. I wouldn't have given him the satisfaction but I wasn't sure if I could make it without twisting an ankle. After so many hours in the same position, my legs were numb. He slid his hands up my arms until they gripped under my armpits and he gently set me on solid ground. "Welcome to the Fiefdom," he said. "Stretch your legs. I'll let Sid out."

The blisters on my feet reawakened as I limped toward the crystal mansion straight out of a modern-day fairytale. Panes of windows, white curved concrete, and multiple rooflines harmonized with the slopes.

A crisp breeze skimmed my cheeks. I stopped and wrapped my arms around my chest to hold back the shivers, though I wasn't cold. I'd never admit it out loud, but I was frightened. I'd finally come to terms with the fact that I wasn't hallucinating. It was real. And if I'd been this blind my entire life, what else was out there that I didn't know about? I swallowed my fear because I had bigger concerns.

Sid ran up next to me and pressed against my thighs, his presence steadying my nerves.

"You better wait. You'll want to be presentable before meeting my family," Raiden hollered.

I turned, my gaze darting over his military-ish appearance. "*You* live here?" There was no way I believed him.

He pursed his lips to the side and shook his head as if he couldn't believe my audacity—or foolishness. I wasn't sure which.

"And why should I care what I look like?" Cleaning up would take too much time. I needed to get home.

"Because my aunt and uncle will be deciding your fate."

"And how will that help?"

He wrinkled his nose. "Well, honestly, you kind of smell, but suit yourself."

A tall gentleman wearing a silver fur vest exited the house. His hair and eyes matched his garment but he didn't look old—probably close to my parents' age. He gave me a quick once-over before turning his attention away. "Raiden. It's been a long time. Glad you're home." He patted him heavily on the back.

"Thanks. I'd like to say I'm glad to be home, too, but you know how it is." They exchanged a look.

"That I do, sir," the man said, glancing down at me. "And this is?"

"Bea—" Raiden paused.

"Walker," I provided, holding out a hand. He stared at it for a beat before he grabbed it, shaking gently as if he might hurt me.

"You're human?"

Not wanting to be rude, I kept my sarcastic comments to myself. "And you are?" I asked.

"I'm Benji. I'm the stable manager and logistics specialist here in the Fie."

"Among other things," Raiden supplied.

Benji nodded in agreement as he took the reins from Raiden and led the horse away, its hooves clacking on the black stone. The barn, not to far away, was constructed from polished concrete and metal with a tall white fence surrounding the paddock. It was weird that they needed a fence when the horses had wings.

Raiden strode toward the huge double doors of pale oak. "Are you coming? Or do I have to carry you in?" He tried to hide the smirk on his face but failed. He opened the door and held up his palm, encouraging me to go first.

Crystal chandeliers, plush white animal hide rugs bigger than an elephant, white leather furniture, mirrors, and vases overflowing with fresh snow lilies made the inside even more glamorous than the exterior. Though the décor was cold, an obsidian fireplace spanned from the marble floor up to three stories high, keeping the huge room toasty. Next to the hearth, on a solid-glass platform, rested a giant-sized gold harp playing all on its own. Goosebumps peppered my arms from the creepy tune. I guess ole' Jack hadn't managed to steal it after all.

"Come on," Raiden said. He gestured up a floating staircase, then followed me up. On the second floor, he knocked on a frosted door with a crystal knob, then opened it. "Ladies first."

A stunning woman with long white hair and icy-blue eyes framed with dark lashes and brows sat behind a glass desk. "Nephew?" Her voice was melodious. She folded her hands together and rested her elbows on the surface. "I wasn't expecting you home for some time."

"Aunt." Raiden bowed his head. "I caught this young lady on our side of the gates." Disbelief painted his voice.

Only a slight twitch of her forehead indicated that she was surprised too. She stood up, and I was shocked that she was as tall as he was. Her trousers flowed breezily around her stilettos as she sauntered around the desk. "Oh, I see," she said, but she sounded confused. She stopped and turned her face away from me, placing her hand under her nose. Multiple diamonds sparkled under the bright ceiling lights. "Raiden, why did you not allow her to shower first? She smells like the barn," she scolded.

"I tried. She refused." He crossed his arms, making his biceps stretch the sleeves of his T-shirt until it seemed as if the material might burst.

"Well, you obviously didn't try hard enough." She tilted her chin toward the door. "Please wait outside," she instructed him. After he closed the door, she turned back to me and paused while staring.

I shrugged my shoulders and widened my eyes, questioning what she wanted. Sid crowded against my leg.

"Child, your name?" She tapped her toe impatiently.

"Ruby Rose Walker, and this is Obsidian, but we go by Bea and Sid." I wasn't sure why I introduced myself like that. Nobody ever called me by my given name—most people didn't even know it—but in the formal setting, it seemed polite.

Her eyes narrowed to a sliver before they grew like something had captured her attention. "Yes, yes," she said breathlessly. "And how did you get here?" She swiped her sleek hair behind her neck.

I recapped my story with a heavy emphasis on the kidnapping and why I needed to get home quickly. If Kevin took out a search party and someone died looking for me, I'd never forgive myself.

"Hmm, I see." She ran a hand over her mouth and pinched her bottom lip between her finger and thumb. "Excellent. You're dismissed." Her heels clicked over the floors as she herded us out.

Her indifference at my grievances and time constraints irked my nerves.

Raiden waited on the other side of the door, leaning against the wall with his hands shoved in his pockets. "Come on." His long legs hurried down the stairs.

"Where are we going now?" I jogged to keep up.

Stopping at the far end of the hallway, he opened a door, and I peeked inside. Against the wall was a plush white bed, taking advantage of the view afforded by the massive windows.

"Don't worry—they're mirrored, so you can see out but no one can see in. There are clothes in the closet. Clean up."

44

He gave me the once-over. His expression said *I told you so.* "Someone will be back to get you shortly."

"What? You're leaving?" Tension gripped my neck muscles. It wasn't that I liked him, but he knew how to get me home.

"My job's done. My aunt and uncle will decide your fate."

"What does that mean?"

His fangs indented his bottom lip as he smiled, reminding me exactly what he was. My heart stumbled.

"I need to know." The knot in my throat caused my tone to pitch upward. I wanted to smack myself for showing any amount of weakness in a house of predators.

His gray eyes softened as the smile slid away. "Don't worry. They're not going to kill you." He reached out and rested his hand on my shoulder, warm and heavy. "Honestly, it's been so long since we've had a human cross into our realm, they'll probably just tell me to take you home."

I inhaled a gasp. "Then why didn't you let me go when we were there?"

He frowned and ran a hand through his hair. "Against protocol. Decisions are above my pay grade."

"So you're not leaving?"

"Not yet," he sighed as he closed the door behind him.

# CHAPTER
# FOUR

I sat on the bed, and Sid jumped up beside me. He pawed the covers, circled a few times, and plopped down in the mountain of blankets and pillows.

All the emotions I'd been holding back flooded through now that I was alone. I put my face in my hands and cried. Hot tears pooled in my cupped palms. I had no way to get back home. Even if I could steal a pegasus, I couldn't find the staircase alone. The only thing I could do was convince someone to take me home. I knew the fear my family was going through—what it felt like to lose someone you loved. Sid whined and buried his head in my lap. I wiped the tears from my hands on the back of my pants and rubbed my fingers over his ears.

Crying wasn't something I did often. The way I'd grown up, it was a sign of weakness. If you wanted to survive, you didn't expose your throat to anyone you didn't trust with your life. I only truly trusted one dog and two people—Kevin and Tee. And even then, I hid my tears from them because when I cried, they got scared.

Since my current options for escape were limited, I snuck into the bathroom and, as suggested, took the longest, hottest shower of my life. In our bunker, we were allotted five minutes. Not because water wasn't plentiful—we had a catchment system in place, and it rained a lot—but because electricity was hard to come by. We had solar panels and some tiny wind turbines, but they weren't enough. If I was lucky, my shower stayed lukewarm. But most of the time, I wasn't.

Reluctantly, I shut off the water and wrapped my hair in a towel. Steam billowed out of the room as I opened the door. Inside the closet, I wrinkled my nose while flipping through the clothes. I settled for a fitted long-sleeved shirt, some trousers, and a pair of wedges. They were comfortable enough, especially since they didn't rub against my weeping blisters, but nothing like the gear I was accustomed to. Cargo pants were my staple—weapons and fishing gear fit in the pockets. And sometimes the occasional rock—just because it was pretty.

Unwrapping the towel from my head, I tossed it on the bed and gave my hair a scrunch before leaving the room. I was supposed to wait for someone to come and get me, so contrarily, I didn't. Sid accompanied me like a shadow.

"Bea—"

I jumped and scrambled against the wall, then threw Sid a dirty look. *How about some warning next time, buddy?*

"Jumpy much?" Raiden said.

I shot him a scathing glare while still holding on to the wall.

"I'm here to escort you to the tribunal."

"Tribunal?" I clamped down on my bottom lip with my front teeth and stopped breathing.

"Not to worry, Red." He lightly tapped me with his elbow before linking his arm with mine and dragging me down the hall. "It's not as bad as it sounds."

"Really? Red? Haven't heard that one before."

"Yeah, well, the other ones I can think of are inappropriate." Humor crinkled the corners of his eyes.

"I'm sure I've heard those ones too." I lived with a rough crowd.

We stopped in front of his aunt's office. "Good luck." He squeezed my shoulder before he left.

I let Sid in first—I wasn't going in alone. Inside stood Raiden's aunt and two men. My shoulders relaxed a fraction. I'd been expecting a courtroom with a judge and jury.

"Ruby . . ." Raiden's aunt paused, looking at Sid with a slight grimace, "and Obsidian, please have a seat." She pointed to a sofa positioned on an ivory carpet. Outside the massive windows, mountains ringed with silvery clouds repeated like rows of shark teeth.

"Bea and Sid, please." I perched on the edge of the couch with my feet tiptoed for a quick escape. Sid sat on the floor next to me, his eyebrows twitching as he tracked the others. Across the room were shelves decorated with some books, crystals, knick-knacks, and marble busts.

"Yes, Bea. I'm Lady Sylvia. This is my partner, Lord Issac, and our son, Loch."

They all bowed their heads and took seats across from me.

Issac, like Sylvia, had a mane of glorious white hair, though both looked to be in their early forties. But hey, I could've been mistaken—maybe they were immortal.

Loch's hair was dark like Raiden's, but long, draping just

past his shoulders. His eyes, framed with thick black lashes, were a bright, glowing teal, the exact match of a glacial river. He was uncomfortably beautiful, and I found him hard to look at. Like his parents, I couldn't be sure of his age. Perhaps he was a hundred years old and had stopped aging at twenty.

Issac sat forward and spoke, his voice deep and powerful. "Bea, you're here to help us."

*What?*

He held up a finger. "Let me explain. For eons, we, the giants, have waited for salvation promised to us in a prophecy told a thousand years ago. We believe you, Ruby, are our salvation."

I was too stunned to even laugh. "Don't be silly. I can barely take care of myself. You're giants. There's no possible way I can help you." I picked at my raw cuticles. From what I'd gathered, they were unusually strong, incredibly fast, and impossible to kill.

"Perhaps. But we giants are a superstitious lot, and the prophecy was foretold by our last living monarch, Queen Dru-Noir. Therefore, we must believe," Sylvia said. I couldn't tell if she was trying to convince me or herself.

"So what does that mean for me?" The skin under my eye began to twitch. It only happened when I got extremely uncomfortable or stressed. I ran my fingers through my wayward curls and flipped them to the other side, attempting to conceal the nervous tic.

"It means you shall live here with us," Issac said. He folded his hands together over his crossed knee, wrinkling his black slacks.

I sat up straight. "Uh . . . no." My core temperature skyrocketed. Heat flashed up my neck and behind my ears.

The idea of never seeing Kevin and Tee again was not something I was willing to agree to. "I'm going home."

"You will do what—" Sylvia was cut off abruptly by Issac raising his index finger.

Loch finally spoke. "Bea, before you panic, hear me out." Everything about him screamed confidence, from his cool demeanor to his flawless wardrobe of black pants, a long-sleeved gray shirt with a fine sheen, polished shoes, and his smooth velvety voice.

I inhaled slowly and exhaled my growing apprehension. "Okay." There was no harm in listening.

"We need you to stay here so you can help us fulfill the prophecy. And don't worry, we'll go get your family so you can all be together. I can only assume that's why you want to go home." His eyebrows raised like he knew that I'd left someone behind, but he wasn't sure who.

It *was* why I was going home but I didn't need to tell him that just yet. There was no need to start a pissing contest if I could get them to take me back willingly. First, I needed information to construct a plan.

My leg started bouncing. "What does this prophecy say?"

Loch glanced at his mother, and she gave him a sharp nod. He rubbed his hands together and clasped them over his lap. "*'When the Earth is on the brink of break, our Salvation lies in wait. The Crimson Jewel it will take for Obsidian the gate to break. Our Salvation lies in wait, for the First-Born son to bond his fate.'*"

I stopped breathing. My leg stopped bouncing. My heart skipped a beat. "Wait! You don't think . . . *I'm* his fate?" I tapped my chest.

"No," Loch said, horror flooding his expression. Now

he'd hurt my feelings. It wasn't like I *wanted* to be someone's fate, but dang, he didn't need to be so disgusted by the prospect.

"So let me get this straight. You think I'm the crimson jewel because of my name . . . and perhaps my hair color?" I tugged on a curl. "And because my dogs name is Obsidian? Your prophecy is ancient and vague. And your argument is weak." I listed all the reasons why I was skeptical.

He rolled his eyes. "Agreed. But you're the most promising lead we've ever had."

"You don't believe any of this, do you?"

He shrugged one shoulder as both of his parents watched with disapproval. "Does it matter?"

"I guess not. Say I agree to live here. What's expected of me?" It wasn't like I was even considering it, but I needed to appear cooperative if I wanted them to take me home.

"Like you said, it's vague. All I know is that I can't take a chance on you leaving now that you're here. Even though I don't believe it, what if I'm wrong? What if you *are* our salvation and I let you slip through our hands? Please, you must understand. As for what's expected of you, that's your choice. All I know is you are required to live here. Honestly, I can't imagine that you wouldn't love it. The Fiefdom is glorious. Plus, if mountainside living isn't your cup of tea," he swept his hand toward the windows, "there are other locations you can choose from."

It was nice here compared to home. Not that Alaska wasn't beautiful—it was visually spectacular, but dangerous on so many levels. At least here, they had food, shelter, heat, and running water.

"What does my family get out of it?" Even if I wasn't hungry or cold at the moment, I had no intention of agree-

51

ing. I planted my feet firmly on the floor, like, if they were solidly connected to the ground, they couldn't stop me from leaving.

Loch cleared his throat. "Let me guess—you have a small group of people that have banded together for safety?"

There was no reason to deny Loch's assumptions. There were thirty-seven of us who worked together to survive. It was a delicate balance, especially because we weren't exactly equipped to handle that many people.

Loch continued. "We know a lot about Earth. We've been watching humans destroy her for centuries. Up here, your family can live amongst us with no fear of starving or being hunted. We will provide them with food and a home. I assure you, the accommodations in our Fiefdom are far nicer than your current living conditions. And if your people wish to work, we will provide a job of their choice and training if need be."

His offer, though very tempting, was starting to sound too good to be true. I glanced at Sid curled at my feet, loyally guarding me. I could count each and every rib under his shiny black coat. The knot on the crown of his head was painfully prominent. The constant threat of starvation was a powerful motivator. But if an offer sounded too good to be true, it probably was.

"Thank you, but I'm going home." My hands got all sweaty, and I balled them into one fist holding the other.

"Look, Bea, I understand you're wary, and you have a right to be, but we're going to have to come up with some sort of compromise. We need your help." Loch tucked a strand of his long hair behind his ear. "We're not here to hurt you. We *need* you. What would you do to keep your people safe? You see, that's what I'm doing here." He patted his chest to emphasize his quandary. "You're the key to keeping my family alive. Just take a minute. Please." He pressed his hands together in a prayer position before he set them on his lap. "Tell us what *you* need in return. What is your price for staying here and helping us?"

He was speaking my language. I would do *anything* to keep my friends and family safe. His plea was loud and clear. Would I kidnap someone and hold them hostage? If it meant keeping my family alive, darn right, I would.

"*If*," I held up a finger, "I agree to this, we get to bring our own weapons. And there are thirty-seven of us," I warned. I wasn't sure how many would want to relocate—we weren't a trusting group.

Loch didn't bat an eye, he just nodded for me to continue.

"If they choose to come, they have the option to return to Earth at any time." That would give my people the opportunity to leave if Loch's promise didn't live up to expectations.

"You're welcome to bring your weapons, but you won't need them. As for the rest, we'll agree to all of it. Except *you* can't leave," Loch said.

"No, I get that choice too."

"No. Our price is *you*. You must stay. And in return, you get my word that those of you who choose to live here will never go hungry. They'll never die needlessly. They'll never have to look over their shoulders in fear again. Our only condition is that you stay."

"And how do I know they'll be safe from *you*?" I wasn't an idiot—giants were dangerous too—but the notion that I could give my family a better, easier, safer life was a huge temptation. I needed to cover all my bases before I capitulated.

"Why wouldn't they be safe? We admire humans."

I scoffed. "If that's true, why did you watch us destroy the Earth and not help us?"

"Because you *heavily* outnumber us. And for the last thousand years, our population has been dwindling. We couldn't afford to help you. We're already facing extinction." He relaxed and rested his arm over the back of the sofa as if we were discussing the weather.

"I don't know. I need to think about it." I was getting in too deep, and I wanted to backpedal to start the conversation over.

"What's there to think about?" Loch asked like I was crazy. Maybe I was. "Here, you'll have food, safety, *and* your family."

He was right. *And* they had hot running water. Everyone had their price.

"Seriously, Bea, you're hurting my feelings." Loch placed a hand on his heart. "Have we not been hospitable so far? According to the prophecy, you're our salvation."

"I just wish I knew how I was supposed to save you." The only savior I was aware of had died on a cross. Though I admired him for it, I didn't want to follow in his footsteps. At least not that part anyway.

I took a deep breath and thought things through quickly. Life in Alaska was difficult. I was tired of barely surviving. And everyone else was too.

Just by looking at Raiden and his family, I could tell they ate regularly. Their faces glowed with vitality, and their living conditions were luxurious. Ours didn't even compare.

"So if I agree," I glanced at all of them, "you personally

guarantee my family's safety so long as I remain here?" How could I *not* agree to this? I could make sure my people were safe from harm and all I had to do was to stay. My freedom —for their well-being. It was a small price to pay. Plus, assuming he was telling the truth, they could leave at any time.

"Yes," they said.

"I have one more condition."

An amused grin spread lazily over Loch's gorgeous face. "I'm sure you do. What is it?"

"I get to go home and get them." When I got home— which was my goal in the first place—I could decide then if I would honor the agreement. I wasn't above lying to protect my family—and my gut told me neither were they.

Sylvia gripped her glass of water tighter, her fingers paling under the pressure. Her eyes darted to her husband.

"I won't budge on any of my conditions." I tilted my chin.

Loch inhaled tightly through his nose.

My leg started bouncing on its own accord again.

He looked from his mom to his dad. They both nodded in agreement, though Sylvia didn't seem as pleased as Loch or his father.

Loch smiled so wide his fangs poked his bottom lip. "Okay. We'll have a legal contract drawn up by tomorrow morning. We can meet back here after breakfast, where you can read through it to make sure it adheres to your require-ments. Then one of us will escort you home. Sound like a deal?"

"Yes." The idea that I got to go over the agreement one more time loosened the tightness in my chest. I wanted some detailed clarification, and I knew there were more questions I needed to ask, but as of now, nothing was set in stone until I signed the dotted line.

Sylvia stood and extended her hand. "But we must insist that our discussion does not go beyond this room. If you tell any giants about this agreement, it will become null and void. I hope you understand. The privacy and sanctity of this room are very important to how our realm functions. This conversation stays here. Do not repeat it," she said slowly, carefully. Though her words were gentle, the undercurrent of a threat was not lost on me.

An old advertisement I once saw in one of my mom's magazines passed through my head—*what happens in Vegas, stays in Vegas*. "Ten-four," I said.

Sylvia's clear blue eyes narrowed in confusion.

"Yes. No problem. But what do I tell someone if they ask? I was under the impression I was going to get punished for crossing your border."

"Simply tell them you came here seeking asylum for your people, and we granted the request," she said.

I frowned. "Yeah, that covers strangers, but what about Raiden? He knows the truth."

Loch placed a hand on my shoulder. "I'll tell Raiden everything, except the part about the prophecy. That needs to be kept secret."

Outside the bedroom windows, the sky morphed from periwinkle to cobalt as the sun slid behind the puffy silver clouds. I kicked my shoes off, relieving the pressure from my blistered feet. Barefoot, I paced over the plush carpet, gnawing on my lower lip.

One second, I was proud of my negotiation skills. The next, I was mortified. They had been far too accommodating of my wishes, which made me question their motives. They were willing to feed and house thirty-seven humans just to get me to stay. Why? The prophecy was vague—as all prophecies were. Or at least, all that I'd read about in my mom's fantasy novels.

It seemed to me that we were getting the better end of the bargain. If I were a trusting person, I'd be pleased. But I wasn't.

Sid rested on the bed, staring at me with his head between his paws. While I was worried, he seemed fine. His lack of concern was the only thing that kept me in the room.

A knock on the door startled me, and I tripped over the edge of the rug, catching myself on the dresser. I needed to get it together.

Sid's tail thumped on the down comforter as I opened the door. Raiden, clean-shaven and smelling like rain carried on a crisp breeze tinged with peppermint, stood outside.

I inhaled deeply.

He leaned casually against the doorframe with his arm above his head, supporting him. His black shirt crept upward, giving me a glimpse of golden skin above his jeans. "So, we'll be leaving at dawn."

A thrill of excitement tingled over my skin. Excitement because I was going home—not because of the specimen standing in front of me. His rippled abs *not hiding* under his T-shirt had nothing to do with it. I had to remind myself I didn't like him.

"I should've known it would be you," I lashed out.

"It's nice to see you again too. Hopefully this time, you won't miss the entire journey, Sleeping Beauty." He winked.

I bit down on a huff and crossed my arms, causing my boobs to lift even higher. It wasn't the effect I was going for, but it was too late to reroute my actions without looking nervous.

Raiden's eyes darted to the pale skin bulging under my V-neck shirt, then back to my eyes. He made a small snort through his nose like he wasn't impressed.

My cheeks caught fire as I slammed the door in his face.

I swear he chuckled on the other side of the thick slab. I muttered what he could do with himself, confident that he could hear me.

Not having given it much thought as to who would escort me home, I'd assumed it would be Loch. He seemed more qualified to convince my people to relocate. I didn't think Raiden was the best man for the job, but hey, what did I know?

What would happen if I couldn't convince my people to relocate? They were a rough crowd. Kevin wouldn't abandon me—I was his first concern—but he wouldn't want to leave the others behind either. His sense of responsibility was bloated.

I sank down into the mattress. Little beasties of panic skittered in my stomach as I leaned back, trying to contain the worry of *what ifs* and *whys* growing inside. I gripped a pillow and hugged it to my chest. The bedding smelled like clouds, if clouds had a smell. Clean. Refreshing. Pure.

Another knock softly rattled my door.

Instead of getting up, I yelled, "What?"

The door opened and Loch stepped inside, looking stylish in a black wool peacoat. With his hair pulled into a low ponytail away from his face, the resemblance to his cousin was staggering.

I jumped off the bed, pulled a wayward curl out of my mouth, and sputtered, "Sorry. If I'd known it was you, I'd have answered the door." I grabbed my tangled mane and tossed it over my shoulder. I'd expected it to be Raiden.

"Don't be silly. I'm here to see if you'd like a tour of my town before dinner?"

*His* town?

"Um, yeah, I guess." Familiarizing myself with the surroundings was a wise move in case our deal went awry and I had to escape on my own.

I slipped my shoes on, and grabbed a navy jacket from the closet.

"That color really brings out the blue in your eyes. Lovely." He stared at me for a beat before I looked away.

My instinct was to roll my *hazel* eyes, betting he said that to all the girls. Unfortunately, it didn't stop me from turning the color of my hair—a pitfall of being a ginger. I could control my facial expressions like a boss, but I couldn't control my blood flow.

"Thanks," I said to the floor.

He held out an elbow and escorted me down the marble hallway. Sid's nails clicked over the floor as he trotted next to me. Abstract photos in black, white, and shades of gray lined the walls. They looked vaguely familiar.

Waiting outside the front door was an open black coach drawn by two white horses without wings. A giant with short silver hair waited in the front seat, holding the reins in his hands.

Sid jumped in with no problem and sat on the seat as if he were human. He was good at adapting. When he was a pup, I'd gotten him used to riding on four-wheelers and snow machines.

"May I?" Loch asked before he grabbed my waist and lifted me into the coach like I was a child. It was the first time since I was young that I was the shortest person around. It made me feel vulnerable and I didn't like it. Not at all.

Once Loch settled in beside me, he grinned, showing off his perfect teeth and pearly canines. They were disconcerting, but they didn't detract from his handsomeness. If anything, the hint of danger made him more fascinating.

60

And now that I knew I was going home in the morning, I began to relax a fraction.

"Are you ready?" he asked.

I was about to say, *born ready*, but around him, that phrase felt unrefined, so I nodded.

The coach took off, rounding the bend and leaving the view of the mansion. Soon, the solid granite turned into smaller cobblestones and vibrated the plush seat below me. A crisp wind tousled my hair around my head. I forced it into a quick French braid and tucked it into the collar of my jacket.

We gently tilted from one side of the carriage to the other as the road began to wind its way downward. I wrapped my arm around Sid to keep me from leaning against Loch and to keep Sid safe. I stared at the dusky mountainside to avoid accidentally looking over the edge.

Rounding the last corner, the late-afternoon sun reflected off the windows of the modern buildings. In the valley, graceful curving streets and clean sidewalks snaked throughout the quaint town.

"All the businesses are centered around the town circle. The rest are the homes of my people." He pointed at the structures built high on the dark slopes. His fingernails were neat and trim, like he'd actually had a manicure.

I slid my hands further inside my jacket, embarrassed by their ragged condition.

Concern creased between his dark brows. "I know this is all new to you and probably frightening. Is there anything you're curious about?"

"You keep saying *your* town, *your* people? Are you . . . like a prince?" I felt stupid even saying it.

"Oh, heavens no . . . Okay, so kind of." He teetered his hand back and forth.

I waited for him to elaborate.

"There are four families who rule the Fiefdom, which is split into four Domes—Fee, Fie, Foe, and Fum."

I shook my head and tried to keep a straight face as laughter bubbled. "No."

Confusion wrinkled his forehead. "What do you mean, no?"

"You're not teasing me?"

"Why would you think that?"

"No reason. Sorry, I interrupted." Apparently, Loch did not have the sense of humor his cousin did.

"No need to be sorry." He reached out and patted my knee before he continued. "There's also the capital, Isle Noir. That's where most of the dual affiliations live; the giant that have more than one bloodline. Hence the name. Those of us that have single bloodlines are known as sole affiliations."

I bristled having read this plot line in many books, but his tone didn't seem to hold any malice or prejudice. It just sounded like he was spitting facts.

"My parents are the Lord and Lady of the Fie. But I run the day-to-day operations."

"And the duals? Who represents them?" I kept my voice steady.

"Well, there aren't many left. When our bloodlines mix, it often goes awry. Anymore, the child doesn't survive. That's why we've segregated ourselves because of the dangers. The youngest surviving dual is Poppy, the assistant palace coordinator, and she's like thirty something."

I couldn't argue with that logic—it was sad—but a solid reason for keeping the Domes separate.

The horse's hooves clickety-clacked around the circle. A behemoth building, directly in the center, took up an entire block. Straight lines bled into curves, concrete morphed into polished obsidian, and the rest consisted of glass.

All the townsfolk smiled and waved at Loch. He tipped his chin in recognition and waved back with a finger as the rest of his hand remained on the side of the carriage. Most of the giants strolling along had stages of salt-and-pepper hair, all the way to pure white. The lack of pigment seemed to increase with age. Flowing skirts, pressed slacks, chic hats, and tailored jackets, all in monochromatic shades, made the sidewalk into a runway show. I was used to people in work clothes, rubber fishing boots, and baseball caps. Not exactly the height of fashion. I shrunk down in my seat despite being dressed appropriately.

Baskets of colorful flowers hung from the storefronts along the main street. The pavement darkened under the containers as if someone had just watered them. A lineup of customers waited outside of a business with *Mountainside Bakery* printed in bold letters above the door. Mouthwatering scents wafted into the air—sugar, cinnamon, salt, butter, rosemary, thyme, garlic. My stomach rumbled at the blend of smells reminding me of distant Christmas memories with my parents. Melancholy filled my chest. I missed them, and if I left Alaska permanently, I'd never find them. But what would happen if we *didn't* leave? How many more of us would die?

I pressed my palm to my belly. "Sorry. I haven't eaten today."

"Are you serious?"

"Yeah." It wasn't like I wasn't used to it.

"Stewart, halt for a moment, please," Loch said to our driver.

The carriage rolled to a slow stop in the middle of the road.

Loch leapt out and jogged toward the bakery. All the patrons waiting in line parted to let him pass. A few minutes later, he came out holding a box with a silver ribbon.

"Here." He handed me the package before he climbed back in. "These are incredible."

I unraveled the ribbon, draped it over my knee, and opened the box. Heat escaped its confines and warmed my hand as I reached inside and drew out a scone.

"Thank you." I offered him the first one.

"No, you need it more than I do." He was right. I was too skinny, as were all my friends, but here, maybe, that wouldn't have to be the case.

"Oh, my goodness," I practically moaned after I swallowed the first bite. Not too sweet, and perfectly flaky, with a hint of lemon and whole raspberries. It might've been the best thing I'd ever eaten. I broke off half for Sid, and he swallowed without chewing.

I pointed inside the box. "Are you sure you don't want one?" I asked Loch.

He shook his head with a smile.

I thought about saving the remaining scone for later, but the drool hanging from Sid's jowls made me reconsider. I split it between us. "Holy cow, that was amazing," I said, wiping the crumbs from my lips.

Loch's teal eyes sparkled. "I know, right? Divine. I do *love* food."

My eyes darted down his frame—like, *yeah, right. Not with that body.*

"No, really. I love to cook and I love to eat, but I do manage to get to the gym from time to time."

"Can you guys read my mind?" I sat forward and narrowed my eyes. This wasn't the first time I'd wondered that.

He chuckled. "Not exactly. But giants are adept at reading body language, and you're an open book."

I gasped at the insult. That wasn't the truth.

"I get it." Loch held up his hands. "Where you live, you're probably pretty good at hiding your feelings. Here, you're going to have to work on it." He took the silver ribbon from my lap and secured it around the end of my unraveling braid. "That should hold. Now let's get you home so we can get ready for dinner tonight. Those scones are only going to last for so long."

Not true. I could survive on dessert for a few days. Easy peasy.

On the way back to the estate—because that term seemed more appropriate than *house*—he told me about all of the Domes.

Fie—the sky—was his domain. They were known for their feats of engineering and architecture. That seemed reasonable, since half of the houses had been built on cliff faces. The only reason his family had a home with a road was because they needed to be accessible to all of its people. Many of the Fie practiced a trade, working all over the Fiefdoms to provide architecture, carpentry, and electrical services.

Fee—the earth dwellers—lived underground, but also had elaborate tree houses. They were known for horticulture and animal husbandry—his word, not mine. They provided much of the Fiefdom's food and materials used for clothing and building.

Foe—the water people—lived on a massive boat that sounded like a hybrid pirate ship-slash-cruise liner. Their passion was marine biology and fishing. Loch may have mentioned they liked to party in excess and their hobbies might've included distilling all kinds of alcohol. They were also a large force in the beauty industry. Their hair and makeup skills were coveted throughout the Fiefdom.

And the Fum—the fire wielders—lived in tents at the base of an active volcano. At first, that seemed unreasonable, but then he explained how easily one could move a tent versus a house. They were known for their metallurgy, especially weapons, and their glass-blowing, but most importantly, they minted all of the Fiefdom's currency.

"When your friends and family arrive, they'll have so many options to choose from," he said.

"How will that work exactly?" I asked.

"First, they'll be provided a stipend and housing wherever they chose to live. Though I assume initially, you'll want to stay together."

"Probably." Safety in numbers and that whole thing.

"But if they chose to work, I have a feeling that once they're comfortable, they'll branch out depending on their career choices. Their earnings will go directly to them. The opportunities here are endless." He sounded truly excited for us. "Bea, everything is going to work out. And if you don't mind me saying, I'm so happy you're here."

I wasn't about to lie and say *me too*. Because *happy* wasn't the word I would use to describe how I was feeling.

"But Loch, what am *I* here for?" I looked up at him.

One side of his lips curled softly. "Honestly, I'm not sure, but does it matter so long as you're safe too?"

Sid, finally tired of the scenery, plopped all one hundred and fifty pounds of himself on my lap. I reached over and held him so he didn't slip off my legs.

"I guess not." I stared into the distance. So far, the Fiefdom sounded amazing. Loch couldn't have painted a better picture. So why was there a pit of emptiness gnawing at my stomach? For once, it wasn't a lack of food.

# CHAPTER
# SIX

Inside my room, spread over the bed, was a high-waisted black skirt, a white crop top turtleneck with no sleeves, and a pair of four-inch-high leather boots. I dressed in the new clothes, though the ones I had on were perfectly clean.

The evening sun flickered over a pair of dangling earrings and a matching bracelet on the dresser. The stones spread a rainbow of light across the wall. The opulence here, compared to home, was significant, and it made me feel like an outsider. I held the bracelet up to admire its beauty, and cringed at the fine line of motor oil staining underneath my fingernails. There was no hope for my nails, so I focused on my hair.

I used the silver ribbon to tie it all together into a ponytail at the base of my neck. It was the best I could manage. I didn't spend time fixing my hair—I contained it. Once, when I was younger, I'd convinced Kevin to cut it off with a set of pinking shears. Bad idea. I'd looked like a clown wearing a wig. Some of the older people started calling me Annie. My blood still boiled when I heard that name.

Displayed neatly on the white countertop in the bathroom was an array of makeup—sparkling shadows, bright blushes, and lipsticks. Tee would be pleased by the selection —not only of cosmetics, but all of it. She loved the finer things in life, and for the last ten years, she didn't even have shoes that matched. In the bigger scheme of things, matching shoes weren't all that important, but it would be nice to *live* for a change instead of just surviving.

A ghost of a smile passed over my face. I missed them, even though I'd only been gone a day and a half. Tomorrow. Tomorrow, I'd get home.

Having never experimented with cosmetics without Tee's help, I decided not to start now. Although concealing the smattering of freckles over my nose and cheeks was tempting. Instead, I settled for a swipe of lip gloss.

Sitting down on the bed, I stared at the heels. They were the final straw of imposter syndrome. You could clean me up, dress me in fancy clothes, and decorate me in jewels, and I still wouldn't fit in. But it was better than starvation or being eaten by a pack of wolves, so I pulled on the ridiculous shoes. Unsteady as a newborn filly, I wobbled over to the full-length mirror. I yanked on the crop top, trying to make the fabric longer.

I glanced at Sid, who was watching me intently. "No, judgment," I chided, not used to so much exposed skin.

Together, we peered out the door, confirming the hallway was empty. With a hand pressed against the wall for balance, my stilettos and I teetered along. I was about to give up and go back to the room to find a different mode of transportation when somebody chuckled. Recognizing the deep timbre, my irritation flared and heat crawled up my cheeks.

I spun around as fast as possible without falling on my derriere. "What? You don't have anything better to do than laugh at me? Don't worry, I'm headed back to the room to change out of these *stupid* shoes."

"No, I'm sorry. I apologize." Raiden held up a hand. "You're just so fierce most of the time, I didn't think a *stupid* pair of shoes would be your demise."

I had to give him an A for effort. He was *trying* to control his laughter.

"Everyone has their kryptonite," I said.

His gaze slid down the length of my body. "That they do." He sounded resigned.

I was surprised he understood the reference, but I didn't have time to ask before my ankle buckled.

Raiden caught me under both arms, gripping almost my entire ribcage with his hands. The weight of my breasts rested on his thumbs. An uncomfortable warmth pooled in my stomach, and shivers skated over my skin. He didn't seem to notice.

"Are you okay?" His gray eyes were level with mine. The pulse in his neck, right above the open collar of his shirt, thumped in rhythm with the rapid beat of my heart.

I took a deep breath and released it slowly. "Yes. Thank you."

He helped me stand, then let go, leaving behind tingling imprints of his hands around my chest. "Do you think if I escort you, you can walk in those things?"

"Yeah, but can't I just go change?" I whined. I didn't like relying on anyone. Besides, being close to him made me feel weird. The force was strong in this one. It wasn't the same

70

as being around Loch—he made me feel self-conscious, like a peasant around a prince.

He glanced down and checked his silver watch. "You can, but being late is heavily frowned upon around here."

"Okay," I said, not wanting to be rude.

He held out an elbow, and when I looped it with my own, his skin was searing hot against mine.

"Do you feel okay?" I touched his arm with my free hand.

"Yeah, why?"

"You're so hot."

A charming but cocky smirk curled his lips. "Thank you."

I smacked his arm lightly. "No. That's not what I meant and you know it. It's like you have a fever."

"We naturally run hotter than humans."

Funny, my temperature ran around 100 degrees, which I'd always thought odd, but my mom had assured me it was normal. She'd convinced me a lot of strange things were normal. Like taking vials of mine and Kevin's blood to work with her. She said she did it because of her job.

"Earlier, you referred to me as a young lady, and now I've been demoted to human again?"

He rubbed the back of his neck. "Yeah, about that. I owe you an apology. I was mad. You interrupted my investigation and I let my irritation get the better of me."

"Is *human* a derogatory term?"

"It can be. Some giants don't like humans. Others, well . . . they like them a little too much."

"What's *that* supposed to mean?"

Redness crept up his neck, staining his face pink. "Oh, for Fie's sake. I'm just making this worse."

I didn't argue.

"I don't *dislike* humans," he clarified.

"Dude, should I get you a shovel so you can dig this hole deeper?"

He snorted, then choked out a laugh, his deep-set eyes all but disappearing behind his wide smile. "Yes, please, so I can finish burying myself."

We turned the corner into the dining room without me falling and breaking my face.

"You know I'm not going to let this conversation go, right?"

He sighed. "Noted. But we'll finish it later."

I scowled at the order.

"Please?"

His begging was kind of cute.

"Fine. But later." I pointed a finger, daring him to forget.

He pulled out a white velvet chair with silver nail heads and gestured for me to sit, so I did. Sid curled around my legs. Even wearing the four-inch heels, only my tiptoes touched the floor. Raiden took the spot next to me. Funny, we were the first ones there. No danger of being late at all.

Light from the five-tiered chandelier sparkled over the glossy table. Bone china contrasted with the ebony surface, and pink roses, nestled in a crystal vase, decorated the center of the table.

A cold sweat crept under my heavy ponytail as I realized this was out of my league. I was used to eating most of my meals from broken dishes or scarred, plastic plates.

Raiden reached over and touched my leg. A faint tingle ran to the tips of my toes. "Don't worry, just follow my lead."

How did he know I was freaking out?

I didn't get a chance to ask before Sylvia, Issac, and Loch

strolled in. Raiden rose from the table but placed a hand on my shoulder, keeping me put.

"Aunt, Uncle, Loch." He bowed his head before sitting back down.

"Raiden. So nice of you to join us. I didn't expect you to be here." Sylvia greeted him politely, but the iciness in her voice led me to believe she wasn't happy to see him. Seating herself at the end of the table, Sylvia motioned to a waiter, who leaned over so she could whisper something in his ear, then he nodded and left.

Loch stared down at Raiden. "Excuse me, cousin, do you mind switching places? I'd like to sit next to our guest."

The muscles in Raiden's jaw rolled.

"You'll have her undivided attention for the upcoming week," Loch continued, "so it's only fair that I have the honor tonight."

Though it sounded like a request, the firm set of his shoulders led me to believe it was an order. A polite one, but an order nonetheless.

Raiden stood up, his chair scraping across the marble floor. Standing next to each other, the resemblance was uncanny. Same dark hair, same jawline, but different colored eyes—icy gray versus aqua blue. Loch might have been a smidge taller, but Raiden was wider through the shoulders. He had a rugged vibe, whereas Loch looked like a cover model.

A young woman poured each of us a glass of champagne, the tiny bubbles darting to the surface before fizzing.

Sylvia picked up her flute and everyone followed suit. "A toast—to new friends." She tilted her head toward me.

I smiled. What else was I supposed to do?

"And to trusting the wisdom of our ancestors," she added.

Raiden looked at me, small lines furrowing between his brows. I shrugged. I wasn't supposed to say anything.

"Here, here," they all said together before taking a sip.

I coughed as the effervescence tickled the back of my nose. I covered my mouth with a silk napkin. The material was finer than anything I'd ever owned.

A few minutes later, a beautiful woman swept in through the open doors. Her straight, raven hair fell halfway down her back and swished in time with her graceful movements. She was tall and willowy with narrow shoulders and hips. Cobalt eyes, framed with long lashes, contrasted beautifully against her golden skin. Even smiling, her lips were full and plump. Painfully cute dimples creased her blushed cheeks.

"Vanessa," Sylvia gushed. "So pleased you accepted my last-minute invitation. I didn't know Raiden was joining us, but I thought you'd love to see him."

I tore my eyes away from her and glanced at Loch.

"Raiden's girlfriend," he whispered.

A cross between disappointment and irritation festered. Raiden had never mentioned a girlfriend. But how should I know? It wasn't like we were close.

Vanessa leaned down to hug Raiden and pressed a kiss to his cheek. He patted her on the back somewhat stiffly, then stood up and pulled out the chair next to him, inviting her to sit.

I unintentionally bristled. What was wrong with me?

The staff served each of us a salad full of greenery and colorful vegetables, followed by a massive plate piled with saucy noodles and protein I didn't recognize.

Out of the corner of my eye, I covertly observed Raiden so I knew which fork to use.

I stabbed the salad onto the correct utensil and took the first bite. My taste buds exploded with flavor at the moment of impact. For fear of what the rich food would do to my digestive system, I only ate a small amount of each dish. Between bites, I discreetly dropped the mystery meat under the table for Sid.

The dining experience was unlike anything I was used to. Tee, Kevin, and I usually ate our dinner curled up on the couch watching TV if we had the spare electricity. If not, we played board games or read books out loud by candlelight.

Vanessa reached over and caressed Raiden's arm as she whispered something in his ear. He smiled, but no joy crinkled his eyes. His gaze met mine and it dawned on me that he was as uncomfortable as I was.

"Bea, how are you enjoying it here so far?" Loch asked, drawing my attention.

"It's beautiful but very different from home." The contrasts between our worlds were stark. Alaska had been devastated by earthquakes and volcanoes. For the first few years, each time we went back to Anchorage to gather what supplies we could find, it smelled like death amongst the ruin and rubble. Here, they had indoor plumbing and electricity. And best of all, there seemed to be plenty of food on their table—and I didn't have to kill it myself.

Loch continued with the small talk through dessert, but after the alcohol, I was having a hard time keeping my eyes open. A big yawn escaped without my permission.

"Please excuse me. I'm so sorry. It's been a long day," I said, shoving my foot in my mouth. "Uh," I stuttered, "but it's been fun." I tried pulling my foot out. I didn't want Loch to think I was ungrateful for taking time out of his day to show me around.

"I'm sure it has," Sylvia said, "but plans have changed, and now that you're leaving first thing in the morning, our breakfast will have to be postponed. Raiden, why don't you escort Vanessa home? I'm sure you'll want to get some sleep," she said, like she wasn't talking about sleeping. "Tomorrow morning is going to come early."

He started to object but with one stern look from her, he said, "Yes, Aunt Sylvia." He set his napkin on his dessert plate and stood up before pulling out Vanessa's chair. Before he left, he placed his hand on my shoulder and squeezed. "I'll see you in the morning."

Strange feelings tumbled inside my stomach. They resembled what my mom's romance books would describe as *butterfly wings*. I brushed them away. The notion was ridiculous.

He offered his elbow to Vanessa and she took it feverishly. Her face was alive with what looked like adoration. Perhaps love? However, I didn't think the feelings were reciprocated. But hey, how would I know? Besides, I didn't care anyway.

Sylvia waited until they exited before speaking. "Since we won't be having our meeting tomorrow morning, I had the contract finished early. We'll give you time to read it, to make sure you approve."

A server filled our glasses. I wasn't planning to drink more, but it was clear that Sylvia was about to make another toast.

"To our mutual arrangement. May it benefit both parties."

We all raised our flutes, and I took a small sip.

Issac added more. "To prosperity." He was a man of few words.

We raised our glasses again, and I took another small sip.

Loch reached out and touched my arm. "And most importantly, to new friends." His gaze traveled over my face, lingering for a moment on my lips, before he raised his glass and downed the rest of his drink. His parents copied.

Even though we'd already toasted to new friends earlier in the evening, I took a deep breath and drank the rest of mine. I didn't want to—I was already fuzzy from the first two I'd had with dinner—but I didn't want to offend anyone either. They were my key to getting home.

A woman dressed in a pinstriped suit swept into the room holding a black leather briefcase. Her stride was long and confident. Tendrils of dark hair with heavy white streaks framed her serious face. "The document you requested, my lady." She stopped at the other end of the table, placed the case onto it before opening it and setting the papers in front of Sylvia.

Her pale-blue eyes settled heavily on mine. The firm line of her lips and the scowl between her brows looked like contempt, but her voice was smooth as she said, "Shall I stay to answer any questions?"

Sid growled. I nudged him lightly with my foot to shut him up.

"No, Penelope. It's pretty straightforward, correct? Nothing too complicated?" Sylvia straightened the contract on the table.

"No, my lady." Penelope's glare didn't break. "I kept it simple." Her lips skewed to the side, suggesting that she thought I was simple. "Just a basic agreement between two parties. If that will be all?"

"Yes, thank you," Sylvia dismissed.

Penelope snapped the case shut, turned, and walked out, her heels clicking loudly over the floor.

I blinked. I was certain Penelope did not like me.

Sylvia slid the papers across the table, along with a shiny black pen that blended with the surface. "Here. Please read the document carefully. We'll give you some privacy, then we'll be back in a bit to answer any questions you might have."

Loch clasped my shoulder before they left the dining room.

The clock on the wall ticked loudly. My dad had always said never to sign a document without reading it in its entirety. I picked up the first sheet and began to read. By the fifth page, my eyes drifted. So far, nothing seemed unreasonable, but I wasn't sure why they needed so many words to convey a simple agreement. Apparently, lawyers were the same everywhere.

Soon, I started skimming pages. My finger whizzed over the words. My concentration waned from time to time, but I was pretty sure the gist of our earlier conversation was there. I would stay—no matter what. My people would be cared for if they chose to live here. Shelter. Food. Jobs. If they decided to leave, they were on their own. Yada, yada, yada.

I picked up the pen, which had been honed from obsidian stone like the stairway and was ice cold in my hands. I started to sign my name—*Ruby Rose Walker*. As if Ruby wasn't colorful enough.

Something sharp pinched the skin over my heart, and I dropped the pen. I slapped the spot like it was a stinging bug before I peered down my shirt. Nothing was there. I retrieved the pen and finished where I'd left off. The bright-red ink stained the stark-white paper, looking like fresh blood. I waved my hand over the signature so it would dry faster.

I pushed the agreement out of the way, crossed my arms, and laid my head down on the table to rest for a minute.

"Finished?"

I jumped and wiped the drool from the corner of my lip. I'd fallen asleep.

Sylvia flipped to the last page. "Well done. Now, in order to convince your people to join you, tell them that you have signed a legal contract that guarantees their safety. And they have the freedom to leave if they choose. Anything that pertains to them, feel free to use in your persuasion. But if you tell any other giant the details of this contract, including Raiden, it becomes null and void."

Her icy blue eyes sharpened and she gave me a curt nod as if to say—*I'll be watching.*

# CHAPTER
# SEVEN

Two winged horses, one black and one white, like opposite sides of a chessboard, stood in the courtyard. They tossed their heads, pawed at the granite, and snorted. Great gusts of fog erupted from their nostrils.

My eyes traveled the length of the beast's feathery, black legs, up its shoulders, to the massive width of its back and the wings folded closely to its body. Apprehension constricted the muscles along my neck, giving me a slight headache. Sensing my hesitation, Sid pressed closer to my thigh. I didn't want to ride one alone. Heck, I couldn't even ride a real horse. We used ATVs, snow machines, and off-road vehicles. I was by no means accustomed to *that* kind of horsepower.

"Don't look so worried," Raiden joked as he strolled out of the house. "You'll ride with me."

"So why are there two—"

"No, Raiden, she can ride with me," Vanessa interrupted from behind us. She was dressed in black riding pants and knee-high leather boots. Her shiny, dark hair spilled down the front of her white peacoat.

I glanced down at my own cargo pants and hiking boots. After I'd gotten back from dinner last night, my clothes had been lying on the bed, folded and clean. Though they were worn and ugly, they were practical. And thankfully, after a night's sleep, the blisters on my ankles and feet had healed.

"Vanessa." Raiden spoke her name like it was a warning.

"Oh, seriously, I'm not going to hurt her." Her eyes landed on mine, and she smiled exposing a set of fangs. "*Much*," she silently mouthed so Raiden couldn't hear her. The dimples that had made her so approachable last night were obviously a farce.

"No," Raiden said, alleviating some of the pressure knocking on my ribs. The idea of her going with us was disturbing enough—riding behind her while at those heights when it was clear she didn't like me—no thanks. He loaded Sid into the basket, and in one swing, lifted me onto the black beast.

I gripped the saddle horn and squeezed my legs to keep from falling. The creature flicked its tail.

Vanessa slipped her foot into a stirrup and pulled herself into the saddle in one graceful motion. The moment she was settled, her mount stretched out its feathery white wings and galloped off the cliff. My stomach dipped and rolled and we hadn't even left the ground yet. I closed my eyes, waiting.

Raiden adjusted the cinch, then climbed up behind me. He wrapped an arm around my waist and leaned in close. "Hang on."

Every muscle in my body constricted hard enough to make me stiffen, and I closed my eyes as the pegasus took off at a gallop and lifted into the air. My stomach undulated with each beat of its wings.

He chuckled. "Open your eyes," he whispered a minute later. His breath was warm on the back of my ear, sending a barrage of unusual sensations to my core.

I shook my head fiercely.

"Come on, Bea. You're braver than that."

Yeah, I liked to think so, but maybe I was wrong. I opened them a sliver, ready to snap them shut. The sharp mountain peaks repeated endlessly.

"Not so bad, right?"

My head swiveled as fear faded. The natural splendor rivaled Alaska in every way, especially from this vantage. Vanessa, just a small white dot in the distance, was far enough ahead of us, I could almost forget about her too. "It's beautiful. Really."

"Yeah, she is. On the other side of the range is the ocean, but we won't be going in that direction today. I want to get this done and over with as soon as possible."

My jaw tensed. I wasn't used to being a burden. I would've been perfectly happy to go home and stay there, but last night, I had signed a contract to return.

Soon, the landscape transformed into large open spaces, broken up by patches of forest and muddy rivers with fingerlike tributaries.

The ebb and flow of the beast's wings almost lulled me to sleep, but I didn't want to miss anything. Once I was more comfortable, I reached down and stroked the black mane of the pegasus. The sun absorbed into his shiny coat, making him hot to the touch.

"Does he have a name?"

"Of course he does. Arnold."

"You named this massive beast *Arnold*?"

"I didn't name him, my mom did, after the actor. She thought it was appropriate."

I laughed. It was. "Your mom has a sense of humor."

"Had," he said softly. "Both of my parents are gone."

"Oh. I'm sorry." I knew the pain of loss, though I wasn't sure if mine were dead. They were gone all the same.

"It was a long time ago. No need to rehash the past."

Gladly, I changed the subject. "You know an awful lot about Earth. At least what it was like before."

"We do. On the whole, our worlds are very similar. Our societies function much as yours once did, minus some technology. Much of it doesn't work for us. Besides, that's a good thing after watching what it did to the human race. The invention of social media deteriorated your already low levels of empathy. The minute people could bully, threaten, say whatever they wanted with impunity, your society was led down a dark path."

He sounded like Kevin, but he wasn't wrong.

"Look, over there." Raiden pointed.

Strange animals with golden coats and huge, branching antlers of glistening silver meandered through the meadow.

"What are they?"

"Elk."

"That's not what elk look like." I was disappointed. I'd expected some mythical, fanciful name for them.

"It is here."

"They look dangerous," I said.

"They are to someone like you."

"What's that supposed to mean? They're dangerous to *humans*?"

"Yeah. You want me to lie to you?"

I ignored him.

Birds, twice the size of eagles, soared next to us. Sunlight bounced off their bronze feathers.

"Are they dangerous too?" I tightened my grip on the saddle horn and leaned further into Raiden's chest. He snaked his free arm around my middle to pull me in closer. The beat of his heart thumped against my back. His thighs pressed closer to mine. I concentrated on our surroundings to keep my temperature in check. His nearness made me comfortable physically—but uncomfortable emotionally. Or was it the other way around?

"Not with me here, but if you were on the ground, you'd be in trouble. They could pick you up and fly away. They'd probably make their nest out of your pretty hair." He yanked lightly on the end of my braid.

I didn't like Raiden much, but I felt safe with him.

Hours later, just as the sun dipped beyond the horizon, we began to descend. Pinks, yellows, and oranges painted the sky in an array of sorbet flavors. I closed my eyes tightly, waiting for the impact upon landing. We set down gently at a lope and came to a gradual halt as Arnold folded his wings in close.

Raiden flung his leg over the side, jumped off, then held his arms out to help me. He caught me under the armpits and lowered me to the ground.

I recognized the valley, but the obsidian staircase leading home was missing. Disappointment, verging on alarm, buzzed under my skin. "Where are the stairs?"

"Relax. They'll be there tomorrow." He tossed me my backpack, let Sid out of the contraption, then pointed to a small grove of trees backlit by the dying sun. "Over there, you'll find camp. Gather some firewood," he ordered. His attitude reminded me of my brother. I was afraid they might get along.

"Aren't you worried something in there will kill her?" Vanessa peeked over Raiden's shoulder. She scooted in behind him and wrapped her arms around his chest, staking her claim.

"The only thing that wants to hurt her is right here," he said, shrugging her off.

"Can you blame me?" She wrinkled her nose.

Did she want me dead? What the heck had I ever done to her? And if she *did* want me dead, how safe were my friends and family going to be?

A cold sweat broke out on my forehead. I'd already signed the contract. And there was no getting out of it now —for me—but knowing that my people still had a choice kept me calm.

Raiden ignored her comment and unsaddled Arnold.

Happy to be on solid ground, Sid and I walked along a partially beaten-down trail through the brush. I skimmed my hands over the long bluegrass. It tickled my palms and weirdly made my nose itch.

A fire pit with log benches waited inside the tree line. I tossed my pack next to the base of a fir tree with a diameter easily ten feet across.

Giant fungus, big enough to sit on, in bright reds and oranges, crawled up the trunks like rungs on a ladder. Tentacles of blackened green moss dangled from the lower branches all the way to the dirt floor. For the most part, the area around the campsite was clear, but the farther away I peered, the denser the forest became.

Venturing into the underbrush, I busted through a spiderweb, invisible in the low light. Its silky strands stuck to my hands and face. I slapped it away fiercely, like I was batting at an invisible swarm of bugs. The willies ran down my back and I shuddered.

Quickly gathering some downed wood, I tried not to imagine the size of the spider that had woven the web. Alaska, for all of its dangers, didn't have venomous spiders or any snakes at all.

After I dropped the kindling next to the fire pit, I dusted off my arms before sitting on a log. Strange sounds—clips, yips, and buzzing—hovered in the breeze. My uneasiness grew harder to ignore as it burrowed deeper. At least when I was home, I knew what to fear.

Raiden started the fire while Vanessa sat across from me and glared. I twisted my tongue behind my teeth. I'd finally had enough of her attitude.

"What? What's your problem?"

She stood. "*You*. You're human. You have no right to be here. If I had my way, we'd roast you over that fire and eat you." She lifted her nose in the air as if she were smelling barbequed flesh.

"Knock it off, Vanessa. We don't eat humans anymore." Raiden sounded bored instead of alarmed.

"Just because we don't doesn't mean we *shouldn't*." The flickering blaze mirrored in her eyes and accentuated the hollows under her cheeks. She lowered her head and rolled her shoulders forward. She took a predatory step closer to me as if I were prey. I wasn't sure if she was doing it to frighten me or if she was for real.

"Vanessa," Raiden snapped. "We talked about this. If you're not going to behave, go home."

She licked the tips of her shiny white fangs, silently challenging me as the campfire crackled and popped. Floating ashes glimmered in the dark.

I waved my hand. "Ah . . . who thinks leaving the lunatic here is a good idea, raise your hand." I didn't want her anywhere near my family.

She was in front of me before I saw her move. Startled, I shied away but didn't fall off the seat.

Sid jumped up, hackles raised and fangs exposed. His were bigger, but hers looked sharper. A guttural growl rumbled from his throat. The beginning of fear prickled at the base of my neck. I guess I had my answer.

"I could snap your neck with one hand, you disgusting filth." Her breath skimmed over my face in a gust of cold air.

Before I could counter, Raiden lunged and grabbed her by the arm, yanking her away. She fell backward, the impact of her crash reverberating through the ground.

"Raiden!" she yelled. "You're going to side with a *human*? I wasn't going to hurt her, but *it* can't talk to me that way."

Sid stopped growling but his hackles stayed up.

"I'm not siding with anyone. My job is to get her family back here *unharmed.* And you're making my job more difficult. One more wrong move and you're gone." He jabbed his thumb behind him, then he pointed at her. "I didn't want you here in the first place."

Her mouth dropped open as she gasped. "Your aunt thought my presence would be an asset."

"Yeah, well, she was mistaken. Aunt Sylvia doesn't know you like I do. She doesn't know how you feel about humans. I tried telling her, but she refused to listen."

Vanessa stood up and dusted off her pants, leaving behind a perfect impression of her butt in the dirt.

"I mean it. One wrong move and you're gone. I. Don't. Want. You. Here." He crossed his arms.

"Raiden." Her voice was soft and hurt. Her lower lip pouted. "You don't mean that." A glassiness coated her vibrant blue eyes.

God, she was beautiful. I hated her.

He ran his fingers through his hair. "Yes, I do, Vanessa. We've been through this. I'm never going to—"

"Okay!" she yelled, holding her hand out to stop him. "I get it!" Her eyes darted to me.

Whatever he was about to say, she didn't want me to hear. I was starting to think she wasn't his girlfriend. I wondered why Loch had said she was. *Interesting.*

"And you." He looked at me. "Keep your mouth shut."

"Excuse me?"

"You heard me," he grumbled.

"I'll do no such thing." I flipped my hair over my shoulder and lifted my chin.

He took a deep breath and exhaled slowly, as if searching for a measure of patience. "Please?"

"Fine," I gave in. Truthfully, it was probably safer for me not to antagonize her. She was a monster, but backing down wasn't my strong suit. I blamed it on the hair color.

## CHAPTER
# EIGHT

T
he next morning, I scrunched my nose, buffering a sneeze as smoke drifted into my sinuses. I yawned and cracked open my eyes. Raiden and Vanessa were curled up on opposite sides of the smoldering camp-fire, still asleep.

After slipping on my shoes, Sid and I strolled to the edge of the tree line. The rising sun framed the far-off mountain peaks and fingers of light spilled into the valley. Only the slight swishing of us moving through the long grass inter-rupted the early hush.

A crisp breeze, carrying the faint scent of dew and wild-flowers, numbed the tip of my nose. I stretched my neck from one side to the other. It was stiff after sleeping on the ground.

To my left, hovering at eye level, tiny pinpricks of light sparkled in the air. Gradually, they expanded to larger spots until they connected. I squinted under the glare, determined not to look away. Like a fuzzy mirage, the obsidian stairwell appeared. I hesitated before approaching.

"It's amazing, isn't it?" Raiden said.

I twitched but managed to keep the yelp on the tip of my tongue buried. For being so big, he moved quietly.

"You're jumpy."

I glanced over my shoulder toward our campsite. "Can you blame me?"

"Not really. Sorry about Vanessa. I don't think she was going to actually hurt you."

I shivered, both from the cool temperature and the confrontation from last night. "Really?"

"Ehhhh . . ." He teetered his head. In one swift motion, he yanked his sweatshirt off, giving me a good view of his rippled six-pack before his T-shirt slid back down. He wrapped it around my shoulders. It reminded me of when I was a kid, before the world collapsed, when my mom would cover me up in a toasty blanket straight out of the dryer.

I buried my face into the soft fleece. It smelled like a campfire, fresh mountain air, spruce trees, and peppermint. And something darker, sensual, musky.

A smirk, and something like satisfaction, flashed in his eyes.

The instant heat of embarrassment rushed to the surface of my skin when I realized what I'd been doing. Surely he wouldn't notice, since my nose and cheeks were already pink from the cold.

"So that's my way home?"

"Yup. That's the door."

"How does it work?" I averted my eyes and busied myself studying the staircase.

"I can open it as soon as the sun rises. But I can close it at any time I choose."

"So when it's open, how come no other humans end up here?"

"We position them in remote locations. And even then, most of the time, humans walk right past them like they don't even see them."

"I don't get it. Are they all in Alaska? How does this work?"

He rubbed his fingers over his jaw. "The best way to describe it, it's like a double bubble. They almost touch in some spots, but they don't invade the other's space. You are the bubble inside the bubble. Some of us know how to poke holes and go through without popping the bubble. We use places of intense energy. Sometimes it's Alaska, when the aurora borealis is strong, sometimes it's near Lake Maracaibo in Venezuela—it's pretty consistent there, since they get over 300 days a year of lightning. The Bermuda Triangle, Stonehenge, the Egyptian pyramids, and there are quite a few more. Just depends on where you want to go."

"Poke holes? I thought you said you didn't use . . . technology?" I said for lack of a better term. Magic just wasn't something I was willing to voice a loud.

"We don't. This is more like magic."

I cringed.

He chuckled at my uncomfortable reaction. "We have some of that here, remember? I thought you said you were familiar with *Jack and the Beanstalk*?"

"I am, but I never took the magic beans *literally*. So, are all of the passages stairs or is there really a beanstalk?"

"They're all stairs. But the story would have been silly if it was called *Jack and the Staircase*. How could he chop it down?" He reached out and ruffled my hair.

Sparks spread all the way to my fingertips. I laughed, but it came out more like a giggle. What was wrong with me?

I started to ask more questions, but he said, "You ready to go home?"

My shoulders sagged with relief. "Yeah, I am."

I was worried about Kevin and Tee. By now, they'd definitely be out looking for me.

He handed me my pack. "Okay, let's do this."

Unease and a measure of fear coiled in the hollow of my throat when Vanessa strolled into the meadow looking as fresh as the day was young. Raiden's lips tightened and irritation flashed behind his eyes.

"Good morning," she called, waving.

He ignored her as he stepped in front of the staircase and entered, Sid following.

I hesitated at the shimmering passageway, knowing it was going to shock me like an electric fence. Raiden and Sid, standing on the other side, looked warped, as if they were underwater. They hopped down about twenty steps, giving me plenty of room. Sid's tail stopped wagging and his ears perked up.

"Oh, for Fie's sake, go!" Vanessa snapped.

"Vanessa!" Raiden screamed, but it was too late.

Vanessa shoved me hard through the doorway. My limbs flailed as I tumbled forward. My head crashed onto the stone and something in my hand snapped, sending a flash of pain up my arm, before Raiden's legs halted my progression. I pulled my knees to my chest and cradled my left hand. I didn't want to look. The screaming sensation in my bones told me it wasn't good.

A warm hand grabbed my shoulder. I flinched. He got down in my face and looked at me. "Bea, are you okay?"

I nodded. I wasn't dead. His eyes were lighter than normal, gleaming like stainless steel, bright and angry.

He let go and ran up the stairs two at a time. "Get out *now!*" he roared, his voice thunderous, echoing off the polished stone. The air was laden with electricity. The weight of it was uncomfortable but left me breathless at the same time.

"Raiden, I didn't mean to push her so hard. It was an accident." Vanessa kept her composure well under the circumstances. I was cringing and his anger wasn't even aimed at me.

"*Leave.*" Raiden's voice was low and soft, far more intimidating than his shouting, which was saying a lot. He stepped up another stair, forcing her to back through the doorway.

"You would hurt me over a . . . *human?*" She looked truly offended and surprised.

"*Leave.*" He raised both hands and said something I didn't understand.

Vanessa and the doorway vanished. The staircase didn't.

He raced back to my side. "Can you get up?"

I nodded, afraid if I spoke, I would start crying.

He helped me sit against the cold black stone as I kept a firm grip on my fingers. His eyes darted toward my protected limb. "How is your head?" He cupped my cheeks with both hands. They practically spanned from the bottom of my chin to the top of my skull. Tiny pinpricks, like static, blanketed my skin.

"My head's okay." I smiled slightly and inhaled a shaky breath, doing everything in my power not to cry. I was used to stress. I was used to living under pressure. I was used to living with very little. I was tough. I *was*. But this

93

was too much. I'd bargained my freedom away for the safety of my people. Now, I wasn't even sure if that was the case. *What if there were more like Vanessa?* And I was tired, I was scared, I was alone, and some hoity-toity bitch wanted to kill me.

My bottom lip trembled.

He pulled me into his chest and rested his chin on the top of my head. My fears gave way, and I plummeted into tears. I sobbed uncontrollably, barely able to catch my breath between waves. Sid nudged me and whined. I tried to pull away, but Raiden refused to let me go. He simply held on until most of my hysteria had passed.

He handed me a handkerchief. "I'm sorry I didn't get rid of her earlier. We used to be friends. I really didn't think she'd hurt you."

"What have I done?" I cried, wiping my nose.

"What do you mean?"

"Are my friends and family going to be any safer in the Fiefdom?"

Gently, he pushed me back and stared into my eyes. "Oh. Yes, certainly. There are a few of us that don't like humans, but the numbers are very small. And our punishment for killing one another—including a human—is execution. Bea, we don't mess around. An eye for an eye is taken very seriously in our realm. I promise, your family will be safe with us. Now, can I look at your hand?" His fingers ran over the sides of my face and tipped up my chin, leaving a trail of heat behind. He tried tucking the wayward curls behind my ears.

Feeling slightly better about my decision thanks to Raiden's assurances, I held out my hand and stared past his shoulder down the stairwell. I was great with other people's injuries and wounds, no matter how grotesque, just not my own.

He sucked a breath through his teeth. "Ouch. You got a couple of broken fingers. I'm going to tape them together, okay?"

"Uh-huh." It could be worse, but the pain was still legit.

He rummaged around in his pack and pulled out some athletic tape. "This is probably going to hurt."

"I have some aspirin in my bag." It was expired, like so many of the medications we had in the bunker.

He dug through my sack and opened the bottle. He tapped out four pills into the palm of my good hand and offered me his flask of water.

As he began to wrap my fingers, a cold sweat broke out on my forehead and down my back. Bright sparkling lights flashed before my eyes before my vision expanded and collapsed.

"Hey, hey." He shook me. I opened my eyes and blinked.

"You passed out." He sat me up and crouched in front of me, his body crowding mine. I stared at the strong line of his jaw, the sharp edges of his lips against the darkening shadow of facial hair. Fire crept up my clammy cheeks.

"Hey, don't be embarrassed. We all have our kryptonite, right?" he joked. He gently tapped the end of my cold nose.

"Yeah," I mumbled. "I seem to have weaknesses, but you don't."

Mischievousness lit up his eyes. "Oh, I have mine alright."

"And they are?" I bit my bottom lip.

"That's for me to know and you to find out. Or not." He winked. His eyes, now back to their normal thundercloud gray, studied my face intently. "You want to rest for a while longer? We can. I want to make sure you're okay before we go farther."

My kryptonite count had climbed another notch even if I wasn't willing to admit it. I averted my gaze from his devastatingly handsome face.

"No," I said, feeling less shaky. It wasn't like I'd lost any blood. I was acting like a baby.

"Here." He handed me some jerky—chicken, I hoped—then tossed Sid a bite before sitting down on the stairs next to me. "You know, you don't always have to be so tough." He bumped me with his shoulder.

"Really? I don't call that tough." I'd just cried—scratch that—hysterically sobbed—and passed out all in one day. Heck, all within an hour.

"So you're going to tell me crying in front of me wasn't hard? I see how stubborn you are."

"It was humiliating," I grumbled.

"You and I have a very different definition of humiliating."

"Do *you* cry?" I bumped him back. The skin on my arm prickled even though I was still wearing his sweatshirt.

"Not often, but then again, I don't have much to cry about. My life . . . it's been pretty good, most of the time."

He hesitated on the last statement. I didn't believe it was as easy as he pretended. His parents were dead, and I had seen how uncomfortable he was in the presence of his aunt and uncle. But I let it slide in favor of a different topic.

"So you and Vanessa?" I fiddled with the edges of the athletic tape holding my fingers together.

"Me and Vanessa, what?"

"Loch said she's your girlfriend."

Raiden shook his head and muttered under his breath,

"Asshole." But he didn't sound angry, more amused. "Vanessa is not my girlfriend."

"Now or ever?"

"Jealous?" His tone took on a teasing edge.

"Don't be ridiculous," I said, even though I knew I was lying. I just hoped he couldn't see through the façade.

"We dated for like five minutes. When I realized she's more interested in climbing the ladder of Loch, I broke it off. She didn't take it too well."

"I can see that." I dug deep into the sarcasm.

"Besides, she isn't what I'm looking for."

I desperately wanted to ask what he was searching for in a relationship, but before I could ease into uncharted territory, he answered. "I want my soul-mate. I know the chances of finding her are slim, but I'm young, and I won't give up hope just yet."

My silly little heart fluttered and did a weird backflip. With my uninjured hand, I rubbed along my sternum attempting to quiet the acrobats inside my chest.

Not comfortable with these strange emotions and eager to get home, I started to stand.

"Wait," he said, helping me up. "I'll go first to break your fall in case you decide to tumble the rest of the way down."

By the end of the day, we were at the bottom.

"We have two choices. We can either camp here or see how far we can get out there—" he nodded toward the thick forest at the base of the stairs, "—before the sun goes down."

"In here. Definitely in here." The things beyond that threshold scared me during the day.

"Good choice." He placed his hands on the stone, its color so absolutely black it seemed to absorb the light around it, making the passageway darker than it really was. He said something in elvish, I was sure. Tiny glitters of light began to sparkle and grow bigger until, magically, a door appeared in the stone.

"Is that giant for 'open sesame'?" I asked.

"You give us too much credit. It's Latin for 'open sesame.' Should I close the door or will that trigger your anxiety?" He clamped his lips together, suppressing a grin.

I shifted my feet. "About that . . ."

"You live in an underground bunker," he finished for me, but he left the door open anyway.

I grimaced. "You knew?"

Sid jumped up on my cot and twirled a ridiculous number of times before settling down.

"I suspected."

"Well, I was trying to escape." I propped my good hand on my hip.

He paused, rolling out his sleeping bag. "Are you planning to escape tonight?"

"No."

"Good. Cause I'd like to get some sleep this time." He sat down and leaned back on his cot, crossing his legs. He still wore his boots.

"You weren't asleep last time?" I untied my hiking shoes and slid them under the bed. There was no way I was sleeping in them since I didn't plan on leaving.

"No. How was I supposed to keep an eye on you if I slept? I have to give you credit, you made me doubt my instincts there for a while."

My eyes darted to the open door, a gesture of good faith. I had no problem honoring his trust because having a giant on the journey home was comforting.

# CHAPTER
# NINE

At the base of the staircase, I closed my eyes, preparing for the shock as I stepped into the open. The zap seemed less intense this time.

My feet sank into the moss. Droplets of water plunked from one leaf to another until they finally soaked into the forest floor, and the heavy aroma of decaying plants hung in the humid air.

Raiden strapped a sword to his back and sheathed a couple of knives before holding out my machete and my precious 9mm.

My fingers were much better this morning so I unwrapped the athletic tape holding them together and bent them a couple times for a good stretch. Raiden cocked his head curiously but didn't comment on why I seemed to heal so fast. For me, it was normal.

"Where did you get that?" I stared at the gun in his hand before I reached out and touched it as if I couldn't believe it was mine. That weapon and I had history, and it ranked high on the list of things I loved.

"I retrieved it last night while you were sleeping." He placed it in my palm.

"How did you find it?" I tucked it into my empty holster and grabbed my machete and slid it into the scabbard on the other side of my waist.

He answered my question with an arched eyebrow as if to say, *really?* "Can you lead us to your home from here?"

I glanced left, then right. "Is this doorway in the same place?"

"Yes."

"Sid, take the point," I said.

He took off in a trot, leaving footprints in the mud. Raiden gestured for me to go first, so I did.

Soon, we hit the ruptured asphalt and followed it to where my Jeep was. Or where it was supposed to be.

Either the On-Grids had taken it or my brother had.

"I guess we're walking," I said.

"How long do you estimate?"

"About four hours."

He glanced at what was left of the mangled highway. "You ready?"

"Yup." I saluted him, then cinched the rucksack around my chest and stomach, and hooked my thumbs into the padded arm straps.

We hiked for hours in silence. It was safer that way. In the old days, people used to carry bells and talk in order to scare the bears away. The bears were no longer scared. Now, any form of noise was the equivalent of ringing the dinner bell.

To the right was the Turnagain Arm of the Cook Inlet, and to the left was the Chugach Mountain range. The uppermost peaks were obscured by low-hanging clouds.

Old railroad tracks, the rusted metal twisted, warped, and separated, ran alongside the ocean like an abandoned roller-coaster ride. Eagles glided in the sky. A pod of beluga whales rose to the surface, their icy-white skin a stark contrast to the muddy ocean. Humans didn't fare as well as the wildlife did on Earth 2.0.

Those of us who'd survived the initial wave of natural disasters, then the virus, seemed immune to anything new. Organic food and fresh air worked wonders for the human body. Not a single person in our group had died from anything other than animal attacks or accidents.

The current head count of our group was thirty-seven people—fifteen adults over the age of twenty-one, fifteen between the ages of fifteen and twenty, and seven children. Over time, our numbers had slowly dwindled. At one point, there had been more than fifty of us. I tried not to think about it, though it was the main reason I'd traded my freedom. Living like we did was dangerous. If the On-Grids didn't get us, the wildlife would. And I couldn't tolerate anyone else's death if I could prevent it.

Loose tendrils of hair slapped me in the face as the afternoon winds picked up through the glacial valley. The tree-tops swayed and the white-capped waves multiplied with a vengeance.

With the gusts at our backs, both Sid and I missed the odor of rotten fish oil and urine, but we didn't miss the angry roar as we came around a bend in the trail. A young brown bear stood on his hind legs, front paws dangling in the air as he swayed his head. He was at least two feet taller than Raiden. He rapidly snapped his jaw open and shut, his teeth chattering.

Raiden swiftly drew the sword from his back. Its sharp

edge flashed even with the lack of sunlight. He held a hand up to keep me away.

I cocked my 9mm and readied my stance. Sid growled and stalked forward, his shoulder rolling and his head down.

"Don't you get in the way!" I yelled.

Sid froze, but continued to bare his teeth and growl.

The bear's beady eyes darted between the three of us.

I moved away from Raiden but didn't get closer to the bear. With every step I took sideways, Sid mimicked mine in the other direction. An older, more experienced bear might've backed down. They were smart and liked the odds to be heavily in their favor—that was why they were such successful killers. It was three-to-one odds and we were most definitely predators.

Once the bear decided who was the greatest threat—Raiden—he launched forward on his powerful hind legs. His speed was unimaginable. Thankfully, Raiden was quicker. He swung the sword up and around, the blade connecting with the bear's unprotected belly. Blood blackened his matted fur. He lifted his head and roared, saliva flinging from his mouth. Seven-inch-long claws swiped at Raiden, missing him by inches. Raiden spun on one foot and ducked out of the way.

The bear faked and started to dash at Sid, but then reversed and slashed with his paw, catching Raiden in the shoulder. His sword flew out of his hand as he was thrown into a sharp boulder. His head smacked the solid surface with a thunderous crack.

Thinking the greatest threat was out of the way, the bear turned his attention to me. Bloodlust glittered in his black eyes.

I gripped the gun tight and aimed for his eye. I was the only person I knew capable of pulling off a shot like that. However, I wasn't sure the 9mm bullet would kill the bear even if I hit it directly in the eye.

Sid snarled, trying to draw the bear's focus.

Before I could make my move, Raiden recovered and flew at the bear with only a small knife. Upon impact, the bear tumbled backward with Raiden on top. Its long canines snapped precariously close to his face.

Indecision needled me. They were moving too fast for me to take a clear shot. But Raiden had already survived a close-range bullet, and he hadn't been hurt. I stopped breathing as I steadied my hold. An instant before I pulled the trigger, Raiden lifted his arm in the air and stabbed the bear through the eye, deep into its brain. Instantly, its muscles relaxed and its head flopped to the side. A fleshy pink tongue lolled between yellow fangs. One last, dying breath rattled under Raiden's weight.

He dropped his head on the bloody chest of the beast.

I shoved my gun back into its holster as I ran over. "Are you okay?" I laid the palm of my hand on Raiden's back. His breathing was ragged.

He nodded into the brown fur before pushing away, straddling the bear before he stood. Blood saturated his tattered shirt.

"Oh my God! You're *not* okay."

He swayed on his feet, and his eyes rolled into the back of his head as he passed out. I sort of caught him before he hit the ground. At least I broke his fall.

The blood couldn't be his. Two days ago, I'd shot him point-blank and he'd remained unharmed.

I shook him, then slapped him hard a couple of times.

We couldn't hang around here with a fresh kill. The bears weren't the only predators we had to worry about.

"Come on!" I slapped him again.

He snatched my wrist. "Is that any way to thank the guy who just saved you?"

I released the breath I didn't realize I was holding.

I rested my head on his shoulder, but when he flinched, I jerked it back again. "Are you okay?" I asked for the third time.

"I'll be fine."

I narrowed my eyes. "Are you hurt?"

"I told you, I'll be fine," he assured me.

I grabbed the neck of his shirt and ripped it open before he could protest. Five long claw marks bloodied his golden skin.

"Wait. I shot you point-blank and you didn't have a scratch on you." I started shaking. I'd almost pulled the trigger, thinking he couldn't be killed. Sure, I had been aiming for the bear, but they were moving so fast, I could've hit either one of them.

He lifted his good shoulder. "I had one hell of a bruise."

"Why?" I pointed to the gaping scratches in his chest. Dirt and hair polluted the cuts. Blood ran freely down his chest, soaking into the waistband of his cargos.

I reached into my backpack and grabbed my clean shirt. I poured what little water I had left over the ragged edges of the wounds. He hissed, exposing the full length of his fangs. My eyes opened wider—they were huge.

"Why do you think giants haven't taken over Earth? Or at least helped you guys when you were trying to destroy her. Here, we're easier to kill."

"Oh . . ." I guess that made sense. Then I slapped his

good arm. "Why didn't you tell me? I almost shot you!" I swallowed back the adrenaline-fueled nausea threatening to come up.

"But you didn't." He smiled and ruffled my mangled hair. His breathing was already back to normal.

I huffed through my nose. *Idiot.* He should've told me.

I started to pull the first aid kit out of my backpack but he stopped me.

"Don't bother." He placed his hand on my arm. "Really, I'll heal just fine in the open air. I said we were *easier* to kill here on earth, but all in all, still not that easy to kill." A sliver of humor crinkled the corners of his eyes.

A feeling of relief settled in my bones, though I wasn't sure why. If he died now, I wouldn't have to go back to the Dome. But the idea of him dying made me decidedly unhappy.

"Well, at least let me clean you up," I insisted. I didn't want his perfectly chiseled chest to scar.

I made him lie down on a large, flat rock to pour the rest of his water over the wounds. I dabbed it off with my clean shirt.

"What?" I said. He was staring at me.

"I was just looking at you." Despite my tone, his gaze didn't waver.

I squinted my eyes. "Why?"

"You're really quite pretty."

"Don't be stupid," I snapped. Heat warmed my ears. It wasn't like people hadn't told me I was pretty before, but I'd never actually cared what they thought.

His eyebrows knitted together. "I'm stupid because I think you're attractive?"

"No. Yes." I let out an exasperated breath. "Yes, you're

stupid. I've seen plenty of giants to know what kind of beauty you're surrounded by."

He lifted himself off the rock and needlessly dusted off his pants. Like that was going to mitigate the blood, gore, and grime. "So you're saying that just because I'm surrounded by roses, I can't think a red tiger lily is beautiful too?"

I turned away before he could see how flustered he made me. I grabbed his sword off the ground and pushed my gun into his hands.

"What do you want me to do with this?" He held the gun pinched between two fingers like it was a pair of dirty underwear.

"Well, it's going to be easier for you to use a gun until all that's gone." I swirled my hand in the air as I avoided looking at his chest, not because I was squeamish, but because I was afraid I would have to wipe drool from my chin. He was big, but not ridiculously bulky like some old-fashioned bodybuilder high on steroids. *This* was au naturel. The perfect amount of hair was sprinkled across his chest and ran down his abs into the top of his low-slung pants.

"Actually, it isn't. Guns don't work for us." He racked my 9mm, aimed at the sky, and pulled the trigger. Nothing happened. "No modern weapons do. Something about the magic in our blood, I guess."

"That doesn't even make any sense," I argued.

"I guess that's why they call it magic." He gave it back to me.

With fervor, I blew a stubborn curl out of my eyes as I holstered my weapon and handed him his sword.

Kryptonite counts one and two—on Earth, giants could be killed, and they couldn't use modern-day weapons.

I braved a glance into his gray eyes. "I won't tell anyone," I said softly.

His gaze lingered on my face for a beat before he reached out and laid his fingertips on my cheek. A strange but wonderful sensation spread over my skin. "Thanks."

I nodded curtly before I spun around and started walking toward home. I reached up and wiped my face where his fingers had been, trying to curb the lingering effects of his touch.

# TEN

We walked up the Alyeska Highway and finally to Crow Creek Road. Hot spots inside my old hiking boots caused the blisters to return. I didn't complain, I just limped the last seven miles or so.

Not once did Raiden ask me if I knew where I was going or when we'd get there. He seemed to trust my judgment. His confidence in me was very refreshing. It wasn't that our group of preppers didn't think I was capable—some of them had admitted to being jealous of my sharp-shooting skills and my fighting abilities—but so many of them were used to doing things on their own. Control freaks weren't easy to manage. I think we had been successful because all the families lived nearby, but not with us. Only Kevin, Tee, and I lived at the bunker full-time. The others stayed with us when the On-Grids were lurking around for long periods of time. So far, we'd only relocated once in twelve years.

My dad, always prepared for the worst-case scenario, had built three secret compounds. The first one was closer to Anchorage. The third one was in Whittier. Along with the compounds, my parents had hidden food and medical caches in these mountains. It was like my parents had had a built-in sixth sense alerting them there was going to be trouble long before it arrived.

The realization that our supplies were no longer needed filled my step with a lightness I'd never experienced. If I wanted to, I could live in a mansion on the side of a cliff, at the base of a volcano in a tent, sail the ocean blue, or live underground in a cave. The last one seemed like the least obvious choice considering where I'd resided for the last decade, though it would probably be the most familiar.

We waded through Crow Creek a few times and continued to hike well beyond where the gravel road ended. Entering the final clearing, a smile broke from my face seeing my dad's Jeep parked under an old woodshed. I knew Kevin was safe, but the vehicle proved it.

I held my hand out for Raiden to stop as Sid bounded up the ravine. Nobody was going to shoot him. He was well-loved. They wouldn't shoot me either, but I didn't want anyone getting trigger-happy with Raiden, knowing he was vulnerable. Some of our people were fair snipers.

"Beaaaaaaaaaaa . . ." a familiar yell echoed through the forest. The sound of running footsteps followed. Tee's braids lifted and settled with the jarring of her feet. She crashed into me, wrapping her arms around my middle. "Your brother is having a fit! He's been secretly freaking out since he found the Jeep."

"Ye of little faith." I lifted her up and hugged her tight. She was six months older than I was, and she hated it when I picked her up. Worse, was when I used the top of her head as an armrest because she was so short compared to my six-foot frame.

She wiggled out of my grasp. "I told him you were fine!" A hint of her Southern accent bled through.

"Where's he now?"

"Trying to fix the side-by-side he busted earlier. Complaining that we should steal some horses."

I glanced at Raiden. He hid a smile behind his hand.

"And who," Tee said, admiration coating her voice, "is this lovely gentleman behind you?" Tee's trust in me was absolute, as was my trust in her. I'd vetted Raiden—therefore she didn't hesitate. She strolled over to him and held out her hand. Though she was an adult, the height difference between the two was immense. "Tee," she introduced herself.

"Pleasure to meet you, Tee. I'm Bea's friend, Raiden."

Her eyes swept from his head to his toes. "I bet you are," she practically purred. I slapped her arm, but she just swatted me back and laughed. "Come on, let's go see Kevin so he can stop acting like a brute. You know you're going to get in trouble for this." She canted her head toward Raiden.

"He'll get over it." He'd have to.

MY BROTHER WAS bent over the engine of the side-by-side with a wrench in one hand and a red bandana in the other. It matched the sunburned color of his neck.

"Let me go first," I said to Raiden.

Tee stayed behind to protect him. Or ogle him. I couldn't blame her. He still didn't have his shirt on, and the claw marks were just five white scars over his muscled chest. He might be easier to hurt on earth, but I was relieved to see he didn't stay injured long.

I stopped a few feet away. "Hey," I said. It was dangerous to startle any of us.

Kev turned with the wrench raised. He dropped it as soon as he saw me, then grabbed me in his sweaty, grease-covered arms and squeezed. I returned the gesture.

"Fuck, Bea! Where have you been?" He pushed me back by the shoulders.

"Kev, it's a long unbelievable story. Meet Raiden."

Confusion appeared in Kev's squinted eyes as he looked up and saw a man taller than his own six foot four inches. He stepped forward and puffed up his chest. "Who—"

"Whoa, whoa! Kev! Give me a minute to explain." I blocked him.

Raiden didn't respond with any aggression. Of course, he was still wearing a sword, two visible knives, no shirt, cargo pants, and hiking boots. *My. My.*

"This is against our policy, Bea. These rules keep us alive." Kev stabbed his finger in the air at my face.

"Kevin Karl," I said, like our mom used to when he was in trouble. "I know the rules! Now if you will give me a second to explain, you'll understand why I broke them. Do you not trust me?" I pressed my finger into his chest, doing my best to avoid the multiple holes in his older-than-dirt shirt.

His eyes shifted from Raiden to me. His tongue played against the inside of his cheek.

"Please," I said.

He pursed his lips and inhaled through flared nostrils.

"Can we go inside?" I wanted to explain the situation before anyone else had a chance to stop by. Some of our friends were the *shoot first, ask questions later* kind of people. Once I had Kevin convinced, the others would be easier.

Kevin nodded.

We followed him up the rickety steps of the old ramshackle cabin. Bright-green moss covered the roof. Mold grew on the gray chinking. Inside, a rusted coffee can and a tea kettle sat on the broken propane stove. The cabin was a decoy, hiding the bunker below.

My brother lifted the corner of the grimy carpet attached to a wooden hatch and opened it. He gestured for us to go first. Raiden, Tee, and I traipsed down the stairs and stopped in front of the concrete door of the bunker..

I opened it, and Sid snaked past.

Feeling along the wall blindly, I flipped on the lights. The LED bulbs slowly warmed up, illuminating the living room and kitchen. We had electricity, but since it came from tiny wind turbines and portable solar power, we were careful with the amount we used each day.

"Do you want to shower first?" I offered and plugged my nose.

We also had indoor plumbing, but the water was always cold.

"Nope. Sit. Now." Kevin's words came out quick and sharp like a shot from a rifle. The tendons in his neck strained. "Tell me what could possibly make you break our rules."

Tension fogged the room.

I motioned for Raiden to sit beside me and Sid, who was already on the sofa in what I called "the dead cockroach position." He was lying on his back with his feet dangling in the air.

Tee opened the cupboard, pulled out two glasses, and filled them with whisky. My dad, who was Scottish, had always said that whisky was life. I disagreed.

My brother threw Raiden a clean shirt off the dining room table a little too aggressively. Raiden didn't take the bait as he pulled it calmly over his head. It was obscenely tight. Every ridge, every muscle, was perfectly visible.

Kevin sat down on the edge of the chair closest to the door, hands folded, elbows on knees. He was trying to appear relaxed. He wasn't fooling anyone.

Tee handed each of the guys a glass of Macallan's. Clasped in Raiden's large hand, the warm amber liquid swirled in the crystal tumbler. They were Dad's glasses and the only two remaining. I loved the smell of whisky because it reminded me of evenings with my family before all of this happened. But I hated the taste. If only my Scottish dad knew, he'd be so disappointed.

My face and Raiden's reflected on the TV screen across from us. A wall of DVDs and CDs surrounded the unit. My parents had left us everything from documentaries to popular comedies and reality shows. I think they wanted us to remember what the world was like before.

Tee sat cross-legged on the love seat. The springs were so worn, she sunk down.

"Kevin, this is Raiden. He's saved my life more than once already."

Kevin arched a reddish-blond eyebrow. I was lucky. My hair was such a deep color I had dark eyebrows and lashes.

I overlooked his disbelief. "Let me explain." I proceeded to tell him of my adventure, though I left out the part where I had been kidnapped. From the beginning, Raiden had insisted he wasn't kidnapping me—he was *taking me in for questioning*. Not wanting to anger Kevin further, I lied and said I went willingly. I also left out the part where I'd signed a contract to return. *Baby steps.* First, I needed him to believe me.

Halfway through, Tee got up, refilled their glasses, and poured herself one in a chipped coffee cup.

When I finished, Kevin said, "How on God's green Earth do you expect me to believe that giants exist?" His eyes slid to Raiden.

Raiden stood up, his head almost reaching the eight-foot ceiling, and smiled, exposing his sharp canine teeth.

Tee covered her mouth as her already doe-like eyes grew bigger. She took a healthy swig from her cup.

"And? This proves what?" Kevin said as his ears flushed.

Raiden used his fangs to cut the back of his large hand. Dark-red blood splashed onto the concrete floor, but almost instantly, the slices healed.

Kevin paled under his freckled skin but his ears stayed bright.

"Kevin, I know this is hard to believe, but I'm telling the truth," I said.

"I need to take a walk." He stood up and shoved his hands into the pockets of his stained jeans, which were four inches too short.

"Do you mind if I join you?" Raiden asked.

Kevin's breathing hesitated as if he were about to refuse.

"I might be able to answer some of your questions," Raiden offered.

Kevin thought for a second, then gave a curt nod. I should've been nervous about the two of them being alone together, but I wasn't.

After they left, Tee's eyes met mine. "So what aren't you telling him?" The overhead lights sparkled in her dark-brown eyes. She knew me too well.

I filled her in on the important parts I'd left out, then reiterated how incredible the houses were, how the people walked around outside unafraid, and how they had enough to eat. I might've mentioned the hot showers more than once.

"Dang, girl, you got yourself in deep. But you know I'm going with you, right?"

I knew she'd do whatever she had to. But her dad, Bach, was the one who worried me. He wasn't my favorite guy. He was useful and sly, but he didn't like Kevin calling the shots.

Eight years ago, Kevin had found him, his wife, and four-teen-year-old Tee living in a gas station off the Seward Highway. He wasn't a hardcore prepper like some of the other members here, but he'd been stationed at JBER. Between that knowledge and the hunting skills he'd acquired in his native Alabama, it had gained his family entrance into our small community. I'd always thought that for someone who was in the military, Bach didn't take too kindly to orders.

Kevin had set them up in a small house not far from us and provided them with supplies until they could do their part for our group. Tee's mom, Kathy, was a nurse. I think she tipped the scale in their favor. Unfortunately, she died four years ago in an avalanche. Bach had been ornery to start with, but after Kathy died, he became unbearable. Now Tee lived in the bunker with me and Kevin most of the time. The arrangement worked for everyone. But there was no way Bach would let Tee go without him. We needed to convince him it was in his best interest to go too.

"I mean it," she repeated. She propped her bony elbows on her knees.

"I know."

"Are all of them as good-looking as he is?" She nibbled on the corner of her full lower lip. I couldn't blame her. Our pickings were limited. Not that the men in our group weren't good people, there just weren't that many.

"So far."

Sid's ears twitched before the door to the compound softly opened and closed. We stopped talking as Raiden walked in first, followed by Kevin. I leaned back on the couch and crossed my legs while pulling a hand-knit blanket over my lap. The bunker was always chilly.

Kevin stopped in front of me and folded his arms, flexing the muscles of his biceps. He was in good physical shape, but he was skinny. We all were. "So when were you planning on telling me the rest of the story?"

I glanced at Raiden who was standing off to the side wearing a slight smirk. *Traitor,* my eyes accused.

Once my focus was trained on Kevin, I said, "Baby steps. You taught me that."

"Nice to know you listen from time to time," he grumbled. "Did you actually *read* the contract?"

"Of course, I did." I didn't tell him I'd been drinking and was exhausted. Now wasn't the time or place for *that* lecture.

"What did it say?"

"We're promised safety, accommodations, food, and careers if we want them. In return, I have to stay with the giants permanently. Even if everyone else leaves." I waved my hand in the air like it was no big deal.

I expected Kevin to look surprised, but instead, his expression turned to stone. "Why do they want *you?*"

With Raiden there, I couldn't tell Kevin the entire truth without nullifying the contract. And honestly, the situation embarrassed me. I was nobody's savior, but by the time the giants figured it out, it'd be too late.

"Because they think if I go, the rest of you will follow."

Loch had mentioned their population was rapidly dwindling, so if I needed to, I'd pull out the *population needs a larger genetic dating pool.*

Before Kevin could harass me further, Raiden spoke up. "Well, she signed in blood. If she doesn't go back, she'll die."

The death part was no surprise. I'd read that passage multiple times before I wrote my name. But the John Hancock signed in blood—that shocked me. A shiver prickled along my neck, making me feel as if that signature might have meant more than just my death. I'd read the contract thoroughly enough. Or at least I'd thought I did. *Shit.*

Before I plunged down that rabbit hole, I lashed out. "What did you expect me to do, Kev?" I raised my hands in question and stood up. "I had an opportunity to give everyone a better, safer life. They have electricity, running water, food." I glanced at Tee, then back to my brother. She was as much of a sister to him as I was. I let what I had to say sink in. "What would you have done, Kevin Walker? How many more people need to die?" The memory of Tee losing her mom upset me, and knowing each of us was often a breath away from dying made it worse.

His stony expression faltered. He would've made the same damn deal. And he knew it.

So, to keep from crying—again—I reiterated, "What would *you* have done to give me a better, safer life?"

His shoulders slumped as he nodded in defeat.

I flicked my hand at Raiden and softened my tone. "They offered. I accepted. The only thing I lose is my freedom."

# CHAPTER
# ELEVEN

Though there were thirty-seven of us all together, only fifteen were gathered around the rickety folding table in the rec room at the back of the bunker.

It was the largest room, and we used it for multiple purposes. It was a bit cramped when we hosted dances or game nights. We did the best we could to not go stir-crazy in the middle of winter. I wasn't going to miss this room at all. It smelled like sorrow, regret, and hardship.

The lights buzzed loudly as people shifted in their metal chairs.

Kevin cleared his throat, managing to silence the chatter. He began the meeting by formally introducing Raiden.

Yesterday, the morning after Raiden and I had arrived home, Kevin went house to house and told everyone about the deal I'd made with the giants—and that they had a choice to relocate with us. Or not.

This meeting was the first time they'd have the opportunity to talk to me or Raiden. I kept my mouth shut as Kevin, again, relayed my adventure, and the offer the giants had made to all of us.

Just as I was about to explain further, Bach pulled out a pistol from under his vest and pointed it at Raiden's head.

Anger seared like a lightning bolt to my chest, only to be replaced by a measure of fear clogging the back of my throat. If Bach pulled that trigger, Raiden would die.

A river of blood flushed Kevin's pale skin, and Raiden's fingers dug into the table, his nails gouging the surface.

Before any of us *mere humans* could react, Raiden stood up, reached across the table, and tore the pistol out of Bach's hand. Or at least I think that's what happened. Because, *damn*, he was fast.

Once the weapon was safely out of Bach's possession, Raiden slowly bent it in half. The metal squeaked in the quiet room as everyone nervously glanced around. He set it down purposely, hard-eyeing Bach before he set it on the table and scooted it back to him.

Frederica, our resident doctor, snorted at the slight and stared at Raiden with open fascination. I was sure the science side of her brain couldn't help it—she analyzed everything. Her husband, Frank, the engineer who kept our electricity and water flowing, was one of my favorite people. His stories were the best and he never complained when I begged him for extra judo lessons.

Frank looked at me, pushed up his glasses held together by duct tape, and asked, "Why? Why you? And what's in it for us?"

*Because of some stupid prophecy.* There was no way I was admitting to that, though. First of all, because it was embarrassing. And second, because I'd agreed to keep that part a secret from Raiden. So I used the only other logical answer I had. "A few reasons, I think. Their population is dwindling and our group has quite a few genetic candidates."

Bach's face, though his skin was dark, turned a shade of purple, but with a stern look from Kevin, he kept his mouth shut.

Bach, Frank, and Frederica were in their early fifties and probably not keen on having kids at their ages. Not that procreating was high on anyone's priority list. Heck, we could barely feed the thirty-seven we already had. And *nobody* wanted to see a child starve.

Before I could continue, Raiden chimed in. "Also, most of us enjoy humans in general. As giants, while very intelligent and capable, we can't create anything. We can play a song only after it's been written. We can draw, so long as we have instructions. And if the plans are already designed, we can build. Somewhere along the way, we missed the creative gene. In the past, we've regularly visited Earth to study. I know we're tall, but it wasn't that hard to fit in on college campuses with basketball and football teams. Though for the last ten years or so . . . well, you know."

Everyone murmured in agreement. Humans had been a mess.

I glanced at Raiden, surprised by the new information.

"What? We don't like to admit our shortcomings," he said.

Frank rubbed his chin. "Interesting. And why do you think this is a good idea?" he asked me. Frank respected my opinions despite my age and lack of education.

"I signed a contract, and in it, not only are you guaranteed safety, but if at any time you want to leave, you're free to do so. At this point, you have the option to try before you buy. Seriously? What have we got to lose? Not that I don't enjoy practically starving every winter."

Everyone but Bach chuckled. Our sense of humor ran dark. Often, we laughed at our tragedy. It was either that or slowly wither away from despair.

Bach finally spoke up. "And if we don't go? Will you give us the locations of the food and medical caches?"

"No," Kevin said.

"You son of a—" Bach started to say, then he shut up when Raiden placed his hands flat on the table.

Kevin continued as if he hadn't been interrupted. "If you opt to stay, I will come back in a year and give you the locations. This guarantees that if anyone returns, they'll have supplies too."

"You don't trust me?" Bach snarled.

Kevin glanced pointedly at the ruined gun and then back to Bach.

Bach huffed and scratched at his growing beard.

"If a few stay behind, our meager supplies will be more than sufficient. You'll eat like a king," Frederica said.

"Do you trust these giants?" Frank asked me.

I teetered my head back and forth. "They act very much like humans, so no. I trust that they follow their own rules. But I trust him." I tipped my chin at Raiden. I wasn't sure why, but I did. "I read the contract, and I signed it knowing this would give us a better life."

Frank's eyes narrowed. "Why did you have to sign a contract?" I knew better than to think he wouldn't consider all of the angles.

"Even if all of you choose to leave, I have to stay behind." I held up my hand to stop Frank's interruption. "I know exactly what I signed, and I was more than willing to do so.

121

If it gives us even the slightest chance at having a better life —you would have done it, too, Frank."

His lips pursed at my half-assed answer but he let the subject drop.

The bunker door opened and Tee popped her head inside. Sid tried thrusting past her and whined when it didn't work. He didn't like to be separated from me. "Everything's ready outside. Are you guys coming?" she asked impatiently. That girl loved a good party—from the planning to the decorating and the socializing.

Kevin held up a finger, and she backed out of the door.

"Bea and I will be leaving in three days. That gives everyone time to think it over. Discuss it with your families. Whatever you need to do to make the right decision," Kevin said.

"Tee and I are *not* going," Bach said.

"Suit yourself. Nobody's forcing you to do anything." Kevin stood up and held the door open.

As everyone left the bunker, I ran down the back hallway and grabbed my gun from my bedroom before heading outside. I felt naked without it.

Under the camouflaged shelter, hidden amongst the trees, the fire pit roared. Some of the younger kids stood next to the open flames roasting moose sausage on birch sticks and then shoveling food into their mouths as fast as they could. They weren't used to having free rein at the table. I chuckled, imagining some of them would come to regret their decision once their shrunken stomachs objected.

A few adults, rifles slung over their shoulders, scattered to the outskirts of the celebration to take their turn on lookout. Thankfully, the On-Grids had already flown over early in the morning. During the last few years, they never made more than one pass but we were always careful. Kevin said it took too much fuel and they were probably running as low as we were. Unless a bear or a pack of wolves wanted to brave fifteen heavily armed people, we were as safe as we could be.

Eclectic vases filled with wildflowers sat on the table between salads, berries, smoked salmon, and mountain goat sausages. The aroma of the freshly baked buns made my stomach rumble. The variety and the plethora were unusual but Frederica had said we were celebrating our good fortune with the deal I'd made—and rationing be damned. Besides, almost everyone had decided to go with us. Plus, we had a special guest—who everybody was staring at.

Something warm stirred inside my chest at the sight of numerous smiles and the overwhelming good cheer. Not worried about wasting food for a change, I gave Sid an entire sausage. He inhaled it and looked up for more. I patted him on his visible ribs and blinked away my tears. Seeing his never-ending hunger always broke me.

On the far table, an old stereo was plugged in with an orange extension cord, playing some random pop song. Tee was in charge of the tunes. She loved music. She'd managed to salvage an old guitar, a violin with only three strings, and a drum set she'd found in someone's abandoned basement. Not to mention the hordes of ancient CDs she'd collected over the years.

"Bea," a deep voice whispered in my ear.

I rolled my eyes before looking at him. Noah.

He pulled his hands out of his pockets and readjusted the baseball hat over his brown hair. He was handsome enough: hazel eyes, a nice jawline, and good teeth. It was his personality that lacked character. He threw an arm around my waist and drew me close.

"Noah, we discussed this already." I pushed him away.

From the other side of the party, Raiden's eyes flashed to mine. He was deep in conversation with a group but it was easy for him to see over the rest of us. I shook my head. He acknowledged but didn't look pleased.

"Ah, come on, babe. You missed me and you know it. Nobody is in the bunker." He lowered his voice and whispered in my ear, "I know what you like."

"Noah, it was a mistake. I'm sorry."

"What? You bring back some dude and you don't think I'm going to fight for you?"

How was I going to get it through his thick skull? A couple of months ago, I'd had a gentle conversation breaking up with him. When that didn't work, I'd told him bluntly I didn't reciprocate his feelings. Last week, I'd been downright rude.

Raiden stepped in front of me. "Is everything okay?" He looked at Noah, who was a couple of inches shorter than I was.

"Yeah, buddy, it's fine. Me and my woman are just talkin', so if ya don't mind . . ." Noah shooed Raiden away with a sweep of his hand.

"Noah, I'm not your woman," I snapped.

"The hell you ain't. You can't sleep with me and not have feelings for me. That's not like you!" he yelled loud enough for everyone to hear.

Heat flared over my face. Nobody knew about me and Noah except for Tee. We'd agreed to keep it hush-hush. Now everyone knew. Even Kevin.

"Oh, excuse me," Noah held his hands up. "Maybe you're

just a slut, and I was the only one who didn't know." He glared at Raiden.

My hand curled into a fist, and I punched him hard in the stomach. He grunted and bent over with his arms hugging his middle, but I didn't care. I stormed into the trees. Once I was out of sight, I ran, Sid at my heels, until I stumbled onto the bridge overlooking Crow Creek. I gripped the cold stone railing and tried to catch my breath.

"Hey, you okay?"

I whipped around. Raiden stood at the edge of the bridge with his hands buried in his pockets.

I swallowed and wiped my nose with a bandana pulled from the kangaroo pouch of my threadbare hoodie. Was I okay? Not really. I was mortified.

"You want to talk about it?"

I shook my head fiercely.

"Do you want me to get Tee?" He gestured over his shoulder with a thumb. "She was inside when it happened."

I shook my head again. Tee had warned me that sleeping with Noah was a bad idea.

Raiden's footsteps were silent as he walked across the bridge and stopped next to me. Heat from his body radiated to mine. "Hey, I'm not here to judge. You can tell me what happened if you want."

I hung my head. "I just wanted to know what it was like before I died."

"What sex was like?" Raiden said openly.

"Yeah."

He said nothing.

"It's just that . . . life is so hard here. So unpredictable. I didn't want to die without knowing. I read about it in books and it sounded . . ."

"Enjoyable," he finished.

"Yeah. And we have so little joy here. It's so much work to survive. I just wanted to know."

"You don't have to explain it to me, Bea. Not if you don't want to."

But I wanted to.

I pulled in a lungful of the cool air. "I chose Noah because he's such a player. He never gets attached to anyone. He's *dated*—" I air-quoted because the truth was crude, "—almost every available female here. Even some that aren't."

Raiden placed his arm around me, holding my shoulder with his hand. Energy trickled from his fingers all the way down my back.

I pinched the bridge of my nose. "He was the only guy not looking for a permanent thing. The only one." I collected my thoughts. "I mean, he's good-looking and is great with a gun. And doesn't try to shuck off the hard jobs."

Raiden's grip tightened slightly.

"And he has a lot of practice in bed."

The pressure of his hold increased.

"Tee warned me. She said I'd be the one he fell for. I asked her why. She said because I'm way too pretty, but mostly because I didn't really want him. I laughed at her." I pressed my hand to my forehead. "I laughed at her."

Raiden scooted behind me and positioned his hands on either side of my hips. Fire pooled low in my belly. The sensation was new.

"I'm so stupid."

He pressed his face in my hair. "Tee's right, you *are* beautiful. Way too beautiful for your own good. And no, you're not stupid, you're just young." His moving lips tickled my scalp.

My heart tripped over the beat. "And you're *so much* older and wiser," I said, leaning heavily on sarcasm.

He laughed into my hair. His breath was hot. "A bit."

"How much older?" I was curious.

"I'm twenty-three."

"In human years or dog years?" How was I supposed to know? Old vampires always looked young, at least according to all the romance novels.

"You're feisty. I'm twenty-three in human years. We do live longer than you guys so long as we're in the Fiefdom. Somewhere around two hundred years, give or take. Here, I suppose our lifespans would be the same as yours."

"Oh good I'd hate it if you were an old man already. It might change the way I think about you."

"What do you think of me?"

Below us, the water gurgled over the rocks. Sid pounced in the creek, trying to catch a small minnow. As far as I knew, he'd never been successful. Birds chirped as the sun began to set. It was somewhere around midnight. The cool breeze shimmied through the leaves and kept the mosquitos at bay.

"I like you." I sounded somewhat surprised, even to myself. I'd known for a while, but I didn't want to admit it.

"Really?"

"Yeah." This time, I sounded sure. The *thump thump* of my heart rang loudly inside my ears. Were we actually having this conversation? And did it mean what I think it did? He *did* say I was beautiful.

"So you don't have feelings for little ol' Noah?" he teased gently.

"Nope, I never did. I just didn't want to die a virgin. I know that seems like a stupid reason."

"No, it doesn't. Life is precarious here." He turned me around slowly and lifted me up onto the edge of the stone bridge. "Don't you ever want to fall in love?" he asked. His eyes glowed a bright silver, almost as if the color swirled like live flames around his pupils.

I nodded. I wanted the fairy tale. I wanted the prince on a white horse—*or a black pegasus*—to sweep me off my feet. I wanted a partner in life. Someone to love. Someone to love me.

A slow smile spread over his handsome face. "Good. Now let's go show *Noah*—" he said his name like it was stupid, "—that you have nothing to be embarrassed by. That dude's lucky to have ever laid a hand on you. And as far as I'm concerned, he'll never do it again."

"Hey." I gently shook Raiden's shoulder, surprised that he hadn't woken up the moment I stepped foot in the guest room. It was used as a storage room, with boxes piled from floor to ceiling. Raiden's huge body was curled up on his side with knees bent and one hand under his pillow, nearly collapsing the sad twin bed.

I stepped back, holding on to the oil lantern. A sleepy smile curled on his lips but he refused to open his eyes. I balled my fingers into a fist, trying to resist the urge to reach out and touch his face.

"What?" he said groggily.

"I'm going fishing. Wanna come?" It wasn't like I *needed* to go fishing since we were leaving in three days. But I needed to say goodbye. While Alaska might've been a harsh place to live, I still loved her. I wanted Raiden to understand what I was giving up, even if I was getting something better for my people in return. Kevin hadn't argued with me last night when I informed him of my plans, but he did suggest I take Raiden with me.

"Definitely." Raiden stood up and stretched his arms above his head, touching the ceiling. I forced myself to look away from the bare, muscled ridges highlighted in the lantern's glow.

"I'll just wait for you out there." I fled the room. He made me feel all mushy and fluttery inside. It was uncomfortable yet exquisite, leaving me confused. Feelings were not my strength.

Ten minutes later, he wandered down the hallway. I shoved a plate of leftovers from the night before into his hands.

"Thanks." He took the plate and tousled my hair at the same time.

A veil of warmth melted over my skin like the glaze on a doughnut. It had been years since I'd had one, but they were still my favorite.

Raiden scarfed down the food, then rinsed off his plate before we went outside.

I slid on sunglasses, shielding my eyes from the glaring sun. "Do you need a pair?" I asked.

"Nope. Thanks. Our vision adjusts to the amount of light available."

"You want to drive?" I waved to the ATV.

"Yeah, but the minute I touch the handlebars, it'll quit. Just another thing here on Earth that won't work for us."

"Well, that sucks. Climb on the back, I guess." I patted the seat after I sat down.

He stepped over the machine and slid his legs alongside mine, his skin searing hot against my bare thighs. I'd chosen a pair of shorts this morning since we weren't going far and

I didn't have to worry about poisonous plants. I clenched the rubber handles.

Sid barked, eager to go, disrupting my blossoming fantasy.

I slowly twisted the throttle, and we shot forward, Sid running beside us. I was headed for my favorite spot on Glacier Creek. Not necessarily the best place for fishing, but it was close. And I wasn't going for the fish.

Ten minutes later, I pulled onto the small beach. Between me, Sid, and Raiden, I wasn't *much* worried about the bears. They didn't hang around that close to where we lived. They preferred to catch us farther away from home when we had limited numbers. And the wolves hunted at night or in the wee hours of the morning. Not that it really got dark this time of year.

Raiden climbed off and explored while I assembled my pole and favorite tackle. With that done, I unlatched the cooler from the back of the ATV and placed it on the ground. While still bent over the icebox, I turned around to see where Raiden was. He stood about ten feet behind me, staring at my butt and legs. His lips were slack and his eyes heavy. The silver color seemed to swirl and dance like flames.

"Uh . . . Hello?" I waved my hand in the air, wiggling my fingers.

His head snapped up and pink flushed his cheeks. He spun around and walked to the water's edge, rubbing the back of his neck.

The idea of Raiden checking me out filled my chest with intense joy. I breathed slowly, trying to contain my racing heart and the weird thing humming in my stomach.

Once my reactions were semi under control, I grabbed

my pole and tacklebox. Rocks grated under my feet as I walked over to where he was standing. "Have you ever been fishing?"

"Yeah, but not here. I'm thinking this might be pleasant compared to what I'm used to wrangling."

My hope was to catch a king salmon.

I cast the line a few times, demonstrating how, then gave him the pole. He cast like he'd been doing it for years. The little red and white bobber floated on the surface, struggling against the current. I sat down on the sand and wrapped my arms around my bent knees.

Raiden sat next to me, his shoulder not quite touching mine. One hand gripped the pole, the other dangled loosely over his lap. Calluses were built up on his palms and the tips of his fingers.

"So, if you don't live with your aunt and uncle, where do you live?" I picked up a small stone and rubbed the flat surface with a finger.

"Most of the time I'm out scouting our perimeters, making sure our gates are secure. But I do have a home at the base of the mountains. It's built into some trees and sits above a lake."

"Is it made of glass and concrete?" I couldn't picture him enjoying that type of environment.

"I built it myself. Hand-scraped logs and all," he said proudly.

"How is that? You said you're only twenty-three." I leaned my head back, tossing my hair over my shoulders to watch the bald eagle soaring in the cloudless sky.

"I started when I was fifteen. It gave me something to focus on other than my parents."

"What happened to them? If you don't mind me asking."

He swallowed. "They went missing ten years ago."

"Mine disappeared twelve years ago," I said, surprised by the coincidence.

"I don't know if they're dead or alive. I've been searching for them for a while now." He rubbed his chin with his thumb and forefinger.

"I wanted to search, but our parents forbade us. They made us promise never—not ever, no matter what—to go looking for them. Early on, I tried arguing with Kevin, but it's a battle I've yet to win."

"I'm sure he's just trying to keep you safe. It's what I would do."

"Yeah, I know. I've heard it all before." Deep down, I held a slight grudge against my parents for going to work that morning, and I definitely held one against Kevin for not allowing us to search for them. Whenever I brought up the subject up, Kevin shut me down. And then he guilt-tripped me into not going out on my own. *What would Tee and I do without you? How would Sid survive your death?* "I guess now it's my turn to keep everyone safe." I still had doubts about whether I'd made the right decision, but since everyone had the opportunity to leave if they wanted to, the positive outweighed the negative.

"That was a pretty brave thing for you to do," Raiden said, watching me.

My cheeks flushed under his scrutiny. I bumped him with my shoulder teasingly. "Pfft, not really. You're not that bad."

"You don't think so?" He didn't sound so sure.

"Well, *I* like you, at least." So far, he was the only giant I'd met that I actually liked. I hoped that wasn't par for the course.

"I like you too." He drummed his fingers on his thigh before he reached out with his pinky and chained it with mine.

The hairs on my arms rose. My toes curled inside my hiking boots. I rolled my hand under and intertwined my fingers with his.

He looked down at me. "Your eyes. They're amazing. Like a kaleidoscope. Where one color ends, the next begins."

I bit my lower lip.

His eyes traced the movement and his pupils dilated. Slowly, as if not to frighten me, he leaned in, his breath cool on my scorching-hot skin. My lips parted.

The damn fishing pole jerked out of his hand. With speed I wasn't able to see, he caught it before it escaped, then leapt up off the ground and yanked the pole hard, setting the hook.

I grabbed the stun stick and waited as he reeled in the heavy fish. Silver flashed under the roiling water.

A respectable king salmon came into view. He dragged it up on shore, and I whacked it hard over the head before pulling my knife and slitting its gills, then tossing it in the cooler. Tonight, we were having fresh salmon steaks.

I ran to the creek and washed the blood off my hands. When I looked up, Raiden's grin was completely uninhibited, as if, for a moment in time, he'd been untethered from his worries. His fangs glinted in the sunlight and I forgot to breathe. He was so beautiful—dark brows framing deep-set gray eyes, that sculpted jawline, and those lips.

When he caught me staring, his smile vanished. In two steps, he was in front of me. He wound a hand into the back of my hair and leaned down slowly again, as if to not frighten me away. His breath smelled like crisp winter air.

Sparks of static tickled my lips before his found mine. They were hot, feverish, and soft. He dipped his tongue into my mouth and explored gently. What started out cautious and tender soon turned into a fire, with gasoline as fuel. We stumbled backward into a sturdy birch tree, leaves and twigs sprinkling in our hair. When the edge of his fang caught on my lower lip and I tasted blood, I moaned into his mouth. He growled and stiffened, but I ignored his reaction, pressing onward. I reached under his shirt and yanked it off with only a momentary pause between fervent kisses. He slid his hands under my tank top and unclasped my bra, his fingers leaving a trail of fire. My breasts sprung free, my nipples hard and pulsing, desperately waiting for his touch. I unbuttoned the top of his pants, and he hesitated as I slipped my hand inside his boxers. He placed his hand over mine and stopped me before I could find what I was searching for.

"We have to slow down," he gasped heavily in my ear.

"No." My body was screaming. My heartbeat pounded between my legs. He was certainly ready.

He chuckled, but I didn't.

"Please. We don't have to stop. I *want* this." The intensity at which my body responded to his was startling. I not only wanted him, but it was like every cell inside demanded I have him.

He rested his forehead against mine. "I do, too, believe me. Every flat surface I've seen in the past two days, I've imagined laying you down and making you scream my name." His voice rumbled over my chest, and I inhaled sharply at his admission. "But I want to take my time and get to know you. I don't want to rush it. I want to enjoy every step." He kissed my forehead with swollen lips. "I don't want our first time to be in a hurry." He kissed my cheek. "It's not like you're going anywhere anytime soon." He kissed my other cheek. "I want to do this over and over until we are so exhausted we can't do it anymore." He kissed the end of my nose.

I tilted my face up, and he placed a finger over my parted lips.

"I want to take you to my home and lay you down on my bed where it's safe. I want to concentrate on every inch of your body without looking over my shoulders for predators. I want to wake up in the morning with you naked beside me."

If he wanted me to stop, he wasn't very convincing. My body clenched tighter with every word he spoke. I stuck my tongue out and licked his finger still pressed against my lips.

The muscles in his jaw knotted. "Not helping," he managed to say without parting his teeth.

"Not trying to," I whispered.

"If I kiss you one more time, I'm going to throw you on the wet sand and take what I want," he said.

"I'm not stopping you," I said breathlessly. I had no problem with it.

"Please, don't make me do that," he begged. "Please."

He was really asking me to tell him no.

My shoulders slumped, though conceding to his wishes didn't extinguish the flames. "Okay, we'll wait," I promised.

But I didn't have to like it.

# THIRTEEN

The next couple of days were a whirlwind of activity. I barely had a second alone with Raiden, but every time he walked by me, he somehow managed to touch me, flaming the inferno raging under my skin.

Finally, Kevin cornered me. "Are you like . . . *dating* or something?"

I sputtered. *Dating?* My brother was as painfully awkward as I was. "I don't know," I said. It wasn't like we'd had a minute to ourselves to label whatever was going on between the two of us. "Do you have a problem with it?"

Kev jutted out his lower lip like his answer surprised even him. "No. I actually like the guy."

High praise coming from my brother. He didn't warm up to strangers quickly.

Wanting to leave it at that, I steered the conversation away. "How's everyone else holding up."

He rubbed his hand over the red scruff on his chin and silently answered me with a shake of his head.

Dissent amongst the ranks was at an all-time high. Bach had been campaigning strongly against going. My brother, calm as always, told everyone to talk to Raiden, who, in turn, was very candid about the dangers of the Fiefdom. Then, once they had all the information, they could make their decision. He wasn't going to pressure them one way or another—which was the smartest way to convince our people to join us.

Tee handled her dad like she always did—by ignoring him. Since her mom had died, they hadn't had much of a relationship. She spent most of her time with me and Kevin.

All the folks here were very independent. They didn't like to be told what to do. Which was why, on the morning we were to leave, most everyone joined us. Bach, Jennifer, and her sixteen-year-old daughter Beth, were the only ones absent. I'd suspected for years Jennifer had a crush on Bach. Her actions confirmed my suspicions.

Tee, the last one to arrive to our designated meeting point at the intersection of the Seward Highway and the Alyeska Highway, pulled up slowly on her ATV, careful to avoid the puddles of water. Raindrops speckled her sunglasses. "If we could get this party started, I'd be much obliged." She snapped her fingers, her freshly painted glitter nails looking beautiful and out of place. Tee and I had often spent our spare time rummaging through abandoned houses looking for small treasures. She collected jewelry, makeup, clothes, and CDs, while I searched for books and weapons. Unfortunately, Girdwood was a tiny town and we'd ransacked most of the places multiple times.

"How did you sneak past your dad?" I asked. I'd already known she was coming with us.

She folded her hands in front of her chin in the prayer

138

position. Her brown eyes sparkled with her mischievous nature.

"Your dad doesn't know, does he?" Kevin said.

"I'm twenty-three. I don't need his permission. But he's going to be very angry when he finally wakes up." She fluttered her curly lashes.

"What did you give him?" I whispered. She had a stash of various medications at her place.

"I baked him some brownies last night." She wiggled her eyebrows. During the summer, we grew a small crop of marijuana alongside our vegetable gardens. "Then this morning, I lit a joint and put a paper sack over his head so he would stay stoned. Not sure how effective that's going to be." Her volume rose. "So if we could kick this into gear . . ." She adjusted the rifle strapped to her back.

We were armed to the teeth, but we'd never ventured out in this big of a group before. The larger the gathering, the easier it was for the On-Grids to spot us. They had an aerial advantage. At least once a day, their helicopter or small plane buzzed overhead. They never kept to a schedule. On the plus side, our numbers would keep the wildlife away.

Kevin started his dirt bike, black smoke belching from the exhaust. The tailpipe was held on by melted duct tape and rusted wire. Frank followed on his side-by-side, with Raiden riding shotgun. The rest of the crew, all doubled up on ATVs or dirt bikes, jockeyed for position somewhere in the middle.

I glanced over my shoulder to take one last look at home. A sting of melancholy tugged my heart. Chances were, I'd never see the place again, which meant all hope of finding my parents was gone. I stared ahead at all the people who'd have plentiful food, real jobs, and less danger in their lives.

139

My parents would have been proud, but it didn't stop the tear from sliding over the edge.

I wiped it away and drew the hood of my rain jacket over my head to hide the bright color of my hair, then kick-started my bike. Kevin ordered Tom and me to hang back so we could listen for aircraft. It was easier to hear if we weren't next to all the other small engines. Plus, Sid and I had sharper hearing than anyone else.

A whiff of salty ocean air hit my face as we turned onto what used to be the Seward Highway. On the side of the road were skeletal remains of dead trees killed by the ever-encroaching saltwater. A large raven perched on a gray branch cawed and gurgled. With nothing but the open road in front of us, we sped up, eager to get to our new home.

---

ABOUT AN HOUR INTO OUR JOURNEY, Sid stopped and cocked his head toward the sky. I signaled for Tom to cut the engines. As soon as we heard the faint whine of an overhead plane, we took off, jumping our bikes over rocks and through puddles. We skidded around the downed vegetation, Sid hot on our tail.

Judy, Tom's ex-wife, who was sitting backward on the ATV, warned everyone with a sharp whistle. Immediately, they stopped their vehicles in a tight grouping while Frank and Raiden pulled the camo tarps out of the side-by-side. The smaller kids huddled in the middle, while everyone else grabbed their assigned corner and covered the caravan. We'd practiced this drill a dozen times in the last three days.

Tom and I sped under the boughs of a large spruce tree,

and I wiped the mud and rain off my face as we came to a stop.

"Do you think it's going to fool them?" I asked Tom.

"So long as they didn't spot us first."

The red and white Cessna flew directly overhead below the cloud cover.

Kev waited until the plane was out of sight before motioning for everyone to fall into formation again as we got back on the road. I kept my eyes and ears focused on the sky for the next hour, knowing everyone else was keeping watch on the ground. If the On-Grids had landed somewhere, we'd know it by now. And they never made more than one overhead sweep per day. It took too much gas. Thankfully, my parents had had the foresight to install an underground fuel tank, but after twelve years, we were running low too.

When we came to the spot where our vehicles couldn't go farther, we left them stashed in the deep brush in case anyone wanted to return.

By that evening, we'd made it to the base of the stairway with only one injury. Noah wouldn't say what happened, but his right hand was bruised and swollen.

Only I could see the magic staircase until Raiden laid his hands over the entrance. He glanced at me and winked as he said something in Latin followed by, "Open sesame." The air shimmered like a mirage, and a weird scent like ozone hovered in the breeze. Everyone ooh'ed and ahh'ed as the stairs appeared from the ground up.

"Ruby, you need to go first," Raiden said. "Everyone else can follow."

I didn't question him, assuming he wanted me to

demonstrate it was safe. I braced myself for the shock, intent on hiding how much it hurt.

It wasn't as bad this time.

I turned to warn them of the impending jolts, but Raiden shook his head no.

"Why?" I whispered.

"Because when you go through, it disables the system."

The older teens and adults inspected the black polished stone as they entered. The younger generation took off running up the stairs, laughing and shouting. After everyone was safely inside, Raiden rested his hands on my shoulder and kissed the top of my head. Warmth poured from his lips, like stepping into the hot midday sun.

A few steps up, Noah clenched his good fist. A part of me wished he'd stayed behind. I didn't want to deal with his drama.

We climbed for a couple hours, just enough time to tire everyone out, before we decided to stop for the night. Raiden touched the side of the obsidian wall and opened a chamber. It was three times the size of the one we'd stayed in. Tee herded the kids inside with the help of Sid. We all had little jobs to help our community survive.

Tee rolled out sleeping bags in the back corner and sat down in the middle. The smaller children gathered around her, sitting cross-legged with their worn pillows propped on their laps.

Tee pulled a book from her backpack and began to read. "*Once upon a time, there lived a poor widow and her son Jack. One day, Jack's mother told him to sell their only cow. Jack went to the market and on the way, he met a man who wanted to buy his cow. Jack asked, "What will you give me in return for my cow?" The man answered, "I will give you five magic beans!"*"

Tee, Raiden, and I busted out laughing. The kids seemed confused but they started giggling too. Soon, everyone but Noah joined in. The humor cut some of the nervous tension lingering in the air.

The moment embraced my emotions tenderly, albeit unnervingly. I wasn't accustomed to my feelings having free-range. Except for Kevin, Tee, and Sid, I tended to cut myself off from the others. It wasn't that I didn't care about them, but keeping my distance protected my heart.

I snuck a glance at Raiden as we rolled out our sleeping bags next to each other. I stripped off my rain jacket and shoes, then scooted into my temporary bed. Sid curled behind my legs as Raiden mimicked my position facing me. The orange firelight sharpened the shadows under his cheekbones. His lips, which I couldn't stop staring at, were framed by the dark scruff on his face.

He'd been right when he said we should take things slow. I'd already opened up to him more than safety allowed, and I worried I'd pay for it.

He reached out and cupped my cheek, stroking my skin softly with his thumb. His fingers smelled like tree sap and wood smoke. I closed my eyes and chewed my bottom lip. The things reeling through my mind were inappropriate in a room full of people. So, with no way to act upon them, I kissed his fingertips and fell asleep holding his hand.

---

I woke up sometime in the wee hours of the morning to people snoring and shuffling in their sleep. When I looked beside me, I was surprised to find Raiden was gone. I pulled on my shoes and snuck outside. I could just make out the outline of him sitting against the cold black stone with his legs straight out in front of him.

"Whatcha doin'?" I tiptoed down the steps. Sid guarded the entrance of the cavern, keeping an eye on me and the others.

"I don't require as much sleep as humans do."

I didn't either. Five hours was my ideal.

He patted his lap as if I should sit. I stepped over him with one foot and he pulled me down, straddling him. His eyes glowed silver even in the dark. The heat from his legs seeped into my thighs.

"You are absolutely beautiful. You know that, right?" He swept my hair away from my face.

I really didn't spend much time thinking about what I looked like, but compared to the Fie, I was downright plain.

Raiden trailed a finger along the bridge of my nose and over my cheeks, the simple act setting my body alight. "You know, I heard a rumor about redheads. I wonder if it's true."

"Uh-huh," I said cautiously. There were many rumors about gingers.

"Every freckle is a soul you've stolen."

It was my favorite. I buried my head into his shoulder and stifled a laugh. I didn't want to wake the others. I leaned back and raised an eyebrow. "Possibly."

I didn't have a lot of freckles, just over my nose and cheeks. Probably because I didn't spend much time in the sun. And when the sun was out, I often wore long sleeves to keep away the bugs and the deadly plants.

"I heard another one." He touched my bottom lip and followed its contour. I closed my eyes and rode the shock wave spreading like wildfire, jumping from one nerve ending to the next. My toes curled and my insides blazed.

"Yes?" I said breathlessly. I could barely concentrate on what he was saying over the sensations snapping over my skin, burrowing deeper into my core with every second.

"I have a feeling I'm gonna want to solve that one on my own." He kissed my neck gently. His large hand cradled my head as he tilted it up for better access. His lips were hot and soft and left a burning path in their wake. He opened his mouth wider and scraped his fangs over my delicate skin. My breath stuttered in my throat. I swallowed hard. My heart beat faster.

His hands traveled the length of my sides, coming to rest low on my waist. Pressing me into his lap, his erection was hard underneath me. I rolled my hips forward, wanting him inside me. My chest bumped against his, and my nipples hardened under the flimsy material of my shirt and sports bra.

His tongue traced the rapidly thumping pulse in my neck before he gently kissed his way up to my lips. He rested his forehead against mine. "The things I want to do to you . . ." His voice was husky. His fingers dug painfully into my waist as he growled.

Desire permeated every inch of my flesh. It pounded between my ears, between my legs, and throbbed inside my very soul. I was alive in a way I'd never been before. It was an awakening—one I never wanted to wake up from.

He stood up abruptly, lifting me up by the waist to set me down. "But not here. Not now." He stepped away.

I was a little surprised at how quickly he'd shut down. It was like he could only get so close to the fire without being charred.

"Okay?" I said it like a question.

"No, you don't understand. Once I start, I'm not going

to be able to stop. It's a weird thing with giants. Once permission is granted, we *don't* change our minds." He ran his hand over the back of his neck and through his hair, messing it up. "I want to make sure we're on the same page."

I stepped forward. "We're on the same sentence."

He kissed the top of my head. "Good," he murmured into my hair. "Because I have plans for us."

I shivered. I couldn't wait.

"Can I ask you something?" I said.

"Sure."

"When did it change? When we first met, it seemed like you . . ." I tick-tocked my head, "strongly disliked me. Now, not so much." I knew all the moments when my feelings had softened toward him, but I couldn't tell when he began to feel the same way.

"I never disliked you. Quite the contrary. I was just irritated. I didn't want to go home. And because of you, I had to. But I never disliked you. Still don't." He winked.

"Why don't you like to go home?"

His answer was interrupted by a child's loud wailing echoing off the granite walls, soon followed by others. I didn't want to go inside but I needed my gear.

Since it was close to dawn anyway, I rolled up my sleeping bag and attached it to the bottom of my rucksack. Once on the staircase, I grabbed a granola bar and some food for Sid. I tossed one to Raiden and we ate in silence, sitting with our arms touching. Even that slight contact made the bees buzz against my chest walls.

As the sun finally peeked over the tall obsidian walls, sleepy-eyed kids stumbled out of the doorway. I shooed them up the steps—it wasn't like they could get lost. It didn't take long for the rest of the stragglers to rise and start walking up the stairs.

After a couple of hours of hiking up and up, all of the kids and a few of the adults began lagging behind.

Raiden picked up Becky's daughter, Sophie, who was four and somehow a little chunky, and threw her on his back. Becky was a wonderful mother and I suspected she often shorted herself so Sophie didn't go hungry. Most of us adults did. Though I shorted myself so Sid had more.

"I'm going to need you to hold on, okay?" Raiden said.

Sophie nodded. Her eyes were big brown saucers framed by blonde pigtails. Her threadbare pink shirt rolled up her belly as she clenched her arms around Raiden's neck. He trotted up the steps, and she giggled.

I'd never thought about having kids before. My world wasn't the kind of place you wanted to raise a child. But Becky's boyfriend, who'd been a wilderness guide, hadn't come home one night. He'd told her about us, and made her promise that if something happened to him, she would go through the Whittier Tunnel and find us in Girdwood. After he'd been missing for a month, she'd realized she was pregnant, and even though she didn't want to leave her home, she did it because of the baby. Thankfully, Sid and I had located her one day while we were out hunting.

Fallon, who was only eighteen, already had two kids. She and her husband, Bristol, didn't care what the world was like. She believed that kids made that shithole a better place.

I stopped and watched as Raiden bounced Sophie up the stairs, her pigtails slapping her back with every step. Her glee rang off the stone walls.

He was going to make a wonderful father someday.

I leaned against the wall and steadied myself with the palms of my hands against the stone. For the first time in my life, I was going to have options. We all were. The realization of possibilities settling in my gut was overwhelming.

Once Raiden had Sophie well ahead of the others, he ran back and hauled the next kid up the stairs, then the next kid. He wasn't even winded.

He stepped in front of Frederica and held out his arms before doing a come hither with his fingers.

"Don't you dare," she warned. But she wasn't serious, because when Raiden picked her up, she started cackling. Tears squeezed between her eyelids. Her light-brown hair, heavy with gray, swayed as he hauled her up the steps and set her down next to the kids.

"Anyone else?" he hollered when he came back. The sun shimmered in his hair like raven feathers, morphing from blue to green to purple. I wanted to run my hands through it, feel the soft texture between my fingers.

Both Emma and Mia, teenagers, jumped up and down with their hands raised. It wasn't like I hadn't noticed all the female attention showered upon Raiden, but he'd given me no reason to be jealous. I liked that.

When I'd first told Noah that I didn't reciprocate his feelings, he began to flirt with Willow. It might've made me jealous if I'd actually liked him, but I didn't. I'd been so happy when he started paying attention to her. Unfortunately, it didn't last long. And now, Willow didn't care for me. Not that I'd done anything to warrant her anger. Noah was the douchebag, not me.

When the rest of us made it to Raiden, we stopped and had some lunch, and when we got going again, Raiden picked up Sophie once more and repeated the process, this time hauling up Chloe and Willow too. None of the guys took him up on the offer, even though a steady line of sweat ran down their red faces. Going up and down mountains was one thing, but going up and up was another.

I lifted my hair off my neck and tried to untangle the dreads forming from curls and sweat. I gave up and tied it into a messy bun that flopped on my head every time I moved.

"Hey, beautiful," Raiden said as I made it to where he stood. "Hanging in there?"

I blew a stray curl off my forehead, and he tucked it behind my ear.

"You want a lift?" he offered.

I rolled my eyes.

He leaned forward. "Is there anything else you want?" he whispered in my ear.

Instantly, blood pounded between my thighs.

"Nothing you can give me." Cocky little beast.

He leaned down and blew on my neck, his breath cool over my sweating skin. Shivers, which had nothing to do with temperature, peppered my arms.

"Oh, I think you're wrong."

Of course, I was. The sound of his voice, the feel of his lips—the anticipation alone was almost enough to get me off.

He kissed the end of my nose before he ran back up the stairs.

Noah passed by me. "Slut."

I didn't take the bait. He wasn't worth it.

Finally, by the evening, we made it to the top—only because Raiden gave so many people a ride.

He made me go over the threshold first, then he declared

Sophie the winner when he crossed through with her propped on his shoulders. Her little round face looked happier than I'd ever seen.

A knot tightened in my throat. It felt like hope. And for the first time, I was absolutely positive I'd made the right decision.

Though I might've been a little concerned about the way Becky, Sophie's mom, was eyeing Raiden like he was stepdad material.

# FOURTEEN

That night, we camped in the same place Raiden, Vanessa, and I stayed five days ago. It seemed like a lifetime away. So much had happened since then.

Leaning against a tree with Sid by my side, I watched Raiden joke around with my small community. The mood amongst the people was cautiously optimistic. Smiles came easier, laughter lasted longer. Even the always-present tension in Kevin's shoulders was loosening.

Noah was the only problem, but everyone ignored his snide comments. He sat down by the fire and pouted as he ate a black bear sausage in two bites. Willow scooted in next to him and attempted a conversation, but he was too busy glaring at me to take much notice of her. Soon, they were both glaring daggers in my direction.

Needing to get away before I flew off the handle, I wandered alone out into the open meadow.

A soft swishing came from behind me. Just from the energy alone, I could tell it wasn't Raiden.

"You okay?" Kevin asked.

"Yeah, I'm good. How about you?"

We hadn't had a chance to talk in the last few days. We'd all been busy getting ready to leave. Probably permanently. The heaviness in my chest from abandoning my parents was already dissipating. I didn't know if they were alive, and even if they were, I knew for a fact that this was what they would've wanted me to do.

He nodded as he subconsciously picked at the corner of his thumbnail. It was endearing because my dad did the same thing, and they weren't even biologically related. It was funny how you remembered the small things, yet sometimes, I had a hard time picturing my dad's face. I often questioned whether my memories were real, or just old photographs I remembered or, worse yet, if I've made them up so I didn't lose the connection.

"I think I'm good," he said. "Everyone seems . . . happy."

They did, but I understood his hesitation. Happiness came a distant second to survival.

"I guess I keep waiting for the other shoe to drop," he said.

"Will we ever stop holding our breath?"

He kicked at the long grass. "I don't know, but I'd sure like to."

Kevin had carried the brunt of our people's welfare much longer than I had. I worried about all of us, but it was Kevin's job to make sure our fears didn't become reality. I could only imagine how substantial that burden was. He seemed more mature than his thirty years.

Our parents had instructed Kevin that if they didn't return home from their government jobs, he was to immediately relocate us to the first of our underground bunkers in

Bear Valley. As soon as they could, they would join. I had spent hours outside, perched in a tree, waiting and watching for their return. Kevin had promised me they would come home.

Three months later, when the entire world collapsed into chaos, Kevin ran into Frank and Frederica and somehow struck up a friendship. They moved into our first bunker with their six-year-old daughter, Willow.

A year into it, and still no sign of our parents, Willie and Martha and their four small girls moved in, followed the next month by Tom, Judy, Noah, and Mason.

When the On-Grids started poking around soon after, we'd hightailed it for the shelter in Girdwood. Along the way, we'd picked up Fallon, Bristol, Owen, Emmett, and Ted. They were all originally part of the foster care system and had banded together for safety.

With the already-crowded living situation, we soon figured out the new bunker wasn't big enough for all of us. Many found cabins or houses close to us and we made it work.

It wasn't like Kevin forced people to stay, but once they found us, they never left. Safety in numbers.

My brother and I'd been holding our breath for a long time, and it felt foreign to let it go.

Kev sighed. "I do like Raiden. He's a good man."

"Yeah, I kind of do too."

"Kind of?" he teased.

I stuck out my tongue.

"I hope the rest of the giants are as sincere as he is."

"Don't count on it. They seem very human in their actions. Though, I think they've learned a lot about what not to do from us. So there's always that."

"Yeah, I got that impression from Raiden. He won't come out and say it, but he's warned me to be cautious. Not fearful, but aware." Kevin hooked his thumbs through his belt loops.

"So what you're saying is, you're still going to be looking over your shoulder for a while." I bumped him with my elbow.

"Yeah. How about you?"

"Haven't stopped. But at least we'll have food, a place to live, and no one actively hunting us."

"There's always that." Kevin reached around and pulled me in for a sideways hug. "Hey, and about Noah, everything cool there? I don't like the way he's been treating you. He's being a dick."

"Yeah, well, I hurt his ego. He'll get over it eventually."

"He better get over it soon before he gets an ass whooping."

"Oh, please." I rolled my eyes. "If he needs an ass whooping, I'll be the one to deliver it."

"Or I will," Raiden said.

Both Kevin and I jumped and spun around with our fists raised.

"How do you do that?" I smacked Raiden hard on the arm.

He shrugged and spun me around to embrace me from behind. I rested the back of my head on the hard muscles of his chest.

"Everyone's down for tonight. They're all pretty tired," Raiden said.

"Yeah, I'm beat. I'll see you guys in the morning." Kevin excused himself.

Raiden turned us toward the sunset, its rays gilding the

meadow. I plucked a thick stalk of rough grass from the ground and ran it through my fingers. The serrated edges cut the tip of my thumb.

I hissed and stuck the wound in my mouth. A sound between a moan and a growl rumbled from Raiden's chest and vibrated the length of my body. He tightened his grip around my shoulders while *something* pressed hard into the small of my back.

Desire, hot and heavy, pooled low in my groin and spread, leaving me breathless.

I wrestled out of his grasp and turned around, but he just looked away. His tensed jaw hollowed out the space underneath his cheekbones and his pulse beat furiously against the collar of his shirt. I grabbed his chin gently and turned his face back to me. Only a small sliver of gray surrounded his enlarged pupils and the light from the dying sun reflected orange in his eyes.

"Are you okay?"

He swallowed and nodded tightly but refused to make eye contact.

I rested my hand on his chest. "Raiden? You're scaring me."

He inhaled a few times before he looked at me. His eyes had returned to normal. "You know the story, right? *Jack and the Beanstalk?* The 'Fee, fie, foe, fum, I smell the blood of an Englishman...'"

My brows crinkled. "So the smell of blood bothers you?" Seriously, who could smell that small of an amount?

*A predator.*

"Some of us. Others, it well ..."

My face flooded with heat as it dawned on me. "Oh."

"Yeah." He shifted his weight from one foot to the other.

"So blood turns you on?" I was beginning to think maybe giants were the base for the myth of vampires. Hard to kill, super-fast, fangs, beautiful, liked the smell of blood —did I miss anything? The sun didn't hurt him, but I didn't know how he felt about crosses or wooden stakes.

His gaze dragged the length of my body. "No. Let me be clear. Just *your* blood. That's never happened to me before."

"Oh." My voice hitched. "But the other day. . ." I recalled our less-than-gentle kiss. Though he did make us stop shortly after he nicked my lip with his fang.

"That was there. Things hit differently here. *Fuck*. I'm frightening you." He swallowed and looked away again.

I didn't want to lie to him, but I wasn't sure encouraging him was wise either, though I was accustomed to living on the edge. "Only a little. But maybe if you could just explain it to me."

"I'm so sorry." He reached out to touch me, but dropped his hand.

I grabbed it and held it in mine. I didn't ever want him to think he couldn't touch me. Even though he was scaring me, I felt safer with him around. Always.

He hesitated, pressing his lips together in a thin line. "I . . . I . . . this hasn't happened to me before. I . . . "

I'd never seen him like this, and honestly, his nervousness was more worrisome than his reaction to my blood.

I placed a hand on his cheek, his stubble grating against my palm. "Raiden, I feel safer with you than I've ever felt in my life. Even now. So whatever it is, I got this."

"Sometimes when giants really like someone, our bodies react to the smell of their blood. It also happens when we really *dis*like someone. But it's not quite the same reaction."

The feral gleam in his eyes excited me almost more than

it scared me and my fear morphed back into desire, with tiny goosebumps skipping along my skin. I licked my bottom lip and tugged on the corner with my teeth. I clenched my thighs together, attempting to relieve the throbbing.

He inhaled sharply as if in pain, and turned his head while gently pushing me away with a hand on my shoulder. "No. I need some time to figure out how to contain this. Please." His voice cracked.

I stepped back and stared at the ground.

"Bea, my feelings for you haven't changed. As a matter of fact . . ." He stopped.

"Matter of fact, what?" I whispered.

He shook his head. "Nothing. Just know that what happened scared me a little bit too. Give me some time to understand how to control this. I don't ever want to endanger you."

"Give me a break. You don't frighten me." I crossed my arms. Physically, he didn't scare me, but emotionally, I was terrified. We'd only been *together* less than a week, and already my feelings for him were stronger than they should have been. But what if he didn't feel the same? Anxiety knocked on my ribs.

"I know. But I'm pretty sure not a lot does frighten you. And it should."

## CHAPTER
# FIFTEEN

Four dappled-gray pegasus grazed in the meadow with their silver wings shimmering in the hazy light, their tails swishing at the long grass tickling their bellies. They were accompanied by two giants, one of which was Benji. The other was a woman dressed in solid black with two silver braids trailing down the front of her long military-style jacket.

A basket, about ten feet square, with a hard floor and woven sides sat a few feet away from Kevin.

"If anyone has changed their mind, now is the time to go back," Kevin said.

Everyone glanced around, but nobody stepped forward.

"All right, then." He opened the gates of the baskets. "Half in one—half in the other. Bea's riding with Raiden on his pegasus, Arnold." His voice lowered a notch, talking to himself. "I can't believe I just said that."

Obviously, Raiden and Kevin had this handled. Exhaustion had taken control and I'd accidentally overslept.

Tee looked over her shoulder to find me and clapped her

hands rapidly in excitement. I smiled and shook my head at her enthusiasm as she stepped inside the contraption. She wasn't afraid of heights.

Once everyone was loaded, Benji and the woman each led a winged horse to either side of the carrier. They attached four long straps to each saddle cinch, then unfolded metal rods that inserted in the side of each saddle to maintain the pegasus's distance apart as they flew. After they repeated the process with the other carrier, each of them climbed into their own saddle. Instead of taking off in a gallop, the beasts just extended their wings and started flapping. Slowly, in tandem, they lifted from the ground, the long grass flattening under the wind pressure. Several people in the carrier yelped and held on to their hats.

"We can hang out for a while. It's going to take them longer," Raiden said after my friends were almost out of sight.

He'd snuck up on me again. It was infuriating. "You need to wear a bell so I can hear you when you sneak up on me."

"That wouldn't be any fun. The faces you make are entertaining."

I tried slapping him, but he caught my hand mid-swing.

"As a matter of fact, all of you is entertaining." His eyes drifted down my face and neck, pausing on the swell of my breast.

A nervous flutter tickled inside. "So, you all good after yesterday?"

"Yeah, I think I've figured things out."

"You planning on letting me in on the secret?"

He yanked me closer, forcing me to look up. "Yeah. I do." His tongue slid over his front two teeth, his fangs still some-what hidden by his lower lip. "I want to do this, but . . . I *need* to do this slowly. I don't want to. Believe me. I want to lay you down right here in this field and . . ." He huffed and glanced away. "I need to take this slow. Is that okay?"

"So you still like me?" I asked hesitantly. I only wanted the answer if it was the answer I wanted.

He raked his fingers through his hair. "Good lord, Bea, *liking you* isn't the problem. Do you understand?"

The elephant that had taken up residence on my chest all night finally moved its fat ass. For the first time in twelve hours, I took an easy breath. After last night, I wasn't sure what was going to happen. If he was scared to be with me, that could present some problems. I was willing to do whatever it took to keep him.

"Look, the emotional part, I don't need to take slow. It's the physical part. I want to know everything about you— who you are, how you were raised, who your parents are, what your favorite weapon is."

"It sounds like you already know me." I patted the 9mm sitting on my hip.

"I'm getting there." He swiped my hair away from my face and kissed my forehead—not exactly the kiss I was longing for, but I wanted to make this easier on him. I couldn't lose him. We'd been together for a very short time, but he was my person. I was sure of it.

Raiden whistled loudly between two fingers. A few minutes later, Arnold soared from the sky. We gathered our things and strapped Sid into his basket before flying home.

*Home.* It felt strange thinking of Fie as home. But I thought, maybe, I could make my home anywhere so long as Raiden was by my side.

Because we had extra time, Raiden flew us over the staircase. From the sky, the sunlight glinted off the black polished stone. I shielded my eyes but I could still see that it traveled down into fluffy coral clouds that somehow connected our worlds.

After we swerved away, we flew over a forest of greens and blues, where most of the trees appeared larger than California redwoods. Birds, the size of eagles and in all colors, flitted throughout the canopy like exotic decorations.

We glided over a swamp thick with vegetation, a dark shadow swimming just under the murky water's surface.

"What's down there?"

"It's a swamp serpent. You'd probably consider it a snake, though it's more like a combination between a snake and a crocodile."

"What? Are you kidding me?"

"No. But most of the animals here are similar to the ones on earth."

"How were we safe at our campsite?"

"All giants have some magic. Wherever I stay, I put up an invisible fence of energy. It's probably one of the reasons I had trouble controlling myself around you yesterday. Some of my defenses were being used elsewhere. When it comes to you, I need all my wits."

"You're not funny." I jabbed my elbow lightly into his rock-hard abs.

"I think I am." He wrapped his arms tighter around me and kissed the top of my head. "So, when we get back, I'd like to make this thing official. I don't want anyone else trying to snatch you up. I'd like to take you out on a date."

A giddiness tightened in my throat. "I'd like that."

"What do you want to do? We can fly to the capital and go to a show. We can take a tour of the Fee-Fie-Foe-Fum museum. Check out some art galleries? Whatever your heart desires."

All of those activities sounded like fun. But honestly, I wanted to get to know Raiden without an audience first.

"I'd like to stay somewhere, just the two of us. Somewhere where you don't have to use your magic as an electric fence."

"You're not afraid I'm going to steal your virtue?" he whispered in my ear.

The simple act of his breath on my neck made my insides scorch. It took every ounce of control I had not to tell him to go there this instant. "I'm counting on it."

---

Hours later, we landed in Fie. Benji walked toward us from the carriage house, his silver hair stuck to his forehead. He wiped at his brow with a bandana.

"What's going on?" Raiden asked after he let Sid out and passed Arnold's reins to Benji.

Benji scowled. "The Fee, Foe, and Fum are here."

"Why?"

"Your guess is as good as mine, but I can tell they aren't happy about something."

A sense of foreboding deflated my joy, and the hope I'd felt earlier began to drain away.

"Where are my friends?" I interrupted.

"Not to worry. They're all settled at the hotel and doing well. I personally made sure of it." Benji's eyes darted to Raiden, then back to me. "Whatever is going on here has nothing to do with your friends. Tonight, your brother and

162

extended family will be escorted on a tour of the town by Ramona, my wife."

I stared at him blankly.

"The woman who was with me this morning," Benji clarified. "She's in charge of welcoming all of you to the Fiefdom. Tomorrow, they'll gather so Ramona can get to know them better. It'll make it easier for her to place them in training or in jobs if they choose. Bea, they're really going to like it here. I promise. Ramona's excited to work with them." Benji pushed his bandana into his jacket pocket.

A shiver-inducing screech, like that of a banshee, echoed from inside the barn. Arnold pinned his ears back and swished his tail.

"Gotta go. That griffin is a handful. And to think, when they arrived, I thought the dragons were going to be the problem." He jogged back to the barn, Arnold trotting after him.

My mouth dropped open. "Dragons? I thought you said all the creatures here were the same as what we have on Earth."

"Well, most of them are." Raiden shrugged, but I could see the smile behind his eyes. "What? Dragons are really big lizards," he teased. He picked me up and twirled me around. "Let's get you inside so I can figure out what's going on."

With his arm clasped through mine, he escorted me inside the crystal mansion and down the long marble hallway until we came to the same room I'd stayed in before. "I'll be back in an hour." He gave me a quick peck on the lips.

Disappointment tugged my mouth into a frown. He hesitated, then pulled me into his arms to kiss me again. This time, his lips swept over mine almost reverently. He curled one hand behind my skull and the other gripped my waist. His fingers dug into my skin almost painfully but his kiss stayed gentle. Fragments of electricity scattered inside me as if I'd pricked my finger but felt the pain in my leg—though it wasn't pain I was experiencing.

A millisecond before I yanked him inside my bedroom, he pulled away, his teeth catching momentarily on my bottom lip. "I'll be back soon." He kissed the tip of my nose and left.

I gently shut the door and leaned against it, trying to contain my smile. I'd never felt this way before. Giddy? Hopeful? Relaxed? All were foreign.

Since Benji had reassured me my friends and family were safe, I took my time getting ready, which meant I spent thirty minutes standing under scalding-hot water. Afterward, I wrapped my hair in a towel so it would dry in nice ringlets while I added a bit of gloss to my lips. I fanned my lashes with mascara, the black making them look bluer than hazel.

My cheekbones protruded more than they should've, but consistent food would fix that issue. I was tired of being hungry. I was tired of being scared. But most of all, I was tired of being lonely. I wanted someone to share my life with, someone to love. I hadn't even realized I was lonely until Raiden kidnapped me and held me hostage. Okay, so looking back, maybe I exaggerated about the kidnapping. He was just doing his job. But I wouldn't have changed a thing.

I'd have given up far more than my freedom if it meant my friends and family had access to food, shelter, and jobs. Here, their options seemed endless. The idea that Tee could find love and have the family she'd always dreamed of pushed me to tears. Unable to control the emotions welling, a sob of relief and happiness made my chin tremble.

I wiped away the budding tears and walked into the closet, needing the distraction of what to wear. I landed on a sleek black jumpsuit and a pair of wedges, knowing they were easier to walk in than regular heels.

A sharp, aggressive knock at the door startled me. I opened it to find Raiden's face seething with rage.

"Are you okay?" I reached for him, but he shied away. My heart stopped—then beat in double time. It felt like it was going to spring from my chest. "Raiden, what's wrong?"

"Ruby." The pulse in his neck throbbed, his tendons straining.

"Yeah?"

"So it *is* your name? And he's Obsidian?" He tilted his head toward Sid, a storm swirling behind his eyes.

"Yeah . . ." I said. I felt like I was being quizzed but answering incorrectly.

"Do you know about the prophecy?" he demanded.

Relief flooded over my fear. He was mad because I hadn't told him I was their salvation.

I inhaled a shaky breath. "I'm sorry. They wouldn't let me tell anyone or the contract would be null and void. I had to save my family."

His voice lowered to a deathly quiet volume. "So you signed the contract knowing exactly what was in it?" He didn't sound less angry—if anything he sounded angrier.

"Yeah?"

"I should've known better than to trust a fucking human. Noah was right about you."

I cocked my head, my breath wedging in my throat. What did he mean? The last time Noah had spoken to me, he'd called me a slut.

Raiden balled his fist and threw a punch at the wall, but

the concrete didn't slow down the speed. Shards of cement flew through the air. I screamed and ducked out of the way, even though I was a little late. Blood dripped down his knuckles onto the white marble floor as he turned and walked away.

"Raiden?" I said, my tone swirling with shock and anger. I was still confused as to what was going on, but I certainly didn't condone of his behavior.

He ignored me and kept walking.

Panic burst inside me like a flame with gasoline.

"Raiden!" I ran after him, but stopped abruptly. Standing at the end of the hallway was Vanessa, wearing a victorious grin. Her dimples cratered deep into her cheeks and her eyes glistened an icy blue.

Sid started barking wildly behind me as if he were trying to help.

Someone tapped me from behind. Having not heard them over Sid's ruckus, I jumped.

"Excuse me, Bea?"

"What?" I yelled as I turned around. A young woman, with her dark hair pulled into a tight ponytail, stared at me with wide eyes as if my outburst frightened her.

"Pardon me, miss. You've been summoned by Lady Sylvia and Lord Issac. They're waiting."

I brushed the woman away as I spun around, intent on following Raiden, but he was gone.

Vanessa laughed, the cruel sound bouncing off the stone walls down the long corridor.

From behind me, the woman's firm hand found my shoulder. "Miss Bea, you can catch Raiden after your meeting is over. I really must insist that we go."

My head ricocheted from her to where Raiden had been.

"Come, now." She linked her elbow with mine and forcibly led me down the hallway.

I wasn't sure what had just happened. Why Raiden would be so mad that I didn't tell him I knew about the prophecy? It didn't make sense. And what in the world had Noah been right about?

The anxiety elephant sat its fat ass back on my chest.

# CHAPTER
# SIXTEEN

L ady Sylvia and Lord Issac waited around a circular
conference table, along with three other couples.
The room was all hard edges of glass and marble
with no art or carpeting to soften the effect.

"Ruby, good to see you," Sylvia said. Her voice was warm
and welcoming, unlike the space. She even smiled at Sid.
*Weird.* "Please, have a seat." She motioned to the office chair
next to her.

I sat down on the edge of the white leather so my feet
touched the ground. My leg bounced rapidly under the
chair.

"Lola, thank you. You may be excused," Sylvia dismissed
the woman who'd escorted me.

"Lola, wait!" I grabbed her sleeve and pulled her down
to me.

Her eyes darted to Sylvia.

"Do something for me? Please?" I asked. Beneath the
table, Sid pressed up against my leg and whined.

Her lips pursed but she nodded. Probably so I'd let her go.

"Go tell Benji not to let Raiden leave," I whispered. "I owe him an explanation. He doesn't understand." Truthfully, I wasn't sure *I* understood what was going on. Did it matter if I was the giants' salvation? Sure, I'd lied to Raiden about it, but I hadn't had a choice. Certainly, he should be able to understand why. My family's safety depended on it. But before he left, we needed to have a conversation and work out whatever *issue* he was having.

"Yes, miss," she said.

I held on to her sleeve. "You promise?"

"Yes." Her pale-blue eyes stayed steady on mine.

"Thank you." I let go, and she rushed out of the room.

"Sorry," I mumbled under the scrutiny of strangers. I patted Sid's back and pointed for him to lie down at my feet.

The set of Sylvia's shoulders led me to believe she wasn't happy with me. Sweat beaded under the weight of my hair, and I started picking at my cuticles with my hands under the table.

"Ruby, let me introduce you to the Foe."

She motioned to the couple wearing winged eyeliner and colorful clothes dripping with beads and jewels. Their skin was dark but their eyes were almost lime green. "This is Lord Ren and Lady Moselle." They tipped their heads toward the table once. Both were beautiful and feminine. If it wasn't for the size difference between the two, I wasn't sure I'd be able to tell which one was Lady Moselle.

"The Fee, Lord Dion and Lady Chantal."

They pressed a kiss to the pads of their fingers. They were dressed much like Sylvia and Issac, in simple but stylish clothes—wool slacks, cashmere sweaters, and simple jewelry. The colors were rich earth tones, olive greens, and buttery creams, as opposed to the monochromatic scheme of the Fie. Lady Chantal's wavy brown hair shimmered a deep moss under the lights.

"And the Fum, Lord Cooper and Lady Sera."

The two with flaming-copper hair looked as if they'd just stepped off the set of the movie *Mad Max* in leather, chainmail, large earrings, and braids. The girth of Lord Cooper's chest was enormous. Lady Sera's was big, as well, but hers was due to her massive breasts. I had to be careful not to stare. A genuine smile broke onto their faces. "Ruby, it's a pleasure," they said in synchrony.

For once, I held my tongue. *Was* it a pleasure? I glanced at the door, hoping they would hurry up. The need to find Raiden overrode my need to be polite.

Sylvia continued, while looking down at the papers in front of her. "We are here to discuss the terms of your contract."

My leg stopped bouncing. "I wasn't aware there were terms to discuss. I'm to stay here. And if I don't, I die. What more do you want to talk about?"

Sylvia lifted her head. "Did you not *read* the contract?" Her words were sharp, echoing in the sterile space like bullets.

My stomach heaved in a large wave. *I thought I did.* "I tried. I was tired. And slightly tipsy." Neither were good excuses.

Her lips thinned until they almost disappeared. "So the answer is no. You signed an unread contract. Did we not give you ample time to read and understand the terms?" She tapped a pen on the table.

The pulse in my neck thumped faster. "Yes, you gave me plenty of time. I was just tired."

"Did I *not* instruct you to read the contract carefully?"

"Yes."

"Did we *not* offer to answer any questions you had?"

"*Yes*, you did." I crossed a leg underneath me and gripped the chair with both hands, trying to sit up higher.

"Then the contract stands as written. Agreed?" She looked at the other couples, who all nodded. "We did not coerce Ruby to sign. She did so upon her own free will. If she didn't read it..."

I shrunk away under her icy gaze. Sweat ran down my spine. I'd done something bad.

"Then that falls on her." Sylvia set the black pen down on top of the contract.

The Foe and the Fee didn't look fazed by my confession, though the Fum were both glaring at the rest.

"Let me get this straight." Lady Sera held up a hand, her eyes glowing amber. "You had a young girl sign a contract while tired and drunk, and you all think this is *okay?*"

"First of all," Sylvia snapped, "Ruby is twenty-two years old. She's not a girl. Second, Ruby, did you tell us you were tired?"

"No," I mumbled.

"Did you tell us you were drunk?"

Embarrassment crept up my chest. "I wasn't drunk, only a little buzzed."

"See?" Sylvia raised her hands in the air.

"Can somebody please tell me what I missed?" I demanded loudly.

"Ruby, you are our salvation," Sylvia said with a huff, as if I was putting her out for needing an explanation. "Foe,

Fee, and Fum agree with our interpretation of the prophecy. I was under the impression you knew exactly what you were getting yourself into. Honestly, I would've made the same decision if I were in your situation. Therefore, I didn't question whether you'd read the document. You're a good person whose first priority is the safety of her people. That is, in my opinion, the most important quality of a great leader."

I swallowed hard. I hadn't read anything about being a leader.

"The legally binding document you signed states you will marry a First-Born son, which was written in the contract in its entirety. We did not hide anything from you. The prophecy says, *'When the Earth is on the brink of break, our Salvation lies in wait. The Crimson Jewel it will take for Obsidian the gate to break. Our Salvation lies in wait, for the First-Born son to bond his fate.'*"

"No. No! Loch said I wasn't anyone's fate!"

Sylvia raised a dark eyebrow, looking displeased that I'd interrupted her. "Loch does not believe in the prophecy. Do you want to hear the rest, since you didn't read it?" She berated me like I was a child who'd made a very poor decision.

I had a sinking suspicion that I'd done exactly that.

"*'Our Crimson Jewel shall be the throne and with the First-Born son rule the Dome until the time has come for the First-Born son and the Crimson Jewel to become one. Only then—Fee-Fie-Foe-Fum—our war on extinction will be won.'*"

The anxiety elephant kicked me in the stomach. Bile burned the back of my throat. My pulse echoed in my ears. So this truly was all about expanding their genetic pool after all. How could I have been so blind? And yet I'd used it as a legitimate excuse to convince my people to relocate.

Now Raiden's anger and reaction made perfect sense.

I didn't think before I bolted out of the room, down the stairs, out the front door, and straight to the barn, Sid leading my way. The wind whipped my hair around my head in a big billowing mass. I opened the door to the barn and yelled, "Benji! Where can I find Raiden?"

I didn't know who else to go to. I didn't know where Raiden was. A frenzy of chaotic energy filled my body, making my fingers and toes tingle. Or perhaps I needed to breathe.

"Bea." Benji rushed over. Something big hit the side of the closest stall. "Knock it off," he said as he thumped the thick panels of wood. "Raiden's gone. He took off right after he saw you." Benji's face said he was annoyed with me. "I'm not going to repeat what he said."

"You don't have to. But I didn't know. I didn't know what I signed." I put my trembling hands over my face to hide my shame. "It's my fault—but I didn't know."

"So you're telling me you signed a contract without reading it? Did your parents teach you nothing?" He crossed his arms.

"My parents disappeared when I was ten. I've lived in an underground bunker longer than I lived in my home. I spent my days hunting and fishing, making sure we had enough food to survive. All while avoiding people who wanted to capture us, and creatures who wanted to kill me. Not reading law books!"

"I'm sorry, you're right. You're young and . . ." He sighed. "You did what you had to, to survive. A formal education wasn't high on your list."

I bristled. "My brother did the best he could, and I studied during the winter. A lot. And this *is* my fault." I hung my head. "I

173

knew better. I have no valid excuse. I may be stupid but I'm not cruel. I wouldn't have started something with Raiden if I was supposed to marry someone else. I— I—" I couldn't admit to the feelings already wedged in my heart. Hot tears spilled over and ran down my cold cheeks, dripping off the end of my chin.

Benji handed me a rag that smelled like a horse as I wiped my face.

"Raiden is under the impression you were having one last fling before you got hitched." He didn't phrase it in the form of a question, making me think perhaps those were Raiden's exact words.

"Probably, but that was *not* my intention." I sniffed.

His pale blue eyes held onto mine for a long, hard moment. "I practically raised that young man and seeing him in that kind of pain, angers me. But I feel the truth in your words, and I know what Sylvia is capable of when she wants something. So what's your next move?"

"I don't know. I ran out of the meeting as soon as I heard what I was required to do. I *need* to tell Raiden. I need to explain."

"Well, you better go back inside before they decide your fate without you present. You're going to need a bodyguard now, and without Raiden here to do it, you're going to ask for my daughter, Liz. Do you understand?" Benji placed his hands on my shoulders and bent over to look me in the eyes.

I nodded. I wasn't sure why I was going to need a bodyguard, but I wasn't about to question him.

"I'm going to find Raiden and let him know the truth. Until then, do what they tell you. I'm assuming they're going to have you choose a First-Born son from one of the Domes."

"I don't know."

"Go." He pushed me lightly toward the door. "I'll take care of Raiden."

I jogged back to the conference room, my shoes clipping loudly over the marble floor and echoing down the hall. I didn't want them making decisions without me. With Sid's help, I found the room and sat down without a word, calmly folding my hands together on the surface.

Sylvia blinked a few times, then jumped right back in, as if I hadn't even left the table. "So, it's been agreed upon that you'll spend one week with each house. There, you will get to know our First-Born sons alone. After that, you'll spend a week in Isle Noir, the capital, in order to carefully consider your options. At the end of the week, we will host a ball in your honor. There, at the stroke of midnight, you will announce your decision on who you'll marry, and therein, officially solidifying the contract."

Five short weeks to decide my entire future. How was I supposed to get to know someone in a week? My thoughts jumped to Raiden. It had only taken me one week to fall for him, but that wasn't normal. I rubbed my forehead between my fingers and thumb, hoping the pressure on my temples would ward off the impending headache from the mess I'd created.

"Okay." I didn't know what else to say. I was between a proverbial rock and a hard place.

"Do not decide on a groom until you've had your week to think about it. That time allows you to reflect on who would be the best partner to rule. And if you copulate with *one*, you're required to do so with all."

Heat exploded up my neck as I stared at the table.

"What?" Now they were regulating my sex life? Not that I had one. *Was that in the contract too?*

Sylvia started to speak, but was cut off by Lady Chantal with a wave of a hand. "We are not here to embarrass you, Ruby. I promise we're not. But from what we know about humans, especially women, when they're intimate with another, something alters their brain chemistry and they form a connection with that partner. You see, if you sleep with one of our sons and not the others, it will give an unfair advantage. It might cause problems. So, to avoid such issues, we've decided it's the best way to keep things equal on all fronts."

"Sure," I dismissed. I wouldn't be that stupid.

Sylvia continued. "The first house you will be spending time with will be the Fum—Lord Cooper, Lady Sera, and their son, Kai. Next, you'll transfer to the Foe with Lord Ren, Lady Moselle, and their son, Trent. Then your hosts will be Lord Dion, Lady Chantal, and their son, Adam. Finally, you'll come back here to spend a week with Loch."

I started to talk, but Sylvia cut me off.

"You have the option to take two people with you on your journey. May I suggest—"

I cut her off this time. "I want my friend Tee and Benji's daughter, Liz."

The skin around Sylvia's eyes tightened as she tapped the pen on the table. "Fine. Your choice."

Tee was the one person besides my brother I trusted, but Kevin needed to stay here with our people, and Raiden seemed to trust Benji, therefore I'd take his daughter.

"You'll be leaving tomorrow morning. I'll make sure Tee and Liz are ready to accompany you."

Everyone thanked me, told me how nice it was to meet me, and left the room. Sylvia stayed behind.

I stood up and propped my hands on my hips. "I'm here to tell you right now—Loch is off the list. You guys entrapped me. You knew *exactly* what you were doing and you counted on my naivete."

"You listen to me, young lady," Sylvia said, towering over me. "We were protecting you. If you had stayed put instead of insisting on rescuing your people, you would be the queen of the Fiefdom already. There are giants that would rather see our race go extinct than have a *human* on the throne. There are also giants that would rather see our race go extinct than have one of the other Domes on the throne. What you've done is give them a bigger window in which to kill you. Once you're the queen, you'll be much harder to get to. Besides, I was hoping once our people realize that you're half giant, the faction that hates humans would dissipate."

I blinked. My hands slipped off my hips and dangled uselessly by my side.

She waved her French manicure in front of my face. "Do you understand anything I'm saying?"

I pressed my fingers against my twitching eyelid. I understood everything. I understood nothing. The lights above faded in and out.

"Did you say I'm half giant?"

"Yes. How do you think you passed through our gates? That shock would've killed a human. And how do you think over the last ten years, no one in your group has gotten sick? No one has died of anything other than accidents. Not even starvation. I'm betting your brother already knows what you are, or at least what your blood can do. I'm also betting that's why the military was after *you* all along. They took your parents because both of them carry giant blood. Your DNA is much stronger than theirs. Or Kevin's."

Air rushed out of my lungs and I struggled to refill them. "How do you know all of this?"

"I suspected, but I didn't know for sure until you signed the contract and the pen funneled your blood. The contract wouldn't have worked unless you carried a significant amount of giant DNA. The rest of the information, well, let's just call it an educated guess."

So many unexplained things about my life clicked into place.

Why I never got sick. Why I healed so quickly. Why I was faster and stronger than everyone else at home. Why my mother stashed vials of my blood in our medical supplies. And why my parents told me—never, not ever, no matter the circumstances, to go to JBER.

It *was* me they were after. And if that were true, my parents might still be alive. Because what better way to lure your prey—me—than with its favorite food—my parents.

My jaw clenched putting uncomfortable pressure on my teeth because as I looked back, I realized Kevin knew about it the whole time. Why else would he have refused to let us go searching for them when we knew exactly when and where they disappeared.

The coach dropped Sid and me off in front of the hotel where my friends were staying. The lobby was decorated with ice sculptures, pussy willows, and abstract paintings. Everywhere the light hit, the white walls sparkled like freshly fallen snow. The front desk, made entirely of a solid piece of glass, came up to my chest. The eyes of the older gentleman behind the counter flickered briefly to Sid. Without argument, he gave me Kevin's room number.

My hand gripped the smooth banister of the grand staircase as I ran to the third floor. At the end of the hall, I knocked on Kevin's door.

He answered wrapped in a fluffy white robe and house slippers. If I wasn't so angry, I might have laughed. My brother in house slippers?

"Hey! I didn't know you were coming with us tonight. That'll be great." He flashed a smile. He seemed so relaxed. His normally alert behavior—eyes searching the area for danger and only half paying attention to a conversation because he was listening for aerial noises or predators—had diminished. I almost hated to destroy his peace.

"We need to talk."

I pushed my way past him and sat down on the edge of the four-poster bed. The white comforter crinkled under my weight.

"Did you know I was half giant?"

His face paled, leaving his freckles stark. I had my answer but I wanted to hear him say it. I wanted to hear his excuse as to why he'd kept me in the dark for the last twelve years.

He walked in front of the expansive window and stared out at the mountains. "Yes. Mom was getting suspicious that the government was on to her, so a few days before they disappeared, they told me everything."

"And now it's time to tell me." Though seething inside, I knew better than to show it. He would treat me like an adult if I acted like one. It took all my control not to scream and throw things at his head. It wasn't as if that hadn't happened before, but if the process were repeated, he wouldn't talk to me until I calmed down. I was simply skipping a step.

"Mom has always known what she is—a quarter giant. She came from a family of scientists. Dad didn't know he had giant DNA until he met Mom. It shows up in genetic testing as Neanderthal. But Mom said she knew something about Dad was different after he broke his leg and was up and walking without a cast or crutches a few days later. She did some testing. He was also a quarter giant. You were about three at the time. She took some samples of your blood and experimented." Kevin threaded his hands together behind his neck. He cracked his fingers and turned around.

"If both of them were only a quarter, I wouldn't be half."

I knew how it worked—I was the daughter of a geneticist.

"Normally, that would be true, but giant DNA is absolutely dominant, according to Mom. Somehow, if both parents carry the markers, all of them are passed on. If you're looking for something more in-depth than my analysis, I don't know what to tell you." His voice held an edge.

"Fine," I said. "Go on."

"You see, Mom's blood, Dad's blood, and my blood—it's enough to keep us healthy for the rest of our lives. We won't die of cancer or any other disease. Our blood will even cure the common cold or the flu. But *our* blood can't cure cancer, reverse heart disease, cure diabetes, or ALS. Yours *can*. Mom said it cured everything it came into contact with. *Everything*."

I crossed my arms, attempting to contain the fury brewing within me. "So instead of using me to help the human race, you guys decide to hide me." *Like I'm some kind of coward.*

"Yes! Don't you understand? The government wouldn't have let you help *just anyone*. There's far too much money to be made by keeping people sick. Your blood would've been auctioned off for the highest price and used to keep the elite alive while others suffered. On the day Mom and Dad disappeared, Mom took samples of all of our blood to the lab," he said.

Over the years, my mom had taken so many samples from us that I remembered Kevin laughing saying if she wasn't careful, his friends were going to think he was doing drugs from all the track marks.

He started pacing. "Mom and Dad planned to leave the samples at her lab at JBER, along with Mom's research, so the government could continue with her work. We were all supposed to go to the bunker *together* that night. They told me if they didn't make it home by dinner, we were to leave. They would meet us when they could. At the bunker, Mom left me a detailed set of instructions for if other people joined us. You know Mom—she liked to cover all the bases. She told me that if I put a few drops of your blood into our water source, no one would ever get sick."

*Gross.* "Not everyone uses the same water source," I said snidely.

"Seriously, Bea? Why do you think we have a mandatory once-a-month social event?" He raised his brows, wrinkling his forehead.

"I can't believe you didn't tell me earlier." I balled my fists into the down comforter.

"I wanted to, but Mom forbade it. She said you would try to do the right thing. You would've run straight to JBER to bargain for their release and martyr yourself for the good of humanity. Which she said was the wrong thing. And now look at us. Give us a few years here and maybe *we'll* be able to deliver a cure to the Earth so everyone can benefit, and you won't have to sacrifice your life to do it."

Hot, angry tears filled my eyes.

"Bea, I'm so sorry. I really did want to tell you. I don't like keeping things from you, but Mom was right. You always try and do the right thing, even if it isn't right for you. I had to protect you from your greatest threat—you."

My chin trembled under the weight of his confession. My parents and my brother had sacrificed everything to keep me safe. But for some reason, I didn't feel an ounce of gratitude. Only guilt. It coated my skin like being dipped in motor oil.

"Bea, please stop."

Kevin sat down next to me. He placed an arm around my shoulder and pulled me close. I tried shrugging him off but he refused to let go. Soon, my tears of anger turned into embarrassment. I cried until I was done, then I told him what I'd gotten myself into. But I didn't tell him my life was in danger.

"You're supposed to marry one of their sons and you'll make him a king? Why?" he asked.

"I don't know. Because their stupid prophecy said so."

Kev handed me a tissue. I blew my nose.

"And Raiden left without hearing your side of the story?" he said.

"When he was asking me questions, I didn't know what I'd signed. So when I answered him, it looked like I'd played him for a fool. But I didn't."

"Damn! Somebody has to find him. He's going to be pissed with himself when he learns you didn't betray him. You're just stupid."

I flinched. His criticism hurt, but he was right.

"Benji is going after him. And you know, I would've signed the contract anyway, even if I'd read the whole thing properly. What's a marriage compared to everyone's well-being? Only I wouldn't have started anything with Raiden."

Though I wasn't sure I could've stopped it. The intensity between the two of us was hard to ignore. But I would've told him the truth from the start. I would've told him I was to be married to another. The mere thought of being with anyone but him broke my heart. It cracked inside my chest walls like ice fracturing over a lake. I didn't know how to keep it together. All I wanted to do was let it shatter into a million pieces. Maybe without a heart, I wouldn't feel the pain.

"We're going to fix this." Kevin squeezed my shoulder.

That's what he always did, but I didn't think there was a way to fix what I'd signed in blood. But someone could tell Raiden I didn't mean to hurt him.

"I have to leave tomorrow morning to go with the Fum. They seem like the nicest of the four, at least."

Kevin stood up. "I'll get my things packed."

"No, Kev, you need to stay here so I don't have to worry about everyone. I'm bringing Tee and Benji's daughter, Liz. Sid has to stay here too. It's safer for him."

Sid sat down in front of me. Even though I was trying to hold it together, he knew the turmoil boiling inside me. The fear. The sadness. The anger. I scratched the scruff of Sid's neck and leaned over, pressing my lips to the top of his head. For the last few years, he'd been my constant companion. He'd slept with me, hunted by my side—heck, I hadn't even been able to go to the bathroom alone. The thought of leaving him behind tied my stomach into a tight little knot. But I didn't know what I'd be facing out there—Sylvia had made it clear that I would remain a target until I was married. Sid was safer here with Kevin, and I had to do what was best for him. Even if it tore me to pieces.

"I don't know, Bea . . . I feel like I should go with you."

"What? So you can chaperone?" I straightened up and rolled my eyes. "Please don't make this any more embarrassing than it already is. Stay here. Make sure everyone is settled. Take care of my boy. You and Tee are the only ones I trust. Find Raiden. I have to go on a four-week dating spree." I pinched the bridge of my nose. It felt like it was going to be a dangerous season of *The Bachelorette*. Except during the finale, I wouldn't be handing out a rose, but a crown.

"Not sure how much help you'll be. I have a feeling you'll be more of a cock block." Besides, I had Tee for that. The girl had good instincts. And for being so small, she was fierce when provoked.

Kevin threw me a dirty look. "As much as I don't want to admit it, you're probably right. I should stay here and get everyone settled." He stopped in front of me and tapped me —not so gently—on the forehead. "But you need to be smarter."

*And here we go. The lecture.*

*Don't sign anything. Don't agree to anything. Keep my eyes open. Trust my instincts. If something is too good to be true, it probably is. Yada. Yada. Yada.*

After he was done, I asked, "What about Mom and Dad? There's a possibility they're still alive."

Kevin pursed his lips. "A slim possibility, yes, but can we please tackle one problem at a time? Just think, when you're queen, we'll have some resources, and if they *are* alive, we might actually have a chance of rescuing them."

He was right. Soon, I'd have the power to find out if my parents were still alive.

# CHAPTER 18
# THE FUM

Two beasts, quadruple the size of an African Elephant, with flaming eyes and elongated pupils, waited in the granite courtyard. A shadowy outline of Tee and I reflected inside their copper scales. Thick, bird-like feet ending with ten-inch black talons gouged the stone. Horns and a mane of spikes twisted into sharp gold tips. It was the foot-long obsidian fangs, edged like daggers, that made my heart race. Both Tee and I stared with open mouths, our hands gripped together.

They were so large, that instead of wearing a normal-ish saddle like the flying horses did, they had four seats mounted to a saddle, each with a roll-up ladder, and a dragon driver wearing a leather duster and goggles on their forehead.

We didn't have luggage because Tee and I had been instructed to assimilate into the Fum culture as much as possible. It was to be that way during each stop, which meant dressing like them. Good thing, because neither Tee nor I had many belongings. Heck, she was still wearing her mismatched shoes.

A hand, nearly the length of my forearm, clasped us each on the shoulder. We both jumped. Tee might've yelped.

"Are you girls ready?" Lord Cooper asked. His voice was gruff as if he smoked. He pointed to the dragons. "This one is Prince Harry and that one there, ladies, is Lucille."

These giants and their fascination with pop culture baffled me.

"Lucille's got a sense of humor, but don't let that scare you. You're in good hands," he said.

Their barbed tails swished slowly over the ground, scraping the surface, making a high-pitched whine. Goosebumps peppered my arms. Smoke, smelling like barbecue meat, rolled from their nostrils.

I swallowed to keep from gagging.

"Oh, not to worry. Dragons have a bad reputation but they're far easier to manage than the *griffins*," he said, like griffins were Lucifer. "All they require is a gentle hand. If you're good to them, they're good to you. Here, let me help you up." Lord Cooper walked over to the beast and rolled down the ladder.

I looked back at Tee, whose expression said, *You first. You're the idiot that got us into this situation, dumbass.* I itched my forehead with my middle finger. She laughed.

I yanked the bottom rung of the ladder to make sure it was secure before I climbed up the side of the dragon. My arms trembled but I made it to the top without falling. I plopped down into the seat and strapped myself in. Two over the chest, one over my lap—just like a race car driver. Tee made it to the top a moment later. Even her dark skin managed to look peaked.

"Thank you, Lord Cooper," I said.

"Ladies, no more of that nonsense!" He waved a massive mitt in the air. "From now on, it's Cooper and Sera. You'll find the Fum far less formal than this stuffy group. No offense, Liz."

Liz, who I'd yet to officially meet though she was supposed to be my bodyguard, ran her fingers through her hair, flipping it to the opposite side. A tiny streak of white framed her upturned blue eyes. "None taken," she said as she climbed up the ladder and settled into the chair next to the driver.

I thought it was strange no one had introduced us, but the Fiefdom ways were still a mystery. Liz didn't seem concerned by the lack of propriety so, I chalked it up to different cultures. I tried to not let it bother me, though if I was being honest, it rubbed me the wrong way.

The dragon driver grabbed a set of goggles from a pouch on the outside of the seat and held them up for us to see. Tee and I dug around and found ours.

I forced them over my hair and glanced at Tee. A wide grin rose on her face before we both started howling—partially because we looked ridiculous, but mostly because of the unspoken nervous energy bouncing between us.

With everyone in position, the beast's great wings lifted into the air and began to flap. Dust and debris swirled over the granite. Slowly, we ascended from the ground and flew into the sky. Our elevation was much higher than when Raiden and I had flown by pegasus. A pang of sorrow burrowed under the barrier I'd erected to protect myself and stabbed my heart like a pincushion. I wondered where he was.

This morning before we'd left, Tee and I had breakfast

with our friends. Their excitement had been palpable as they talked about what they wanted to be when they grew up. Frank was over the moon. He, with his expertise as an engineer, was sharing his knowledge with a group of giants mostly from the Fie. Frederica, a doctor, had plans to study alongside an herbalist from Fee. Becky, and her daughter Sophie, wanted to tag along with the herbalist, since Becky loved gardening. Noah, obsessed with weapons, had planned a trip to visit Fum. Seeing everyone so happy had hope blooming in my chest, like a tiny seed pushing through the soil.

Of course, all of their adventures would take place after their four-week course on Giant 101. I was a bit disappointed to miss the classes, but it seemed as if Tee and I were about to get some hands-on education. Kevin promised me he would take care of everyone in my absence and instructed me not to fret. Truthfully, I wasn't worried. Kevin had been taking care of them far longer than I had.

I'd hugged him fiercely, then got down on my knees and buried my face in Sid's fur. He smelled like the outdoors. I stared into his dark eyes, and his cute little eyebrows twitched. He licked my cheeks. "I love you, too, buddy. I'll be back in a month, okay?"

Just the memory of leaving Sid brought forth pain, constricting my breathing. Bringing him with us might've been safer for me, but I couldn't put him in unknown danger. Having Tee with me was worrisome enough. I reached over and grabbed her hand. I squeezed, and she squeezed back. We didn't need words. The heat from the dragon's core warmed the seats, but the fierce wind kept conversations to a minimum.

Soon, the mountains changed into a thick forest. Veins

of navy-blue trees grew amongst deep-green ones, creating an ocean-like effect of long, lazy currents. Valleys morphed into sweeping prairies with grasses bright as limes. Up here, details were less distinctive, but colors more obvious. Everything was a few shades from what I thought of as normal.

I tried staying awake, but after a couple of hours, exhaustion, stress, and a warm backside got the better of me.

WHEN I AWOKE, the sun, which had started out behind us, chased the horizon. Late-afternoon light drenched over the vast dunes. Golden mounds oscillated between the dark pockets of sand as if a wind were blowing heavily at the ground level. The mountains in the distance, backlit by the sun, were as jagged and black as the dragon's teeth. It was beautiful, like something I'd only seen in pictures. Fie reminded me of Alaska, while this made me think of Africa. Not that I'd been there, but we did have a collection of *National Geographic*s in the bunker.

As we neared the foothills, we lowered in elevation. The dunes turned into scrubland with cactus, scantily clad trees, and plots of determined grasses.

Up ahead, some kind of industrial unit was built around the base of a jagged volcano. Orange and red light glowed through the openings like eyes inside a cave. Farther away from the mountain, a city of beige tents spread through a wide valley.

As we landed softly in the desert sand, Lucille roared. I covered my ears, but still the screech pierced my eardrums and vibrated from my seat up into my chest cavity. She tossed her head and snorted, a coil of smoke swirling from her large nostrils. The dragon driver slipped down the ladder and patted her on the side of her neck until she purred.

Tee and I climbed down and backed away slowly, never losing sight of the beast—the same thing we would have done if she were a bear. A predator was a predator.

Cooper and the chauffeur each led a dragon to a sandstone building far away from the tents.

"Having dragons near fabric isn't a wise idea," Sera said, motioning for us to follow her. She walked quickly toward the labyrinth of tents connected by wide wooden walkways. I double-stepped to keep up while Tee jogged through the shifting sand.

The tents themselves were more like elaborate yurts—a hard frame covered by canvas. Each unit had round walls connected to other units with round walls and multiple roofs. As the sun faded behind the mountain, colorful lights glowed on the fabric and on the wooden walkways surrounding the tents.

"How do they get electricity here?" I hadn't seen a single power pole or conversion station.

"Giants generate an electrical field. All we have to do is be near and the lights will have power," Liz said. "For the other appliances, they have battery packs to store the energy we create. That way, when we aren't around, they still work." She spoke without looking at me. I assumed she was shy—probably not the best candidate for a bodyguard, but if Raiden trusted her, I did too.

"Nifty," Tee said.

We briskly walked around the edge of the camp, our feet

sounding hollow under the wooden path. Voices and laughter escaped the cloth walls.

We stopped in front of a tent and Sera opened the flap. "Please." She gestured for us to go inside. As she followed in behind us, she switched on the lights, the glass globes slowly flared to life. A leather couch dominated the central room. Some kind of animal hide lay on the wooden floor under an iron coffee table. A skylight at the top of the conical roof revealed a glimpse of the sky. A small kitchen curved around an island with a countertop of black obsidian.

"Things in Fum are different from the other Domes. Since it's so hot during the day, we sleep from nine-ish in the morning to five-ish in the evening," Sera said. "If you girls would like, you can have a few hours of downtime to either rest or use the facilities. They're out your door and to the right. They're the tents surrounded by greenery. I'll come get you in a few hours. Liz, if you would accompany me?"

"My tent is right next door. I'll be back soon," Liz reassured us before she left.

I took off my shoes and set my backpack on the bed directly off the main room. We decided to use the facilities since neither one of us was overly tired, having slept part of the way. We slipped into some flip-flops, grabbed towels, and wrapped ourselves in the fluffy white robes that were draped over our beds.

On our way to the bathrooms, I asked Tee, "What do you think of Liz?"

"Well, I'm not sure. She seems okay, but distant? Very unlike Sera and Cooper. But she's Fie, so I suppose, her standoffishness is normal."

"Yeah, kind of what I thought too." I was pretty good at defending myself, so I shelved my worries for another day.

The bathroom was located in a small green oasis. Tropical trees and plants surrounded individual showers. I hung my robe on a branch and stepped onto the smooth pebble floor. Steam mixed with the spicy scent of the shampoo and conditioner. Showering was my new favorite thing—particularly when the water was hot. After I finished, I twirled my curls around my finger and wrapped my hair in the towel to dry.

Once back in our tent, Tee dressed in a gauzy white gown, while I picked a black one. We layered them with leather vests cinched in at the waist and gladiator sandals, then added hammered silver bracelets and dangling earrings. Tee insisted she put some makeup on my face, and I knew better than to resist. I'd learned to pick my battles with her.

"There," she said, satisfied as she added the final coat of mascara to my lashes. "It's crazy—your eyes are almost gold today."

"Isn't that what hazel eyes do? Change colors with our moods?" I snarled a lip with feigned irritation. She knew I didn't like to wear makeup.

She batted her lashes and smiled, her plush lips a flattering shade of coral.

Minutes later, Sera and Liz stepped through the doorway. Liz was still wearing the typical Fie attire, but with a dagger strapped to her chest. Sera had on a short dress made entirely of chainmail with knee-high brown leather boots. Hanging from a belt around her waist was a sword inlaid with gold scrollwork and emeralds.

Outside, voices and raucous laughter rang in the air.

We followed Sera over the boardwalk through the town. As we got closer to the base of the volcano, businesses—restaurants, bookstores, and retail vendors—overtook the homes.

At the base of the mountain, she led us up a set of winding stairs. Sweat beaded on my skin and began to run down my back before Sera stopped in front of the first wide-open door. A wave of hot air blasted my face. Lava flowed into carved trenches and reflected off the polished black walls of the obsidian cave. Redheaded giants wielding huge hammers pounded on glowing metal. Clinking, clanking, and banging shuddered the smoky air.

"This is the forge. Here, we make everything from weapons—" she patted her sword, "—to furniture, to jewelry."

A few of the giants paused what they were doing and stared openly. Bulging, monstrous muscles, sheened with sweat, glistened in live flames. Their eyes shined like molten gold coins.

Once we had our fill, she escorted us to the next door.

"And over here, we have our treasury. We mint all the currency used in the realm."

The heat was stifling, and I didn't envy anyone who had to work near the mountain. Sweat seeped through my dress, and I fanned my face with my hand to cool my skin.

"And finally," she said with a soft smile on her face, as she held open another door, "don't tell anyone, but this is my favorite."

A woman had her mouth over the end of a long pipe. At the other end of the shaft, a bubble of glass formed. She rolled the pipe and blew some more as it expanded. When she was satisfied, a man wearing leather gloves carefully knocked it off the end and held it up for us to see. Tee ooh'ed and ahh'ed at the treasure, practically jumping for joy.

We'd spent most of our lives with chipped glasses and plastic dinnerware. I'd never minded, but Tee hoarded beautiful things in life. She took immaculate care of everything she cherished, from nail polish to her rifle.

Upon her reaction, the guy brought it over and held it out.

She swallowed hard. "For me?"

A shy smile tugged the corner of his lip, and he pushed it into her hands.

She blinked fiercely, trying to contain her tears. "Thank you!" She hugged it to her chest as if it were a precious child. We were not accustomed to receiving gifts just because.

When we got back down the mountain, Liz offered to take Tee's treasure to our tent. Tee hesitated, but let it go with a firm promise from Liz that nothing would happen to it.

Minutes later, we found ourselves standing in front of a tent palace. While all the other abodes had only one story, this place had multiple levels, all with domed roofs, some looking like castle turrets. All the sections had slatted windows and greenery planted in hanging iron boxes. Lighting draped around the edges of the roof made the tent wall awash with a rainbow of colors, and everything from cactus to tropical foliage surrounded the base of the structure.

A beautiful redheaded man with biceps the circumference of Tee's head waited for us at the front door. Sera introduced us to her son Kai, and then immediately excused herself.

"Ruby," he welcomed, his arms stretched as wide as his

smile. He wore a plethora of jewelry, a white tank top, and a pair of black leather pants that brushed the tops of his bare feet. His eyes darted momentarily to Tee, his grin slipping slightly before he caught himself. Forcing his attention back my way, he took my hand and kissed it. Blood-red rubies sparkled from his military-style ring.

"Tee," he said as he replaced my hand with hers and kissed it gently. The size difference between the two was stark—a David and Goliath kind of comparison. "It's a pleasure to meet you."

I could have sworn Tee blushed, or maybe it was just the colorful lights.

She had a weakness for redheads. For years, she'd had a crush on my brother, but he'd always thought of her as a little sister and I didn't think that was likely to change.

"Come on in." He slid the massive door open and gestured for us to enter.

Clear round globes hung from wooden beams illuminating the entryway. Weapons—swords, daggers, axes, and spears all made of Damascus steel, their hilts inlaid with precious metals and jewels—decorated the canvas walls. My fingers twitched, wanting to grab one to test its balance.

"Things are pretty informal around here," Kai said. His eyes were topaz yellow and his hair was almost the exact shade as mine, though instead of curly, it was straight and shaved on the sides, the rest pulled into a ponytail. "I thought we could hang out in my quarters for a while, then maybe go out on the town later?"

Tee and I exchanged glances. "Sure."

We wound our way up the circular staircase to his room. A floating bed hung from the ceiling beams by stout black chains. Posters of musicians and actors lined his wall

—a fair few of which were beautiful hip-hop and pop singers. The rest were superhero movies. Musical instruments, including a drum set, were scattered throughout the room.

"You have a thing for American pop culture," I stated the obvious.

He smiled, the cleft in his chin deepening. "All of us do. We love the music, the movies, the books. Pretty much everything."

He and Raiden had something in common, though I'd never been to Raiden's home. I wondered what it looked like. A sharp stab to my already-pulverized heart made me flinch.

Kai scratched his jaw. "I'm particularly fond of the twenty-first century."

I cocked an eyebrow and tried to hold back a chuckle. "I'd have never guessed."

He laughed.

Tee was busy admiring the mahogany violin hanging from the wall. It was bigger than a normal violin, but so was the guy who owned it. When he stepped beside her, her head barely hit the middle of his chest, but she wasn't intimidated in the least.

"Have you ever played?" Kai asked her. His voice was soft and smooth. I imagined he had a beautiful singing voice.

She looked up. "No, but I'd love to learn. I can play the guitar a little, but that's about it. Do you play?"

"Yeah."

Tee's voice took on an air of amazement. "All of them?"

"Yeah." He somehow managed to say it with humility.

She stared, her lovely lips agape. "Wow." Her breath came out wispy. I'd never seen the girl speechless before.

"Tee's into music," I said. "She's always in charge of our playlist."

"Really? What's your favorite?" Kai asked, zeroing his attention on Tee.

And that was my cue to tune them out. I meandered around Kai's room and then to the other upstairs spaces while those two held a steady conversation about music. I found a deck outside and sat down on a bench. Almost every tent was glowing. The cacophony of conversations, laughter, and insects blended together, creating a peaceful ambiance. I gazed at the sky and watched the stars flicker as my thoughts drifted to Raiden. I wondered if Benji had found him. I hoped so.

"Bea!" Tee hollered, one decibel lower than yelling.

"I'm out here."

"Oh, this is nice." She stepped onto the deck, Kai following behind.

We sat for hours and visited. I learned a lot about Fum and the other Domes. They bought their water supply from the Foe, their food from the Fee, and all of their tents were built by the Fie. All of the units were easy to disassemble— even the palace, but if there was an emergency, it was designated as the last tent to be deconstructed. The contents were more important than the actual structure. Kai said he didn't want his people to lose their homes in order to save his in the event one of the volcanoes erupted.

After a while, Sera brought us some food and asked if we planned on hitting the town. We'd been having so much fun, we'd lost track of time.

Kai pulled on a pair of boots and escorted us to the club. It was a tent with the sides rolled to the roof. A polished obsidian bar surrounded the center skylight. Around the periphery were tables filled with people drinking from beautiful glassware. A live band played on a raised platform as people dressed in leather, chainmail, buckles, straps, corsets, and tights danced. I'd heard the tune before but I didn't know who sang it. It reminded me of an eighties punk rock venue.

In excitement, Tee jumped up and down. The delight in her eyes twinkled even in the poorly lit room. Not only did she know the song—she loved the song.

After Kai found us a table, he held out a hand and offered me a dance.

I wrinkled my nose. I wasn't the world's best dancer, and I wasn't planning on having any liquid courage to help me with my moves. "Take Tee." I cocked my head at my best friend, who was having a hard time standing still. "I'll get us some drinks. Can I just put it on a tab? I don't have any money."

"Nah, you're with me. It's covered."

I grabbed their drink orders and headed to the bar, watching slyly as Kai placed his hand on Tee's shoulder and led her to the dance floor. He fist-bumped everyone he passed on his way. They stared down at Tee, but she just smiled, seemingly oblivious to her diminutive frame amongst giants.

The bartender pointed at me. "Bea?" he said. His head was shaved bald but his long beard was strawberry-blond, threaded with braids and black beads. His eyes were more of a green-gold than a true yellow.

"Yeah." I was surprised he knew my name. But perhaps I shouldn't have been.

"What can I get ya?" He wiped his hands on the towel hanging from his black-and-white-striped apron.

"Two beers on tap, whatever Kai drinks. And something that looks like alcohol but isn't." I wanted to make sure Tee had a good time and wasn't in any danger. I planned on keeping my wits about me.

"Sure thing. How about some regular iced tea?"

"With sugar?" I said hopefully. Sugar was hard to come by at home.

He smiled widely at my enthusiasm over the simple treat, showing a set of fangs that were longer than I'd yet seen. "Do you mind if I water your friend's drink down a bit? The beer is potent."

"Yeah, thanks." I appreciated the warning.

A few minutes later, feeling like a German bar wench carrying huge glasses, mine filled with sweet tea, I forced my way through the crowd to our table. Miraculously, no one had nabbed our spot. Must have been the company we kept.

Tee and Kai danced up a storm under the flashing strobe lights. Tee was a better dancer than anyone. I'd always chalked it up to her lower center of gravity. She said it was because she had actual rhythm, unlike me.

Soon, she was teaching the others her mad skills.

Eventually, the sweaty couple made it back to the table and sat down. Kai swallowed a big gulp and wiped the foam from his upper lip.

"Seriously!" Tee said. "I've never had so much fun!"

"Really?" Surprise wrinkled Kai's forehead.

"Yes, really," Tee said. And she meant it.

By the time they cooled off, Tee wasn't going to take my no for an answer, so, reluctantly, I followed them to the dance floor. We danced amongst the crowd, with strangers, with each other. We danced until the sun rose over the desert sands. And Tee was right. I'd never had so much fun. Ever. Probably because nothing was trying to kill me. *Yet.*

Kai escorted us home and made sure Liz knew we were safe.

I flopped on my bed and thought about Kai. Could I see myself married to him? No. Not because he wasn't a great guy. He truly cared about his people and put their needs above his. He was attentive to both Tee and me. She seemed to like him, which was high praise. He was painfully sexy in a rugged *I could kill you with my little finger and look like a rockstar doing it* kind of way. His sense of humor had brought tears—in a good way—more than once. He was fun with a capital F. But if I was being honest, the chemistry between us was lacking. Or maybe it was just because I *wanted* someone else.

Thankfully, I'd have some time to get to know Kai better and even longer to ponder my situation. With luck, by the end of the four weeks, my broken heart would have had a chance to mend. And with a crown on my head, maybe then, I could find my parents.

# CHAPTER
# NINETEEN

T hrashing in the sweaty bedsheets, I tried to escape the tangled mess I'd created. The sleeping mask slid from my eyes and partially onto my forehead. I paused and squinted. The light was bright. Having lived in Alaska my entire life, you'd think I'd be used to sleeping in the daylight, but for the last ten years, I'd lived in a pitch-black, underground bunker.

A tall figure stood off to the side of my room. I was having a hard time seeing with only half an eye exposed.

"Liz?"

"Shut her up," a woman whispered as a large hand clamped over my mouth. It smelled like fried food and spices. I struggled, only to find my wrists and ankles tied. Someone steadied my head and stuffed a rag in my mouth before I could scream. I gagged. I couldn't breathe. I was going to suffocate.

A man with a deep voice whispered in my ear, "Breathe through your nose."

Inhaling slowly, I pulled extra oxygen into my deprived lungs.

I was lifted from my bed by my legs and arms. I squirmed, not sure if this was some sort of hazing ritual or what.

"Stop resisting," the dude said.

"What does it matter?" a female voice replied. "We're going to kill her anyway."

My heart stuttered and then fled like a rabbit on the run. I swallowed, but my throat was as dry as our surroundings.

Someone tossed me over their shoulder like a bag of feed. I bucked, twisting my hips one way and my torso another. Someone pinched me aggressively. But they were going to kill me, so I fought harder.

"Will somebody pop her?" the giant carrying me requested.

A shock of electricity preceded a flash of light, circling stars, and blackness.

---

THE SENSATION of floating in the air then falling like a stone woke me up. My eyes were no longer covered but my hands and feet were still tied. I blinked fast but I couldn't process the chaos.

I crashed into something. My skin ripped on jagged edges as I tumbled down, scraping along a rough surface. My head slammed into the ground with an excruciating thump, stopping me violently fast. Overwhelming pain exploded everywhere. Bile shot up my throat and I swallowed for fear of choking. The gag was still in my mouth. I concentrated on calming my spasming stomach muscles. A haze of dizziness washed over me and my vision faded.

Lifting my head from the warm surface, I blinked and squinted. A shred of nothingness clouded my brain. No memories whatsoever hovered in my thoughts. Having had enough outdoor survival training, panicking was the last thing needed. I stayed calm and counted to ten. Then to twenty. Slowly, things came back.

My name was Ruby Rose Walker.

I was from Alaska.

My brother was Kevin.

I was half giant.

The rest miraculously appeared.

Lying on my back, I stared at the conical opening high above me. A few pearlescent clouds scooted across the periwinkle sky. The inside walls of a mountain obscured everything except for the circle of blue. About five feet to my right was a sharp drop-off. Gingerly flipping onto my stomach, I put the front of the gag on the ground and rolled it down my chin. I inhaled, then instantly regretted it. Not only was the air scorching and noxious smelling, but the side of my chest stabbed with the pain of broken ribs. I mentally scanned the rest of my body. Besides my skin feeling as if I'd been scrubbed with a wire brush, I'd managed to escape further injury.

I crawled to the edge of the precipice. Steaming orange lava bubbled deep inside the heart of the volcano. A stuttered sob caught in my throat as I scooted away from the drop-off.

They'd meant to kill me. But instead of a quick, painless death, I was to die slowly of dehydration. Or suicide—if it came down to it.

The inverted walls of the mountain looked impossible to scale from this angle. I certainly couldn't climb thirty feet to the top without falling. But it was only thirty feet. So close, yet so far away.

There was no need to panic. At some point, people had to come looking for me. I clung to that thought. Giants had incredible hearing, and I could scream. For now, I wouldn't waste my energy. I'd wait until the sun set. By then, they would know I was missing.

I braced my arms over the edge of the cliff and rubbed the restraints on the sharp rock. The piercing in my lungs from my busted ribs made it difficult to breathe. I bit the inside of my cheek and ignored the agony. Gradually, the material frayed. They'd used torn strips from my bedsheets. I clung to the positive—with my sheets destroyed, Kai, Tee, and Liz wouldn't waste time thinking I'd gone exploring on my own.

Eventually, I'd created enough room to wriggle out of the binds. My hands prickled with pins and needles as the blood rushed back. When the feeling returned, I untied my feet. I tossed the fabric to the side in case I needed it later.

I scooted back against the mountain wall and waited as I drifted in and out of consciousness.

When the sunlight mostly disappeared, I held my ribs together with both hands like a bandage to mitigate the pain and screamed for help. My tongue felt thick and my voice soon became hoarse. Panic coated my skin in another layer of sweat. Why hadn't someone heard me?

Exhaustion weighed heavily on my shoulders since my kidnappers had deprived me of a day of sleep. I tried swallowing, to scream again, but no saliva was there. Giving up, I took some loose rocks and placed them on the cliff edge, hoping they would wake me if I rolled.

---

LATER WHEN I WOKE, the sun shone on the far side of the mountain, the obsidian wall sparkling in the light. My eyes were gritty. My jaw trembled. Nobody had found me in the night.

The back of my nose burned with tears, but they refused to fall as my body was already dehydrated. What would happen to my family if I died? Would the giants hold up their end of the agreement even though I hadn't completed the bargain? I couldn't remember the particulars of the contract because the only thing I could focus on was the thought of cold water sliding down my parched throat. I licked my cracked lips. It only took seconds for the moisture to evaporate in the stifling heat. It was like trying to breathe with your head in an oven.

I drifted off to sleep again, only to wake up to a black sky dotted with bright stars. I tried yelling but it came out a whisper. I needed liquid if my voice was to work. There were only two choices—urine or blood.

I grabbed a rock and sliced open a spot on my forearm. I hesitated before clamping my lips over the wound. My blood tasted like metal and salt. I managed to get some down before gagging, just enough to wet my throat.

Then I screamed for all I was worth, repeating the process until hope deflated like an escaped balloon.

Defeated, I stared over the edge of the cliff in contemplation. The ebb and flow of the fiery colors mesmerized me, a caldera of bright orange swirling and popping around crimson and gold. How easy it would be just to roll off the side and be reborn like a phoenix from the ashes.

---

I AWOKE to the sun glaring in my eyes. It was high in the sky and at just the right angle to blind me. Shielding my face with my hands, my vision took a moment to adjust to the intense brightness. Volcanic ash gritted between my teeth and scratched my corneas. My ribs felt better, though. I could take a semi-deep breath without cringing.

I estimated I'd been in the caldera for three days, and if I was going to die, I was going to go out fighting. I wrapped my fingers with the ripped bedsheets and found a grip spot in the wall. I pulled myself up slowly and located a nook for my bare foot. The sharp rocks dug into my flesh, slicing as I climbed. My free hand searched for a crevice or a shelf of some kind, and once found, my bare foot searched for another. I scaled about ten feet up the wall before sliding back down and rolling off the side of the cliff.

Terror ripped from my raw throat as I tumbled. At the last second, both of my hands caught the edge of the platform. My fingers clawed into the surface and my feet dangled, scrambling to find hold. Because of the cone shape of the mountain, they found only air. My arms trembled under the strain of no food or water for days. Slowly, I inched my hands forward, finding a better grip. Once I was more secure, I lifted my leg until my toes caught the edge of the precipice, and I shimmied my foot over the side.

With one last heave, I pulled myself to safety and collapsed into a ball.

# CHAPTER
# TWENTY

The growling of the volcano vibrated in my ears and chest, but I ignored it. Growing up in Alaska, we were used to the rumblings of earth.

I opened my sandpapered eyes, fully aware of my delusional state. Under the full moon, carrying me in his strong arms, was Raiden, his eyes glinting silver in the moonlight. His pulse rapidly beat in his neck. He was fierce and beautiful. And I was happy knowing his face was the last one on my mind as I drifted off.

A whisper softly floated over the cool air. "Dude, relax. She's safe now. We're going to take her home."

I wondered if my parents were dead and would be waiting for me in heaven. I assumed that's where I was going. I hadn't done many bad things in my life. If we were keeping score, I probably had more pros than cons. But what if they were alive, and now I'd lost my chance to find them?

But my will to persevere was gone. I'd spent most of my life fighting tooth and nail to survive. And I was tired.

My eyes fluttered shut and I coasted off to oblivion,

where there was no pain, no sorrow, no anything. Only a dull *thump thump . . . thump thump . . .*

Until a spray of cold water shocked me out of my journey to the afterlife. One minute, I was on fire, the next minute, encased in ice.

"Ruby." Someone lightly slapped my face, but I scrunched my eyes tighter. "Ruby, don't be a coward. Open your eyes."

Did he just call me a coward?

I blinked into a stream cascading over my head and shoulders. It soothed my eyes, and I opened my mouth, letting it run down my aching throat.

Bright emerald plants surrounded Raiden as he stood under the shower with me. Rivulets of water washed away the dust streaking his beautiful face.

Again, it didn't surprise me that visions of him clouded my final moments. He was my unfinished business.

"Am I dead?" It was the only logical assumption I could grasp.

"Not yet. You gotta wake up and tell us what happened." He pushed my hair out of my face and cupped my cheek.

I tilted my head toward the skylight and reached out to touch his wet face. I ran my thumb over his soft mouth. "Is it really you? Or am I dreaming?"

He kissed my forehead, his lips scorching like the volcano's fire. "It's really me, Bea-bea."

I fell into him. I wasn't dead. Somehow, he'd found me. I wanted to cry, but exhaustion prevented a breakdown. I had no energy left. I'd survived twenty-some years in Alaska and one week in the Fiefdom was enough to destroy me. I guess I wasn't nearly as tough as I thought.

He turned off the shower and dried me as best he could.

I rested my head on his shoulder as he lifted me and carried me back to the tent. I didn't like being incapacitated, but I decided to give myself a break. I'd been thrown into a volcano. It couldn't hurt to let him take care of me for a bit.

As I put on a fresh tank top and shorts, he stood at the bedroom door with his back turned.

"Do you think you can tell us what happened or do you need some rest first?" he asked.

My muscles tremored under my skin and my stomach roiled with queasiness. "I'm okay."

"Liar." He turned and took two massive steps before wrapping his arms around me. His breath shuddered on the inhale.

"I'm sorry," I croaked. Despite the cold water, my esophagus felt as if I'd swallowed broken glass. "I didn't read the contract carefully. I didn't know I was supposed to be married."

"I know. Benji told me. Then Kevin told me not to hate you because you're an idiot."

A laugh burst from my mouth. "He's right. I *am* an idiot."

"Maybe a little. But you were tired and they were pushing alcohol on you. But I told you earlier—we're dangerous. I guess I should've specified that we're dangerous in more ways than one."

I looked up. "You saw Kev?"

"Yes, just a few days ago. Everyone's fine. I didn't mention your predicament because I didn't think you would want them to worry until there was something to *really* worry about."

"Thank you." Kevin would be mad when he found out I'd kept this from him. "Do you think they're going to be okay?"

"Yes. They'll be fine. It's you they want dead." His jaw flexed.

A knock on the bedroom door made me balk. It opened, and Kai stuck his head through. "Hey, Raiden."

Raiden's head whipped around and a predatory growl rumbled through his chest.

Kai held up both hands. "Bruh, you're going to have to get that—" he swirled a palm in the air, "—under control. If I were any other First-Born son, you'd have a challenge on your hands. Plus, if you keep this up, they will *not* allow you to be her bodyguard. You feel me?"

Raiden's shoulders slumped as he nodded.

"What's going on?" I glanced between the two.

"Nothing," Raiden said.

"Grouchy much?" I slapped him in the chest and followed Kai out the door.

Despite having giant blood that allowed me to heal quickly, I was emotionally spent and needed a nap. But if they were going to find out who'd tried to kill me, they needed answers.

In the living room, Tee flew into my arms, then pulled away and smacked my back. "Don't you ever scare me like that again!" she yelled.

"Wasn't my intention."

I stepped away, but she had other ideas. She dragged me over to the couch and placed a glass of water and a snack in front of me. "Drink," she demanded as she sat next to me.

Liz hovered behind the kitchen island. A huge smile bloomed when she saw Raiden, then dimmed when she saw me. "Bea, I'm so sorry," she said.

"For what?"

"I kept an eye on you all night at the club and everything

seemed okay. No one gave you a hard time or even looked at you wrong." She rubbed her hands over her face and stared at the countertop. "The Fum tend to like humans. I honestly thought you'd be safe here. I'm so sorry."

"Don't be. This isn't your fault. I'm fine now." I picked up the water glass, leaving a sweat ring on the wood table. I took a big swig to get Tee to stop side-eyeing me. Her mom had been a nurse, and that apple hadn't fallen far from the tree. It was easier to do what she wanted.

Raiden sat down on the other side of me with his knee touching mine. Kai raised an eyebrow but didn't say anything as he flopped in the chair across from us.

"So, Bea, do you remember anything?" Kai asked. He folded his hands and tapped his thumbs together.

"As far as I could tell, there were two of them. A guy and a girl."

"Did you see their faces?" Kai asked.

"No, my sleeping mask was on the whole time."

"Okay. Try and remember everything. What did they smell like? Were they clean? Dirty?" He sat forward, placing his elbows on his knees.

I closed my eyes and replayed everything in my head. Raiden rested his hand on my thigh. The sparks spreading from his touch made concentrating difficult.

"One smelled spicy? The other like fresh air?"

A knowing look passed between the three giants in the room.

"What? What does that mean?"

"Come here and give me a hug," Kai said, staring hard at Raiden as he said it.

"Okay . . ." I agreed to his strange request.

Raiden's fists tightened, his veins standing out against his golden skin.

Kai stood up and wrapped his arms around me. "What do I smell like?"

I inhaled deeply. "Clean, spicy, with a hint of fire or smoke."

He nodded. "Go give Liz a hug."

She opened her arms, and I leaned in close to smell.

"You smell like fresh air. A lot like Raiden, only with a hint of flowers, where he normally smells of mint. What does that mean?" I sat back down on the couch. Raiden wrapped his arm around my shoulder, pulling me close. I folded my legs underneath and snuggled into his embrace.

"It means one giant was probably from here, the other from the Fie. They knew you'd be vulnerable without Raiden. I must say, I'm pissed." Kai patted over his heart. "We like humans. Unless you're assholes—then we don't like you. But you and Tee—" his eyes glowed when he looked at my best friend, "—are definitely not assholes. As a matter of fact, Tee was with us searching the entire time. I didn't know humans could be so resilient."

Tee blushed. I was sure of it.

"Yeah, what she lacks in size, she makes up for in stubbornness." I jabbed her with my elbow.

"You're one to talk." She returned the gesture.

That's why we got along so well. We understood one another.

"So, do you know who tried to kill me?"

Everyone but me flinched.

"We have our suspicions," Raiden said.

I covered my mouth and tried to stifle my yawn.

"Come on, I'm going to put you to bed. We can finish this conversation tomorrow," Raiden said.

I didn't argue. A fuzziness clouded my brain, and I wasn't sure how much more help I could be anyway.

Raiden went to scoop me up, but I stopped him. "I can walk the twenty feet to my room."

His nostrils flared, but instead of arguing, he wove his fingers with mine.

---

THE MINUTE my head hit the pillow, I fell asleep, only to be woken later by voices outside my tent. I didn't know what time it was, but sunlight illuminated the canvas walls. Every nerve ending flared with fright. My muscles tensed for fight or flight—until I realized it was Raiden and Kai whispering.

I kicked off the sheets, my sweating skin cooled by two ceiling fans whirling on high.

"How are you going to do this?" Kai whispered. "You can't keep your hands off her. And if I even get close to her, your hackles go up. If you aren't in the possession stage, dude, I'd be shocked."

"I'll be fine. I'll figure it out," Raiden snapped.

"You'd better do it soon. She's only got two days left here since the lords and ladies voted to not extend her stay."

"That's unfair. She was gone for four days. You didn't even get a chance to know her," Raiden said.

"Yeah, I'll spend the next two days with her." I couldn't see or hear what happened, but Kai said, "See? Man, you're fucked."

"Well, I guess I have two days to figure it out then, don't

214

I?" Raiden said a little louder than he should've if he was trying to be quiet.

"Or you could find out what happened to your parents?" Kai prompted gently.

"Don't go there. I've spent *years* searching for the truth. There's nothing to suggest anything other than an accident."

"You know better than that, Raiden."

"Yeah, I do. But I can't prove anything. Hunches and feelings aren't proof," Raiden grumbled.

"There's always the *other* way," Kai said.

"You know that's not going to happen."

Heavy footsteps creaked on the boardwalk, then inside the tent, moving toward my room. The mattress sagged under Raiden's weight as he laid down beside me. I didn't say anything because I didn't want him to know I'd been listening.

Feeling safe with him beside me, I let go of my worries and fell back asleep.

---

THE NEXT TIME I woke up, it was to an empty bed.

I wandered to the living room. Raiden was in the kitchen cleaning up.

"Aren't you up early, or late, or whatever?" I was having a hard time figuring out the unusual sleep schedule.

"Yeah, but I couldn't lay there any longer."

I stretched my arms above my head and then back behind my neck, pushing my chest forward. My sternum popped, releasing the pressure. All the scrapes and scratches on my skin were already healed. It was amazing what a good long nap and having giant DNA could do.

Raiden's eyes darted down my body and then back to my face as he gripped the edge of the countertop. I blushed as heat coiled deep in my core.

He tore his gaze away and threw down the kitchen towel. "I'm going for a walk."

"Can I come with you?"

"No." He didn't even glance my way as he stormed out the door, barefoot and without a shirt. The muscles in his back and shoulders were beautiful—roped and well-defined all the way down to the two dimples above the waistband of his pants.

I was slightly confused as to what I'd done to make him leave, but I didn't have time to think about it before Tee stumbled out of her bedroom all sleepy-eyed.

"Do you want some coffee? I made iced."

Normally, I didn't care for coffee, but a cold drink sounded good. "Please."

Tee pulled a pitcher out of the fridge and poured some over ice. She handed me a glass, then walked behind the sofa and opened a tent flap. Outside was a small deck with two chairs and a table.

Though I was warm, I welcomed the afternoon sun on my skin.

Tee sat down and curled her legs underneath her. I had a hard time reaching the floor with my feet. For her, it was impossible.

"Soooo," I dragged the word out. "What's going on between you and Kai?"

"Nothing," she said too quickly and too sharply.

I scoffed. I didn't believe her.

"Really, it's nothing." She crossed her arms.

I took a sip, the flavor of sweetened coffee exploding on my tongue. It wasn't half bad iced.

"You wanna try that again?" I set my glass down and crossed my arms, mimicking her body language.

"Ugh," she groaned. "Nothing's going on." She twisted one of her small braids around her finger.

"Come on, Tee. I see how he looks at you. I saw you blush last night. If it would've been me blushing that hard, my face would have matched my hair."

"Nothing's happened. We just became close while searching for you. He knew how worried I was."

"So you're not going to have a problem if I marry Kai?" I baited her.

"Nope." She lifted a shoulder like she didn't care.

"You're not going to have a problem if I kiss him?" I formed my lips into a pucker.

She shook her head.

"Or if I nuzzle his neck, then make my way down his glorious chest. If I slip off his pants . . ."

She gripped her glass tightly.

"And run my lips—" I circled my tongue over my glass.

"Okay!" She slammed hers down on the table. "I might have a problem with it."

Laughter bubbled in my chest. I snapped and pointed at her. "See. I knew it! Why do you think you can hide things from me? You know better."

Her eyes in the sunlight were lighter, the same shade as freshly tilled earth.

"Pishposh." I waved my hand in the air. "There's no way I'm marrying the guy my best friend wants to play hide the sausage with." I wiggled my brows.

"You're gross." She glared.

I laughed.

"But he's a good man. He would make an excellent king. I can't stand in the way of that." She tilted her chin up with her high moral standards and noble bearing.

"And I won't marry him."

"But—"

"Not happening. There are three other guys to pick from."

"What if they are all jerks?"

"Then at least I know you'll be happy," I said seriously.

"Bea, that's not fair. Kai would make a good, kind ruler." The genuineness in her voice made me sad. She meant what she said.

"How does he feel about marrying *me*?"

"We haven't talked about it. But I did tell him you're the best person I know," she said.

That wasn't true. The best person was sitting next to me. "Has anything happened between the two of you?"

She scrunched her nose.

"*Spill*," I demanded, slapping my thighs for her to get on with it.

She looked off to the horizon. "We kissed."

I sat forward. "And how was it?"

"It was like nothing I've ever felt before. I didn't know it could be that good," she said breathlessly.

I smiled. "I know, right?" I leaned back and crossed my legs.

"What about you and Raiden? I hadn't realized things had gotten so serious until he got here. He was crazed, insane, trying to find you. I don't know how it happened so fast, but that boy loves you."

I looked over at her. "You don't know how, huh?" It seemed to me that she had already fallen for a certain redhead.

She ignored my comment and wiped the condensation from her glass.

I pushed up from the chair. "I have to get ready. I'm supposed to spend the entire day—I mean night, *whatever*—with Kai. Is there anything I should tell him for you? That you love him and want to make babies with him?" I teased.

She squinted her eyes in false irritation. "No."

But even though she said no, I knew better. Tee was a romantic. Always had been. I'd do anything to see her happy, even if that meant marrying a jerk.

# CHAPTER
# TWENTY-ONE

An hour later after I finished getting ready, I found Raiden standing next to the kitchen counter eating the last of an apple. He tossed it in the trash. "Are you ready?" he grumbled without making eye contact.

"Yes." I held out my elbow so he could escort me to Kai's palace, but he didn't take it.

"Walk in front of me." He thrust his chin forward.

"Okay? Is there a problem?"

"Just do what I asked."

Pain stabbed my chest, and I pressed my hand against my collarbone, hoping to dull the hurt from his words—mostly the tone in which they were said.

"Screw you." With that, I took off without waiting for him.

The sun hovered on the horizon, just about to set, as I hurried toward Kai's place. Though I couldn't see Raiden, his dark shadow strolled next to me.

Once we got there, he said, "I'll be here at eight in the morning to escort you back."

"Don't bother. I'm sure Kai can manage." A vice constricted my lungs like a belt cinched too tight. What had happened between yesterday and today? In my entire life, I'd never experienced this kind of turmoil. The constant upheaval of my emotions left me unbalanced as if I were trying to ride a four-wheeler with only three tires.

Kai answered the door in time to see Raiden walking away. He smiled a tight-lipped smile. "You wanna go get something to eat?"

My stomach growled.

"I'll take that as a yes." He held out an arm. "I know a great breakfast place."

We wandered until we came to a small café below the forge on the mountainside. The smell of coffee, bacon, and cinnamon rolls wafted from the tent.

Kai ordered us food, and we found a spot to sit outside. We were the only ones there besides the staff.

"So, how are you feeling?" he asked.

"Good," I sort of lied. Physically, yes—mentally, well debatable.

We sat there in awkward silence, clearly both wanting to ask questions, but not knowing where to begin.

When the pressure built to the point I couldn't stand it, I said, "You and Tee?"

Kai's golden eyes rounded at my bluntness. I wasn't known for my tact. He swallowed, his Adam's apple bobbing.

I laughed. "I'm not mad. I'd do anything to see her happy, but I think we need to talk about it."

He sighed. "I didn't mean for anything to happen."

"Kai, we're past that. I'm sure you didn't. *'The heart wants what it wants—or else it does not care.'*"

221

That used to be my mom's favorite quote by Emily Dickinson. I didn't always understand poetry, but I loved it. And art. Though I'd never had much time to appreciate it at home. I hoped that here, I might have a chance to expand not only my education, but my emotional needs as well. They'd always come second to survival. Food over frivolity. Most people didn't understand how *true* survival could warp a person's development. Tee, Kevin, and Sid were my lifelines. Without them, I shuddered at the person I might've become.

"Ain't that the truth," Kai said.

"At this point, I can't pick you even if you are the best man for the job. Which, by the way, Tee insists that you are."

His face softened at her approval.

"So I propose you help me figure this out. I'd ask Raiden, but talking to him about who I should marry hurts too much. Because if you haven't figured it out by now, I have feelings for him."

"You mean you love him."

"No, I don't." I rubbed my forehead.

"Yes, you do."

"Not possible. I haven't known him long enough."

He tapped the table thoughtfully. "You'd be surprised at what's possible here."

"Yeah, well, it doesn't matter. I signed a contract in blood saying I have to marry another."

"Perhaps."

"You're being evasive. What's that supposed to mean?"

"Talk to Raiden about it."

"Oh. My. God! Can any of you giants just be open and honest?" I grabbed my hair at the roots and squeezed.

We stopped talking as our food arrived. I had a

cinnamon roll, while Kai had bacon, large eggs—the yolks were the size of my hand—toast, pancakes with a strange-smelling syrup, and tea. It surprised me how much their food and culture matched humans'. Sure, some things were different—like, I wasn't going to ask what the bacon came from or if he was eating dragon eggs. Sometimes it was better not knowing.

But some things I needed to know.

"What happens after I marry someone? Like at this point in time, I'm in the dark. I know *nothing* about *anything*. Please. I need *someone* who will tell me what's going on. What's expected of me? Tee trusts you. Can *I* trust you?" I licked the delicious glaze from my fingers.

"Yeah, you can. Let's start at the beginning. You'll live in the capital and try to unite the Fee, Fie, Foe, and Fum."

"And how's that going to go?" I asked with a trace of sarcasm. I already knew the answer.

He used his toast to mop up the yolks. "It's been a while since we functioned as a healthy unit."

"I guess what I'm trying to figure out is why they need to be united. What's the problem everyone is facing?"

"Have you not noticed our lack of children?" He looked at me like that was impossible.

I'd long ago guessed that they needed an expanded gene pool, but beyond that, I hadn't paid much attention.

"About a thousand years ago, our population began to dwindle. The prophecy that has you bound was foretold by Queen Dru-Noir on her deathbed. She had no children, therefore no person to pass the throne on to. Lordships or ladyships can be passed from brother to brother, son to son, to daughter, to sister, but the throne can only be passed to an offspring. After she died, we went to war with each other.

Every lord thought they should be appointed ruler. You can imagine how well that went. *We're on the brink of extinction, so let's kill each other.*" He cocked a brow at the irony. "Eventually, we figured out our stupidity and enacted a peace treaty. We survived like this for a time, but then strange things began to happen to our children. You see, kids born with parents from different Domes were born . . . conflicted." He took a sip of coffee, giving me time to let the information sink in.

"They were so confused as to where they belonged in the world, droves of them committed suicide or killed others. When the Fie reproduced with the Fum, it was like the air stoked the fire and made the kids mentally unstable. Fee and Foe, it was like the water drowned the earth and made the children depressed. Don't let me get started with the Fum and the Foe. Most of the kids were born with physical defects and mental problems. Because of their violent tendencies, most of them were . . . euthanized."

My breath hitched at his blunt admission, but I didn't interrupt. What kind of people did something like that?

"Eventually, everyone slunk home and segregated themselves within their Domes. But even producing kids among themselves became difficult. They aren't born with the same issues, but they aren't born often. Our death rate heavily outweighs our birth rate. As a matter of fact, I'm the youngest person in the Fiefdom. Raiden, Loch, Trent, Adam, and I were all born the same year."

The weirdness of the situation dawned on me. I really was here so the giants could repopulate. Horror collected behind my ribs, making me nauseous as I realized I'd been in denial.

"If we continue at this speed, we'll become extinct." He tapped his finger on the light wood table.

I inhaled and exhaled slowly from my mouth. "So you basically think we're here to help you repopulate? That's what the prophecy means. *'Our Crimson Jewel shall be the throne and with the First-Born son rule the Dome until the time has come for the First-Born son and the Crimson Jewel to become one. Only then—Fee-Fie-Foe-Fum—our war on extinction will be won.'"*

Naively, I'd had it in my head that I was here to do something amazing and biblical in proportions, not become a broodmare.

"If I were to guess, the answer is yes. And possibly to open up communication between humans and giants. If our prophecy is to succeed, we're going to need more of you. Thirty-some people is a start. But there are going to be plenty of giants who don't like the idea."

I balled my fists as I struggled to control my temper. "So basically, we're targets and breeding machines?"

"Don't be so black and white. That's unfair. Everyone's looking for love. Most want children. And when our DNA is mixed with yours, the children don't get sick."

He wasn't lying. I'd never been sick once, nor had my brother. Injured, yes. But even then, I healed faster than normal.

"They don't die from disease or malnutrition. We have just as much to offer humans as you have to offer us." Though he didn't sound upset, it felt as if I was being scolded.

I simmered down. He was right. Our group of people hadn't gotten sick because they'd had my blood in their water. But what about other humans on Earth? I didn't know for sure, but I'd bet they struggled with more than just crafty wildlife.

"Do you guys spend a lot of time on Earth?"

He set his cutlery on the side of his plate and slid it to the edge of the table. "We used to. But now, it's more dangerous. There, bullets can kill us almost as easily as they can you. When you shot Raiden, he was still in the stairwell, affording him protection." Kai paused and blinked pointedly. I had shot his friend.

I shrugged and threw him a look of *devil may care*—I hadn't killed him, and currently I was a little bit mad at him.

"Now, you guys shoot first and ask questions later. Prior to ten or fifteen years ago, that wasn't the case. Ergo, it was safer. Besides, Earth really isn't that fun anymore. There are no new movies, no new works of art. Believe me, all the good stuff we grabbed early on."

I clasped my hands in a triangle shape over my nose and mouth, breathing as I processed. "What do you think of humans, personally? Please be honest. I'm sick of the lies."

"You saw my room. It's not like I could've collected all of that stuff in the last week. I've been fascinated with humans since I can remember. Especially your music. A lot of us are," he said.

"Why?"

"Because humans can create. Giants can only replicate. While I can play all those instruments, I cannot write the music. We can do the simple stuff, but nothing too complicated. We can learn, but not create. That's why we used to go to Earth—to steal all your ideas. What we couldn't do, we hired out."

My mouth dropped open.

226

He chuckled, not concerned at my reaction. "But there's a dark side to humans that I find fascinating too."

"And what? You guys don't have a dark side?" I'd been here less than a week and someone had already tried to kill me.

"Oh, yeah, we do. But we're predictable. When we love, we love. When we hate, we hate. It doesn't change. Humans are fluid. You can love someone one minute and hate them the next," he said. "You love, you hate, you forgive, repeat." He punctuated each statement with a drop of his chin.

"It's not that simple."

He flared his fingers. "Exactly. That's what I'm trying to say. Humans are not predictable."

He was wrong. Humans, for the most part, *were* predictable, but I wasn't there to argue that point with him.

"Moving on. What are your feelings for Tee?"

"Girl, you don't pull punches, do ya?"

"I don't have time."

Kai scratched his head and took a sip of water. "Given what I know of her right now, I can see spending the rest of my life with her. Is that what you wanted to know? Or were you wondering, if you and I were to marry, would I always pine for her?"

"God! No. Don't be stupid. We're beyond that. And that's not why I'm asking. Her happiness is my priority." After my parents disappeared, I closed my heart off to everyone except for Kevin. When Tee came along, she shattered that barrier over and over again, even though breaking through my glass shield often resulted in her pain. Eventually, I gave up, let down my guard, and welcomed her friendship. She hadn't given me much of a choice—and I loved her for it.

"Tee's my best friend—my sister really—and she's the only person besides my brother I truly trust."

His forehead wrinkled. "What about Raiden?"

"I don't know. One minute he seems to care for me, and the next, he bites my head off. It's confusing. Do I think he would hurt me? Physically, no. But emotionally, it looks like we're having a competition to see who can destroy the other first. But again, that's not my point. When I become queen, do I get to choose a board of advisors, per se?"

"It's been so long since we've had a monarch, I think once you're queen, you get to make up the rules. But traditionally, you would appoint someone from each house."

"What about the king?"

"*You're* the Crimson Jewel. The line of royalty is passed *only* through direct descendants. So, I'm assuming, somehow, that's you. Therefore, you can give the king whatever authority you desire."

I had a feeling that level of power wouldn't endear me to the giants. If one of them randomly inherited the Earth to rule over all others—yes, I'd have a problem with it. How could they understand our struggles? Or what was best for the human race? But if I could stay alive long enough to pick a partner to rule beside, then I'd be free to lead a "search party" to go to Earth to gather more humans for the cause. But secretly, it would be a rescue mission for my parents, and if others wanted to join us, I wouldn't stop them. It could be a win-win for all of us.

"So I can pick you for a cabinet position?" I asked.

"If you wish."

"I can appoint Raiden?"

He stopped to think for a minute. "I don't think that would be fair. After you choose a First-Born son and you're safely on the throne, it would be in Raiden's best interest for you to let him go. I know you said a second ago that you didn't know how he feels about you—and *you* accuse *us* of lying." He clasped his hands together and rested his elbows on the table sitting closer to me. "You know exactly how he feels. Put yourself in his position. What if *he* had to marry someone else and you had to make sure he survived long enough to do it? I'm not trying to be cruel. I'm trying to be fair."

"Yes, and I appreciate that." The idea of me marrying anyone still felt like a bad dream I couldn't wake up from. But the idea of marrying someone who wasn't Raiden was a nightmare I couldn't allow myself to feel. Because once I traveled that road, I was afraid I wouldn't return. Buried inside, my heart wept blood, but in order to protect my friends and my family, I had to keep it together. Getting to that altar alive seemed to be the key.

"Can I appoint humans to be my advisors too?"

"I think we should expect it, even if some giants won't approve."

"So my point is, I want Tee by my side the entire time. But I'll only do that if I know she's safe. This week has quickly opened my eyes. I want to know if I can count on you to protect her. I didn't realize coming into this that their lives were going to be in *this* much danger. Don't get me wrong, we're used to it, but up here, I'm dealing with a whole new set of rules. I need to know who's on my team."

He reached across the table and grabbed both of my hands, his skin searing hot. "As long as I'm alive, no harm will ever come to Tee. I promise. And when giants make promises, Ruby, we keep them."

229

# CHAPTER 22
# THE FOE

For miles upon miles, the vast ocean tossed violently. Twenty-foot waves rose like sea creatures out of the depths, then crashed back into the blackened sea. Lightning flashed, bolts fanning throughout the sky, and thunder cracked the heavens. The smell of ozone snapped sharp and clean. Rain soaked through my jacket and my teeth chattered. Raiden hunched over me, shielding me from the worst of it, but the torrent pelted us from all directions. Looking down from Arnold's back curled my toes in terror so I shut my eyes.

Apparently, it didn't matter if we had to fly through a storm. The agreement was not to be trifled with. That was the reason I didn't get to stay with the Fum longer, even though I'd been missing for four days.

Leaving Tee behind had turned ugly. She'd stomped on the wooden floor, her braids shuddering with every step. "You are *not* going anywhere without me!" she yelled, balling her fists.

"I can only have three bodyguards." They'd upped the

number because of the attempt on my life. In addition to Liz and Raiden, Kai had advised me to take his friend Grant, the bald-headed bartender with the impressive beard. The Fee and the Foe, however, weren't pleased that I had chosen two from the Fie and one from the Fum. "Raiden and Grant are far more capable than you are!" I yelled back. If I had to hurt her feelings to get her to stay, I would. I didn't want to, but I'd do it.

"Y'all are being unreasonable!" she'd hollered, her accent more pronounced.

Kai had stepped in to save me. "Tee, Bea's right."

She'd turned her anger on the huge man behind her, pointing at him with a red polished fingernail. "Shut up."

"Tee, don't be rude. Raiden and Grant can protect me. *You* can't. Do you want me to get hurt?"

Her head had snapped around, her braids flying. "Don't be like that!" she'd hissed. "You know I don't want anyone to hurt you. That's why I have to come with you."

I understood her anger. I would've done the same thing if the roles had been reversed. She could've come with, but then Raiden, Grant, and Liz would have to protect her, too, making their jobs more difficult. But that wasn't why I wanted her with Kai—I wanted her there because he'd promised to protect her with his life. I believed him.

I'd brought my people here for their safety. Raiden had assured me they were secure where they were. At the moment, everyone, including Kevin, was taking classes on Fee, Fie, Foe, and Fum history, taught by instructors from each clan. Next, they were going to dive into career options. I was jealous but happy for them. The fun they must've been having, dreaming of their opportunities for the future—at least I'd given them that.

"I'm coming with you," Tee had repeated. She'd crossed her arms and planted her feet.

This was not a battle I was prepared to lose.

"No, you aren't. You're staying here."

She'd inhaled sharply. "Ah, bless your heart," she said, which was the Southern equivalent of *fuck you*. She placed her hand on her chest. "You're not the boss of me, *carrot butt*." She'd modified the insult during our childhood, seeing as carrot tops were actually green.

*Oh*—below the belt. I hated it when she called me that. My hair wasn't orange and she knew it.

I'd gritted my teeth and pissed her off by saying, "Actually, I am. And the last time you were on watch, I was kidnapped and thrown into a volcano to die." I hadn't wanted to say it, but I had to. It had to end with her being mad at me. It was the only way she'd stay. I didn't blame her for my kidnapping, but she didn't know that.

Her face caught fire. If looks could kill, all of us in the room would have been instantly incinerated. "Bitch," she'd hissed.

Angry Tee was one of my favorites, but normally, her wrath wasn't aimed at me. I knew her well enough to know the foulness going on in her head was not coming out of her mouth.

She'd whirled away and stormed out the door, and Kai had nodded to me before he followed. *Brave man.*

I left a letter with him, asking for her forgiveness. It would be a while before she was ready to read it. She'd have ample time, since I was going to be away for three more weeks. Kai had promised they would meet us at Isle Noir, the capital of the Fiefdom, when the time came.

"You're going to want to see this," Raiden said.

I wiped the rain away from my face with the back of my already-wet sleeve and opened my eyes. Up ahead, a massive ship rode the squall with ease. Flashes of lightning illuminated the sails billowing from the tall masts. Lights glowed from round windows inside the hull. It looked like a modern cruise liner had had a baby with a pirate ship.

We descended slowly, and Arnold's hooves slid to a stop on the wet deck. Liz and Grant landed behind us.

A group of giants quickly gathered around. Raiden helped me down, and I stayed near him as a groom took the winged horses away.

A woman cloaked in a blue trench coat that matched her eyes escorted us down a long corridor inside the ship. Gray wood doors, carved with ocean themes, were evenly spaced apart in the teal hallway. She pointed to a door and informed me that I'd have four hours to nap and get ready to meet Trent, the First-Born son of Lord Ren and Lady Moselle.

I found it strange that despite not being able to produce children easily, each one of the ruling families *just happened* to have a son close to my age. Kai had said that made the prophecy more plausible.

"I'm right next door," Raiden said. "Grant is on the other side, and Liz is across the hall. Don't eat anything without our approval."

"Why? Do you think someone is going to poison me?"

"It's possible. And lock your door. Both Grant and I have access to your suite from our rooms," Raiden ordered before he shut my door.

What made him think I wasn't going to lock those doors too? I wasn't—but it would have served him right.

I flopped down on the emerald bedspread. Colorful

pillows of all sizes, some embroidered, some beaded, were tossed on the bed and the magenta love seat. Gold velvet curtains hung from the round windows, framing the darkness outside. Artwork with gilded frames lined the damask-patterned walls. The light sconces, shaped like seashells, spread a warm glow over the room. It was luxury with a touch of something dark, something sexy.

The swaying of the water was surprisingly gentle compared to what was going on outside. I laid my head on a pillow as the waves rocked me to sleep.

———————

SOMETIME LATER, Raiden gently shook me awake. I rubbed my eyes. The material hanging above the four-poster bed changed with the position of my head, from green to blue to purple, almost like the inside of an oyster shell.

"Come on, you need to bathe and get ready." His hand was warm on my shoulder.

I glanced at the clock on the wall. "Ain't no way it's going to take me two hours. Go away." I slapped a pillow at him and pulled the covers over my head.

"Oh, it's *definitely* going to take you two hours. You're not good at doing hair and makeup, but here, it's pretty much required. Do you want me to fetch Liz? Though, if I'm being honest, she's not much better at it than you are."

I groaned as I sat up. My hair was curlier than normal from all the humidity in the air. I shoved a wayward lock away from my face but it stubbornly flopped back and hung between my eyes.

Raiden suppressed a smile as he shoved his hands into the pockets of his black slacks and waited. He looked formal in his pressed pants and tight black sweater. And beautiful beyond belief. The stark color made his gray eyes pop and his skin glow.

"Fine," I huffed. "What am I supposed to wear?"

He walked into the oversized closet and pulled out a shimmering green dress with a small keyhole cutout in the front and a larger one in the back. He hung it on the closet door. "Go take a bath. You smell like a wet horse."

My brows puckered, and my mouth fell open at the insult. "And you don't?"

"No. I took a shower while you slept, princess."

I didn't know if he used that term sarcastically or sincerely. I scowled but let the comment slide.

My bare feet sunk into the opulent carpets scattered randomly over the wood floor as I walked to the bathroom and closed the door behind me. Steam swirled from the wooden Japanese soaking tub. It was large, probably meant for two. Pink rose petals floated on the surface, perfuming the air.

I tiptoed over the chilly tile and stepped into the hot water. As I dipped deeper into the tub, the temperature eased the knots in my back and shoulders. With my head leaned against the side, I closed my eyes and released a long sigh of momentary contentment.

I jumped when Raiden knocked. "Did you fall asleep again?" he asked through the door.

"No!" I said when I really should have said yes. I couldn't have been too long; the water wasn't even cool. I dried off and wrapped a white towel around my hair and one around my body.

Raiden's posture stiffened as I exited the bathroom and went into the closet to slip on the dress. It fit like it was made for me. The front showed just enough cleavage to be sexy but not sleazy. The color made my eyes greener than hazel.

Raiden sat with one leg crossed over the other on the love seat with a pillow propped on his lap, reading a book. He avoided looking at me.

I realized this was hard for him—that was, if he actually cared about me. At times, I was certain he did, but other times, not so much. Kai had said that Raiden loved me, but I wasn't sure if I believed him. His demeanor toward me had changed, and we hadn't said more than a few sentences since the morning after he'd rescued me. On the other hand, I could barely contain my feelings for him. They nudged under the surface of my skin, begging for release. I kept them firmly contained to keep from embarrassing myself. Because what if he no longer felt the same? What if he'd come to terms with the situation, even though I hadn't.

In the bathroom, I piled my hair on top of my head and stabbed it in place with a few hair sticks. I pulled some curls down around my face to soften the effect, then swiped on some blush, lip gloss, and mascara.

Raiden poked his head in. "Ah, you might want to try some eyeliner and actual lipstick."

"Why?"

"You'll see."

"Just tell me, will you?"

"The Foe are quite dramatic. You'll find you probably feel slightly underdressed—" an eyebrow cocked as his eyes dipped to my cleavage, "—or overdressed, as it may be."

"Well, which is it?"

He just smiled. "Here. Let me help you with some makeup."

"Seriously? You know how to do makeup?"

He sat down on the stool next to me and grabbed an eyeshadow brush, one I hadn't even attempted to use. "I used to watch my mom. Close your eyes."

"You better not screw this up."

He swiped something over my eyelids, then blended it with his finger. His touch was gentle, perfunctory. But it didn't matter. Flames ignited and my nipples hardened. Just the friction of my dress swiping over them sent a barrage of tingles between my thighs. Desperately, I tried to think of anything but him.

After he was satisfied, he took a pencil and lined my eyes. Then he took another pencil and concentrated on my lips, outlining the edges with a soft nude color. I stared at his dark arched brows, the high edges of his cheekbones, and the almost perfect nose, except for the small bump on the bridge. His lips, the bottom one slightly fuller than the top, were set off by the neatly manicured edges of his dark scruff. I sighed again, trying to banish the throbbing deep in my core and the delightful shivers peppering my skin. It was as pointless as attempting to control the beat of my fluttering heart.

"Done." He glanced up, his stormy eyes holding such intensity when he looked at me, it instantly transported me deeper inside my fantasy. His eyes widened slightly before his pupils dilated. Bolts of desire splintered along the contours of my mouth as I tilted my chin upward to meet his lips.

He shoved the stool out from under him, and it toppled loudly on the floor. He fled through the door and slammed it behind him.

A dry sob caught in my chest but I managed to smother it.

I stared at my reflection in the mirror. I almost didn't recognize myself. Smoky shadows paired with heavy black eyeliner made my eyes an olive green, but sorrow dulled their shine.

I stood up and straightened my dress before I stepped out of the bathroom. Raiden's hands were deep in his pockets as he stared at nothing but blackness out the port-hole window.

"Are we going to talk about this?"

"There's nothing to talk about. I'm here to keep you safe until you're wed." His breath fogged the glass.

"So that's it then. We're not even going to discuss options?" I said softly.

He turned abruptly. "*Options*? What do you mean *options*? There are no options. You're bound by blood to another. At this point, who you choose makes no difference to me," he said coldly, but the undercurrent of anger edged every word. He stepped away. "I'll be waiting outside when you're ready."

I gulped fast and heavily, but the air thinned and getting sufficient oxygen seemed difficult. It was like he'd stabbed my soul with his words and left me to slowly bleed out.

But he was right. What did I expect?

My head started to sway, so I sat on the edge of the bed, clasping my hands over my lap and concentrating on breathing before I passed out. How embarrassing would that be? Passing out because of a boy? *Not going to happen.* Even if it felt as if my heart was cracking—breaking, shattering—beneath the weight of his rejection.

# TWENTY-THREE

T hree bodyguards waited outside my room. Raiden joked with Grant as if nothing had passed between the two of us. If he could do that, so could I.

I linked arms with Liz, which warranted a curious look from Grant. I still wasn't overly steady in a pair of heels. We walked down the hallway and caught an elevator. In the crowded space, the abalone tiles shimmered and the mirrored ceiling reflected our images. It came to a smooth stop and the door whooshed open. A gust of cool ocean air snapped at the hem of my dress. It smelled different here out on the open water—less fishy, and more like salty seaweed, oiled wood, and rain.

A young woman, waiting outside the elevator, introduced herself as the head of security. "Carrisa," she said, emphasis on the first syllable and a tongue roll toward the end. She looked exactly how she sounded—sexy. Her brilliant aqua eyes and full lips coated with a bright-red stain stood out against her rich skin. Perfect ringlets cascaded down her back in a waterfall. Unlike my rowdy curls.

"There has been a change of plans," Carrisa said.

Both Raiden and Grant crossed their arms.

"Nothing to fret over." She placed a hand on Raiden's arm.

I dropped my eyes to the floor. Liz tightened her grip on my arm.

"Trent has requested time alone with Ruby." My name sounded delicious rolling off her tongue. Her gaze finally landed on me. If she hated me or liked me, I couldn't tell. Her facial expression was professional. Bland, if a face like that could ever be bland.

She escorted us outside. Standing on a small platform in the middle of a water fountain was the First-Born son of the Foe. Lightning flashed in the distance but the rain and violent winds had stopped. Puffy clouds skated quickly in front of the full moon.

Liz grabbed Raiden by the arm and ushered him into the shadows while Grant followed, leaving me alone with Trent.

Trent waved and stepped onto the water before proceeding to walk—on the water—over to the edge of the fountain to greet me. The slacks he wore under his long blue tunic didn't get wet.

Thick bracelets, in a rainbow of metallic shades, clinked on his wrist as he scooped up my hand and gently pressed a kiss to my skin. His smile was warm and sincere behind his full lips, complete with a pair of pearly white fangs. A set of dreadlocks rested at the base of his neck, tied into a pony-tail. "Ruby, it's a pleasure to finally meet you. Come." He had an accent, too, but it wasn't as pronounced as Carrisa's. He helped me up the small set of stairs onto the fountain. I hesitated at the water's edge. Multiple shades of blue and green illuminated the warbling liquid below.

"It's safe, I assure you."

Tentatively, I tapped the tip of my shoe on the water and was surprised to find a panel of glass below.

Trent lifted my hand high in the air and spun me around in a circle. "You look lovely, Ruby." He was as tall as Raiden, but slimmer through the shoulders, more like a dancer. And there was something immensely attractive about his dark skin with light-green eyes.

"Thank you," I said with less sincerity than I should have.

He laughed as if he knew I didn't believe him, but he didn't press the issue. He clasped my elbow in his and led me to the middle of the platform. With a snap of his elegant fingers, a fine spray of water around the outside of the fountain shot up into the air.

I wondered if Raiden was lurking somewhere near and if he was going to have an issue with not being able to see me. A swallow lodged in my throat. After our last exchange, I doubted it.

Trent released my arm and faced me. "Sorry about the change of plans, but I wanted to be able to speak with you freely."

I shook off my melancholy. "About what?"

"Well, I thought we could start this relationship with some honesty." A half-sided smirk tugged at his lips as he fidgeted with a ring on his index finger, twisting it around and around. "Even if we don't end up together, this will still be a relationship regardless, since you'll soon be queen. And eventually, I'll be lord of the Foe. Unless of course, we can just forget this whole thing and you can make me your king now." He winked.

I blinked.

Again, he snapped his fingers and a table made of water rose before us. I started to question how that table came to be until my eyes focused on the bottle of wine and two glasses that sat on the sloshing surface. I stepped back.

"Oh, love, have a sense of humor." He laughed and poured us each a glass, then handed me one. I accepted it, but didn't drink. He took a long sip of wine, holding on to the delicate stem. "You've been with the Fie for too long." He rolled his eyes. "Have some wine." He gestured for me to take a sip.

I shook my head, set the glass on the table with a splash, and crossed my arms. Fool me once, shame on you—fool me twice, shame on me.

"Oh, forgive me. I heard how the Fie got you drunk and tricked you into signing a contract you probably wouldn't have signed if you'd been given adequate time to read it."

"While I don't like what the Fie did, the blame is mine. It takes a special kind of stupid not to read a contract."

"Sweet Ruby, don't be so hard on yourself. I'm sure you were tired, probably a little frightened, and drinking. It's a mistake anyone could've made. But now I'm curious— would you have signed it anyway?" He didn't sound convinced.

"Yeah. The Dome offers better and safer opportunities for my friends and family. Wouldn't you have done the same thing?"

"Heavens, no," he said with a wave of his hand. "I'm not that good of a giant. Honesty—that's my strength. Even if my boyfriend doesn't always appreciate my candor."

I'd never met anyone who put me at a loss of words so quickly. It was like standing in the shallows of a river on one

242

foot trying to maintain balance so you didn't get swept into the rapids. I wasn't sure if I liked him or not.

"So . . . you're gay?" How was that going to work if I married him? I started to stick my finger in my mouth to mangle a cuticle but caught myself at the last second.

"No, bisexual. I told you we were going to have an open conversation. I have a boyfriend. But since I'm a First-Born son, it's frowned upon. Not because our society has a problem with it, but because our family lines seem to have less trouble producing children. So, in order to keep our population alive, I, along with the rest of the First-Born sons, have a duty to spawn." He said the last few words as if the mere idea bored him.

"Is your boyfriend going to have a problem with you marrying someone else?"

He poured himself more wine and drained it before setting it down next to my untouched glass. "Yes, but we've talked about it and it's going to happen one way or another. So here's my proposal."

I cocked my head. That was a bit abrupt.

"Love, not *that* kind of proposal. Not yet, anyway." He chuckled and held out an arm for me to take.

We walked to the edge of the fountain as the water lowered so we could pass through without getting wet. Stepping onto the stairs, I glanced around for my body-guards but didn't see them.

Trent guided me toward the massive white sails flapping in the breeze. "I have to marry a woman, but nothing says I have to love her. You have to marry a First-Born son, and nothing says you have to love him. I don't want to rule. It's tedious. If we were to marry, I'd leave ruling the Fiefdom in your hands. Josha and I can continue our relationship, and you'd have the freedom to do the same. Rumor has it, you may already have someone."

I tossed him a startled glance and stopped. How did he know? And it wasn't necessarily true. I wasn't sure what I had.

"And children?" I held up my hand in a stop position. "Not that I'm in a hurry." As a matter of fact, I wasn't sure I wanted *any*, but I didn't think I was going to get away with not having them. At least eventually.

Trent's gaze slowly studied my face then flashed to my cleavage. "Oh love, I'll have no problem putting babies in your belly."

My face, normally able to control its expression, failed me. "Gross!" I spouted uncontrollably. I slapped my hand over my blathering mouth.

He tilted his head back and laughed. "There won't be anything gross about it. I have no doubt we'd both enjoy it. You are quite innocent, aren't you?" He leaned against the mast with one foot propped on the creaking wood. Long shadows crept along the deck from the light of the moon.

I had a feeling that even though I wasn't a virgin, the answer would be yes in his opinion.

"I think you underestimate how fun I can be." The gleam in his eyes was terrifying. If I had to guess, I'd say he was enjoying himself.

"I think you overestimate how much fun I can be," I said dryly, twisting my hands.

"It's not my intent to scare you, Ruby. I just want you to know where I stand. What my priorities are."

"And what exactly *are* your priorities?"

"I live to have fun. I love the finer things in life. I enjoy traveling, socializing, meeting new people. The usual."

"Why would we bother getting married? It sounds as if you have everything you want already."

"I do. But I'd love to wear the crown. It's the easiest way to make my parents happy." He twitched one shoulder as if this conversation wasn't serious in the least.

"I'm going to be honest—your honesty is exhausting."

He laughed again. The sound was infectious, and I found myself joining.

He wiped the tears from the corner of his impossibly green eyes. "You see? This—" he motioned between the two of us, "would be fun. When you're not busy ruling the Fiefdom," he said as if that were no big task, "we could travel, see new places, meet new people, dance, dine. And after we have our first child, you could bring along whomever you choose. I believe after spending the week with me, you'll find my personality might be exactly what you need. I'm charming and charismatic. And no offense, I'm thinking your talents do not extend to, ah, shall we say, people."

He was right. People were not my strong suit. But I wasn't sure how he knew that already.

"And I'm not marrying you because I want to rule the Dome. Plus, you'll always know where I stand. I promise."

"And how does your boyfriend feel about all of this?" My curiosity couldn't be contained.

"Josha is well aware of the situation. Our arrangement —" he pointed between the two of us, "—if you agree, gives both of us the freedom to live how we choose, love who we choose, or simply *do* who we choose."

I choked on my spit. Once I cleared my throat, I said, "Well, you've given me a lot to think about."

"So you'll think about it?"

"Of course." His proposal, while unorthodox, wasn't unreasonable.

A big smile bloomed on his handsome face. "Good. Tomorrow night, we shall party. I can introduce you to my friends." He clapped his hands together in front of his face.

"And Josha?"

"Him too."

How was that going to go? If I were in Josha's shoes, I certainly wouldn't like me. Just what I needed, another target on my back during an already deadly game of dating.

CHAPTER

# TWENTY-FOUR

The next evening, Liz offered to help me get ready for the party, but Raiden refused her before I had a chance to speak.

Liz scowled. "It's not appropriate for you to be alone with Ruby." The words sounded angry, and the way she said my name made me wonder what I'd done to irritate her.

Raiden shooed her away, then shut the door, leaving the two of us alone.

Nervous bees bounced around in my stomach. I wanted to talk to him about Trent's proposal of sorts, but how? What did one say when asking someone if they wanted to be your mistress? I'd reversed the roles in my head time and time again, and in all honesty, I wasn't sure what I would've said, let alone what Raiden would think.

Would I be okay if Raiden were to marry someone else and keep me on the side? Even if he didn't love that second someone? Knowing they were sleeping together? Knowing they would be raising children together? The thought had my fingernails digging into the palms of my hands.

Raiden pulled out a pair of navy slacks and a white silk tank top from the closet for my approval. Several draped strands of pearls held the open back together. It was beautiful, but what I really wanted to do was to stay in my lounge clothes, lay around on the bed, and read a good book. Anything to take my mind off the current situation.

Earlier in the day, Liz and I had toured the ship with Carrisa. It was a city on the ocean propelled by massive sails and electric engines, and they had pretty much anything I could think of—restaurants, clothing boutiques, salons, banks, even a movie theater, which was ironically playing a blockbuster pirate movie.

"Ruby? Do you like this one?" He shook the tank top impatiently, the strands of pearls rattling together.

"I guess." The pants looked comfortable enough.

He looked as if he were about to say something, but instead, laid the outfit on the bed with a matching pair of shoes and pointed me toward the bathroom.

He applied my makeup in silence. The tension in the small room was charged like the air before a storm. With every touch, my nerves flared, sending sparks along my skin. Warmth pooled deep in my belly. The feeling was incredible and uncomfortable at the same time.

I was losing confidence that he felt the same way about me. It seemed like years ago when he'd said liking me wasn't the problem. I'd thought that maybe that meant he liked me a lot, but now, I wasn't so sure. Had his feelings changed that drastically over our misunderstanding?

I stared at his face as he outlined my mouth in a berry-red stain. I wanted to run my fingers through his dark hair, wanted to taste his sculpted lips. I sighed. What I wanted and what I could have were two different things. Unless I offered Trent's proposal.

"Stop moving," he ordered.

I swallowed down the impossible proposition.

"There. Done. I'll wait outside while you get dressed." He turned abruptly and left the room.

I ducked into the silk top, which didn't allow for a bra, and slid into the strappy stilettos. I was getting better at walking in them, but in no way did I enjoy it.

Raiden knocked before he opened up the door between our rooms. "Here. This will look nice with that outfit." A silver pear-shaped gem, the exact shade of his eyes, hung from the platinum chain like a raindrop. His fingers burned on my clammy skin as he clasped the necklace at the base of my skull. "Are you okay?" He came around and touched my cheek with the back of his hand.

I turned my head away, afraid if I looked at him, I'd break down and beg him to run away with me, despite the death warrant hanging over my head if I didn't uphold my end of the agreement.

"I'm fine." I fiddled with the necklace and let it fall from my hand. It landed heavily right between the swell of my breasts.

He placed his fingers beneath my chin and forced me to look at him. He canted an eyebrow and waited.

"I don't want to do this anymore," I whispered. I was completely exhausted. My days were normally filled with hunting, fishing, and training with weapons. Not people.

His stony expression softened and pain flashed, his eyes warring with intensity. "I don't want you to either. Fuck it," he said quietly. He cupped my cheek before sliding his hand into the base of my hair. Gently, he pulled, positioning my head as his lips skimmed against mine. His breath filled my mouth, the kiss slow and long like a hot summer day. I gripped one hand around his neck and the other against his back, pressing into him. His heart beat rapidly against my chest—or was that my heartbeat? I couldn't tell. Tiny bubbles of happiness whizzed to the surface of my skin.

I stretched on my tiptoes, trying to get closer. The hard length of him pressed into my stomach. The ache between my thighs deepened.

A loud knock on the door made me jump.

"Are you guys finished? Ruby's going to be late," Grant hollered from the other side.

Raiden's shoulders drooped and he rested his forehead against mine for a few breath-catching seconds. "Here. Let's fix your lipstick." He wiped the smudges off my face with his thumb.

I sat down on the bed, my legs trembling, while he fetched the lipstick from the bathroom.

"There," he said, as he swiped the color over my lips.

"You know there's something I've been meaning—"

I was interrupted by more loud banging at the door.

"Later." He shushed me with a finger pressed against my mouth. "Come on." He held out a hand and pulled me off the bed.

THE PARTY WAS in full swing by the time we arrived. Sheer curtains hung from the rafters of the large wooden pavilion, swaying under the breeze, making the humid air pleasant instead of sticky. Several sunken rooms, filled with colorful pillows and people holding drinks, were scattered randomly about. Outside, a lagoon with in-ground lights and tiles morphing from green to blue to aqua snaked between the fluttering white sails. Large tropical birds, in and around the pockets of lush greenery, vines, and bright flowers, sang almost obnoxiously. Scantily clad giants played a game of water volleyball while others sat on the edge of the pool visiting with friends.

"Ruby!" I heard from across the room. Trent hurried over with a beautiful bald man on his arm. He pushed a curtain of dangling crystals out of the way as he leaned down and kissed me on both cheeks.

Liz grabbed Raiden and yanked him to the other side of the pavilion to lurk in the background. Earlier, Raiden had told me that if I planned to eat and drink anything, he needed to taste it first.

Trent wrapped his arm around the man standing next to him. "This is my boyfriend, Josha."

"Ruby, it's so nice to meet you." Josha kissed the back of my hand. His smile, which crinkled the corners of his eyes, seemed to be sincere. He was smaller than Trent, and his features more feminine—a softer jawline, rounder eyes, and two diamond studs piercing his full lower lip. He, like so many of the Foe, wore colorful makeup. His aqua-colored eyes glowed under the pink winged eyeliner and purple mascara.

"Come on." Trent chained one arm through mine and his other around Josha before whisking us into the middle of the party. If I married him, was this how it would be? A throuple? And could I live with it?

Trent introduced me to so many giants that I couldn't remember anyone's name. But everyone seemed genuinely interested in my story. So I repeated them—repeatedly.

251

"Here." Trent offered me a glass of wine.

My throat was dry from talking, but Raiden's warning flashed in my brain. I accepted the glass, not wanting to be rude, but he quickly noticed I wasn't drinking it.

"You don't like the wine?" he asked.

"Um . . ." I searched the room for Raiden.

Trent smirked. "Let me guess—someone told you not to eat or drink anything?"

I nodded.

Trent grabbed my glass and took a sip, swirled it around in his mouth, and swallowed. "It's safe." He handed it back to me.

"How do you know? I've been told you're pretty hard to kill." I was a bit more cautious now that I knew someone wanted me dead.

"We are, but our senses are more developed than yours. If this glass contained poison, I'd be able to taste it, even if you couldn't. And I promise, it's safe. But don't drink too much—it's stronger than what you're used to."

I took a small sip. The carbonation stung the back of my nose and bubbled in my empty stomach. I wanted to guzzle the whole glass because I was so thirsty, but the last time I did something like that . . .

Josha traded my wine for a sweating glass filled with ice and a colorless liquid. "Water," he whispered in my ear.

"No poison?" I asked. He *did* have a reason to want me dead.

He held the glass out for Trent to take a sip, then handed it back to me.

"Thank you," I mouthed, before draining the entire glass. "Sorry for being paranoid."

"No worries. I'd be cautious too if I were you," Josha said.

For the rest of the evening, Trent introduced me to a dizzying number of people. There was no way I was going to remember any of them except Josha. He stayed at Trent's side, whispering in my ear who was who and who was doing who. He was funny in a reserved, quiet sort of way—exactly the opposite of Trent, who was loud, boisterous, and very entertaining. Everyone wanted to be near him, to stand in his circle. And it wasn't just because he was heir to the lordship—but because his personality was magnetic. He made you feel as if you were the most important person in the room. He managed it with everyone, which honestly made it difficult for me to trust him. But in the grand scheme of things, as a king, he'd be the perfect choice if it were a popularity contest. I just wasn't sure what kind of contest it was yet.

I rubbed the back of my neck, sore from looking up all night. I was the shortest person in the room, and I wasn't fond of it. If I heard, *"you're such a tiny little thing,"* one more time, I was going to scream. The Foe, while tall, weren't as tall as most of the Fie and not nearly as wide as the Fum. They were built like dancers—well-muscled but lean.

"Your neck hurt?" Josha asked. He laid a soft hand on my arm. His long fingernails were painted dark at the base and white toward the ends.

I nodded.

"If you're ready to call it a night, I'll gladly escort you back to your room. These parties can be exhausting sometimes."

"I'll take her," Raiden interrupted from behind us.

A knowing smile curled on Josha's gold-glitter lips.

"Take care of her," he said to Raiden. "I'll see you tomorrow, Ruby." He glided next to Trent and clasped his arm. Trent pulled him in close but kept his attention on everyone around him, even as Josha's focus was directed at Trent. It was obvious Josha was head over heels for Trent, even to a novice like me. As for Trent, he seemed to be smitten with everyone—which led me to believe maybe he was just smitten with himself.

After the elevator stopped on our floor, I asked Raiden, "What do you think of Trent?"

He threw me a side glance and shook his head. "I'm not a fan."

"Why?" It seemed as if everyone else liked him.

"Because he's a player. That's his game. How would he run a kingdom?"

"I don't know. He's really good with people. And I'm . . . not so good."

Raiden unlocked my door and pushed it open, holding it for me to enter.

While I'd been out, someone had straightened the room. The bright pillows were back to their original spots on the bed.

"Give yourself more credit. You're not *that* bad," he mocked.

He caught my hand in mid-air as I tried smacking him. I yanked it away, but his grip was ironclad. He tugged me closer. The pulse in his neck thumped above his collar. He just stood there, silently holding my wrist and studying my face.

Nerves skittered inside my chest cavity as he reached up with his unoccupied hand and pushed a wayward lock of hair over my shoulder. Tickles of electricity sparked over the delicate skin on my neck. I shivered.

The muscles along his jaw flexed. A fleeting look of pain pinched his face before he abruptly dropped my hand and turned away.

*No*—I wanted to scream. *Don't pull away.* The need to be near him was almost obsessive—possessive. I might've been concerned about my stalkerish feelings toward him if it wasn't for the overwhelming intuition he was about to leave me permanently.

"Wait. Please," I said breathlessly.

He stopped, his shoulders rigid and tight.

"Do you still have feelings for me or was that a lie?" I said, the words bursting out of my traitorous mouth. I wanted to hide under the mound of pillows on my bed.

"It wasn't a lie," he said with his back to me. "But you know there's nothing that can be done. You signed a contract in blood. Whether I like it or not, in a few weeks, you'll be wed to another." The tendons in his neck strained.

"That's true," I said. "But there may be another way."

## CHAPTER
# TWENTY-FIVE

"Y ou want me to *what*?" Raiden yelled. The color of his eyes whirled like molten silver as red flushed up his neck. "If you think I'm going to share you with another man, you're fucking crazy. At this point, I couldn't do it even if I wanted to."

Before I could explain further, he stormed across the floor, wrenched open the door to his room, and slammed it behind him. I heard the lock click into place.

That conversation had *not* gone the way I'd hoped. But if I was being honest, I hadn't expected it to go well. The mere idea of being a "mistress" was repulsive to him. I didn't blame him. It *was* repulsive. But the reality of not having him in my life was worse.

I stumbled to the bed and curled up on my side. Tears wet my pillow as I stared at the door, hoping he would come back through but knowing he wouldn't.

SINCE SLEEP DIDN'T COME EASILY, by morning, I was exhausted. When I couldn't pretend to sleep any longer, I got up, showered, and dressed, prepared to have a civil discussion with Raiden. I hoped that with some time to think about it and cool off, Raiden would consider my proposition. Even as unorthodox as it was. It wasn't ideal—me married to another, while he and Josha stayed on the sidelines—but it was a solution. Maybe not the one I wanted, but the notion of not having Raiden at all was too painful to imagine. I was willing to do whatever it took. Hopefully, he was too.

I knocked gently on the connecting door, my forehead pressed against the cool wood. I waited for a second, then knocked again a little harder. He didn't answer. My temper flared. I twisted the handle. It was still locked. I pounded harder, banging until my hand was sore. He'd better answer the door.

"What are you doing?" Liz startled me from behind.

"I need to talk with Raiden." I propped my hands on my hips.

A fleeting look of irritation crossed her face before she said, "He's gone. He left last night."

"*What?*"

"He's gone," she said slowly, like I didn't understand her the first time.

"Why?" I whispered. Until that moment, I'd been under the—apparently naïve—impression we could fix the situation.

She waved a finger in the air. "I'm thinking it has to do with this racket you're making."

The vice in my stomach twisted another notch. "He left me *again?*" I tried, unsuccessfully, to hide the hurt in my voice. "Can you at least tell me if he's coming back?"

Her eyes hardened as she inspected me from head to toe. "It would be best if he didn't. I'm not trying to be mean, but there's no hope for the two of you."

"So he *didn't* tell you where he was going? What he's doing? If he's coming back?"

Her eyes darted away. "No. I'm just here to ask if you want to go to breakfast. But I can see that you probably shouldn't be out in public right now."

"What gave that away?" I asked snidely.

She backed toward the door with her palms facing me. "Don't go anywhere without me or Grant as an escort. I'll be back to get you this evening. There's another party you must attend." She softly closed the door on her way out.

I attempted to distract myself. But there wasn't much to do. I read. I exercised. I bathed. I ate the lunch delivered to my door, even though no one taste-tested it. I was feeling rebellious. Angry. Hurt.

Raiden had left. Again. No goodbye. No reason why.

Our fight hadn't given him a legitimate excuse to leave. Not without finishing what we'd started.

As the day wore on, my sorrow lessened and my anger increased. By the time Josha knocked on my door, my rage had boiled over. Raiden was a prick and not worth my time. Besides, in the end, there was no way for us to be together. So tonight, I would give Trent the attention he deserved. In a little over a month, I was to be married. I needed to make a wise decision. And if my heart didn't get its choice, then my brain would.

"Hey." Josha poked his head inside the doorway. "Liz said you might need some help? Do you mind?"

He sauntered in with clothes draped over his arm and a

bag slung on his shoulder, walking far more gracefully in his knee-high leather boots than I'd ever manage. His black spandex pants captured the light as if they were wet. He wore a white shirt with a low-cut neckline and lace cuffs layered under a purple Victorian-style jacket. A necklace of diamonds and amethysts draped around his neck.

He rolled a display rack out of the closet and hung up the clothes, then pulled a slinky blood-red dress that glittered like ruby slippers from the hanger and held it up to my shoulders. He pursed his shiny lips before he shook his head. Next, he picked an orange dress the color of fall leaves with a cutout over the stomach showing *a lot* of skin.

"The color's good, but it's not quite the look I'm going for," he muttered.

"What *are* you going for?"

His many bracelets clinked together as he pressed a finger to his lips. "Shhhh."

He held up a few more in various shades and shapes before he grabbed the last one from the rack. Tiny crystal gems glittered over the transparent black material.

"No." I shook my head to solidify my answer.

He smiled and ignored me as he pulled a pair of black panties and a bra out of his bag and dangled them in front of me.

I crossed my arms and stood my ground. "No."

"Please." He pushed his bottom lip out, pretending to pout. His piercings glittered.

I narrowed my gaze at him.

"I promise," he said with his hands pressed together in a prayer position, "if you don't look amazing, I won't make you wear it."

I rolled my eyes and snatched the undergarments out of his hand while I reached for the dress.

"Darling, don't bother. There's no way you're getting into that without my help."

I disappeared into the bathroom and returned wearing only the underwear. My boobs, a reasonably adequate size on their own, were stacked practically to my chin in the satin bra.

He slipped the dress over my head and shimmied it down my frame then stood back to appraise with a pinky finger pressed to his lips. "Yes." He escorted me to the mirror.

It seemed as if a spider had woven a perfect web made of minuscule crystals over the fabric. It was incredible. Because there was so much going on, the dress wasn't near as sheer as I'd imagined. I rolled my eyes, knowing I'd lost. "Fine. You were right. It's gorgeous."

"Alright, makeup time." He rubbed his hands gleefully.

I sat on the chair in the bathroom and let Josha create. The whole thing reminded me of Tee. She and Josha would get along like peas in a pod. I had to hold back the emotions twisting at the base of my throat. Another check mark under Trent's name, compliments of his boyfriend. Who would've believed?

What kind of man had the confidence to help the woman who might marry the one he loved? I didn't know if I had the character to behave with that much grace.

"Thank you," I uttered with my eyes closed while he was in the process of gluing on fake eyelashes. I hoped they weren't as big as the ones he currently wore.

"No need. Decorating people is kind of my thing." He

fanned the drying lashes with his hand. The smell of his sweet yet masculine cologne swept under my nose.

"Well, that too. I suck at it. I haven't had much practice. But really, what I mean is—thank you for being nice to me. If the roles were reversed, I'm not sure if I could be as good as you are."

His hands paused. "You're welcome."

After a few more minutes, he said, "Now open your eyes."

I blinked rapidly a few times, adjusting to the weight of the lashes, and stared at myself in the mirror. "You're a magician."

I was almost as pretty as he was. Though he'd kept my makeup classy—smoky purple eye with winged liner, bronzer, and a perfect burgundy lip. I looked like a different person. My eyes glowed positively emerald against my creamy ivory skin.

He fluffed my hair, then threw in a few braids, but left it dangling down my back in a cascade of raucous curls. He started to reach for the necklace Raiden had given me, but I stopped him. I shook my head. While I was mad at Raiden, I wasn't ready to let go just yet.

"Suit yourself." He dangled a pair of black stilettos with diamond ankle straps in front of me. "Are you ready?"

"I guess." All this socializing was taking its toll. I wasn't used to it and I didn't enjoy it. But I stuffed my feelings down because this was about keeping my friends and family safe. And planning for a future rescue mission.

"Good. But before we go, let me warn you, tonight is bound to get wild. Be cautious and don't drink too much, okay? I don't want you to regret anything come morning."

A sense of dread coiled in my throat and spiraled to my stomach. I was racking up regrets like notches on a belt.

Liz and Grant followed closely behind us, both dressed in their usual black attire. Liz avoided eye contact as I threw her a dirty look. I was still angry with her for not telling me where Raiden went.

Instead of going up, we rode the elevator down. When the doors slid open, we stepped onto a lush eggplant-colored carpet leading to a door at the end of the long hallway. Victorian light fixtures glowed a dim yellow over the black-and-silver-striped wallpaper.

Grant opened the ebony doors for us to enter. It was very different from the bohemian style on the upper levels. The only similarity to the rest of the ship was the sheer luxury. Candle chandeliers hung from the antiqued mirrored ceiling. The soft light glimmered over a polished obsidian stage built into the bow of the ship, the stone pouring down the edges and morphing into the dance floor surrounding the platform.

Behind us was a bar with bottles of liquor lining floating shelves. Two women in white corsets, contrasting beautifully with their skin, concocted drinks. A shirtless man wearing white pants and an apron placed the cocktails on a silver platter and whisked them away.

Velvet chairs with gold nail heads and mercury glass tables were scattered across the herringbone floor. Intimate couches crowded the outer edge of the room, full of people laughing and relaxing. They were dressed in everything from S&M garb to Victorian steampunk to elegant gowns. A band, consisting of a cellist, a violinist, and a pianist, played a vaguely familiar tune. It was like pirates and vampires in the middle of a Victorian rock concert. It felt dark and dangerous. And intoxicatingly sexy.

My initial dread flickered with a hint of fear, and though the temperature was cool, sweat steamed under my curls. I was out of my depth.

Pops of the Fum red hair and the light skin of the Fie stood out amongst the crowd. I was curious as to why they were here. And a bit nervous. After all, there were giants trying to kill me. Couldn't they wait their turn?

Liz and Grant faded into the background as Josha escorted me across the floor. Along the way, he lightly brushed hands with some of his friends but didn't stop to visit. He offered me a spot on the love seat nearest the stage.

A server placed a burgundy drink on the end table next to me. Smoke whirled from the crystal glass.

Josha leaned over and placed a hand on my arm. "Drink slowly," he cautioned, his diamond-studded lip piercings sparkling under the candlelight. "So, what do you think?" he asked me over the haunting melody.

"Not what I expected. But I'm not sure I had a clear vision of expectations either. Do you guys do this all the time?" I rubbed the crimson armrest with my fingers, making designs on the velvet.

"No, only for special occasions."

"What's the occasion?"

He fluttered his lashes. "You."

I heaved out a slow breath of resolve. "Where's Trent?"

"You'll see soon enough."

I took a tentative sip of my drink, expecting it to be warm since it was smoking, but instead, it was so cold it almost burned. If pleasure and regret had a flavor, this would be it.

There were notes of cinnamon and clove, a hint of sweetness —perhaps honey—but underneath the flavor was something bitter. Not unpleasant, just unusual. I set it down before I drank the entire thing. With everyone *trying* not to stare at me —but not succeeding—I could've used some liquid courage, but I took heed of Josha's earlier warning. Plus, drinking too much got me into this whole mess in the first place.

White fog rolled under the velvet drapes and spiraled upward as they slowly parted. The cacophony of noise faded as the cello hit the first long note. My heart leapt with recognition. It was one of my mother's favorites—"Wicked Game" by Chris Issac. Distance wise, I was farther away from them than ever, but, when I was crowned queen, I vowed to remedy that.

A deep voice I recognized crooned the first verse, pulling me away from my thoughts. Trent stepped out of the mist onto the middle of the stage.

His eyes, lined with smudged black coal, glowed emerald green as if they'd been lit from within. He wore black leather pants, boots, and thick silver cuffs around his wrists. Two identical tattoos of sea serpents circled his large biceps and spread over his chest. Loose dreads hung almost to his pierced nipples. His smooth, hairless stomach was etched like that of a Greek god—Poseidon, if I had to guess.

Goosebumps peppered my entire body when he hit the chorus and stepped down from the stage. If sex, drugs, and rock and roll had a definition, it was stalking toward me with a predatory gaze. He crouched in front of me, one hand on my bare thigh, and sang the second verse.

He squeezed my knee before rising to finish the song as he wove through the crowd. They were all mesmerized by his every move. When he was done, the audience screamed and hollered.

"Thank you," he said. "But from here on out, I'm going to let the band take over. Tonight, I plan on showing a friend a *very* good time. Maybe give her a reason to stick around." He glanced at me and winked.

People cheered and catcalled. I took it as a good sign—maybe the giants attending this party didn't want me dead.

# CHAPTER
# TWENTY-SIX

T rent plopped down on the love seat between me and Josha, throwing a warm arm over each of us. He smelled like smoky coconut, citrus, and rum.

"Wow. That was incredible. Your voice gave me chills." I rubbed my arms.

He dipped his chin. "Thank you. I enjoy it."

"I know the song." As I thought of the lyrics, Raiden's face popped into my head uninvited. Grief twisted, and I swallowed a big sip of my drink. A warm numbness spread pleasantly from my stomach to my extremities.

He cocked his head. "You do? It's kind of old, isn't it?"

I shrugged. The song was like an anthem for my relationship with Raiden. I took another sip of my drink. The taste was growing on me. "Yeah, maybe. But my mom was a fan."

He unclasped his arm from Josha's shoulder and gently tipped my face up with a finger. "Well, your mom has excellent taste."

A server balancing on impossibly tall platform shoes

swept over and handed Trent a smoke-swirling drink. She bent over, her cleavage and tight curls bouncing, and placed a red-lipstick kiss on the side of his cheek.

"Thanks, love," he said. He downed the entire cocktail and handed the glass back to her.

Trent pointed to the dance floor with his thumb. "You want to dance?" he asked.

"Uh, sure?" I said like it was a question. I really didn't want to dance in front of a crowd of giants. They weren't paying attention now, but they would be in a second. It seemed as if everyone in the room had one eye or ear on Trent, like he was true north. Thinking about it, I could have said the same thing about Kai.

Trent helped me up, pressing his palm low on my waist as he directed me toward the dance floor. Once there, he took my hand and swirled me onto the obsidian surface. "You look spectacular," he said as he caught me on the way back. He pulled me in close and effortlessly led me around the floor.

"Thanks," I said, but I didn't mean it. I felt like a rock amongst a sea of gems.

"No really, you're quite a stunning creature."

Heat crept up my skin. I wasn't comfortable with compliments.

"And your hair, it's the color of fresh blood." He pulled gently on a loose strand and twisted the curl around his finger before he let it spring back. He licked his lips. The heat in his eyes made me nervous.

"Yup." I smiled tightly.

He tossed back his head and laughed, giving me a glimmer of a tongue piercing. "I can see you're not one to be won over with flattery. How refreshing. But what I said, it's true whether you like it or not."

When the song ended, we made our way through the growing crowd back to the couch. Just as we sat down, a server placed a drink in my hand.

Trent grabbed my glass with my hand still attached and took a sip. "Yup, it's safe." His lashes were long but tipped blond at the ends as if he spent ample time outside in the sun and salt water.

"Do you guys ever dock this boat and live on land?" I asked.

"Not really. We crave the feel of the ocean. Though we do moor the ship in coves often. Most of us enjoy surfing and exploring the reefs, but we always sleep on the ship. Some of the creatures out here are dangerous. We make monthly stops at the capital to get fresh water and restock, but for the most part, we're self-sufficient. We have a large garden, big enough to supplement what we buy from the Fee. It covers an entire floor. It's quite impressive. I'd love to show you. Maybe tomorrow afternoon depending on how we feel." He finished his drink.

"How many live on this ship?"

"There are about a thousand of us left. We used to have three ships, but now we only need one. As I'm sure you've heard our deaths outpace our births."

"Apparently, that's what I'm here for." The idea left a sour taste in my mouth. I didn't want kids. At least, I didn't want kids with Trent. I washed away the regret—and anger—by downing some more of my cocktail.

His gaze traveled over my face. "Oh, I think you're here for more than that. It'll be fun to figure out what it is, don't you think?"

"I guess."

He took my hand, intertwining his fingers with mine. "Think of it like this—it's an adventure, right? Soon, you'll be queen. You can do whatever you want, however you want, whenever you want. You'll be in charge of your own destiny. Your choices will be endless. Starting now. You get to choose whom you'll marry. Sure, it's been narrowed down to four of us—the four most eligible bachelors in the Fiefdom." He blinked deliberately, letting that fact sink in. "I'm not trying to toot my own horn, but there isn't a single woman here—and a few men—" he glanced at Josha, sitting at a table laughing with friends, "—who wouldn't trade places with you right now."

"I know," I said a bit defensively.

"But your stubborn heart still resides somewhere else, doesn't it?" He tapped the end of my nose with his finger.

I crossed my arms and bit the inside of my bottom lip.

"And where is he? I heard he left after the two of you had an argument. I bet I can guess what that squabble was about. What an idiot," he said under his breath. "But there's no way Raiden will ever share you with someone else."

I took another sip of my drink.

"It's not in his constitution. I wish it were, because I feel like that's the only way you'd accept my proposal."

"That's not true."

"It's not?" The expression on his face said he didn't believe me in the slightest.

"No. Sure, I wanted Raiden to say okay, but I knew he wouldn't. Couldn't. Whatever." I tossed the last word away with the wave of my hand. I picked up my glass and drank more. "Now I need to narrow it down to the person best suited for the job."

Trent's eyes slivered. "So you're saying that if we were to marry, I could still have Josha? And you wouldn't have a problem with it?"

I watched Josha interact with his table of friends. "No, so long as you afforded me the same privilege."

The idea of marriage without love saddened me. My parents had been beautiful role models on what love should look like. Though I knew the odds were slim, I'd always held on to the hope that someday I would have what they did. Maybe that's why I'd fallen for Raiden so quickly. I devoured romance novels. When I'd finished my mother's collection, I'd read my favorite ones again and again until the spines were broken and the pages tattered.

Even though I knew better, I finished my drink because it blocked the feelings threatening to shatter me like crystal on concrete. The waitress swept it away and quickly replaced it with another.

"Of course I would. But there's nothing that says we can't be friends—" he paused and licked his bottom lip, "—and a little more."

"Are you in love with Josha?"

A tiny frown appeared, then disappeared quickly as he shook his head. "No. But giants aren't wired like humans when it comes to many things—love being one of them. I love Josha, but no, I'm not what you would define as *in love* with him." He air-quoted the last part.

I waited for him to elaborate. "And?"

He shrugged.

"You can't say you're wired differently, then not explain."

"Okay. What would you like to know about us?" He propped his arm on the back of the couch, his fingers almost, but not quite, touching my shoulder. My skin hummed despite the lack of actual contact.

"You say humans aren't wired the same. What do you mean?"

"Huh. Where to begin?" He rubbed his forehead. "Well, for starters, have you noticed that all of the music you hear is from humans? And have you recognized any of the artwork? You see, giants can recreate, but we can't create."

He repeated what I'd already been told by Raiden and Kai, but I didn't interrupt.

"We can be taught anything, but we cannot create out of the blue. There is a big difference between learning and creating. I think that's why giants have always been fascinated with humans. Some of us are mesmerized by it, while others are intimidated and jealous because of it. I find I'm somewhere in the middle."

"Okay? What else?" I wanted new information.

"When it comes to love, it seems we are very black and white. When we're truly in love with someone, we become very possessive. It's hard to explain, but we form a particular bond with the other person. I'd say humans compare it to a soulmate. Even here, it's very rare. Some of us wait a lifetime looking for it. Others, knowing the odds aren't good, marry someone they love or at least like. Sometimes they use marriage as a business relationship. But once the blood bond is sealed, the chance of finding your soulmate is nullified. You could be standing right in front of them and you'd never know it."

"Then what are the odds?" My voice cracked, knowing I'd already found my soulmate—and knowing, that no matter how we felt, we could never be together. I took another drink, stupidly trying to numb my heart.

"The only bonded pair of the leaders are Kai's parents, Lord Cooper and Lady Sera. My parents love each other, as do Lord Dion and Lady Chantal. Lord Issac and Lady Sylvia have a business relationship. So, going by that, it looks like the chances are around twenty-five percent. Good enough that some will waste a lifetime looking for it. But bad enough that seventy-five percent will never find it."

"That's sad," I said. But the alcohol had finally dulled some of my morose emotions.

"It is, so I'd rather talk about something more interesting. *You.*"

"Oh, don't get your hopes up. It's not like I'm able to create anything either. I don't paint, I don't sing, I can't write. Do you think that's because I'm half giant?"

"No. A lot of humans are useless."

My eyes rounded, but the look on his face said he was teasing me again. I tried smacking him on his chest with the back of my hand, but he snatched it out of the air before I could make contact. He brought it to his lips and kissed it instead. They were hot, even against my warm skin. My core tightened and clenched. I mentally chastised myself at the physical reaction.

Trent gently pulled me next to him, my dress sliding easily over the velvet. "There. That's better."

I put my thumb in my mouth, chewing on a cuticle, though they looked much better after Josha had pampered me with a manicure. Trent grabbed my hand out of my mouth and held on so I couldn't destroy them further, then proceeded to ask me a million questions—everything from how we survived, to who I lived with, to whom I'd actually slept with. He was so open and non-judgmental, he was easy to talk to. During the conversation, I managed to plow through another drink. I wasn't drunk, just warm and tingly. I was of the mindset that the first bad decision was an accident, while the second was a choice. But really, what could go wrong? I'd already signed the contract.

"So you've only had sex with a human?"

"Yup."

"Well, I'll be more than happy to remedy that for you." He slid his hand to my thigh, tracing over my leg with a finger. Bolts of electricity shot deep in my groin. My nipples contracted. The muscles in Trent's jaw flexed.

His voice was husky when he said, "I'm not going to lie. The things going through my mind are wicked."

I swallowed. The things going through my mind were also wicked, but I couldn't go that far with him unless I wanted to sleep with all of the First-Born sons. I would never do that to Tee.

But the temptation to anesthetize the weeping, gaping wound in my heart, in my very soul, was overwhelming. I needed to forget.

Forget that Raiden had left me.

Forget that no matter how much I loved him, he'd never be mine.

Forget that I had made a deal to save my people.

Forget that if I ran away with Raiden, I would die, and my friends would be left on their own in this dangerous world.

So, for a small window of time, I wanted to pretend that I was a regular girl and Trent was a regular guy. Besides, I reasoned, it was smart to sample some of the merchandise. Right?

# CHAPTER
# TWENTY-SEVEN

A s the server passed by, she set another drink beside me. I downed the entire thing and pushed it away. The liquid cooled my throat and warmed my stomach.

"Hey, go easy on those. We have all night," Trent chuckled.

"Whatever." I dismissed his advice. It wasn't like I'd ever suffered from a hangover. Now knowing that I was half giant, that probably explained why. I stood up and held out a hand.

"Living life dangerously, I see." He grabbed it, and I pulled him off the swanky couch. With a flick of his wrist, about half of the candles atop the chandelier mysteriously extinguished, black smoke swirling from the wicks. My eyes bounced between the candles and Trent with a fair amount of *WTF*.

He laughed. "The Foe have an affinity for water. That includes humidity in the air."

"Oh." I nodded like I understood. "I feel like I need to take a 101 class on giants."

"Probably wouldn't be a bad idea. But for now, I'll fill you in on what I can." He clasped my elbow as we wove our way onto the dance floor.

"We control water, the Fie are air, the Fee are earth, and the Fum are fire."

*Water. Air. Earth. Fire. Got it.*

"We all have an affinity with electricity. Our bodies produce more energy than humans, and we learned how to harness it eons ago."

The closer we got to the music, the louder it became. More and more bodies had piled onto the shiny floor, making conversation nearly impossible. The music changed to something techno-punk with perhaps a dash of rap or R & B. I wasn't sure. Music wasn't my thing. It didn't matter, though, because the beat pulsed inside of me, making it easy to keep the rhythm. Trent stepped in close, our bodies touching. He wrapped one hand just shy of my butt, and the other rose into the air. I threw caution to the wind and joined him. The alcohol, having been given a few minutes to hit my bloodstream, dulled my ability to care what others thought, and at the same time, heightened my awareness of those around me. I kept my eyes closed but could feel bodies beside me, behind me, everywhere. Soon, I wasn't only dancing with Trent but with a tall, beautiful woman with cobalt eyes, then a gorgeous bald man with pierced dimples and eyes so pale green they were almost mint, joined in. When the song ended, they disappeared, only to be replaced by two others equally beautiful. The guy, with braided cornrows, placed his hands low on my hips and pulled me in tight. Normally, that might've bothered me, but

I'd lost my basket of *give-a-shits* somewhere along the way. And I was in no hurry to find them. Trent wrapped his arms around my shoulders from behind and pressed his entire body to mine. Through the sheer dress, I could feel his leather pants and bare muscled chest.

"Damn, she does smell good," the other guy said to Trent over the music.

"Right?" Trent tightened his grip. He buried his face into the side of my neck and kissed and nibbled his way to my ear. I was already warm, but a throbbing inferno spread to my nether regions.

The stranger leaned into the other side of my neck and repeated the gesture. Though I'd never met him—heck, I didn't even know his name—my body responded anyway. Tingles, almost painful, like tiny volts of electricity, hardened my nipples.

He lifted his head away and growled. "Dude, how can you stand this? Her scent is a fucking aphrodisiac."

He wasn't talking to me, but I didn't care. All I cared about was the pounding of the music and the pounding of my blood.

"Unique, I know," Trent answered.

As the next song started, the guy drifted away. The woman who'd been sitting at the table earlier with Josha slid in front of me. She smelled like a tropical drink. She wasn't quite as tall as the others because she was barefoot. She lifted my chin with a finger and rubbed her long thumbnail over my bottom lip. Her eyes were a brilliant turquoise framed with ebony lashes and perfect eyebrows. I'd never kissed a woman before, never even thought about it, but staring at her lovely coral lips, I wondered how they felt. I parted my lips and wrapped a hand underneath her waist-long spirals as I gently pulled her to me. She bent her head and her mouth met mine. She tasted as good as she looked —like sugar and fruit. Trent wrapped his arms around her back and pulled her closer, her full breasts rubbing against mine. I moaned. Trent gently bit the side of my neck and my moan turned to a whimper. I was hesitant to let her go when the next song began.

"Until we meet again," she whispered. She kissed her fingers and then pressed them to my lips before she danced away.

I lifted the hair off the back of my neck to cool down. "Who was that?" I asked Trent.

He spun me around. "Bali." His eyes were glued to my mouth. "My turn," he said.

There was nothing shy or hesitant about his kiss. His tongue tangled with mine, his piercing strange but intoxicating. I dug my fingers into his shoulder blades. The hard length of him pressed against my stomach. He knotted his fingers through my hair and pulled my head back, giving him access to my throat. He licked his way from my collarbone to my earlobe, where he whispered, "Do you want to go somewhere private?"

"Yes," I said breathlessly, almost as if my voice belonged to someone else. Someone who didn't care. *Yes, I did.*

"Don't let go." He dragged me through the sweating, undulating mob. Along the way, people reached out and touched us, but they didn't try to stop us.

He stayed somewhat amongst the crowd as he maneuvered us toward the back of the room near the stage, not by the doors where Liz and Grant stood guard. They didn't look like they were having any fun, leaning against the wall with their arms crossed in identical fashion. Somewhere in the back of my mind, I thought I should tell them I was leaving. It was their job to protect me. But was it my problem if they weren't very good at their jobs? Raiden would've never let me out of his sight. A sliver of guilt stabbed my heart and then twisted into despair. A breath later, the ache burst into a burning rage. He'd left me—alone—when someone wanted me dead. So as far as I was concerned, he could screw himself.

I might have not really meant that, but I was doing everything possible to forget. In order to erase him from my head, I was going to have to rip my mangled heart from my chest. The thought had crossed my mind a dozen times in the last few hours. And that's what I was attempting to do.

I caught Liz's gaze for a millisecond before she looked away as if she hadn't seen us sneaking through the crowd. Trent pulled me along.

In the shadows, we slipped onto the stage behind the satin curtains. Backstage, he led me into his dressing room, complete with his name on the door with fancy gold lettering. He slammed it shut and rested against the frame.

"Whew, I think we made it without your jailers noticing."

I laughed. *But had we?* It felt good to rebel. I was safe with Trent.

I placed my palms on his dark chest and dragged my fingers downward. His breath flinched as I tweaked his nipple rings.

A smile, slightly wicked, curled on his lips. He picked me up and draped me over his shoulder, one hand holding my butt. I squealed before laughing.

"I can walk, you know," I said into the hot skin of his muscled back.

"Yeah, but I can get you there faster by carrying you."

"And where is it we're going?"

"My room." He paused. "Any objections?"

"Nope."

He opened a door at the back of his dressing room, then shut it behind us. The darkness was absolute. I couldn't see two inches in front of my face. Trent held on tight as we ascended one flight of stairs to the next.

"How are you seeing anything?" My voice bounced with every step up.

"We have decent night vision."

At the top, he stopped, not even breathing heavily after carrying me at least twenty flights of stairs, and gently put me down. I found the wall and leaned against it. Trent's breath swept hot on my face before I felt his lips. His hands drifted down my neck, past my shoulders, to my arms, brushing my breasts. Between the liquor and the sight deprivation, every nerve in my body flared on high alert. My pulse raced, thumping so hard I was afraid he could hear it. They obviously had far better senses than humans.

His fingers curled around the neck of my dress and he yanked, the fabric ripping apart like Velcro. Gems fell like raindrops, tinkling onto the floor. He slipped one side off my arm, then the other.

I could feel his gaze travel over my almost naked body like a static shock. Seconds passed with only the sound of the groaning and creaking of the ship.

"You're exquisite. What I wouldn't give to have an artist carve you from marble. The way your breasts curve, narrowing to your waist, then swelling into your hips. And that hair."

That was high praise coming from perfection. He'd gone

a bit far, but hey, I was in no shape to protest. Despite my four days in a volcano, I'd managed to put on some much-needed pounds.

He caught his fingers under the straps of my bra and tugged gently before he slid them off my shoulders. He kissed my collarbone, his lips like fine silk gliding over my skin before he unsnapped the front closure. I reached up and held on to the material.

"If you're not comfortable, please, just tell me. We'll stop anytime you wish. Though I'm not going to lie, I'll do what I can to tempt you." His voice lowered a note.

My bra dropped to the floor.

I heard him inhale sharply and exhale slowly.

My breasts heaved with anticipation. The fire in my groin strained. A hot tongue flicked the tip of my rock-hard nipple. I flung my head back into the wall behind me and moaned.

A scorching hand lifted the weight of my breast into his mouth. His tongue swirled and flicked and sucked. He ran a finger over the outside of my panties, where I was already wet with desire. A growl vibrated against my skin. Slowly, a hand inched under the material and a large finger slid inside me. Time ceased and all I could concentrate on was the motion—in and out—while his mouth feasted on my breasts, his hand rubbed against my clit, and his amazingly large fingers coaxed me home. I arched my back and screamed as waves of pleasure rocked my core.

Never had anything felt so good. I had suspected it would be amazing, but even the foreplay was better than the sex I'd had with Noah. Hands down, no comparison.

"You taste even better than you smell," he whispered.

"You okay?" he asked as his lips found mine. I could hear his smile even if I couldn't see him.

"Absolutely."

I ran my hands down his sides, stopping at the top of his leather pants. I traced them around until I found the button fly and unbuttoned it one by one. I kissed my way down his chiseled chest, my mouth reading his abs like braille, and slid his pants to the floor. He wasn't wearing any underwear. I skimmed my fingers over the length of him. He did not disappoint.

I knelt in front of him and placed my lips over the tip. I shouldn't have been surprised to feel the metal stud against my tongue. He groaned and dug his fingers into my hair as I took his velvety shaft deep into my throat as far as I dared and squeezed the rest of him in my hand.

I wanted to make him scream the way he'd made me scream.

Once I'd accomplished my goal, Trent lifted me up with my legs wrapped around him. I heard him tap around until he found what he was searching for—a door knob—and threw open a door and then another one. He gently laid me down on the huge four-poster bed in the middle of his room. My eyes adjusted to the soft glow of the nightlight, allowing me to see Trent fully naked. He was as beautiful as I'd pictured. And I was nowhere near done with him—nor was he done with me from the looks of his huge erection.

"I'm thirsty. Do you have anything to drink?"

He walked barefoot over to a fridge and pulled out a bottle of something, taking a deep swig before handing me the bottle.

I didn't even ask what it was. I didn't care.

Tiny bubbles, tasting strongly of strawberries, fizzled down my parched throat as I drank the whole thing.

"Whoa, that's pretty strong. Go easy."

"Too late." I set it down on the side table.

He chuckled. "Still living dangerously, I see."

"No regrets," I lied. I tossed my arms over my head as I laid back. The comforter was soft and cool against my over-heated skin.

Trent stood at the foot of the bed. "Good to know." He slowly crawled on top of me, his hips directly above mine, his hard penis resting on my stomach.

My head swirled around, pleasantly muddying my thoughts.

"You still going to tell me when to stop."

"Who said we're going to stop?" I reached down and cupped my breasts, my thumbs flicking my already-taut nipples.

His eyelids drooped heavily, momentarily masking the bright-green color. "Remember, if you sleep with me, you have to sleep with all of the First-Born sons," he gently reminded me.

It wasn't like I'd forgotten, but my body didn't give a rat's ass. I needed to forget, and this was the only solution that had presented itself.

"Do we have to tell them?" I whispered.

He shook his head. "Nope."

# TWENTY-EIGHT

T he early morning sun crested the horizon, streaming ginger light through a large porthole. Beams splashed over a watercolor painting of a mermaid with dreadlocks and an eyepatch. I collected a fistful of sheets and pulled them up over my bare breasts, the emerald green stark against my pale skin.

*Of all that was holy, what did I do?* Guilt twisted in my stomach, followed by a strangled half-sob in my chest. Garbled scenes from last night flashed through my brain, leaving me feeling like I'd cheated on Raiden, even if, in reality, I hadn't. He'd left me alone with no hope of a future together. But that didn't stop the embarrassment and shame from scorching my insides. I had only planned to sample the goods—not scarf down the entire meal.

Trent rolled over and opened his eyes. A beautiful, sleepy smile tugged his lips—until he saw my face. "Bea, what's wrong?" He turned onto his side and propped himself up with an elbow on his pillow.

"Did we . . . ?" I asked, even though I knew the answer. I'd broken the cardinal rule. We'd had sex. And if we didn't keep it a secret . . .

Slashes creased between his brows and horror painted his expression. "Please tell me you remember?" He rested his head on his hand, frustration obvious. "Please say you remember," he pleaded, his voice low and soft.

I nodded, though my memories were fuzzy.

He exhaled heavily and reached out to pull my hand from the death grip I had on the sheets. "I was afraid for a minute that you thought I'd—"

"No, I remember. I was a willing participant. No worries there. I just can't believe I was such an idiot." My chin trembled while hot tears pooled in my eyes.

"Well, now you've hurt my feelings." He sounded like he was being serious.

"No. That's not what I meant. Last night was *unbelievable*." So unbelievable that the replay in my head was making my skin tingle even as my heart chastised me like an angry mom.

"Thanks. I thought so too. I've never slept with a human before—man *or* woman. It was . . ." He blew air through his puckered lips. "Intense."

"Yeah," I said tightly.

His gaze leisurely skimmed my curves. His eyes dilated. "I'm game for round five." He scooted closer and traced his middle finger over the exposed skin on my thigh.

I pursed my lips. Physically, everything inside screamed at me to do it again. Mentally, I felt like a broken, battered little bird that had thrown itself out of the nest. Only instead of dying of guilt and shame, I would have to live with my mistake.

"What are we going to say if someone asks what happened last night?" The panic in my tone grew.

"We're going to tell them you had too much to drink and you passed out before anything happened. Besides, you'd already told me we couldn't because you didn't want to sleep with all of the First-Born sons. And to keep me in check, you said if we slept together, you wouldn't pick me. That should give the people who know me a reason why I wasn't able to seduce you. Don't you worry. I've got all the bases covered." His grin held an unmistakable air of cockiness.

I waited for my brain to process his words, but I was having trouble concentrating due to his touch traveling higher and higher. "Yeah, I guess that sounds plausible, on both accounts."

"Good. Now that we have *that* settled . . ." He slid his hand slowly up my leg.

I held my breath, remembering what his hands were capable of, what his mouth was capable of, what the rest of him was capable of. I shook my head like an Etch A Sketch. If Raiden really wanted me—*us*—he would've stayed. Right?

"I can't. I shouldn't have." I swallowed hard.

"Oh." He pulled his hand away and sat up. "You and Raiden. There's something deeper going on there, isn't there?"

"Not anymore," I said firmly.

"Do you want to talk about it?"

I shook my head, fearing that if I started, I wouldn't stop. Instead, I asked, "Can you give me a crash course in Giants 101? I could seriously use it."

He snaked his arm around my shoulder and slid me over for a side hug. "You bet," he sighed, sounding disappointed.

The bedroom door burst open, and I yelped as I yanked the satin sheets up to my neck.

Trent's muscles tensed and his fingers dug into the flesh of my bicep. "Mom? Dad? What in the Foe's name are you doing here?" By the pitch of his voice, his parents were the last people he'd expected to crash this party.

Though it was early, Lord Ren and Lady Mosella were flawless in their appearance. Each wore matching tunics and trousers in a bright canary yellow. I wanted to shield my eyes from the glow, but that would mean I'd have to let go of the sheet I was so desperately clinging to.

His mother's lips pressed into a flat line as if she were disappointed, but not particularly surprised. His dad slid his hands into his shimmery trousers while taking a deep breath.

Though I didn't feel like I had a hangover, my brain seemed to be processing slower than normal, and it took me a second to comprehend the situation. And the impending ramifications. Though Trent had an explanation about how and why we *didn't* sleep together, sweat pooled under my breasts and at the small of my back.

"Get out!" Trent yelled. "Now." He stood up, bare-ass naked, and pointed to the door. Hanging from the corner of his four-poster bed, he grabbed a silk robe and threw it on.

Josha stepped out from behind Lord Ren, his expression that of the spider that had eaten the fly. A knot constricted my throat. It was too late, I realized I was the fly—and I'd walked right into his web. The corner of my eye started twitching. I squeezed them shut, hoping to stop it.

"Son," Lady Mosella said, "this is not our choice. We've been ordered by the Domes, a vote of two to one."

Lord Ren grumbled under his breath and turned his head, looking behind him.

Just when I thought the situation could not deteriorate further, Lady Sylvia and her attorney, Penelope, scooted through the door, their shiny black stilettos clicking on the wood floor. Though I couldn't see my face, I was positive it had morphed from crimson to purple.

"We have to ask you and Lady Ruby if you've had sexual intercourse. With each other," Lady Mosella clarified. "And we've also been ordered to invoke the parental promise." She zoned in on Lady Sylvia, and if looks could have killed, Sylvia would've perished. "You know the consequences of lying to us once the promise has been invoked. I don't understand why this is such a big deal. So, can we hurry up and get this over with? Did the two of you have sex?" Lady Mosella repeated.

Trent turned back to me. "I'm sorry, Bea. I . . . . I never in a million years saw this coming."

Trent had promised he would stick to our lie. *We did everything except for intercourse, because if we slept together, I wouldn't pick him as my king.*

Though we'd been found in a compromising position, I tried not to fret. The sweat rolling down my back indicated my efforts were wasted.

Trent stormed over to Josha and stabbed a finger into his chest. "You did this, didn't you?"

Josha tilted his nose in the air like he was too high and mighty to answer. He straightened the dainty scarf tied around his neck and blinked pointedly, ignoring Trent.

"You thought if you could get Ruby out of the way, you could have me all to yourself again. Well, it's not going to work. Because I don't love you."

Josha's eyes rounded, his fake lashes touching his brow bone.

"And now I never will. Because from this moment, you're banished from the Foe."

The arrogance on Josha's face crashed as he reached for Trent's hand. "Trent! No!"

Trent stepped away. I sat forward, the sheets still clenched in my hands. Trent was overreacting as far as I could tell. Josha may have told Trent's parents of his suspicions—I mean, I *was* in bed with his boyfriend—but I really couldn't blame him for getting mad.

"You don't mean that!" Josha cried. "You're angry. I get it. But what I did, it was for us. You and me. Give it some time, please. You'll see." His desperation hung in the air like sour sweat in a dank bunker.

"No. You did this for yourself. Your true colors are now apparent." Trent swirled his hand around Josha. "My mom said you were a snake, I just couldn't see it. And now that I've spent some time with Ruby, I realize I harbor more feelings for her in only five days than I have for you after an entire year." Trent turned toward his parents and nodded his head once before he said, "Lord Ren, Lady Mosella—I stand by my decision to banish Josha from the Foe."

Tears streamed down Josha's face, streaks of eyeliner ruining his flawless complexion. His hands trembled. "You'll pay!" he screamed at me before he fled the room.

*For what?* Nobody could prove a thing.

Trent looked at me. "Ruby, please forgive me." Then he addressed his parents. "To answer your question, yes, Ruby and I had sex."

My stomach shot into my throat and twisted, cutting off my ability to breathe. Betrayal mule-kicked my heart, sending it spinning. Not waiting to hear the rest, I wound the sheet around my chest, bolted to the bathroom, opened the door, and locked it behind me.

Trent's leather pants and boots, along with the destroyed remnants of my dress, were scattered on the stone floor. Apparently, the secret door we'd come through last night led to the bathroom. I'd been too busy to notice. Nausea churned and my head spun. I sat down on the edge of the tub, propped my elbows on my knees, and rested my face in my trembling hands.

*What did I do?* Tee would never forgive me. Could I blame her?

I was swearing off alcohol permanently. Every time I drank, I ended up in a heap of trouble. And the only person I could blame was myself. Trent had warned me. Even the bastard Josha had warned me. *But no.* I'd ignored them. I was so stupid that I hadn't learned my lesson the first time. I wasn't fit to be a friend, let alone a queen. Tears streamed down my cheeks and vomit burned the back of my throat.

"Bea," said Trent after gently knocking on the door.

My jaw quivered as I gnawed on a fingernail.

"Bea, I know you're mad, but let me explain." He tried the doorknob, but I refused to unlock it, needing a few minutes alone to wallow in self-pity before I was willing to talk.

"Okay. I get it. But I know you can hear me. And knowing how little you know about us, let me explain to you what just happened. A crash course in Giant 101, even if it's a little late."

It seemed like he was waiting for me to acknowledge him, but I didn't.

"Anyway, I can't lie to my parents after they invoke the

parental promise. And never—not once in my entire life— have my parents ever invoked the promise. I had no reason to think they'd start now. And they wouldn't have if Josha hadn't sent messages to all of the lords and ladies. A lover scorned. I should've known better." Fists pounded on the door. "Damn it! If I'd lied, I'd have lost the title of First-Born son and my parents would have lost their standing as well. I would've lied if it was just my title at stake, but I couldn't sacrifice all that my parents have done. I'm so sorry. I want you to know that. I had no intention of telling anyone. I really didn't. And now . . ." He paused for a long minute. I heard his head lightly thump against the door. "And now, I'm afraid I've lost you. I meant what I said out there. I've developed more feelings for you in the last five days than being with Josha for a year. You fascinate me. And to be honest, you scare me a bit too."

I wasn't sure how I could possibly scare him, but I didn't ask. I was afraid that if I opened my mouth to talk, sobs would break free.

"I'm going to wait right here. Even if you never forgive me, I owe you a face-to-face apology. Please," he whispered.

I stood up and let go of the sheet, the green satin slith- ering to the stone floor. My feet tingled from lack of blood flow. Pinpricks had me limping as I grabbed the cotton robe hanging next to the shower. I slipped it over my shoulders and tied the belt around my waist, its length dragging on the floor.

If Trent had really planned to keep our secret, then I owed him a conversation. How was he to know Josha would stab him in the back? Heck, I'd thought Josha was one of the nicest, sincerest people I'd ever met. He'd fooled me.

Seconds before opening the door, I caught a glimpse of someone wearing a hooded cape reflected in the bathroom mirror. I inhaled to scream, but it was too late. An electrical shock zapped the back of my head, and I fell to the floor as I passed out.

# CHAPTER
# TWENTY-NINE

My eyes flew open upon impact.

I inhaled sharply to catch the air that had been knocked from my chest. Mistake. Icy waters choked me as they dragged me under. Panic delved its ugly claws into my mind. My arms thrashed about, unaware of what exactly was happening. I couldn't breathe. I couldn't see.

My dad had always said, "Fear will keep you alive, but panic will kill you."

I forced my muscles to relax and willed my mind to stop. I focused, noticing where sunbeams penetrated the deep-blue water. I kicked my legs and paddled toward the light.

Agony engulfed my lungs, screaming at me to breathe. I broke the surface at the same time my body won the argument to inhale. Saltwater spewed violently into my mouth and nose, burning the mucous membranes. I hacked and coughed, all the while trying to stay afloat. My swimming skills were mediocre at best.

After I expelled most of the liquid from my lungs, I frantically scanned the area while treading water. *Those bastards,* I thought as I caught a glimpse of billowing white sails as the ship disappeared over the horizon, leaving me alone with nothing but miles of vast blue ocean.

I floated on my back to reserve energy, hoping I was harder to kill here than on Earth.

Time soon became meaningless as the sun leisurely traversed the periwinkle sky. Through its arc, it scorched my pale skin. Over the mindless hours, instead of focusing on my fear, I occupied myself by belittling and berating my character. I was no one's savior. I was a useless harlot, lacking the ability to make wise choices. At that moment, I couldn't have hated myself more. I probably deserved the punishment someone had doled out, but I still wasn't ready to die.

Dark-gray clouds lined with pale pink moved in sometime during the late afternoon and the sky morphed to purple. If I hadn't been stranded in the middle of the ocean, I might've thought it was beautiful. Until the wind picked up. Whitecaps tossed me up, then let me down like a roller coaster. My stomach churned from swallowing the briny saltwater that splashed into my face. The robe sloshed in the angry waves but I refused to let it go. It was my only protection against the sun.

I flipped over, because if I didn't, I was sure to drown. From this new angle, the waves were like little tsunamis, hovering for a long moment in the air before crashing down. Panic hummed beneath my skin, and for the first time, I thought I might die.

Pain exploded as something bashed me in the back of my head. I sank under but looked up, hoping whatever it was, it wasn't alive. Spindly branches attached to a log shone black against the sky. Kicking hard and reaching out, my fingers grabbed the tail end of the mangled roots. I fought my way to the surface and held on for dear life. I rested for a few minutes before loosening the robe belt and tying myself to the log.

Lighting flashed in the sky, and once the sun finally set, the temperature plummeted. Shivering took hold, my teeth chattering loudly. Soon, my eyelids drooped closed, and I surrendered to the darkness.

I WOKE up on the sand, still draped over the log with water sloshing over my legs and feet. It rolled to and fro every time the surf washed up on the beach like rocking a baby.

Spitting the salty strands of hair out of my mouth, I untied myself from the log. My exhausted muscles strained as I pulled it all the way on shore, not wanting to let it go. It had, after all, saved my life. Relief surged as I bit down on a dry sob. I could celebrate my survival later.

I hung the wet robe over a branch to dry and sat down on the sand to gain insight on the situation. My bleary eyes, tired and heavy, stared vacantly as the vista transformed from bronze to gold. Dawn bloomed gently over the land. The crescent-shaped beach, rocky on one side and black sand on the other, was protected by a wall of gnarly bushes with six-inch thorns and tall trees.

Once my limbs were rested, I got up and peered into the thicket behind me, but there was no way I was venturing in until the sun was higher in the sky. I listened but heard nothing other than the gentle waves lapping on the shore and the wind swishing through the boughs.

The sandy beach was as beautiful as it was useless, so I explored the tide pools on the other side for possible food sources. Small silver fish darted into the shadows, wicked-looking urchins with black spikes languished on the clear bottom, and a few colorful starfish with a plethora of legs stuck to the edges. I tiptoed carefully over the sharp volcanic rocks and around the corner. A small cave hollowed into a sheer cliff face sat far away from the shoreline. It was dry and uninhabited as far as I could tell.

I stood inside the shaded opening and stared longingly at the ocean. I tried swallowing but my throat was parched. *"Water, water everywhere, but not a drop to drink."* While I might have been part giant, I was pretty sure I could still die of thirst.

Desperate for potable water, I shook the sand out of the damp robe and put it back on. I packed some small rocks in the pockets and found a large stick in case I needed to defend myself.

The stillness at the jungle's edge made my instincts balk, but I had no choice. My lips cracked and bled with the slightest twitch and my cheeks were hot and tight from the sunburn. I staggered on a trail through the brush, hoping it would lead me to a creek, praying the eerie silence wasn't because a predator was lurking in its dark recesses.

I tripped over an exposed tree root and skewered my shoulder on a six-inch thorn. Its razor-sharp edge sliced through the robe and my skin as if it were butter. I cussed loudly as I yanked it out, blood staining the would-be dagger and soaking into the white terrycloth. I snapped it off the branch and stuck it in my pocket. Dehydration was making me careless. At home, that mistake might've cost me my life. But besides a slight sting, the thorn didn't seem to contain any poison. The wound didn't go numb or tingly. Both good signs.

A faint gurgling from ahead propelled me onward, directly into the path of a small creek. I fell to my knees, buried my face into the clear stream, and gulped. I drank so much that thirty seconds later, I projectile vomited. My throat, already sore from salt water inhalation, spasmed and burned like a mother. I gave it a minute, then drank slowly, tiny scoops at a time.

A few feet away, the creek flowed into a large pool. The reflection of massive trees, foliage too green to be real, shimmered over the slow-moving surface. I crawled to the side, leaving my robe behind, and slid feet first into the icy bath. I hissed at the cold, but once I was submerged, it was comfortable. I flinched as I cleaned my wound, thinking what I wouldn't give for a nice shower or a glorious waterfall. I leaned my head back, prepared to rinse my hair, only to have a deluge pour down my face. I sputtered and twisted around, rubbing my eyes as I blinked sharply. A wall of water rose from the surface of the creek and rained down like a showerhead made from nothing but air. I slowly backed away and crawled out of the creek. The illusion crashed as if it had never been there.

I shook my head and thought, *Whatever*. A side effect of dehydration was confusion. I slipped on my discarded robe, and along the way back to the cave, I scouted for dry wood.

High-pitched, tinny laughter floated in the breeze. Whipping around, my ear cocked toward the sound. I froze as the underbrush vibrated. What kindling I'd managed to find, I piled on one arm and backed up slowly until my feet sunk into the hot sand. I reached into my pocket and pulled out a rock, throwing it hard into the jungle. Noise, like bursts of static, fluttered from one location to the next.

A creature, around three feet high walking on two legs, stepped out of the bushes. It had neon-blue skin and splayed fins where its ears should be. It growled, exposing tiny black fangs. I retreated and carefully made my way to the cave. Reaching the entrance, I turned to find at least ten of them stalking me. I did a quick dodge and fake, and they scattered quickly, only to group back together like a school of fish.

I dropped the wood and aimed a few more rocks. A scream, like nails on a chalkboard, burst from the direct hits. They backed off but didn't leave. Their little heads swung like pendulums but their beady black eyes never left my face.

Most creatures were afraid of fire, and I hoped these were no different because I was running out of rocks.

I crouched down and rolled a branch vigorously against a larger piece of wood. Fire-making had always been my strong suit. I could coax a flame from damp tinder on a rainy night. The Fum were probably my direct relatives. My mom was a redhead with brown eyes, though my dad had black hair and blue eyes. His skin had taken on a beautiful golden glow in the summer, which meant he could belong to the Fee, Fie, or Foe.

A curl of smoke wafted from the friction and caught fire a moment later. I gently blew on the ember, keeping an eye on the creatures skulking closer. When they got too close, I threw my hands in the air and roared. They jumped. Skittish little things, but ballsy.

Once the fire was going, they backed off, whispering to one another before they disappeared.

I plopped down on the sand, not ready to succumb to relief just yet, and planned on what to do after my wood supply ran out. I only had five logs, six rocks, and a thorn.

My stomach growled. If I could just hit one of them hard enough to kill it, I could roast it over the fire. I was sure I'd eaten worse. Desperation and starvation would do that to a person.

Movement from the edge of the cave caught my attention. They were back, their cheeks bulging. Coordinated, they shot water out of their mouths like fish fountains, straight at my fire. I palmed two rocks and rushed forward before they extinguished my hard work.

"Cowards!" I yelled with my fist raised.

One cocked his head, its voice like an unclear static radio. "Princess," it said, picking something out of its teeth with a shiny black talon. Pale-blue light spilled through the webbing on his fingers. The others stepped forward.

My tongue weighed thick, jumbling the words as I shouted for them to leave. I stumbled behind what was left of the fire in a desperate attempt to keep the creatures at bay. I tossed my final log onto the flames, sparks flying. My eyes tracked the red-orange hues of the sparks as they faded in and out. It was as if I were drunk or hallucinating, and they'd magically transformed into lightning bugs. I reached out with a heavy hand to see if I could touch them.

"Princess," another repeated, startling me. Somehow, I'd forgotten they were there.

A different one with pink fin ears broke out into a song from the movie *The Little Mermaid*.

*Strange.*

I shook my head and slapped my face, forcing myself to concentrate. Sweat poured from my brow. But the tune was catchy, and I found myself bopping to the beat. Feeling uncharacteristically uninhibited, I broke out my best moves. When the creature finished singing, the rest applauded. Apparently, I had mad skills on the dance floor. I bowed, one hand under my waist, the other straight out to my side like the starlet I was.

They introduced themselves all using familiar dwarf names from the movie *Snow White*.

Their little fin ears perked up. "Do another!" they chanted.

My head swam with euphoria. I'd never felt this free. This alive.

I danced madly as they sang the soundtrack from *The Phantom of the Opera*, where I twirled over the sand using my robe as a cape and my hand as a mask.

I was so impressed. They knew every word of every song. While I wasn't a music buff when it came to actual songs, I was a huge fan of musicals.

Tee often made fun of me.

Soon, I started singing along and acting out the scenes using the driftwood that had saved my life as my partner. The little sea creatures jumped up and down and applauded. Their enthusiasm was invigorating.

Without their prompting, I broke into my own rendition of my absolute favorite musical—*Beauty and the Beast*. I had been fascinated with the beast the first time I saw the animated cartoon, half in love when I watched the live-action movie, and positively in love with him after the live version. Which, not so strangely, made sense.

As I leapt and twirled, a large black horse with wings landed on the beach, interrupting the chorus. Sand flew everywhere as Raiden jumped from his back before Arnold came to a complete stop. I coughed and sputtered, prepared to whoop Raiden's ass. How dare he interrupt my award-winning performance?

I tossed my hair over my shoulder and stomped through the sand dramatically, stopping in front of Arnold.

"Bea-bea, what have you gotten yourself into?" was the last thing I heard before I crumpled to the ground.

# CHAPTER
# THIRTY

I dug my fingers into the black sand as I vomited again and again. Yellow bile dangled from my lips.

"Bea, what is this wound from? I need to know." Raiden shook my good shoulder.

I couldn't answer him as I dry-heaved, so I reached inside the robe pocket—though I didn't remember putting it back on—and dropped the thorn that had stabbed me.

"Shit! Shit! Shit! That's a thornberry. You should be dead! Do you know how long ago it happened?"

I lifted my wrist, looked at my nonexistent watch, and flipped him off. How was I supposed to know?

My little friends waved from a distance. I managed a weak smile and a wave before I dry-heaved again. Blood dripped from my lips, darkening the sand.

"Fuck! Fuck! Fuck!" he said, each with a different inflection.

"Water," I whispered, even though I knew it wouldn't stay down. But throwing up water was easier than blood.

"Water isn't going to help."

My arms collapsed. I flopped to the ground, not caring that I was lying in filth.

Raiden scooped me up and carried me to the cave. My head lolled back. From my upside-down position, I could see that my fire was dead. Not even a curl of smoke rose from the ashes.

He sat down and leaned against the cave wall with me still in his arms.

"Water," I whispered again, more insistent this time.

"How do you get yourself into these situations?"

I stared up at the bottom of his chin. He hadn't shaved in at least a week. Even like this, he was the sexiest thing I'd ever seen. And probably the last thing I would ever see. There were worse ways to die.

"I love you," I slurred, knowing he wasn't really there. Or if he was, at that point, I was dying and I had nothing left to lose.

"No, no, no!" Raiden slapped my face. "Please let this work," he said with a strangled voice. He sat me up higher in his arms and sliced his teeth over his wrist. He shoved his bleeding skin to my mouth, but I turned my head away. I wanted water.

"Bea, just fucking drink."

He held my head and didn't give me a choice. Once some of the warm, salty blood slid down my throat, I didn't care if it wasn't water. Liquid was liquid. I latched my lips to his wrist and sucked.

Every muscle in his body tensed and he groaned in pain. Not wanting to hurt him, I stopped and looked up.

"No, keep going," he said, both his voice and face were strained.

I shook my head. If he could just get me some water.

He held my face to his wrist and forced me to drink more. His breathing became heavy and labored until finally, he'd had enough and pushed me off his lap. He fled from the cave as I nodded off to sleep.

WHEN I WOKE UP NEXT, Raiden was sitting in the sand, leaned up against the wall of the cave with his eyes closed. Light and shadow flickered over his cheeks from the dancing flames of the fire.

The muscles around my stomach protested violently as I sat up. I looked down to find I was dressed in a long-sleeved shirt and rolled-up pants with rope as a belt. The vomit had been washed from my hair.

"Hey, you're awake," Raiden said, opening his eyes but avoiding my gaze. He almost seemed shy, hesitant.

"Yeah. What in all that's holy happened? How long was I out? And where are my friends?" I bombarded him with questions.

Raiden watched me warily. "Ah, probably no more than a day, or you'd be dead. And what friends?" He glanced around the cave.

"You know, those little blue creatures with the funny ears." I splayed my hands on either side of my head and wiggled my fingers.

He shook his head. "There's no one here but us."

"Yes, there are," I insisted. "They spent the entire day with me."

"Bea, I hate to tell you this, but you were hallucinating. Your little friends don't exist. You were stabbed by a thornberry plant. You should be dead. You're half human. Though to be honest, I'm starting to question that. You survived a volcano, a day in our ocean, and a substance so toxic, it's one of the only things that can kill a giant."

I frowned, saddened to hear the little creatures were hallucinations. "So how about you tell me what happened then?" I snapped.

"You first." He got up and handed me a canteen of water.

My cheeks started to burn, remembering the last thing I'd said. And the last thing I'd drank. Why did it feel personal? Intimate? Something that couldn't be taken back.

Where was I supposed to begin? This was going to be the world's most awkward conversation. My cheeks, already sunburnt, blazed.

"Come on, Bea, out with it."

I narrowed my eyes. "Someone threw me off the ship."

"Uh-huh. I gathered that. How about you start right after I left?" He sat across from me and submerged his bare toes in the soft, dry sand.

I crossed my arms over my chest as if I could physically hold myself together and stared at the crumbling wall. He waited.

"I wanted to talk to you. I *needed* to talk to you. I didn't like the way we left things. It felt wrong. But you ran. Again."

He licked his lips and shifted uncomfortably at my harsh tone.

"Josha was nice to me. Helped me get ready for the evening." I bit the inside of my cheek, attempting to contain my hurt. I thought I'd found my first *giant* friend. How stupid was I? On a scale, I was damn near at the top. "They threw a party. I danced. I drank. I did everything I could to forget about you." I stared at Raiden's face, wanting to see his reaction. "You know, Trent's a way better guy than I gave him credit for. After we slept together—"

"*You what?*" Raiden sprung up from the sand and backed slowly out of the cave with clenched fists. The veins along his roped forearms bulged.

Sometimes my redheaded temper liked to aggravate situations, and I lashed out knowing I was being mean. But truthfully, I hated myself for what I'd done—and now he could too. Maybe it would make our separation easier.

"What? What did I say?" I yelled after him. Which wasn't a smart idea, since my throat felt like I'd been gargling rocks. I took a sip of water and waited for him to return.

"Better?" I asked when he slipped back into the cave a few minutes later. My sarcasm was hard to miss.

He ignored the question, shoved his hands in his pockets, and told me to continue.

I told him the rest but didn't go into detail. He was struggling with the abridged version as it was. He wasn't going to make it through the actual story. The guilt weighing on my shoulders threatened to drown me. I hated myself even before I even said the words. But I was mad. He'd left me all on my own to deal with monsters.

"I figured I'd better test-drive the car before I bought it. I learned a lot."

A gambit of emotions passed over his face too quickly for me to read, then settled on anger. "Are you purposely trying to make me mad?"

"Why would any of this bother you? I was under the impression you didn't care." I shrugged. I was angry too. Angrier than I'd ever been. After spending years with my brother where screaming and yelling hadn't accomplished anything, I'd learned how to be passive-aggressive with the best of them. It wasn't my favorite means of communication, but effective if I wanted to piss someone off.

"You know what, Bea? The truth is—I *don't* care about you." He turned away, his shoulders tense and his head bowed.

My bottom lip trembled. But better that I knew it now. Besides, after what I'd done, he had no reason to care.

He swirled back around, fury and pain seething behind his silver eyes. "I'm in love with you. You are my soulmate. You are my fate. Why *the fuck* do you think I'm here!?" He dug his fingers into his hair and pulled.

I stopped breathing.

"You want a lesson on giants? When we find our fate, which is rare, it's jokingly called *possession*." He paced between the cave walls, wearing a path in the sand. He stopped abruptly and leaned into my face. "Because that's what it feels like. Like you're possessed. And my fate?" He clasped his chest. "I. Can't. Have." He stood up and tossed his hands into the air, hitting the ceiling, rocks crumbling to the ground. "Correction. I could have her, but it would require me to kill my cousin because he took my spot as First-Born son when my parents disappeared."

My mouth hung open. He'd won this battle. I'd come to a gunfight with rocks, a stick, and a six-inch poisonous thorn.

Tears clouded my vision and my chin trembled. "Please slow down. I don't understand."

He paced for a few more steps then came over and crouched in front of me, his hands clasped over his knees. He flexed them a couple times, almost as if he were afraid to touch me. "Ruby Rose Walker, I love you. Completely.

Eternally. Unconditionally. I can't pinpoint the exact moment it happened, but I'm thinking somewhere between when I found you in the hallway trying to walk in those ridiculously high-heeled shoes—" he turned his head to the side, trying to hide a slight smile, "and when you gave up your freedom for the people that you love. You don't let fear stop you. Even surrounded by danger, you run headfirst into the fire. It's very frustrating, you know."

"How did you find me?"

He lifted the gray stone hanging around my neck.

"What is it?" I pressed his fingers to my chest. My heartbeat raced as if it wanted to jump into the palm of his hand.

"There's a tiny amount of my energy fused into stone. With it, I'll be able to find you anywhere. That is . . . until you blood bond to another, then it will lose its effectiveness." He cleared his throat and pulled away.

"Wait." I grabbed his hand, preventing his escape. "You can't lay all of that on me, then act as if nothing was said. Don't you want to know how *I* feel?"

He shrugged, sadness etched on his face.

"I love you too." Although, love might not have been a strong enough word for how I felt.

He closed his eyes to hide the pain, though it did nothing to mask his hurt. "Even though you slept with Trent?" The pulse in his neck jumped.

"I could ask you the same thing. How could you love me after what I did, even if it was an accident?"

His eyes slivered. "How is something like that an *accident*? Did he—" He practically snarled.

I didn't want to tell him I'd spent the entire night drinking every time I saw his face in my head. And I'd managed to get myself drunk even though I'd vowed never to do that again.

"No! No, I'm to blame. The fault lies completely with me. Do you really want to talk about it?"

He shook his head and waved his hand, brushing the problem aside for another day. Assuming I lived that long.

And because of that, I knelt and placed my cold hands on his warm scruffy cheeks. "I love you. I love you. I love you." The last part came out as a whisper and a prayer.

He leaned forward and rested his forehead against mine. A current of electricity danced on my lips. If I hadn't spent the last two hours puking, I would've kissed him. I would've laid him down on the sand and made him scream my name. But I had a feeling that would make things between us even more difficult than they already were.

"And now, what were you saying about you being a First-Born son?"

# THIRTY-ONE

After I cleaned up, we ate a small meal of crackers with cheese that he'd pulled out of Arnold's saddlebags. Raiden insisted I get something into my ravaged stomach before he told me his story.

He had been thirteen when his parents disappeared. After having been gone a little over a year, they were declared legally dead. His Aunt Sylvia and Uncle Issac assumed the position of Lady and Lord of the Fie. When Raiden and Loch turned fifteen, they'd decided Loch was more suited to be the First-Born son.

At the time, Raiden had had no interest in claiming his title, as his main objective had been finding out what happened to his parents—giants were particularly hard to kill, and two of them even more so—so he'd willingly forfeited the position to his cousin. His best friend. Now, the only way to regain his title was to challenge Loch to a duel —a duel to the death.

"And if I challenge him, I'll win. I've spent years perfecting my skills. You never know what you're going to run into out there. I had to be prepared for whatever nature threw at me." He fiddled with the sapphire ring on his finger.

"Why didn't you tell me?"

"I didn't tell you in the beginning because it didn't matter. I had no idea you'd been bound by blood to wed. And after, what difference would it have made? It would've given you false hope. And now—I didn't want to tell you because if you asked me to—" He swallowed. "I'd do it. I'd kill my own cousin to be with you." The guilt twisting his face was almost unbearable.

"I would never ask you to do that. I'd give almost anything to be with you, but not that. I love you, but if I had to kill Kevin to be with you—I couldn't do it."

"So you see my conundrum." He shifted restlessly.

"Isn't there any other way? Can't we just run away together?"

"If you don't choose a First-Born son by the agreed-upon date, you'll die. When you signed that contract in blood, it embedded a small amount of energy over your heart. If a decision has not been reached, that energy will be released, instantly stopping your heart. I can't let that happen."

I was already aware that if I didn't fulfill my end of the bargain, I would die. I just didn't know how. As deaths went, cardiac arrest sounded more pleasant than most that I'd witnessed.

I sat up on my knees, getting closer to him. "And Trent's proposition?"

He squeezed his eyes shut. "It's too late. Every cell in my body screams to possess you. If any other man touches you while I'm around, I'll kill 'em."

"And what would happen if I just take what I want, right here, right now?"

He smiled, but it was fraught with pain. "Once I have you, there's no way I'll *ever* be able to take you back. And you'll die." He lifted a hand as if he wanted to touch me but instead squeezed it into a fist and pressed it to his mouth.

"So what do we do?"

"We behave like adults and do what's best for our families. I take you to the Fee and let you continue this journey. I go back to searching for answers about what happened to my parents . . . Unless you ask me not to."

I rose and turned away, my forearm to my chest, fearing it would explode as my already-fractured heart shattered. He would do it. He would kill Loch—his own blood—if I asked him to. The knowledge catapulted me into a realm of despair, dragging me down to rock bottom. A jaded huff escaped my chest. And to think, I'd thought I'd already found rock bottom. While I'd discovered there was farther to fall, I wasn't prepared to exchange murder for my heart's desire. That price he asked of me was too high for either of us to pay. As much as I wanted him, knowing that I'd love him until the end of time, I had to let him go.

As I walked out of the cave, the ocean breeze hit my face, cooling the tears streaming over my cheeks.

He followed and stepped in front of me.

Though I knew I shouldn't, I pried his folded arms away from his chest and buried myself in his embrace. "I would never ask you to kill him to be with me."

He gripped my waist, his fingers digging in painfully. "What if I wanted you to?"

"You don't. Not really." But for one night, I could pretend

that we didn't have to sacrifice our wants for the well-being of others.

I snaked my hand up his firm chest and rested it over the beat of his heart. He stood so motionless that if it wasn't for the thumping under my palm, I might've thought he was made of stone.

I fisted his shirt and dragged him down, but he shied away.

"Please," I whimpered. "Just one last kiss." I wanted to keep the memory of him tucked inside—a picture in a locket that I could look back on for eternity.

For a split second, indecision racked his expression before he crashed into me. His lips roamed, hot and demanding, while he grabbed my hair at the base of my skull, positioning me to his best advantage.

I latched on to his shoulders and pressed myself against his firm chest.

A groan rumbled in his throat as he released my hair and slid his hands down my back, electricity following the path of his fingers. They crept lower until he cupped my butt, lifting me from the ground. I wrapped my legs around his waist.

Not breaking contact with my lips, he carried me inside the cave. The feelings and emotions battering my body were like nothing I'd ever known. I couldn't tell if I was floating or falling. All I knew was that with him, no matter the trajectory, I'd always be safe.

He knelt on the sand and sat me on the discarded bathrobe. With deft fingers, he grabbed the hem of my shirt and slipped it over my head. My breath lodged in my throat, losing myself in his silver-gray eyes, hypnotized by the swirling colors.

His gaze dropped to my naked chest. My nipples constricted deliciously under the heat of his stare, aching to be devoured. He swallowed, his Adam's apple bobbing, as if he was thinking the same thoughts. Reaching for the collar of his shirt, he tugged it off in one fluid motion.

His abs rippled as he pressed a finger to my breastbone and pushed me all the way down onto the robe. His hand slid between my breasts, grazing along my stomach, and untied the rope holding up my too-large britches. A fire threatened to consume me as he pulled the pants down my legs and tossed them aside.

I laid before him naked, throbbing with desire. My heartbeat quaked in my chest and beat violently yet exquisitely between my thighs.

He scooted alongside me and reached out hesitantly, as if the act of touching me would scald him. His fingers hovered above my stomach, tingling on my skin, though he wasn't making contact.

I grabbed his hand, guiding him to where I wanted. A strangulated groan tore from his lips as his nails dug into my skin. I held tight, refusing to let him go. Tiny wisps of blue electricity danced over our hands, arcing onto my stomach.

He clenched his eyes tightly shut.

"Are you okay?" I whispered.

He nodded.

"If you don't want to do this, we don't have to." Insecurity crept in.

He opened his eyes and stared before pulling his hand away and clenching it into a fist. "Ruby, that's not the problem." His voice was strained.

"Then what is?"

"Nothing," he lied. "I just need to touch you. Feel your skin next to mine."

I bit my bottom lip. I wasn't about to stop him.

He positioned his body between my legs and slowly leaned forward, his chest meeting my breasts, his skin blazing with heat. He laid his head into the crook of my neck, and with his every exhale, strands of my hair tickled my skin.

I caressed the back of his head.

His erection, hard and long, pressed against the inside of my thigh. Wetness spread between my legs.

His body stiffened. Afraid he was about to push away, I searched for his lips.

His mouth engulfed mine and time ceased to exist. I couldn't tell where I ended and where he began. Rays of light flared behind my closed eyes in a kaleidoscope of colors, and pleasure followed the path of my nerves, fracturing like lightning across the sky. I ran my fingers down his hard-muscled back and caught the waistband of his cargos. I tugged gently, hoping he would take my hint.

He froze and ripped his lips from mine. Icy air brushed the cool, wet skin on my mouth as I whimpered.

He shoved off of me so quickly, I didn't see him move. He slammed against the cave wall, dirt and rocks crumbling to the sand from the impact.

"Raiden?"

A growl rumbled from his throat. "Ruby, we can't do this. I thought I could control myself long enough to just have a taste of you, but I was mistaken."

I sat up and covered my breasts with his discarded shirt. "I don't want to stop."

His ragged breathing made his bare chest tremble. "We have to."

"Why?"

"Because if we do this, something inside of me will irrevocably change. Right now, I love you so much *I don't* want you to die. Your life means more to me than anything in the universe. But—" he scrubbed his face with his hands, "—if this goes further, I would sooner take you away and hold you in my arms as you die because after this—after I change —I would rather you die than see you with another man. It's how possession works. And I cannot allow that to happen."

# CHAPTER 32
## THE FEE

Arnold flew us quickly over the island, toward the home of the Fee. My soul wallowed in misery as miles passed by. Ocean turned to beaches, then to vast prairies, the pale-gold grasses undulating in the wind. In the distance, rolling hills, with random pockets of forest, grew larger.

As the trip progressed, Raiden tightened his grip, his strong arms wrapping me in a steel cage—one in which I was happy to throw away the key. It took all the willpower I had not to beg him to keep flying. Fly until we were out of reach. Fly until I died. But he would no more fly until I died than I would make him kill Loch.

My anxiety increased as we coasted lower. Arnold's hooves skated over the ground as we touched down with a soft jar.

Rounded mounds, like rabbit holes with huge wooden doors, peppered the land. A man with rich-brown hair stood outside with his hands deep in the pockets of his worn jeans.

I waited for Raiden to dismount. Instead, he clasped his arms around my entire body and rested his face in my hair. He inhaled deeply and refused to let me go. I brought his hand to my lips and tattooed a soft kiss onto his golden skin.

"Ruby, I'm afraid eternity would not be a sufficient amount of time for me to hold you. I will love you forever, Bea-bea."

I swallowed the sorrow and choked out, "If you find us a way, Raiden, one that doesn't require you or me to kill someone we love, I *will* choose you." My words stumbled under the agony. "I'll always choose you."

"I know." His breath warmed the back of my head. "And you could do worse than Adam. He's a good man, and the only son who doesn't want the position."

*But he's not you.*

"Since I'm not going to be around to protect you, I'm going to need you to take this." He pressed a dagger with a scabbard to my chest. "This blade has the power to hurt us. Keep it with you at all times. *Please.* Promise me."

"I promise."

"You know when giants make a promise, we keep them."

"So I've heard," I whispered.

He gently lowered me to the ground without dismounting.

I looked up to say something, but stopped when I saw the mixture of pain fraught with fury twisting his expression.

"Ruby, don't. Please just go."

Tears spilled down my face as I turned and walked away from the love of my life. My heart's desire. The light of my soul.

Life was a cruel mistress and so often, we were just

pawns in a larger scheme. I didn't want to go on without him. But where would that leave Kevin? And Tee? And my precious Sid? The thought of them allowed me to place one fucking foot in front of the other.

The tall man waiting for me handed me a handkerchief embroidered with delicate pink roses and green vines.

"Thank you." I wiped the tears from my face and balled the soft material in my fist.

"Let me escort you to your room," he said with a slight Gaelic-like accent.

I nodded. He didn't mention the dagger I clutched to my chest, and I didn't question who he was. If he was here to kill me, I didn't care.

He opened the door and gestured for me to go first. The inside was bright and clean. I didn't know why I'd expected rock walls and a dirt floor. Closing the door behind him, he escorted me down a hallway lined with colorful artwork, tapestries, and weapons. At the end of the hall, he opened a solid wood door with rounded corners. "These will be your accommodations for the evening."

A large bed with a dark-wood headboard sat on a plush carpet. Crackling flames from the fireplace warmed the soft taupe walls, making the room welcoming and cozy. Three large paintings of massive longhorn cows with pink flowers nestled between their ears rested above the rustic mantle.

A small measure of familiarity burrowed past the pain because I immediately felt at home. No windows, very few doors—similar to our underground bunker. Though much nicer.

"Ruby, if you don't mind, I'm going to sleep on a cot outside your door. I want you to get a good night's rest without worrying. When your dinner gets here, I'll taste it

318

first. If there's anything you need, just open the door and let me know. Okay?"

I nodded.

"We'll see you in the morning." He softly shut the door behind him.

Reluctantly, I set the dagger on the bed and stared at it until curiosity won me over. It softly hissed as I pulled it from the scabbard. The ivory hilt was warm and fit into my palm as if it had been made for me. The black blade, carved from obsidian, glowed silver in the firelight. With my free hand, I reached up and gripped the necklace he'd given me. I held on, thinking it was all I'd ever have of him.

Under the crushing weight of reality, I stumbled to the bathroom and stepped inside the shower. I slid down the natural rock and crumpled on the floor, wrapping my arms around my legs, pulling them close to keep myself from shattering. Sobs, one wave after another, rocked my shoulders as the hot water muffled the sounds and washed my tears away. How was I to do this? How was I to sleep with another, marry another, when my heart, body, and soul belonged to Raiden?

My brother had once told me, "Emotions get you killed —logic doesn't." I didn't care if I survived. But I did care if Kevin, Tee, Sid, and the others lived. And their best shot for a healthy, happy life was for me to stop whining, stop feeling sorry for myself, and logic the shit out of this miserable situation.

As I shut off the water, I locked my heart behind iron bars and threw away the key.

THE NEXT MORNING, I stuck my head outside the door.

"What are *you* doing here?" I asked Liz, my tone harsher than necessary.

She was sitting outside my door in a rocking chair knitting some kind of scarf, the pale-blue yarn pooling on the stone floor.

"Making sure no one goes into your room. I relieved Adam when I got here. We've decided that you'll have a guard twenty-four seven."

I also had my new dagger strapped under my shirt.

"That was Adam?" I was surprised the First-Born son had taken it upon himself to sleep outside my room all night. I tried recalling what he looked like, but other than tall with brown hair, I couldn't conjure his face.

"Yeah. And about the other day, I'm so sorry. I'm a terrible guard." She missed a stitch.

"No, you're not. I snuck away." Though I was pretty certain she'd seen me leave with Trent.

She stood up and stuffed her yarn into a bag. "You need to stop doing that. Can't you see someone really wants you dead?"

I ignored her. I got it. Someone wanted me dead. Probably a lot of someones.

I followed her down the hall to the dining room. A few high windows allowed natural light to pour into the space. Golden sunbeams spread along the white walls, over the hand-hewn table, and onto the rich-brown hair of the man sitting there, legs crossed, a book in one hand and a large bite of pancake with blue syrup in the other.

Too late to turn back now, he shoved the bite into his mouth and washed it down with a drink of milk. Pink tinged his cheeks. "Ruby." He stood up and wiped his hands on a napkin. "Did you sleep well?"

"Yes, fine. Thank you."

He held out a large hand. "I'm Adam."

"Bea," I clarified, and shook his hand.

"Sit. Have some breakfast. The syrup was made with fresh blueberries this morning."

My mouth watered.

I propped myself on the edge of a chair and slathered my pancakes in butter, then smothered them in syrup. I closed my eyes as I bit in, flavor bursting in my mouth. A ghost of a smile crept forth. Blueberries tasted like home. They were plentiful in Alaska, if you were stupid enough to brave the bears.

"Good, right?"

I opened my eyes and nodded. I didn't speak because I was afraid my voice would crack.

His hair curled over his ears and on the back of his neck. The color was deep, rich like the earth, as were his eyes. "It's my favorite."

I stared rudely. How had I not noticed he was this beautiful last night? Because of his natural coloring, he could almost pass for human. His skin was a lovely shade of olive, his eyes were deep set, chocolate brown, and mysterious, and his clean-shaven jawline begged to be celebrated for its masculine perfection. I wanted to puke.

"Are any of you just normal looking?" I snapped rudely.

He rubbed his hand over his lips, which were also irritatingly perfect. "I'm going to take that as a compliment." He cracked a smile, again showing off his perfect set of dimples.

I scowled and huffed. *Dimples too? Seriously?* "You do that," I mumbled.

"So how are you today? Are you game for a tour of Fee?"

"Absolutely." *But not really.* Though I'd locked away my feelings, they were just under the surface, raw and damaged, waiting to escape. Any activity that might keep my mind occupied seemed ideal.

After finishing breakfast, we started with his accommodations, which was where I was currently staying. Everything was neat and tidy. Multiple fireplaces kept the underground spaces warm in the winter, fur area rugs broke up the stone floor, and fresh, vibrantly colored flowers the size of dinner plates decorated every room, including the bathrooms.

We wandered down a hallway to a back door.

Outside, the sun blinded me. I shielded my eyes until they had a moment to adjust. In front of me was a glorious wonderland. Trees, easily twenty feet in diameter and hundreds of feet tall, spread between stone walking paths. Staircases carved into the mahogany timber curled in and around the massive trunks. Suspended walkways made of wood planks and ropes spanned from one platform to the next. Smaller vegetation, including trees with branches draping to the forest floor and colorful flowers taller than Adam, wove amongst the pathways, perfuming the air with their sweet aromas.

Birds sang from above, and brown-and-yellow-striped bees the size of my fist flitted from one blossom to the next, their flight pattern erratic like they were drunk on pollen. I dodged a coconut-sized pine cone thrown at my head by a thirty-pound squirrel hollering profanities.

"Don't mind Charlie. He doesn't like strangers."

I laughed. "No worries. I don't either." I picked up the pine cone and twirled it.

"Then you two will get along just fine."

Adam clasped his hands behind his back as we strolled through the park while he explained that the Fee lived in underground houses. His parents' abode was connected to his by a long corridor. And all of his people equally enjoyed the garden and treehouses.

We emerged from the magical forest into an immense grove teeming with fruit trees. Adam reached up high and popped a ripe purple fruit from a branch. He peeled it and handed me half. Juice, sweeter than sugar, ran down my chin. I groaned in pleasure and licked my fingers.

He waved to the workers as we passed through the orchard on our way to the barn. I met the curious glances with a timid wave of my own. Many of the men and women tipped their wide-brimmed hats that shielded them from the sun. I heard one of them whisper, "It's the Crimson Jewel!"

My instinct was to yell back—"My name is Ruby!" The constant scrutiny didn't settle well with my character, and it incensed my nature to lash out. Sometimes the pressure made it hard for my lungs to catch a full breath, leaving me exhausted and cranky. Lack of sleep, a broken heart, and the constant looking over my shoulder to see who was trying to kill me wasn't helping either.

Oversized chickens and turkeys with grand plumage scratched the dirt, hunting for bugs. I pointed toward the swans and geese gliding seamlessly over a large pond in the distance. "Do they lay golden eggs?"

He snorted as a grin formed. "They might."

Cows looking as if they partook in a daily dose of steroids meandered in lush meadows, alongside pigs, goats, and sheep.

"We keep the more dangerous creatures on the other side of the farm." He stopped and rested his arm on top of the white-slatted fence. A cow, its horns spanning at least ten feet, wandered over.

"And what, exactly, are the more dangerous creatures?" I stared at the sharp tips of her horns as Adam dodged out of the way when she pressed her ear into his hand, looking for a scratch.

"Well, the griffins, for one. They can be temperamental, and they do enjoy stealing bacon from time to time. We also keep the bulls and the boars separate. The rams aren't too bad if you remember not to turn your back to them. They're opportunists, like the goats. If you give them an opening, they'll take you down."

"Noted."

The underground accommodations and the outdoor life, both of which I was accustomed to, eased the tension binding my ribs. So far, nothing was trying to kill me.

"This is amazing." I climbed up on the fence to pet the cow. Adam pressed something into my palm and motioned for me to feed her. Her long tongue scrapped roughly on my skin. I expected it to be soft and smooth, but it was rough like a cat's.

"I love it here. I can't imagine being anywhere else. Come on, I'll show you my lab."

His lab was none other than a greenhouse where he genetically engineered plants. He combined species, as well as bred ones that were bug resistant, drought resistant, sweeter, larger, and so on.

As the overhead sun poured through the glass, butterflies in brilliant colors, lady-like bugs, and bees worked their way between plants. Tomatoes the size of basketballs dangled from green vines, and peas curled their wisps around latticework, the pods the length of my hand. Fresh herbs and flowers thrived in the hot, humid enclosure, as did many other vegetables I didn't recognize.

Adam removed his sweatshirt and offered to hang up my sweater. Underneath, he wore a white tank top that complemented the amazing color of his skin and clung to his wide chest and washboard stomach. I averted my eyes.

He tossed me a pair of gloves, slightly too large, and instructed me to deadhead the wilted flowers. I focused on the varying smells and colors, creating stories for each bloom in an attempt to occupy my mind. The greenhouse was massive and it took hours to complete my assignment. At the end of the final row, sweat dampened under my curls. I lifted them off my neck for some relief.

Adam appeared around the corner carrying a basket of bulbous tomatoes and fresh herbs over one arm. He handed me my sweater. "Here. Thanks for your help."

I tied it around my waist. "Anytime. That was actually very relaxing."

We stepped outside, the breeze cooling my sticky skin. In the distance, I could hear the lowing of cows, but there wasn't a giant in sight. "Where is everyone?"

"I asked them to make themselves scarce." He scratched his nose, leaving a trace of dirt behind.

"Why?"

"I don't know. I figured, maybe after spending time with the Fum and the Foe—they're very social—" he said like that wasn't a positive attribute, "—you could use some downtime. And having heard your background, I thought maybe you'd like some peace and quiet. If I'm wrong, please let me know."

One of the crevices in my heart might have miraculously healed in that moment. How kind of him to put in context what I was used to in order to make me comfortable. "No. You're spot-on. Thank you."

"Though I can probably only keep them at bay for so long. How about I cook you some dinner tonight and we hang out? If anyone stops by, I won't let them in."

The ever-present bind loosened again, and I sighed with relief. "That sounds amazing."

I cleaned up, showered, and changed into a pair of trousers and a green cashmere sweater. I left the dagger behind on the bedside table, figuring if I wasn't safe with Adam, I wasn't safe anywhere. I followed my nose to the kitchen, the scent of mysterious herbs leading my way. I offered to help but he shushed me onto a bar stool and slid a goblet of deep-purple liquid in front of me.

"It's grape juice," he said before I could decline.

He nudged a plate of cheese and crackers within my reach. I picked as we talked, artfully dodging the elephant in the room. He kindly acquiesced.

He was funny and shy and as comfortable in the kitchen as he was in his lab.

He dished us up a plate and set it on the small dining room table. "I kept it simple."

Roast chicken, leafy greens with fresh tomatoes, a balsamic dressing, and a side of creamy mashed potatoes. I sliced a pat of butter and squashed it into the mound, the golden liquid melting over the side. I hadn't eaten this well since I was a child.

We ate in silence, but it didn't feel uncomfortable. It was more like an extension of our camaraderie in the greenhouse.

I wiped my mouth and placed my napkin beside my clean plate. "Thank you. That was incredible."

"You're welcome. Everything we raised here on the farm." Pride clung to his words.

"You don't want to be king, do you?" I blurted.

He pressed his lips into a thin line. "How can you tell?"

"Because you belong here. It's obvious. Plus, Raiden said you wouldn't want the position, so that's why you would be perfect for it." A knife sliced through the center of my heart upon saying his name. I shoved the feeling away but the sting remained.

"He'd know. Neither of us want it. He found a way out. Now I'm thinking he's regretting that decision?" He raised both brows.

I glanced at my plate. "Does it matter?"

"I don't suppose it does."

"So if you don't want the job, I won't make you take it. Even if you do end up being the wise choice."

He ran his fingers through his dark hair, pushing it out of his eyes. "Can I let you know after our week is over?"

"Sure. I've got no problem with that."

We headed to the living room and sat on the suede couch. I slipped off my shoes and curled my legs underneath me. He threw a blanket over my lap, then crouched down and started a fire in the hearth.

"The temperature stays cool here all year long. Doesn't matter what it's doing outside."

I understood. Our bunker was cold even on the hottest days, and the same in the winter.

He regaled me with tales from the farm, and I reciprocated with my life in Alaska. After I was more comfortable with him, I decided it was time to address the elephant in the room.

The tips of my ears warmed from impending embarrassment. "So I'm sure you heard what happened with the Foe. Me and Trent . . ."

"Yeah." His eyes shifted around the room.

"I didn't mean for it to happen." I twisted the blanket in my fingers.

"Well, Trent has that effect on people."

I snorted. "I'm as much to blame."

"If you say so," he said skeptically.

"I do."

"You know, I'm not going to force you to sleep with me. I don't care what they agreed to. If I lose my status as First-Born son, so be it. Worse things have happened."

"What do you mean you'll lose your status?" I'd assumed that somehow, they would punish *me* for my faux pas, not one of the First-Born sons. This new development was concerning.

"Well, if we don't sleep together, I'll have to step down. My half-brother Leonardo will inherit my title because I don't yet have kids."

"I don't want that to happen," I said.

"And I don't want to sleep with someone who isn't willing."

I allowed my eyes to drink in his appearance. "I'm sure that's never been a problem."

"Yeah, well, despite what you may think, I'm not a big hit with the ladies." He crossed his legs.

I quirked a brow. *Yeah, right.*

"Something about me caring more for my job than

women. Or at least that's the rumor. And it's kind of true. I've yet to meet a girl that's captured my attention."

"And the boys?"

A hearty laugh exploded from his chest, flashing his perfect dimples. "I'm not Trent. So, if at any time you find yourself interested," he held his hands up innocently, "don't hesitate to say so. I'm more than willing, but I won't make the first move. I don't want you to feel pressured."

I didn't know what to say. He was prepared to lose his title before he forced me to sleep with him even though I'd already agreed to the bargain. *Sort of.* I never thought I'd be stupid enough to find myself in this situation.

"Thanks, but there's no way I'm letting you lose your title because I'm an idiot. Besides, you're not *that* hideous. I could probably manage." I shuddered, faking disgust. It helped hide the sadness hovering near the surface.

He chuckled but his cheeks flushed under his tanned skin.

We sat up late into the night getting to know one another, and by the time I headed to bed, I was thoroughly impressed. He was kind, thoughtful, introverted, and one heck of a chef. Like Raiden had said, I could do worse. And like my brother had said—logic was the key to survival. It was time to put my heart aside and think with my head.

Could I sleep with him? *Yes.*

Did I want to? *No.*

But I'd never tell him that. He was a good man, and I wasn't about to punish him for my mistakes.

# CHAPTER
# THIRTY-THREE

M y eyes peeled open as someone gently shook me by the shoulder. "Hey, do you want to come with me?"

I blinked a few times to see Adam standing in my room outlined by the ambient light coming from the hallway. "Where?"

"I have to feed the livestock."

"Don't you have people to do that for you?"

He shrugged, his hands in the pockets of his worn jacket. "Our larger operation has a foreman, but the animals here, I like to care for myself."

I stretched my arms above my head, forcing myself awake. "Yeah, can you give me a minute? I'd love to go."

"I'll wait in the kitchen."

I brushed my teeth and braided my hair, then threw on tights, a T-shirt, and a pair of rubber boots before I strapped the dagger to my waist and pulled on a zip-up sweatshirt.

Grant, my other bodyguard, was stationed outside my bedroom door nursing a steaming cup of coffee. I mumbled good morning and stared at his beverage longingly. Though coffee wasn't my favorite, I needed it. He pointed toward the kitchen.

Having people guard my door bothered me. Relying on anyone made me feel guilty. Like I should be able to protect myself. But here, obviously, I wasn't.

Ignoring my feelings of helplessness, I found Adam waiting for me with a thermos of coffee. I clasped my hands into the prayer position, and he shot me a dimpled smile.

We walked down another lengthy corridor. At the end, jackets and hats hung along the wall and a collection of dirty boots lined the floor. Adam opened the back door, sending me straight into the barn. The air was cool and smelled like manure.

A couple of goats, perched on top of a hill of hay, looked up and paused their chewing.

"Shoo, little bastards," Adam said as he chased them out.

When he came back, he filled four tin buckets with grain. We each carried two out to where the cows were lined up against the fence waiting for their breakfast.

I took a deep breath, attempting to control my fight-or-flight reaction. Sure, they were just cows, but their shoulders were in line with my head. Their enormous horns, brown at the base and cream in between, gently looped upward until the tips turned black. One wrong move on my part and I'd be skewered like a marshmallow on a roasting stick. Their long eyelashes and gentle manner did little to comfort me.

I stayed behind while Adam went inside the fence, artfully dodging the massive horns. "Easy now, Elaine, Lizzie, and Lee," he said to the three pushiest cows. He poured his buckets into the bin before coming back for mine. After they were emptied, we headed back to the barn. Adam filled an enormous wheelbarrow with loose hay. I filled mine halfway up and followed him back out to the pasture. The cows, deep in the grain, ignored Adam as he dumped it over.

We repeated the process four times before we finished.

"Good job." Adam poured each of us coffee, then climbed on the fence and held my cup as I scrambled up beside him.

The morning sun, a deep persimmon, peeked through the distant trees, making it look as if they were on fire.

"I'm pleased you came out here with me. I was afraid you wouldn't."

"Why wouldn't I?" I sipped the coffee. It was much smoother than I was used to. Plus, he'd spiked it with cream and sugar. I could get used to it if it tasted like this all the time. Sugar had been a precious commodity in the bunker, and it was heavily rationed. Adding it to our gross coffee was considered wasteful.

He shrugged.

I tapped on the steel cup, and it clinked under my finger-nails. "Oh, come on. You have your reasons. You might as well come clean. We only have a few days to get to know one another."

"I thought you might want to sleep in." He fiddled with the frayed hem of his coat.

"And?"

"Well, if you did, it would tell me you're more suited to life with the Foe."

"You mean, the up-all-night, sleep-all-day kind of life?" I spread my hands around the cup, absorbing the warmth.

"Something like that." He finished his coffee and dangled the cup in his hand while holding on to the edge of the fence.

"So this was a test. How did I do?"

His lips twitched. "Surprisingly, you passed with flying colors."

"Why surprisingly?"

"Well, I thought maybe you'd gotten used to the extravagant lifestyle of the Foe."

"I actually prefer this." I drank down my last sip, then stared into my empty cup, disappointed that it was empty.

"You do?"

I *pfttt* out through my teeth. "Absolutely. Don't get me wrong, I had fun. For the most part, they're nice people. But I'm not cut out for that kind of life." My shoulders sagged. "It actually scares me to think maybe it doesn't matter what I'm cut out for. I don't want this. But now, I don't have a choice. I have to make the best of it. And I'm not saying that it's not worth it. I'd do anything to give my family a better life, but it doesn't mean I have to like it." I bit out the last words.

"Wow, you're an incredible person."

"You got all of that from a few sentences?" I said insincerely.

He lightly shoved me. "Yes. I did."

I shoved him back harder. He tossed his cup to the side and pulled me off the fence. My empty mug went flying, landing next to his.

He carried me, kicking, hollering, and laughing, all the way to a pile of loose hay and threw me in. The goats, who'd returned in our absence, scattered.

I stood up and brushed myself off, curling my tongue

over my front teeth as I planned my retribution. "I'm going to make you pick the hay out of my hair like a monkey hunting for lice," I threatened while smiling.

"And how, exactly, do you plan on managing that?"

I quirked my finger at him. "Come here and I'll tell you."

He stepped forward, only inches away from my chest.

With the judo moves I'd learned from Frank, I hit him hard with my shoulder and swept his legs out from underneath him. He grunted in surprise as he crashed to the ground.

I jumped onto his stomach, straddling him. "Do you yield?"

He raised his hands. "Yes. Yes." He was laughing so hard he could barely speak.

Both of us knew he could outmuscle me in a heartbeat. It was chivalrous for him not to.

I collapsed onto his chest, my face near his neck. He smelled good, like leather, earth, and lavender. His heart pounded against mine. I rolled off to one side, uncomfortable at the thoughts traveling through my head. I shouldn't be thinking things like this. There was no way I was over Raiden. Wasn't sure I ever would be. He owned my soul. So for now, it seemed like it was just my body and impending crown for sale. How depressing.

But . . . there was no way for us to be together. And I needed to decide between three other men. Adam deserved a fair shot. As far as I could tell, he was a good man. Given the proper amount of time, I could like it here. A pang of guilt and betrayal pierced my chest. I shoved the feeling back inside its incarceration.

Adam clasped his hands behind his head. "Where did that come from?" He sounded impressed.

"When you grow up where I did, you learn to use any advantage you have. I'm not above using deceit or leverage."

"I'll keep that in mind."

I propped myself up on my elbow and looked down at him with an eyebrow raised in jest. "Probably wise."

His gaze slid down the side of my cheek, to my mouth, where it paused for a second before it hitched on the unzipped sweatshirt doing nothing to hide the cleavage heaving under my tank top.

My bottom lip caught between my teeth as I stared at his mouth. His pout was not overly full, but symmetrical and heavenly shaped. Though he looked more human than Raiden, Loch, Kai or Trent, I thought he was the most beautiful.

Suddenly, my head snapped forward and my forehead slammed into his chest, but not of my own accord. Tiny hooves jumped up on my back and pranced around.

We both busted out laughing.

"Khaki, get down," Adam scolded. He reached around me and slapped the goat off my back.

"Well, I guess we know who's boss." I got up and dusted off my hands.

"Damn goat. He's going to be a handful when he grows up," he grumbled.

And like I'd predicted—Adam picked every last bit of hay out of my hair.

---

AFTER A FULL DAY of showing me the farm, how it worked, and trying to convince me to ride a griffin—which I'd refused since only one person could ride at a time—we made it back to his house to find two notes waiting for us on the table. The first one was a message from my brother.

HEY BEA,

    *Everyone is having a grand time without you. Even Tee. She finally read the letter you wrote and has sort of forgiven you for leaving her behind. But I think it's because Kai is the perfect distraction. I just wanted to let you know that we are all thriving. Sid misses you and pouts daily. People feel sorry for him so they feed him way too many treats. You might have to put him on a doggy diet. Hell, you might have to put all of us on a diet.*

    *We'll see you at the capital in a couple of weeks. Hang in there.*

    *Love, Kevin*

I SNORTED as I read it—because it sounded just like him. It was nice to hear everyone was happy with the decision they'd made.

The second note was an invitation to have dinner with Adam's parents.

He'd confessed earlier that he'd made a bargain with his people. If they would agree to give us the week alone, he promised that after I was crowned queen—whether he was crowned king or not—I would spend a few days getting to know the Fee. I told him I would gladly spend a few days with them. *Later.* Anything to give me a slight reprieve from peopling.

"Plus," he said, "after two attempts on your life, I thought it safer to keep you away. Our people are good, but there's always a rotten apple or two. Once you're on the throne, it'll be harder to kill you."

"Thanks." I leaned into the sarcasm.

But his parents and older brother weren't included in the bargain.

"I'd like it if they could get to know you." He tossed the invite into the garbage, while I slipped Kevin's note into my pocket.

"Another test?" Anxiety quelled in the pit of my stomach at the thought of spending time with people who were about to judge me on my merits as a wife and queen.

"I'd be lying if I said it wasn't. Though my parents *do not* make decisions for me. But I do respect their opinions."

"So how is it you have an older brother and yet you're the First-Born son?"

"We only have the same dad. Leonardo's ten years older than me. And it's my mom's family that the title passes through."

"Did his mom die?"

Adam lightly kicked the floor. "No. It was a bit of a scandal."

I waited for a few beats before I said, "So?" I didn't want to go to dinner unprepared.

"When my dad met my mom, they fell in love. But he was already married." Adam pursed his lips to the side. "Once you've blood bonded, divorce is frowned upon. Anyway, he got divorced, then married my mom, and miraculously, I came along. Though now, seeing as you're here, it makes more sense why the First Families all had sons about the same time. As for Leonardo, you might have to ignore him. He hates me. I'm pretty sure he dreams of my demise so he can inherit my position."

"How does that work if the title passed through your mom's lineage?"

"My dad's ex-wife demanded it as the price for their divorce. The Domes granted it since there are so few children. When my dad married my mom, he became a lord, granting Leonardo the spot if anything ever happened to me."

"Why is he coming to dinner?"

Adam quirked a lip, a dimple creasing one side of his cheek.

Leonardo was coming because of me.

"No pressure," I grumbled.

"Don't worry. You're going to love my parents," Adam said.

*But will they like me? And what about his brother? Why is he really here?* My level of trust was at an all-time low.

I walked to my room to get ready. It impressed me that Adam was vetting me as much as I was vetting him. If we married, he definitely wouldn't be marrying me for a title. He didn't want the crown. Which made me kind of sad. I enjoyed being with him. The chemistry wasn't explosive like it was with Raiden. I expected that was a once-in-a-lifetime connection. I'd had chemistry with Trent, but it had been fueled by alcohol, a broken heart, and bad decisions. And because I'd been thrown overboard, I hadn't had time to explore it further. But deep down, Trent's lifestyle wasn't one I wanted, though I could see us being friends.

I changed into a brown wrap dress with a cream sweater. In this darker light, my eyes adjusted to the hue of the material. I finished the ensemble with a set of dangling topaz earrings that clashed with my necklace. I gripped the icy-gray stone in my hand to take it off, but panic sliced under my skin. I wasn't ready to let go of it. It was the reason I was still alive—*he was the reason I was still alive.* Sorrow washed through my heart in a dizzying wave. I waited until it passed, mostly, and left the bedroom.

Adam escorted me to his parents' home connected by another long underground tunnel.

Lord Dion and Lady Chantal's house was much like their son's—neat, tidy, and tastefully decorated. Lady Chantal was, by far, the most beautiful decoration in the room. The waves of her brown hair shimmered with an undertone of olive green under the fireplace's dancing light. Her eyes, the same shade, reflected the flames. On anyone else, her skin would look sickly, but on her, it was ethereal. Adam looked like her—his deep-set eyes and sharp cheekbones—but he'd got his dimples and coloring from his father.

"Ruby, it's nice to see you again," said Lady Chantal. Her accent was slightly thicker than her son's. "I hope you're enjoying your time here." She gave a side glance to Adam. "Please, let Adam know that putting a woman to work on a farm may not be the proper way to woo her."

"I'm enjoying my time here. Honestly, Adam may be on to something."

Lady Chantal's face lit up. "You're really enjoying it?"

"Immensely."

She clasped a hand over her chest. "We've got ourselves a farm girl here." She sounded so proud.

"I like the cows but the goats are questionable." Adam and I locked eyes and laughed. "The griffins terrify me."

"Yes, well the griffins can be a bit to get used to. But I have no doubt you're up for the challenge."

I wasn't sure she was right, but I didn't correct her.

Adam's parents held hands as they led us out into the

garden. Flickering lights bobbed around the long flowing grasses and the bottom-most branches.

"Fireflies," Adam whispered into my ear. A chill that had nothing to do with the temperature tickled my spine.

As we climbed a winding staircase carved into an enormous tree, the firefly light faded, replaced by glowing lanterns hanging from the boughs. A fine sheen of sweat broke out over my top lip by the time we stepped onto a platform hollowed out of the expansive trunk.

Leonardo—I presumed—sat at a round table in the center of the room. He didn't bother getting up to greet us.

A bouquet of flowers, red roses, pink lilies, yellow sunflowers, and greenery decorated the surface. A crystal pitcher filled with water, ice, and slices of lemons glinted in the candlelight on the elegantly adorned table. The scent of grilled meat and vegetables perfumed the air.

I peeked over the side of the glass banister to the ground below as we made our way to the table. My head swam. It was a long drop, and I wasn't fond of heights.

Adam pulled out a chair for me and sat down with his knee touching mine. "Leonardo, this is Ruby," Adam said.

Leonardo's dark eyes assessed me. "Nice to meet you." He traced the top of his wineglass with his finger, sounding bored. He was handsome, like his brother, but his expression suggested our mere presence was inconveniencing him, and he had much better things to do than waste his precious time with us.

"You too," I replied.

The conversation flowed naturally, despite Leonardo's lack of involvement. He seemed content listening. Though more often than not, the hairs on my arms raised under his intense scrutiny.

I was amazed how easily everyone else ignored him. Feeling slightly sorry for him, I asked, "So Leonardo, what do you do?"

"I oversee operations at Isle Noir." A lock of dark-blond hair fell over his forehead. He brushed it aside. "What do *you* do?" His tone was slightly caustic.

Adam squeezed my knee.

"Right now, you could say I'm between jobs, I guess."

Everyone but Leonardo laughed.

"But before this, I was a hunter. Mostly large game." I smiled politely but I made sure it didn't reach my eyes.

"You don't even know what large game is." He picked up his knife and cut off a slab of meat, shoving the whole thing into his mouth.

"You might be surprised." I was done feeling sorry for him. It was obvious he was only here to make me uncomfortable. Though, I wondered, suppressing the cold tingle running down my spine, if that was all he was here for. I checked to make sure the dagger was secure under my sweater.

After we finished eating, Leonardo stood up and threw his napkin on his plate. "Thanks for dinner," he said to Lord Dion, completely ignoring Lady Chantal and Adam. "Ruby, it was a pleasure. I'm sure I'll see you again at the capital. And a word of friendly advice—watch your back."

Adam flew out of his chair, and it tumbled to the floor as he pointed a finger in Leonardo's face. "Leave now, before I take this outside," Adam growled.

Lady Chantal grabbed Adam's hand. "Don't," she said.

Knots worked along Adam's jaw.

"Leonardo," Lord Dion warned.

Leonardo tipped his chin at me and walked out.

341

After he left, the tension in the air dissipated. Lady Chantal excused herself, and disappeared through a curved doorway, coming back seconds later carrying a cake sprinkled with nuts.

Not wanting to be rude, I made room for a slice.

Soon, everyone was laughing and having a good time. It reminded me, not painfully, what my family used to be like. And by the end of the night, I thought they would be happy if I joined them. Emotions twisted in my throat. I could see a future with all of them.

Curiously enough, Lord Dion had human ancestors a few generations back, making them far more amenable to the human side of me.

"Do you know what faction of giant DNA runs through your lineage?" Lady Chantal asked. She held a glass of wine delicately between two fingers. A ring with a large orange gemstone set in gold glittered in the candlelight like a live ember.

"Not for positive, but I'm betting Fum is in there somewhere." I pulled on a curl.

"To be sure," Lord Dion said. "But I wouldn't be surprised if you had a drop or two of Fee blood as well with your brown eyes." He wasn't a man of many words but his face spoke volumes. He adored his wife and was extremely proud of Adam. Leonardo—not so much.

After we finished, I said, "I want to thank you for everything. The last time I had a meal and a conversation this wonderful was before my parents disappeared."

It wasn't as if we hadn't had good times in the bunker. We had. But survival had always been at the forefront of our minds, making everything else second. I could see many of my friends, and especially my brother, settling down here and creating a wonderful life.

Lord Dion and Lady Chantal welcomed me as if I were family. They made me feel at *home*—which was something I hadn't felt in a long time. They'd make extraordinary grandparents. Not that I wanted kids anytime soon, but I was warming up to the idea of knowing that here, they would have a good life. Possibly a less dangerous life if I played my cards right.

# CHAPTER
# THIRTY-FOUR

T he earth trembled. My eyes popped open, and reflexively, I gathered the sheets in my hands, prepared to dive under a doorframe.

"Whoa. It's okay," Adam said, shaking my shoulder.

I relaxed. It wasn't an earthquake.

"Stay here," he demanded.

"What?" I sat up in bed.

"I need you to stay here, okay?" Panic hovered in his voice.

"Okay? But what's wrong?"

"Our crops are on fire. I've got to go help. I'm taking Grant with me, but I'm leaving Liz outside your door. *Please* promise me, no matter what happens, you won't leave this room."

"You don't think this is about me?" I asked.

He shook his head but didn't seem convinced. "No, but I can't completely rule it out. Your track record—"

"Go," I said. "I'll be fine. I promise I won't leave the room."

Setting the fields on fire seemed like an extreme measure in order to get me alone. After all, every faction counted on the Fee to provide their main food stocks. It would be the ultimate cut off your nose to spite your face.

Just in case, I opened the drawer to the bedside table and pulled out the dagger. I adjusted the scabbard so I could buckle it under my armpit for easy access to the weapon. Over it, I threw on a zip-up sweatshirt and asked Liz if she wanted to come in. She declined, saying she had a better view out there.

I paced the floor for what felt like hours. When my stomach started growling, I estimated it was sometime around noon.

There was an odd thump outside my door, and my pulse skipped a beat.

With a hand on my dagger and an ear to the wood, I asked, "Liz, are you okay?"

An eerie silence ensued.

"Liz?" I said louder.

The doorknob twisted. A nervous sweat dampened my brow.

"Who's there?" I demanded.

A tune whistled from the space between the door and the stone-tiled floor. I recognized it as the song Trent had sang on stage.

"Trent? Is that you?"

Something slammed into the door. The nearby artwork clattered to the ground. The light fixture flickered before it extinguished with a pop and hiss.

I jumped away and slipped my hand under my sweatshirt, resting it on the dagger. Before I had time to pull it, the door busted open, wooden splinters flying. I deflected them with my forearms.

Josha stood haloed by the hallway light, dressed in solid black, complete with smudged eyeliner and false lashes.

I didn't know why I was so surprised. My shoulders relaxed a fraction. How dangerous could he possibly be? Then I internally chastised myself—he, while not the scariest of giants, was a giant. It was like thinking just because he wasn't the biggest, oldest bear, he wasn't deadly. Plus, I'd already underestimated him once, and look how that had turned out.

He sneered a ruby-red lip before he stepped in, his combat boots silent on the stone, and pointed a finger toward my chest. His midnight nails glistened like an oil slick. "You're mine," he whispered. Fine webs of electricity sparked between his fingers.

I expected him to monologue before knocking me out.

I was wrong.

THIS TIME, I woke up with the midday sun blaring down on me and a headache pounding at the base of my skull. Shadows of tall trees swayed with the breeze. I crawled onto my hands and knees and slowly pushed up from the ground. I was tired of getting zapped by these assholes.

Josha rested against a tree trunk, filing his already-sharp nails. He stuck the file in his pocket and stepped into the light.

"What are you doing here?" Pungent smoke hazed the grotto. I scrunched my nose, trying not to sneeze.

"I'm going to kill you."

I flicked my hands in the air and shook my head like *Yeah, I know, can we just get on with it?*

"Out here, I can take my time. Savor the moment. Plus, I plan on flaying your body and nailing you to a tree. I saw it in a movie once. So much more dramatic than the Fee finding you dead in your room."

Josha did have a flair for the theatrical. Seriously, who wore false eyelashes to an assassination? But the *Silence of the Lambs* image he painted made my pulse race. I was afraid my heart was going to spring free without any help from Josha. I needed to calm myself and treat him like any other predator. I inhaled through my nose, slowly out through my mouth.

"And how do you plan on killing me? You don't have any weapons."

"I don't need any to snap your neck with my bare hands." He cracked his knuckles and stretched them backward.

Okay, so he didn't believe I was any threat to him. An advantage. Not much, but I was willing to use anything.

"Just so I know, why kill *me*? It's not like Trent's at the top of my list. You could've simply waited."

"Well, he should be! He's the only choice. You're too stupid to see it. You can't pick Kai since your best friend is boning him."

He was trying to bait me, but two could play that game.

"And everyone knows Adam doesn't want the job," he continued. "So all you have left is Loch. And *that* arrogant fool doesn't know the first thing about romancing a woman. He assumes they'll fall at his feet just because of his title. So by default, you'll pick Trent."

347

"So what you're saying is . . . I'm damned if I pick him, and I'm damned if I don't?"

"No, what I'm saying is, you're dead. I'm going to watch the light drain from your eyes as I choke the life from you with my bare hands." He started forward, one foot in front of the other like he was a supermodel on a catwalk.

"Eh, whatever you say. I guess I shouldn't have expected more from someone like you." I curled my lip and flipped my hair over my shoulder, matching his energy.

"What's that supposed to mean?" He stopped and pressed his hands to his hips.

"Well, you can't create anything. Even the dress you picked for me was someone else's design. A *human's*. But I do need to thank you. Trent loved it. Better off than on." I giggled.

His shoulders tensed. His eyes narrowed. "Don't you speak his name. When you're dead, your hold over him will be nullified. I don't know what kind of witch you are, but he loves *me*."

"And you called *me* stupid," I muttered under my breath, knowing full well he could hear me. "If he loved you, I wouldn't have been able to steal him in less than a week. You were simply a placeholder. At best, a bookmark. Unfortunately, you're not very interesting. You're kind of boring."

He snarled. It wasn't attractive.

"Now *Trent*." I paused, gauging the situation. The only way I could win was to get Josha to lose control. I needed to stoke his jealousy. "That man's not boring. Especially in bed. I didn't know it could be like that. He was my first giant. He said it was the best sex he's ever had. If I recollect, *intense* was the word he used."

I inwardly cringed at my words as I cataloged Josha's

every tick—the whitening of his knuckles, the flare of his nostrils, the slight twitch of his mouth—to know the exact moment of attack. That, I had practice with. But I would only have one shot because giants moved at the speed of light. I'd have to strike without being able to see my target, and if the timing was wrong—I was as good as dead.

The split second before he launched, I sprang forward, tucked my head to my chest, and rolled to the ground in a somersault. I came up on one knee, keeping my body low, and swiped the dagger across the inside of his upper thigh with all my strength. The weapon effortlessly pierced his leather pants and his flesh. Salty blood sprayed like a hose over my face. I zigged the knife in the opposite direction over the soft spot beside the knee, then zagged over to his Achilles tendon and cut it in half.

He screamed and toppled to his knees. There was no time to waste. Giants healed fast. If he were human, he'd be dead already. I'd severed his femoral artery in two places.

I jumped up and pulled his sweating bald head back against my chest. He reached up, but not before I sliced the dagger across his throat, hot blood gushing over our hands. A wet gurgle escaped, along with more blood. His slickened palms pushed my face away and electricity danced before my eyes.

---

IN ANOTHER ROUND of déjà vu, I woke up, dazed, lying on my back with the upper half of Josha's body weighted on top of me. I scrambled out from under him onto my knees, adrenaline feeding my strength. Was he dead?

Tentatively, I reached out and felt for a pulse on his

wrist. The red gaping wound on his neck and his ice-cold skin suggested there was no need. Though he'd tried to kill me, remorse heaved inside my stomach.

I collapsed onto my hands and knees into a tangle of exposed roots and swallowed back the bile shooting up the back of my throat. I could've sworn the ground was smooth and manicured. But, at Josha's feet, it looked like twisted roots had burst from the earth in order to trip him as he attacked me.

I rocked back and wilted into a seated position before gathering my dagger in my lap and staring off into nothing. Burning tears ran down my face and dripped pink from the blood staining my skin, onto my formerly cream-colored pants.

The punishment for killing a giant was immediate execution. I wasn't sure if that extended to self-defense or not.

But I guess I was going to find out.

# CHAPTER
# THIRTY-FIVE

"Ruby." Adam's face hovered in front of mine, his hands gently placed on both of my cheeks.

I gazed into his eyes, feeling lightheaded and queasy.

"Ruby, are you okay?"

I blinked and nodded. Though I guess it depended on his definition of okay. I was alive. Which was more than I could say for Josha.

I tried turning my head to make sure he was still dead—it had been a while since I'd checked. I could hear other people talking and whispering, but Adam purposely blocked my view.

It wasn't like I needed to see what Josha's body looked like. The image was forever stamped into my psyche. His aqua eyes had faded significantly, as if his life was somehow connected to the brilliant color. They stared ahead at nothing now, one false lash askew and his eyeliner smeared across his skin like an aging rock star. Blood and gore congealed at the hollow of his throat and stained the ground.

And even though I couldn't see his face, I could see his polished combat boots. At some point, the plant vines that had snaked around his feet and ankles had vanished as if I'd imagined them. I shivered, wondering *had* I imagined them? I could've sworn . . .

"Ruby," Adam repeated, shaking my shoulder.

I refocused. "Is Liz . . .?" I flexed my fingers into fists against the sticky dried blood.

"She'll be fine when she wakes up."

"And the crops?"

"We saved most of them. It was just a distraction to get me away." Adam turned his head toward the disembodied voices. "You guys got this?"

Even though I was six feet tall, he swept me into his arms and carried me to his house, to his bedroom, then into his bathroom. He carried me down a set of stairs to a cavern under the floor. The obsidian walls glowed as if the black rock was embedded with waves of neon. Steam whirled from a small turquoise pool carrying whiffs of sulfur.

He set me down on wobbly feet, holding me steady by the shoulder. He held a hand out for the bloody dagger still clutched to my chest. "You're okay now, Ruby. You can let go of it."

I hesitated, but gave it to him. He set it down before he grabbed my sweatshirt and pulled it off, followed by my shoes, socks, and pants, leaving me in my underwear and bra. He stripped down to his bright green boxer-shorts before he picked me up again. Gently, he stepped into the steaming water and slowly made his way to the bottom of the waist-deep pool.

The hot temperature stung my cold skin as he placed me on a submerged bench carved from stone. While he cleaned the blood from my face and body with soap and a washcloth, pink frothy bubbles swirled then rushed away.

After he finished scrubbing the mess, he sat down next to me, his body not touching mine. He reached out and held my hand, but it wasn't enough. The seriousness of my situation was setting in, and though I was immersed in scalding-hot water, my body refused to stop shaking. I crawled onto his lap facing him and wrapped my arms around him with my head buried in the crook of his neck. He smelled strongly of smoke.

He stroked my hair and snaked his other hand around my waist, pulling me in tighter. He simply held me and let me work through the emotional trauma.

During my twenty-two years, I'd killed more wildlife each month than most people would in a lifetime. But I'd done it because I had to, not because I wanted to. Though I'd enjoyed the hunting, I had not enjoyed killing. But families had to eat, and we all had our duties.

This was the first time I was positive I'd killed a person. Sure, I'd shot people before—though they'd all shot at me first—but as far as I knew, I'd never actually killed any of them. Besides, there was a distinct difference between shooting a stranger from a distance in self-defense and slicing the throat of someone you knew. Someone who'd helped me dress, someone who I'd thought for a time might become a friend.

A trembling whine caught in my throat as I tightened my grip around Adam. The steam from the hot spring had washed away the scent of smoke, leaving behind earth, leather, and lavender. I nuzzled closer and inhaled deeply, concentrating on how lovely he smelled instead of the visual horrors on replay in my mind. Momentarily, he stopped caressing my hair, his fingers pressed into my scalp.

God, he smelled so good. As I tentatively kissed the warm skin below his ear, his pulse jumped under my lips. Receiving no resistance, I continued along the edge of his jaw, his scruff rough on my skin. I stopped and pulled away, my hands on either side of his head. Humidity dampened the ends of his hair, curling it over his forehead. I brushed it away from his beautiful brown eyes. Trailing my fingers behind the back of his head, I fiddled with his curls as I licked my bottom lip, catching it between my teeth. He let out a breath and ran a finger over my naked thigh. My nipples hardened under my sports bra. His eyes darted to my chest, and heat curled between my legs.

He'd already told me I was going to have to make the first move. I'd thought I had, but he seemed a tiny bit shy. I twined my fingers into his curls and pulled him to me. His lips were soft and gentle, as was his kiss, but as I pulled away, he caught my bottom lip between his fangs before he let go.

"Do you really want to do this? Or are you doing it because you know it's what *I* want? Or are you simply trying to forget what happened out there?" His voice was rough, as if the smoke inhalation had finally caught up with him.

"Yes," I said, holding his gaze. Did I want to? *It was complicated.* Was it what he wanted? I didn't know for sure, but I did know that he didn't deserve to lose his title because I'd made a mistake. And did I want to forget what had just happened? *Absolutely.*

A dark eyebrow quirked. "Yes? To all of it?"

I swallowed and I nodded. Adam was kind, hard-working, beautiful, and I was sure, in time, we could build a relationship upon those qualities.

"Are you sure? I don't want to do this if you don't want—"

I cut him off with a finger pressed firmly to his lips. "I want to. I promise."

He flipped me around so fast that I didn't have time to scream. He straddled me where I had been only seconds ago. His hands ran down my arms, and he intertwined his fingers with mine, then pulled them high into the air and stood up over the top of me, pinning them to the cave wall behind me. The shy boy from a minute ago had disappeared. He stared, his gaze searching, from the curve of my cheek to the swell of my breasts, as if he were mapping out a plan.

He released my fingers and slid his hands down the sensitive skin on the inside of my arms, past my chest, skimming the outsides of my breasts. Every nerve ending flared despite the hot water.

Grabbing the hem of my sports bra, he pulled it over my head and tossed it aside, where it made a splat on the dry stone. A lopsided grin deepened a dimple as if he liked what he saw. He reached behind me and pulled my body toward the surface of the water as if I were floating.

"Hold on to the side," he ordered. He knelt on the bottom and slid off my underwear before lifting my legs over his shoulder. He spread his hands over my butt cheeks, holding me afloat as he planted a kiss on the inside of my thigh. I moaned, though it might have been more of a whimper. I could hardly breathe as he spread my thighs further apart. He swept kisses up the inside of my leg, his mouth searing hot on my throbbing skin. Blood thumped deliciously in my core as my fingers gripped the edge of the stone.

Normally, in this kind of position, I might've felt exposed on both a physical and personal level. I wasn't sure if I was just that comfortable with him or if my emotions were burnt out and on a temporary hiatus. Either way, it didn't matter. Any coherent thoughts vanished as his tongue flicked over my hot, pulsing nub, sucking and feasting on my delicate flesh. Lights flashed behind my closed eyes as he brought me to climax almost immediately. I arched my back and screamed, clawing at the side of the pool.

When he finished, he rested his head on my leg and chuckled before slowly submerging me back into the water and drifting closer. "We can stop here if you want." He was so sincere, so honest—so clueless.

The pounding deep inside insisted I was by no means finished with him. I grabbed the back of his head and pressed my lips to his, tasting myself on his tongue. Any hesitation he had was vanquished by that kiss. He hoisted me into his arms and carried me up the stairs to his room, leaving a trail of water behind. He tossed me onto the bed and stepped out of his boxer shorts. My breath stuttered. He was large—not grotesquely massive like some of the romance books I'd read. But certainly larger than poor Noah, the only human I'd ever been with. Staring with open fascination, I rose to my knees, the mattress firm under my weight, and ran my hand over his tanned chest. I toyed with his skin, over to the defined ridges of his stomach and down to the dark curls hugging the base of his cock. I trailed a finger over the soft skin, which jumped at my touch. I laughed nervously and glanced up to his eyes. They were closed, his jaw tight with tension.

I reached around and gripped the firm muscles of his buttocks and pulled him close to me as I dragged my tongue along his velvety shaft. A growl rumbled from his chest. His eyes, now opened, were a fathomless black pool staring straight into my soul.

Tingles skated along my spine.

He pushed me down on the bed with one hand on my shoulder, the other above my head. He positioned his wide body between my legs and coaxed my thighs open. The tip of him nudged inside, finding me slick with want and need. I spread my legs further, bowing my back, begging him to enter fully.

He rocked forward slowly, letting my body adjust to his size. I had to relax my muscles in order to receive the entire length of him. The sounds coming from my throat might've been embarrassing if I was in a mind to care.

He nuzzled his face into my neck, then kissed over my collarbone to the swell of my breasts to the tip of my nipple. Sparks of pleasure fanned over my skin as I bucked beneath him. All reason disappeared and the only thing I could focus on was the desire possessing my body. He held me in place, nipping and sucking, while his hips picked up the pace.

He grabbed a handful of my hair and pulled as cries tore from my throat. I let out my breath and opened my eyes to see a satisfied, perhaps triumphant, smile on his face.

Without warning, he pulled out and flipped me over, coaxing me to my knees with my hands under me. He slid back inside and held my hips steady with an iron grasp. This new position hit areas I didn't know existed. It felt as if my entire being was filled with his length and girth. I grabbed a pillow and hugged it tightly, my head bumping against the headboard. With every thrust, I moaned until my body convulsed under the barrage of sensations and my moans became screams. I buried my face into the pillow to muffle the sound.

As I came back down from that high, he rested his head on my back and kissed it gently. But he was still hard as a rock. I shimmied out of his grip and made him lay back on the bed.

Climbing onto him, I slowly slid myself onto him, surprised that pleasure still existed after I'd come so many times. What was it going to take to make him climax? Focusing on his eyes, I gently undulated back and forth. He turned his head away, but I grabbed his chin, bringing his gaze back to mine. My thumb rubbed over his bottom lip as I leaned forward, my breasts grazing his chest, stopping just short of our lips meeting. I inhaled his breath and rocked harder, deeper. I rested my forehead against his and kept my rhythm slow, steady, frustrating. A strangled groan escaped from his lips.

Though I'd already been satisfied—thoroughly and completely—twice, and that wasn't counting the episode in the pool, I was close again. My nipples rubbed against his chest and my clit throbbed from the friction.

"Please," I begged. I wasn't sure if I was pleading for him or me. "*Please.*"

His hands gripped around my waist, almost spanning the circumference. I sat up to see his beautiful face. He looked vulnerable and perhaps a bit frightened, though I couldn't figure out why. I slid my fingers up my sides until the weight of my breasts rested heavily in my hands so I could circle my nipples with my thumb as I kept my rhythm, slow, steady, and deeper. His groans became moans and his fingers dug into my sides. I rode him faster and harder, never breaking eye contact, until I threw my head back and screamed in unison with him.

Collapsing on his chest, I deduced that a connection was his weakness—or strength—and if I was being honest, I should've known. To most giants, it seemed as if sex was just sex, but to Adam, this was personal.

I'd planned on sleeping with him from the minute he'd informed me he would rather lose his title as First-Born son than have sex with an unwilling participant. He was a gentleman—one who still hadn't told me, when the time came, if he'd be willing to marry me.

# CHAPTER 36
# THE FIE

The more I relaxed, the better the griffin underneath me responded to my guidance. We cut through the dense clouds, down toward the ground, skimming only feet away from the tops of the trees. Birds dove out of sight in fear of Delila's black talons and sharp beak. I reached out and ran my fingers over her bronze feathers gleaming in the sunlight. They were silky, but not as soft as the golden fur covering the rest of her body.

She angled sideways, mimicking Adam's beast. Despite my fear of heights, I leaned into the turn without the worry of falling. We'd been practicing the last few days, and it was as if the air cradled me in her soft hands and held me steadily in place.

In the distance, jagged peaks surrounded by a ring of pink clouds grew from the meadows. The last few days with Adam had sped by with ferocity, and I'd enjoyed every moment with him—from learning how to ride a freaking griffin to the evenings spent with his parents and the quiet moments we shared alone. We had held hands, snuggled, and even slept together in the same bed, but we didn't have sex after the first time. I think he was waiting for me to initiate the intimacy, but I couldn't bring myself to do it. Not that I didn't enjoy it, or him. I did.

But guilt plagued me. Not so much the guilt of loving Raiden and sleeping with someone else. I had to accept the fact Raiden and I could never be together, even if my heart refused to acknowledge it. It was the guilt that I would harbor later for sleeping with Adam if I didn't choose him as king in the end. He was a good man—who I didn't want to lead on. He was my first choice, and I didn't expect that to change. Okay, so he was my second choice. But I couldn't have the man I really wanted.

A stab of longing escaped its bindings as thoughts of Raiden lingered. I pushed through the torment, concentrating on the positive. Even though I couldn't have my heart's desire, I was still alive and could protect my family. I'd been afraid of what my punishment for killing Josha would be, but Adam said it was self-defense. Never, in their entire history, had a human killed a giant on their own soil.

"I'm not sure *how* you managed to kill him," he'd told me before we left his home. "It should be impossible for a human to do. Are you sure you're half human? I'm starting to question it. You survived a volcano, the ocean, thornberries, and now Josha. I think there's more to you than we understand."

His statement reinforced Raiden's earlier suspicions.

Truthfully, Adam had said it would help my street cred when it came to some of the giants who remained on the fence about my impending coronation. My actions had fueled whispers that I might have the strength and the figurative *balls* needed to rule the Fiefdom.

But I knew I had only been able to best Josha because he hadn't believed me to be a threat. I pressed my hand to the dagger hidden inside my shirt. What small advantage I had —the giants underestimating a mere human—I feared was lost, and I desperately wanted that advantage back.

As we flew closer to the mountainside city, my stomach flipped and flopped at the thought of spending a week with Lord Issac, Lady Sylvia, and their son Loch, Raiden's cousin and doppelgänger.

The griffin's wings shifted as we drifted to a smooth stop, Delila's talons clicking over the granite. Adam helped me down and waved to Loch, who was standing outside the door of the modern mansion. He pulled a hand out of his wool jacket and acknowledged us with a two-finger salute.

Patting Delila's neck, I thanked her for not killing me. She blinked, her honey-colored eyes and oblong pupils reflecting my windblown image.

I glanced at Loch, who was waiting patiently, then back to Adam. "I don't want to go."

"I don't want you to either." He stepped closer and planted a kiss on my lips. If I had to guess, the kiss was a bit possessive, as if he didn't want me to forget. He lingered with his forehead pressed against mine before he turned away.

"Adam, wait."

He turned his head but kept his back to me.

A tight ball wadded in my throat, making it hard to talk. "You never did answer me. When the time comes, are you willing to give up what you have to be king?"

He shook his head. "No."

Unwanted tears smarted the back of my nose.

"I understand," I whispered. I wasn't sure I would have been able to give up his small corner of paradise either.

"But," he said as he faced me, "I'd give up what I have in order to marry *you*."

I closed my eyes and suppressed a shudder of relief.

"Though I need you to answer a question for me. If Raiden were on the shortlist and you had to pick now, would it be him or me?"

Adam and his beautiful face, his kind heart, and his generous nature—he was a good man and I could see us having a wonderful life together. A happy life. I'd even go so far as to say that given enough time, I could find it in my heart to love him.

But if given a choice, I'd choose Raiden.

Every.

Single.

Time.

I wanted to lie to Adam, but I couldn't, because he deserved the truth.

"I'd pick Raiden. Though I want you to know, in time, I'm not sure my answer wouldn't change. I enjoyed every second with you and your family."

A measure of disappointment, or maybe irritation, flattened his lips. "I see. Do you mind if I give it some more thought? I'll let you know when we get to the capital."

I swallowed hard and nodded. "Though I want you to know that you're my first choice amongst the First-Born sons. You're so far ahead of the rest, they're not even in the race."

Without another word, he stepped into the stirrup, effortlessly threw a leg over his griffin's back, and flew away,

Delila following. I watched for minutes, waiting for Adam to look back, but he didn't.

"Ruby."

I jumped and turned at the sound of Loch's voice. I'd forgotten he was there.

"It's nice to see you again." His slight smile and the twinkle in his blue eyes suggested he really was pleased to see me.

I huffed with disbelief and glanced away. He was painful to look at. Plus, his family was the reason I was in this debacle. Okay, so sure, I'd signed a contract without reading it, but the contract wouldn't have been necessary if it wasn't for their greedy ambitions. Sylvia had said she did it so I would marry Loch and be safely on the throne. I didn't buy her excuse for one second. She didn't care about my safety, she only cared if Loch—the *false* First-Born son—was crowned king.

Somehow, Penelope, their attorney, had slid that one little detrimental sentence past me, and I was going to spend the rest of my life kicking myself about it.

He held up his hands. "Whoa, what gives? Are you angry about something?" Lines creased between his perfectly manicured brows. Though he and Raiden looked like brothers, perhaps twins, Loch was the cover model for a fashion magazine, while Raiden was the real-life version of a mountain man.

"Sure, I'm angry. Your family's the reason I'm in this situation."

He tilted his head, a strand of dark hair escaping his ponytail and trailing across his face. "I think what you mean is, *my parents* are the reason you're in this situation. Not me. I had no idea what was in that contract. I didn't read it until after you left. And here's a bit of advice—next time, read the shit you sign."

"Oh, so you expect me to believe you had *no clue* what was in that contract?"

He crossed his arms. "At this point, I don't expect much from you." His eyes darted down my frame. "I can see now that you've already decided I'm the enemy. So enjoy your week with my parents. When you're ready to fuck, just send me a message."

"What? You really think I'm going to sleep with you?" I fumed.

He shrugged his shoulders with his arms still crossed. "I assumed so. I thought you'd probably want to use your free pass with Kai, but hey, what do I know? And FYI, I'm *not* Adam. There's no way I'm losing my title because you don't want to hold up your end of the agreement."

"I didn't agree to sleep with *anyone!*" I shouted.

"The minute you knocked boots with Trent, you did. Now I'm going home. If you need anything, don't ask me."

He stormed toward the barn, leaving me alone outside his parents' house. I didn't know what to do. There was no way I was bunking with Lady Sylvia and Lord Issac. And where were Grant and Liz? They were only supposed to be a few minutes behind us.

Knowing that my friends and Kevin were staying at the local hotel, I decided to walk to town. There was a lightness in my step despite Loch's ugly words. He'd mentioned I had a free pass with Kai, and I assumed, from the letter Kevin had written me, Tee didn't know of my misstep yet. When she found out the mistake I'd made, she was going to be angry. Perhaps an understatement.

Today was my chance to set the record straight. Plus, I

was dying to see how Frederica, Frank, and the rest of the gang were doing for myself. I could only imagine they were having the time of their lives. And Sid. I missed him fiercely.

I double-checked over each shoulder and cocked an ear toward the sky, looking and listening for danger, then, as an extra precaution, I unzipped my sweatshirt for easy access to my dagger. Without other options available, I set off in a jog, anxious to see my family.

Not long after, the clip-clop of hooves stopped me in my tracks. Instinctively, I rested my hand along the hilt of my dagger and spun around, preparing to fight. My hand dropped away when I saw Benji perched upon a dapple-gray pegasus.

"What are you doing?" He hopped down, dust puffing around his huge feet. "It's dangerous for you out here alone. Where are Liz and Grant?"

"I don't know. They were supposed to be right behind us."

Benji searched the skies. "Loch told me you decided to stay with his parents?" His eyes slivered as if he didn't believe it.

"No. I'm going to stay with Kevin."

"Kevin and your friends are in Isle Noir. Lady Sylvia didn't want them around to be a distraction."

My jaw twisted with anger. *What a bitch.*

"So what should I do? I don't want to stay with them, and Loch made it perfectly clear I'm not wanted."

Benji raised an eyebrow which said he questioned my assessment.

"Okay, so I might've been slightly impolite," I spit out.

"Well, staying with him is your safest option at the moment. To him, you hold value."

My breath caught in my throat. "That's rude."

"The truth often is. Do you want to stay with him or should I take you back to the estate?" He hopped on the pegasus.

I didn't think I had the constitution to control my temper around Sylvia. "Fine. Take me to Loch."

Benji held out a hand and yanked me into the saddle. The beast took off at a gallop and spread his wings as he leapt off the edge of the cliff. My stomach hovered in the air before it slammed into place. We flew over a few peaks before we set down outside of a house cantilevered over the side of the mountain.

"You'll be safe here. I need to find Liz and Grant," Benji said. He quickly dropped me to the ground. He was obviously worried about his daughter. Guarding me was a dangerous job.

With gritted teeth, I packed my pride into my pocket before knocking on the modern front door.

Loch answered wearing lounge pants, a T-shirt, and a pair of fleece slippers. My face must have given away my surprise at his attire. "What?" He folded his arms. "I'm not dressed up all the time. This is my home. What are you doing here?"

"I don't want to stay with your family." I stared at my shoes. To get back in his good graces, I probably needed to apologize, but the words stubbornly caught in my throat. Instead, I admitted to the second most humiliating thing about my circumstances. "And Benji said I'd be safest here with you." Reluctantly, I met his gaze.

He shook his head and closed his eyes. The set of his lips and the small lines between his brows indicated he wasn't any happier than I was about the situation.. "Well, come in."

He gestured flippantly with his hand. I wanted to flee but there wasn't anywhere to go except cliff diving.

Inside was very Scandinavian—pale-wood floors with minimal furniture, muted decorations, and a freestanding wood stove with a roaring fire sat in the corner. The walls over the portion of the house that extended past the mountain were all glass.

I'd expected his house to be more like his parents'—cold and sterile. Though it was minimal in nature, there was thought and love behind its intention, making it feel warm, like a real home.

He scooped up a sweatshirt hanging over a kitchen chair and picked up a pair of discarded shoes, before throwing them both into the closet next to the door. "Your room is down there, to the left."

I slipped off my coat and shoes and put them neatly in the closet before heading down the hall. Family pictures hung on the walls. I stopped in front of a particularly interesting one. Two young boys with dark hair and no front teeth stood with their arms thrown over each other's shoulders. One had eyes the color of a tropical ocean and the other one had eyes like a tropical storm. Dozens of photos of them together lined the walls. My heart fractured. It really seemed as if they were brothers.

A lump settled in the hollow of my throat as I thought about the fact that Raiden was almost willing to kill Loch just to be with me. The weariness resting on my shoulders grew heavier, knotting the muscles to the point of pain.

With a big exhale, as if that would release my mounting tension, I opened the door to the bedroom. A quilted picture of mountains and a river hung above the simple wooden bed frame. A yellow comforter, silk pillows, and a desk with fresh white flowers completed the décor. He had definitely planned for me to stay here. Why else would there be a bouquet in the room?

Replaying Benji's words in my head—*to him, you still hold value*—I tucked the dagger inside the drawer of the bedside table.

Though I knew I had to apologize, I wasn't ready yet. So instead, I utilized the incredible steam shower since I smelled like a barn after riding the griffin.

Dressed in jogging pants and a long-sleeved shirt that was softer than air, I proceeded to take my walk of shame. I hated apologizing, especially when I wasn't sure it was warranted.

The smells wafting from the kitchen were divine. I laid my hand over my growling stomach, hoping to muffle the sound.

"Hungry?" Loch stood in front of the kitchen cabinets holding a knife.

"You could say that." I sat down at a barstool on the backside of the obsidian stone island where he worked. "Is there anything I can do?"

"Can you cook?"

"Not really. It wasn't one of my tasks at home. I pretty much hunted and fished. But I'm competent with a knife."

He stopped chopping and deliberately stared. "So I've heard."

I held up my hands. "Hey, it was self-defense."

"I've no doubt," he said dryly. "How did you manage it anyway?"

"I used the dagger R—Raiden left me," I stuttered. Even saying his name hurt.

"Well that explains it."

"Explains what?" I said with an edge to my voice. He, like all the others, didn't think I was capable on my own.

"Knowing Raiden, he infused some of his energy into the blade and didn't tell you."

"Oh." What little self-esteem I had left blew away like a dandelion puff in the wind. I'd been under the impression that maybe my skills as a fighter and a hunter had saved my life. But no, again, it was Raiden. How was I supposed to do this without him?

Loch's gaze caught mine and held it for a few seconds. "It's illegal for us to modify weapons that way. But with him in charge of our border security, he gets a certain amount of leeway. Just to be safe—don't tell anyone you still have it. Who knows when you might need it again."

"Thank you." I appreciated his willingness to bend the law. "And I owe you an apology." I kind of expected him to interrupt and contradict me, but he didn't. "I shouldn't have assumed you were in on the deception. For that, I'm sorry."

"Apology accepted. And I'd like to apologize on my mother's behalf, even though I'm sure she's not sorry. And even if she was, she'd never admit it."

I wondered if he knew that his mom and Penelope had been there when I'd been accused of sleeping with Trent. I was ninety-nine percent sure they were the ones who had insisted Lord Ren and Lady Mosella invoke the parental promise, forcing Trent to tell the truth instead of lying like we'd agreed upon. My cheeks flushed just thinking about it. No way was I bringing up that situation. At least, not yet.

"I'm not sure that's how it's supposed to work," I said.

"Me either. But I'm sorry my mother is the queen of manipulation. Try being her kid sometime." He turned with a set of pot holders in hand and pulled something from the oven.

My stomach growled louder.

"Doesn't anyone feed you?" He set the dish on a metal grate protecting the counter.

I shrugged. "Sometimes I forget to eat."

"I'm assuming old habits die hard?"

"You could say that."

"Well, if nothing else, you'll eat well while staying with me." He dished up a couple plates with casserole. Golden cheese, crispy at the edges, stringed onto the countertop. He scooped it up on his fingers, then licked away the evidence before sprinkling the fresh herbs over the top and setting a dish in front of me. He leaned against the counter and ate while standing. "We kind of got off on the wrong foot. Can we start over?"

"I'd like that," I said, then pointed to the food. "This is amazing. Thank you."

He tipped his chin up in acknowledgement. "So, while you're here, is there anything you want to do? Anything you want to learn?"

The answer came quickly. "I want to learn how to fight. Can you teach me?" I wasn't sure how competent he was, but he was a giant so he had to be better than I was. Plus, I didn't know how to use a sword, just a knife. At home, I had been a force to be reckoned with—the top dog—but here, I was just human. And judo could only get me so far when my opponents were bigger, stronger, and faster. It was like a child fighting a professional boxer.

His brows raised. "Okay, not exactly what I expected. But yeah, I'm not half bad. I'm probably the second-best fighter in the Fiefdom thanks to Raiden's endless practice sessions he forced me into. I'm not him, but then again, nobody is."

I tried to keep my expression neutral, but something gave me away.

"Dang, you really do have it bad for him." He tossed his plate into the sink without rinsing it.

"I don't want to talk about it." I slid off the barstool and rinsed both dishes. I hated dried-on food. Kevin did that all the time, and it irritated me to no end.

"No problem. I don't either."

# THIRTY-SEVEN

"We are *not* vampires," Loch said for the third time.

"I don't know. The more I learn about you, the more I'm convinced you're vampires." They were almost impossible to kill, especially in the Fiefdom. On Earth, they needed to be stabbed directly to the heart, their heads severed, or their bodies burned. They didn't get along well with technology or weapons, they had fangs, they were faster than the eye, and not too long ago, humans were considered a delicacy. Though sunlight didn't kill them and they didn't sleep in coffins, the similarities were frightening.

We sat on a blanket in an open field eating gourmet sandwiches. We'd gotten here via a secret passage that led from his house into a tunnel of obsidian carved through the mountain, ending in this beautiful meadow. Snowcapped peaks, long flowing grasses, and purple flowers begged me to sing *The Hills are Alive* from *The Sound of Music*. But the last time I performed a musical, I had been nearly naked on a beach, dying. I rubbed the scar on my arm where I'd been stabbed by that thornberry thorn and fought to keep Raiden's face out of my head.

Earlier, Loch and I had made a deal—he would train me to fight if I would give him a fair shot to prove he was the best fit for the vacant position. He'd made it perfectly clear he wanted to be king. At least he wasn't lying to me.

A light breeze cooled the sweat-saturated ringlets on the back of my neck. I reached for my sweatshirt and pulled it on over my head. "If I took a picture of you, would you even show up on film?" I re-braided my hair.

He didn't bother hiding his grin. I might've been irritating him with all my questions, but he thought I was funny.

"Of course. You've been in my house."

I was teasing him. I'd spent more time than appropriate looking at the pictures hanging on his walls. At times, I'd had to drag myself away.

Loch stood up and brushed off his athletic pants before holding out a hand and pulling me to my feet. My muscles protested. I folded the blanket and threw it on top of the picnic basket before I picked up the sword with a groan.

"Let's try some hand-to-hand combat," he said.

"That seems pointless." I stabbed the end of the blade into the soil. "The minute one of you gets a hold of me, it's game over," I whined.

"Only if they want to kill you."

I threw him a look that said he was being stupid. "That's what they keep trying to do."

"Haven't you noticed they keep throwing you into things instead of simply breaking your neck?" He raked his fingers through his hair and pulled it into a messy bun on the back of his head. Sunlight warmed the color to a deep espresso. It was dark, but not black, like Raiden's.

Now that he mentioned it, he was right. "Why is that?"

"Because the penalty for killing you outright is execution. For throwing you into a volcano or over the side of a ship—attempted murder—it's banishment. Most of us would rather take our chances with exile. While we don't like living on Earth, we can." He stepped closer, shifting his weight to the ball of his front foot.

Frank was a judo master and always happy to share his knowledge, therefore I had a fair amount of training in martial arts. I readied my stance, and in two seconds flat, I was on my butt. My head—and ego—slapped the earth with a hollow thump, Loch straddling me.

"You need to be faster. Get up," he demanded.

I tried squirming out from under him but he rested his full weight on me.

"You're heavy," I complained.

"And you're not trying very hard." He leaned forward and pinned my hands down. "Do you think you can hurt me? Do whatever it takes to get away." He licked my cheek.

"What the—"

A grin reached his eyes. It was the first time I'd seen a genuine smile from him. A pang of familiarity pierced my throat. He looked too much like his cousin.

He licked my other cheek.

"What are you doing?"

"It's either that or I dangle a loogie over your face."

"Are you twelve?"

"No, but that's what Raiden and I used to do to motivate each other," he said.

"Gross!"

He licked the end of my nose. I shook my head wildly. I tried prying my hands from his iron-like grip. I kicked and bucked. He just laughed harder. He was enjoying himself. Which, of course, aggravated me. There was nothing I could do to get away. He had my legs and hands completely under control. Finally, I relaxed my exhausted muscles and let out a deep, surrendering breath.

"That's it? That's all ya got?" A lock of hair flopped across his face, making him appear younger, more playful.

I didn't move until his hands softened their grip slightly. Years ago, Frank had taught me to use my perceived *disadvantage* as a female to my advantage. Here, with the giants, that perceived flaw was even more pronounced. But not because I was a girl, but because I was human. At least part of me.

I yanked hard with my arms and twirled my hands around to grab his wrists. He jerked away from me—which was the plan. I threw my right leg up and anchored it around his neck using his backward motion against him. I pushed until my leverage was stronger, then I thrust hard with my other leg, knocking him off of me. Quickly, I crossed my ankles and flipped from my back to my stomach, planting my weight on all fours and mule-kicking with my left leg, catching him hard in the nose as he rose to subdue me. I scrambled forward and almost made it out of his reach. If I were only a second quicker. He caught my ankle and yanked me flat on my stomach, then shimmied onto my butt and snatched my flailing arms. He gathered them in one hand and held them in the small of my back.

"That was pretty impressive. I don't know why you need *my* help," he leaned down and whispered in my ear.

"If I didn't need your help, I wouldn't be stuck here." I banged my head against the ground.

He let me go and helped me up. Blood ran from his nose, over his lips, and down his chin.

"Oh, crap! Are you okay?" I grabbed a napkin from the picnic basket and pressed it under his nose to stop the bleeding.

"Thanks for your concern, but it's healed already." He cleaned the blood from his face. "Though I must admit, that stung. You have a wicked back kick."

"Not wicked enough," I muttered.

"You're not giving yourself enough credit. You surprised me." He chuckled, then felt the bridge of his nose with his fingertips. "I never expected that. So we're going to keep this training on the down-low. I don't want anyone else finding out about it. Even though you killed Josha, giants are going to think it was a fluke. And that's probably still your greatest advantage."

We practiced for another hour, but I couldn't get the drop on him. The speed in which he attacked left me frustrated. It was hard to defend what you didn't see coming. Training with a sword was easier because Loch was teaching me the basics so he went slow and didn't use an ounce of his real strength.

Eventually, he blindfolded me, explaining that, maybe, if I used my other senses, it might help. It didn't. By the time we gave up, I was feeling pretty defeated. I'd spent most of my life being better than everyone else at fighting. Here, I was now eating humble pie.

On the way home, I picked grass, leaves, and twigs out of my hair. My fingernails needed a thorough scrubbing. I was thankful he didn't BS me, telling me that I'd get better with practice. I was already better, but not by giant standards.

When we got back, he allotted me nap time, which was humiliating, but I used it anyway.

---

LATER THAT AFTERNOON, Loch offered to show me what occupied his days. We flew to town and walked down the spotless sidewalks to his office. Baskets of flowers lined the storefronts, lending pops of color to the monochromatic scene. We passed by everything from a hair salon, a bank, a home goods store, and an art broker. Loch's office was in the large building that took up an entire city block—glass, concrete, sweeping contours. Across the street was the delicious bakery he'd introduced me to a few weeks ago. My mouth watered at the savory and sweet scents even though I wasn't hungry.

Inside his office was much the same, with clean elegant lines, vases of fresh white flowers, corridors and ebony staircases leading to workplaces. Loch's department was on the top floor overlooking the entire town. In a way, it reminded me of Santorini in Greece, with all the little white houses perched on the hill.

We spent the afternoon going over the ins and outs of running a city. Loch gave me a quick look at what he did all day, from balancing the city's budget to approving work orders to handling people's complaints. None of it was accomplished on a computer. He was like the mayor of old school. Everything was done by hand, on paper, and stored in file cabinets.

After a couple of hours, when I started to nod off, Loch

gave up. "Come on." He bumped into me and I almost toppled over. The gesture reminded me of something Kevin would do, sending a pang of melancholy to my heart. I missed him. I missed Tee. And I missed Sid. I couldn't remember a time when we'd been separated for this long.

Loch snatched my arm to steady me and took a long look at my face. I didn't know what he saw, but his expression changed from teasing to one of concern. "Let's get you home. You look beat."

When we got there, I changed into fleece pajamas while he warmed up dinner. I curled up on the couch, exhausted, physically and emotionally, and admired the evening sky. For most of my life, I'd lived underground. Though the bunker had made me feel safe, this made me feel free. Like if I stared long enough at the stars scattered in the heavens, they would magically transport me to a place where I no longer bore such a heavy responsibility. But today was not that day.

I sat there and fidgeted with my necklace—I never took it off—and fretted about Liz and Grant. They still hadn't arrived. They were giants and they were hard to kill, but I worried anyway. Did someone kidnap them? Kill them? And why? Though I probably knew the answer. With them gone, I was an easier target.

Loch had assured me I was safe. Though that didn't stop me from taking my dagger with me when we left his house. He'd promised not to leave my side, even if there was an emergency. He had staff equipped to deal with any situation. He'd said as long as I remained with him, nobody would dare touch me.

However, his reassurances didn't stop the constant

worry. Vulnerability chipped away at my self-esteem. I hoped it wouldn't always be the case.

The flickering fire, reflecting in the floor-to-ceiling windows, was hypnotizing, and my eyes began to droop. But I had a question I'd been dying to ask Loch. I gnawed at my cuticles. "When I got here, you said something about a free pass. What did you mean?"

He crossed his legs and relaxed deep into his chair. "Wow, I'm surprised you held on this long."

I threw him a fake smile.

He chuckled. "Since you killed Josha, you got yourself a free pass of sorts. Your act garnered you a certain amount of respect. If you want to opt out of sleeping with one of us, you could probably get away with it without losing too much support. I assumed you'd want to use it for Kai, not me, but the choice is yours."

"So really, there's no such thing as a free pass, but because I killed a giant, you believe most of your citizens will look the other way if I choose not to sleep with one of you?" Relief loosened my shoulder.

"Pretty much. And honestly, sex wasn't in the signed contract, though we are very serious about our promises here."

I couldn't believe it. Hope bloomed like a wilted flower receiving water and light. I'd found a way out of sleeping with Kai. And if it meant I had to sleep with Loch, then so be it. I'd do it if it meant not harming Tee. I could only imagine how angry she was with me right now. She was such a traditional romantic that there was no way she was going to be okay with her best friend sleeping with her boyfriend. I wasn't okay with it either.

"So would you really lose your title if we didn't—ah, um . . ." I circled my finger in the air.

"Not likely. My life would be *difficult* for a while until something new came along to distract them. I'd be more worried about what it meant for you. Being human, you're already on unstable ground. If you can't keep your promises, well, for a lot of giants, that's a deal-breaker."

I'd already slept with Trent and Adam. In the grand scheme of things, what was one more? I would simply logic the shit out of the situation. Put on my big boy pants and think like a man. Sex was sex—not love. One might think that him looking just like Raiden would make it easier, but it made matters worse. Much worse.

"What about Adam? He said he would lose his title?"

"Adam, being the good guy that he is, would've willingly stepped down even if he wasn't forced to."

"Is that a compliment to Adam?"

"No. We're giants, and while he's a good man, he's never going to be a strong leader. You've only been here a short time, and most of us have been on our best behavior." Though his message was serious, a teasing smile curled his lips.

My mouth opened like a fish out of water and I cocked my head as if I hadn't heard him correctly.

"Yeah. Can you imagine what we're like when we're not behaving?"

# THIRTY-EIGHT

I reached down for my bottle of water, filled with ice and slices of lemon and lime. Everything Loch did in the kitchen was go big or go home. Just as my fingers wrapped around the glass, a flash of movement caught my attention. I didn't have time to respond before I was knocked to the ground, again, for the hundredth time. But I did manage to land a punch to Loch's stomach before falling. Not that it harmed him. It was like hitting a brick wall. I sat up with my knees to my chest and shook out my fist, trying to abate the sting.

"Wait," Loch said, leaning over the top of me. "Did you see me?"

"I saw something out of the corner of my eye. And you cheated!" I smacked his arm. "You're not supposed to attack me while I'm drinking." I wiped the sweat from my brow and chugged some water.

"Come on." He pulled me up. "I have an idea."

*Here we go again.* So far, none of his *ideas* had worked. My body had the bruises to prove it. What I really wanted was to go back to his house and take a scalding-hot shower. I was so cold, my bones hurt. It had rained intermittently all morning and I was wet from head to toe and covered in mud.

I readied my stance, my weight settled lightly on the balls of my feet and my hands in the defensive position.

"Don't look at me." He bounced up and down on his toes.

"What?" I actually didn't spend a lot of time looking at his face. I usually stared at his chest. His white tank top was drenched, leaving little to the imagination. His body was sculpted to perfection. His athletic pants draped precariously low, and I was worried they might fall down. I hated —hated—how much he resembled Raiden. It was confusing. Especially when he was being nice. Which was most of the time. Loch was pleasant to be around. A little business-like and slightly uptight, but the more I got to know him, the less stuffy he became. From time to time, I even got a glimpse of humor.

"Stare hard at that peak to your left." He pointed.

I shrugged and capitulated. The mountaintop was obscured by dark-gray clouds with a hint of magenta, as if there was blood pumping within.

Out of the corner of my eye, an object blurred toward me. At the last second, I stepped out of the way. A breeze grazed my cheek, followed by the scent of spearmint. I was pretty pleased with myself—until a millisecond later, when my feet were catapulted out from under me. I sprawled in the mud with Loch laughing on top of me.

"Would you like to tell me what's so funny?" A muddy piece of hair gritted between my teeth.

"I think we've figured it out." He pushed up on his

hands, staring down at me. His eyes were glorious—different shades of blue, from cobalt to periwinkle to aqua, blended together in striations of color. "You can't see me move when you look directly at me, but you get a sense of motion when you're looking elsewhere."

I clasped my mouth. "Oh! I think you might be right."

"Let's try one more time." He helped me up, his hands toasty compared to my frozen digits. "Then we're going to get you home. You're cold and you need a shower." His eyes traced the path of mud. "A long one."

*See? Humor.*

It worked. I was to catch his movement, even if I couldn't see him, allowing me to avoid his attack—until I looked at him. Then I tumbled to my butt again, but this time he went down with me.

"I think, from here on out, we can make some progress. You're already a great fighter, better than most of the giants I know. And now that you can see us move, well, you might become a giant after all."

Weirdness fluttered inside my chest from his praise. I didn't need his approval, but it was nice nonetheless.

He threw an arm over my shoulder and we stayed that way until the tunnel narrowed, only wide enough for one person to pass.

Back at the house, I stripped out of my filthy clothes and stepped into the shower. Hot water scaled in thick rivulets over my body. Steam almost obscured the mud swirling down the drain. I stood there for a good thirty minutes.

Finally warm, I threw on an ivory sweater, a pair of leggings, before I found Loch sitting on his couch drinking some hot tea.

He pointed to a steaming mug on the counter. "I thought

today we could do something different. I'm sure you're bored of my repetitive lifestyle. Besides, I think you could use the distraction." He crossed his legs, the top one tapping to an unheard beat, and stared out one of the massive windows.

I wasn't bored with watching him work. The man was efficient and his staff respected him. Which spoke volumes.

"Sure. Whatever you'd like." Swallowing the last bit of tea, I picked up his cup and set it in the sink next to mine.

An almost imperceptible smile twitched the corner of his lip as he rose from his chair and opened the closet door. He handed me a pair of black leather boots and helped me into a wool jacket.

As we stepped outside, he stuck his index finger and thumb in his mouth and whistled. Less than five minutes later, a snow-white pegasus swooped over the ridge and landed in front of us.

My eyebrows practically disappeared into my hairline.

At my surprise, Loch gestured behind me. "The community barn is just over the ridge. During the daytime hours, the grooms have them ready and waiting."

Once I was seated in front of Loch, we flew toward town. My eyes scanned the rugged terrain. I was worried about Liz and Grant. They hadn't been found yet, but there wasn't anything I could do. And I had so many things to worry about at the moment, I had to trust they were okay, until I learned otherwise.

We landed near a concrete stable, and Loch helped me dismount. A groom grabbed the reins and led the pegasus away.

When Loch held out his hand, I hesitated. I wanted to take it. But then again, I didn't want to. My eyes flashed to his face, and I almost missed the fleeting expression of hurt. I grabbed his hand but he tried pulling away.

I'd anticipated his rejection and gripped tighter. "Please don't. It's just hard. I'm sorry."

His fingers relaxed as we walked in the opposite direction from his office, past multiple boutiques. One selling beautiful stationery and old-fashioned typewriters caught my interest. Inside the window were hand-torn papers with gilded edges, fancy pens, and black machines with ivory keys. It was charming.

We turned onto a long sidewalk leading to a marble building with gray veining and few windows. Milky white statues decorated the green lawns in between curving gardens filled with shrubs and flowers. It smelled like mountains in the summer. A few giants sat on scattered benches eating lunch. Most looked up and waved or nodded to Loch. I did a funny half wave, not wanting them to think I was rude.

"Come on," he said. "The good stuff is on the inside."

We stopped in front of the massive arched doors, which were covered in equal-sized squares depicting some kind of people and events sculpted in shiny bronze. I squinted, knowing that I should recognize them, but I glanced at Loch for clarity.

"These are the Columbus Doors. They used to be in the east wing of your capital."

"What are they doing here?" I touched the metal cautiously, as if I might be burned for not identifying a treasure so iconic.

He opened one for me to step inside. It took a moment for my eyes to adjust to the muted light.

In the middle of the room hung a collection of paintings.

At least a hundred spanned the length of the white wall. I stepped toward them hesitantly, then faster until I was at a jog.

My mouth dropped open and tears collected in my eyes. I rushed to wipe them away to see clearly. Water lilies, bridges, soft muted colors. Photos in art history books had not done them justice. The light was otherworldly, like it had been captured by an angel and painted onto the canvas.

"Are these . . ."

"Yes. They're real."

Claude Monet. They had *the* collection of Claude fricking Monet here in Fie. I studied them down the line, wanting to stop and stare forever, yet anxious to move on to see what else they had.

Loch slipped his arm around my elbow and pulled me down another corridor full of van Gogh, Renoir, da Vinci, Michelangelo, and many more from artists I didn't recognize.

I was still in a minor state of shock by the time he escorted me into a restaurant inside of the art museum.

"The usual," he said to a man with salt-and-pepper hair pulled into a ponytail.

We sat at a table next to panoramic windows overlooking the cliff. Outside, giants on their mounts flew in through the canyons and valleys. We sat in a comfortable silence until our food was delivered.

"So?" he questioned with a fork full of lettuce, dressing dripping back onto his plate.

"It's. . . ah. Wow. How did you come by all of it?"

He finished chewing before dabbing the corner of his mouth with the white cloth napkin. "When Earth started taking a turn for the worst, we thought it would be a good idea if we saved as many as we could. What a tragedy to have lost them forever."

At first, I'd been kind of irritated that they had stolen them, but he was right. At least they were safe here. "Are there more?"

"Yes. Most of the art is shared between the Domes, but the ultra-precious ones are at the palace—the *Mona Lisa*, *The Starry Night*, *The Last Supper*, the statue of *David*. Plus, more."

"The statue of *David*?"

"Yeah, it wasn't easy."

A sob stuttered in my throat and tears ran down my cheeks. I covered my whole face with my napkin.

"Bea? Are you okay?" He tugged on the corner of the cloth.

I held up a finger. I needed to get a hold of myself. But to think, these treasures had been saved and someday, I would get to look upon the creations.

Inhaling a trembling breath, I said, "I'm sorry. I just thought they were gone. Destroyed. So many beautiful things lost. And to find out they're safe is a bit over-whelming is all. In a good way." I dabbed at the tears but they refused to stop.

"I had no idea this would affect you so deeply." He reached over to squeeze my hand.

"Honestly, I had no idea it would either. But the magni-tude of a discovery like this . . ." I patted my chest, not knowing how to describe the impact.

"Yeah, I can see how it would be intense. I want you to know how valued and loved these works of art are here in the Fiefdom. Since we're not able to create on this level, we appreciate them in a way humans might not understand.

And, if at any point, people get their shit together, these works of art will be returned to the rightful owners. But until then, we believe it's a great honor to keep them safe."

I'd spent much of my life ignoring my emotions—not because I wanted to, but because I had to. Here, all those emotions were free to roam, and at times, it was almost debilitating. "Thank you." My voice cracked.

"Ruby, I'm going to be frank. I'm very pleased with your reaction."

"Why?"

"Because I feel strongly about them too. It also makes me question my earlier assessment of you." He shifted in his seat.

"Which was?" My pulse kicked, suspecting what he was about to say might irritate me.

"That you lacked a certain amount of depth."

I clasped my chest. "Ouch."

"I know. But I think, maybe, you keep that part buried deep inside. Why is that?"

I sipped some water and defied my instinct to lash out. How could he know what life in Alaska had been like? Instead, I opted for a sliver of vulnerability and a measure of trust. "Because, where I come from, there isn't much time to explore our wants and desires. For the last twelve years, 'kill or be killed' dominated my life. It's not like the thought of losing such beauty didn't bother me, but I had to prioritize things."

His thoughtful expression twisted with pity. "Understandable. But I'm really glad I brought you here."

"Me too."

He folded his hands on the table. A diamond, set into a wide silver band on his finger, sparked in the beams of sunlight penetrating the windows. "So I'm curious. Where do I stand in the lineup?" He tapped his thumbs together.

My eyebrows shot upward at the boldness of his question. "The lineup of who I'm going to choose?"

He nodded.

"I thought I wasn't supposed to talk about it?" I paused with my fork swirled into the spaghetti.

"You're not supposed to *decide* until next week, but there's no reason you can't give me feedback. I'm not going to lie, I'm very competitive, and I'd like to know what I can improve upon."

I laughed. "How are you with constructive criticism?"

He teetered his hand.

"Kai doesn't count, and Trent's at the bottom—not because I don't like him, because I do, but he's a party boy. I fear I'd be left to my own devices. If I'd been born here and knew all the rules, I'd be okay with the situation. The two of us have good chemistry." Though I wasn't sure if it was because I'd been drinking or if it really existed.

"Currently, Adam's my top pick, but he's yet to tell me if he's willing to leave the life he loves to become king. I feel as if he would *help* me rule, and we *definitely* have chemistry. And you're floating somewhere in the middle. Watching you run this city makes me think, logically, you're the best choice. And you've been very patient in training me. You're an exceptionally good instructor. But . . ." A flush rose up my neck, settling on my cheeks. I pressed my cold hands to my face, attempting to hide my discomfort.

"But?" he pressed.

I avoided his eyes as I blurted, "We *lack* a certain amount of chemistry."

"You mean we lack *sexual* chemistry?" He didn't wait for

me to confirm. "Well, it's kind of hard to form any kind of chemistry when you refuse to look at me."

I bit down on the inside of my cheek. He'd noticed.

"Looking at you confuses me." I stared out the window.

"Because I look like Raiden?"

"Yeah. Sometimes when I catch a glimpse of you, my heart stops. And then I have to remind myself you're not him. And then I feel bad for you because it's not your fault. Ugh! It's not your fault, but it's exhausting." I rolled my eyes and puffed out a deep breath.

"You have strong feelings for him, don't you?"

"Yeah. And sometimes I don't even know why. Can you really fall in love so hard, so fast?"

"Can you look at me?"

I reluctantly found his gaze.

"Do you know that if Raiden wanted to, he could challenge me for the title of First-Born son?"

I nodded.

"You do?" His forehead wrinkled with surprise. "If you love him that much, why don't you encourage him to challenge me?"

"He'd have to kill you."

"True. And he'd win." If Loch was concerned about dying, he hid it well.

"I would never encourage him to kill you in order to be with me. I don't want you to die. And I don't want him to kill you. I would *never* do that to him. Or you."

"Why?" He rubbed the sharply trimmed five o'clock shadow on his chin.

"Because I love him too much to make him do something so awful. You're his cousin. If the roles were reversed and I had to kill Kevin or Tee in order to be with Raiden, I couldn't do it." I leaned forward and practically snarled, "I *wouldn't*."

"That's good to know. I'm not ready to die, and he's the best warrior of our generation. While I've spent the last few years running a city, he's been out searching for his parents. The creatures out there—" he ticked his head toward the window, "—are formidable, and he's still alive." He traced a pattern on his sweating water glass before he took a drink. "So what's it going to take for you to look at me? I feel like, if you could just get to know me, you might actually like me." His elbows rested on the table while his fingers flared apart. "I mean, seriously, Raiden likes me. Shouldn't that be a clue? Look, I've been honest with you—I *do* want to be king because I think I'd be good at it. But I don't want a relationship like my parents have. I mean, come on, it's got to be pretty clear they didn't marry for love. Hell, they don't even *like* each other. I should know. While I'm not ready to profess my love for you, I'm coming to respect you. You have determination, fire, and today, I learned you have heart. Far more than I expected. And in the future, if you choose me, I'm hoping the respect can grow into more. But first, you have to give me a chance."

He was right. I was being unfair. I just didn't know how not to.

# THIRTY-NINE

The sun, having risen above the mountains, warmed my black sweatshirt, its light spreading across the valley like the slow flow of maple syrup over fresh pancakes. Yes, I was hungry. We'd been out here for hours. Loch had insisted we start practice in the dark, where I didn't have the disadvantage of using my eyes like a normal person.

I kicked a stone out of my path, only to catch a flash of movement to my right. Instead of backing away, I stepped forward, my leg extended near the ground. Loch tripped and fell ass over teakettle. It was like watching a massive rag doll cartwheel over the ground in slow motion, from the surprise widening his eyes to his hair flinging in his face, to his long arms and legs no longer under his control.

Laughter exploded from my chest. I bent over and held my stomach. I was going to pay for my actions, but sometimes the pain *was* worth the gain.

Loch tackled me and twirled me around in the air, my

limbs flying outward from centrifugal force. I laughed harder until we both landed on the ground. I tumbled to a stop and closed my eyes, trying to erase the dizziness. The sweet smell of flowers, grass, and dirt fragranced the air, followed by the crisp scent of spearmint.

A shadow darkened behind my closed eyelids, and I opened them to find Loch propped over me, studying my face. He picked something from my hair and licked his finger to wipe mud from my cheek. The slight fluttering of my heart made me shy away. It was complicated when the man you were *dating* looked exactly like the man you loved.

"Don't," he whispered, almost like a plea. He grabbed my chin and forced me to look at him. The sun reflected on his hair like melted dark chocolate. The blue flames in his eyes danced as he ran a thumb over my bottom lip. It was cold compared to the warmth of my mouth. I concentrated on the color of his eyes, the only thing that didn't remind me of Raiden.

It wasn't as if I didn't like Loch—I did. I'd never imagined dating four different guys in four weeks would be so difficult. Awkward, yes. Emotionally taxing, not so much. I'd thought there was no way I could develop feelings for someone in a week, let alone multiple someones. Now, a future with either Loch or Adam actually seemed plausible. I'd never been so confused in my entire life. I wanted to bury my head in the sand and deny this was happening. It wasn't like kissing Loch was going to be a chore—though it would be easier if I could pretend he was Raiden. Over the last few weeks, I'd proven I was stupid—but I wasn't cruel.

So I pulled up my big girl pants and decided Loch, as himself, deserved a fair shot.

He ran the backs of his fingers down the side of my

cheek. I closed my eyes and enjoyed the tingles feathering over my skin. When I opened them again, the intensity of Loch's gaze excited me. My instinct was to push the emotion away. Instead, I leaned into the distress and lifted my lips toward his. He cupped his hand behind my head and met me halfway.

His lips were gentle, tentative, as if he were waiting for me to change my mind. The thought occurred to me for approximately two seconds before I forgot what I was thinking entirely. When he realized I wasn't going anywhere, he deepened the kiss, his tongue exploring my mouth, and a knot of longing twisted low in my stomach. I didn't want to desire him—the guilt was soul crushing—but my body didn't care what I wanted.

Too soon, he pulled away and laid on his back next to me. He shimmied his arm under my neck and I scooted in close. He intertwined his free hand with mine. Neither of us spoke. We laid in the grass, listening to the wind swish through the valley and the birds sing. An enormous dragon-fly, with triple sets of wings and eyes the size of nickels, landed on our clasped hands. Its wings shimmered in the light like an oil spill on water.

"They symbolize transformation or resurrection after hardship," Loch whispered.

"That's poetic," I said dryly. "I honestly wish it was over already."

"Really?"

"Yeah." I wanted to tell him I was tired, confused, ashamed, and I felt all alone. There was no one for me to talk to, no one to get advice from who didn't want something from me.

"I guess I can see that. I mean, at first, it might seem fun

—choosing between the Fiefdom's most eligible bachelors. But if I really think about it, that's a lot of pressure. You get one week to decide who you trust the most."

"I never thought of it like that, but yeah, you're exactly right."

The dragonfly buzzed off, and I sat up, facing Loch and crossing my legs. I picked a yellow flower, then another, and started weaving a dandelion chain.

Still lying on the ground, he clasped his arms behind his head. "And how well can you really know someone after only a week?"

"I'm not sure your situation is any better." Kai, Trent, Adam, and Loch seemed like pawns in a thousand-year-old prophecy. Where was their choice?

"I don't know. It could be worse. I kind of like the girl I'm seeing right now. Though she did just try to eliminate me from the competition." He quirked a dark brow.

I kicked him softly. "You're the one who told me to play dirty."

He sat up and knelt in front of me, resting his hands casually on his legs. Dirt was embedded under his manicured nails and his hair was a tattered mess, subsequently making him even more handsome, if possible. "And I hope you plan on using that advice wisely." He leaned in, his lips just shy of touching mine. His energy buzzed over my sensitive skin, his breath warming my face.

I didn't want to like him. *I didn't.* It made me feel foolish, indecisive, and sleazy. What was it about these giants? And why did I feel some sort of attraction to each one of them? Okay, so they were ridiculously good-looking, but I wasn't a shallow person. I respected people who were hard workers, those who went above and beyond what they were required to do. People who cared for others more than they cared for themselves. And looking at Adam and Loch, they both had these traits. Trent, not so much, but he was so charismatic, he was easy to like, though he was my last choice because of his carefree attitude. I was going to need all the help I could get if I wanted to succeed. Adam—our chemistry was off the charts, and I adored his parents. Loch—if only he didn't look like someone else. Someone who, every time I closed my eyes to sleep, showed up in my dreams as if to remind me of what I couldn't have.

"You know, you think too much," Loch whispered.

"You're one to talk."

He grabbed the flower chain I was weaving and placed it on top of my curls. He smiled like he thought it was cute before he reached up and tangled his fingers in the hair at the nape of my neck. He drew me the last remaining inch and bit my bottom lip gently with his teeth. I sighed and gave in. It wasn't like my body didn't want him. My skin tingled, my pulse raced. I wanted him—I just didn't *want* to want him.

He paused as if he could sense my hesitation. I rose up on my knees and snaked my hand behind his neck, refusing to let go. His lips paused over mine before he kissed me again, harder this time, like he meant it. His hand squeezed, pulling on my hair. I gasped as his other hand skimmed over my waist, landing in the middle of my back, drawing me closer. My breasts pressed against his muscled chest, my nipples puckering in response.

A growl escaped from Loch's throat before he pulled away and glanced at the sky. Out of the corner of my eye, I saw a white pegasus dip below the tree line.

"Come on, I'm not keen on having an audience." He

helped me off the ground. "Let's go back, shall we?" he asked, a cautious hope in his eyes.

I nodded. I had to get this over with some time. It might as well be now.

He held my hand all the way through the tunnel, even though it was only wide enough for one of us at a time. He opened the back door to his house and stepped aside so I could squeeze past. He stopped me and placed a kiss on my cheek beside my ear before he said, "I'll be back in fifteen minutes, tops. You're welcome to check out my room if you want."

Heat rushed up my neck.

I shut the door behind me and leaned against the wood. I had to shake the guilt I felt over sleeping with so many guys in such a short time. I always made fun of Tee for being such a romantic, but if I was honest, I was probably a bit of a romantic too. I need to logic the shit out of this situation. Take comfort in the fact that I'd found a way *not* to sleep with my best friend's boyfriend.

Knocking the back of my head against the door, I decided to reflect while showering. Two birds, one stone.

After I finished, I wiped the steam from the mirror with a towel and stared at my reflection. Over the last few weeks, a few pounds had stuck to my bones. I could no longer count my ribs and the hollows of my cheeks were filling in. The dark circles under my eyes had vanished, making my irises look bluer than normal.

I dressed comfortably and paced the floor, waiting for Loch to get back. What was taking him so long? Fifteen minutes had passed fifteen minutes ago. I threw on my shoes, tucked my dagger into the waistband of my jogging pants, and snuck into the tunnel, leaving the door open in case there were people out there trying to kill me. But I was getting worried.

Darkness blinded me until my eyes adjusted. I trailed my fingers over the damp stone and stepped carefully. I stopped and tilted my ear forward. Angry whispers resonated down the narrow passage.

"Whatever! But we're doing this for *you*," a female voice said.

"What, exactly, are you doing for me?" Loch replied.

"I'm here to kill Ruby."

My heart tripped. I should've run, but I stood frozen in place. My fingers curled over the hilt of my dagger.

"What?" Loch said loudly. "Get the fuck out of here. Now!"

"Loch! Stop and listen to me! They found Liz and Grant this morning. They'll know I'm in on the assassination attempts. The crown should be yours. You've said it yourself. And if Ruby doesn't choose you, then it'll be lost forever. If I kill her now, we can find another way for you to take the throne."

"And what makes you think she *won't* choose me?" Loch said with a hint of arrogance.

"Because when Liz and Grant get here, they'll tell everyone it was me that tried to kill them. And *everyone* knows I do whatever you say. I always have. You give the orders, I follow."

"Then follow this order, Vanessa—Leave. Now!" His voice bounced off the tunnel walls.

My free hand turned into a fist. *Bitch!* I knew I recognized that voice.

"Loch?" She sounded hurt.

"You heard me. Now go! And don't come back. I have this under control."

A cold sweat broke out over my face and neck. He was letting her escape before Liz and Grant had time to accuse her of attempted murder. Did he know she had been behind the attempts on my life the entire time? Or was *Loch* the mastermind behind the assassination plots? I shook my head. It didn't make sense. But then again, he hadn't denied it either. And why was he letting her go?

What was I going to do? Flashes of light blurred the outer edges of my eyes. I blinked tightly and concentrated on taking slow, deep breaths before I hyperventilated and passed out in the tunnel where Loch could find me. Then he'd know that I knew he might be behind everything. Or at least that I knew Vanessa was involved. Unless . . . he was truly angry and didn't know anything about Vanessa's plans. But then why had he let her go? And what exactly did he have under control? It wasn't like I could ask if he was the ringleader, an accomplice, or an unknowing bystander without possibly endangering myself. Once my mind darted down that rabbit hole, it tumbled like a rock rolling down-hill, picking up speed along the way.

A gust of wind whipped through the tunnel, slamming the open door shut. Shit. They'd find out I was there. I scuttled away, my hands against the stone as a guide. Tiny pieces of dirt and rocks sprinkled on the floor behind me. I found the doorknob by exploring blindly and opened it quietly. Once on the other side, I ran to my room.

What was I going to do? How could I sleep with someone who wanted to kill me? I hoped that wasn't the truth, but how could I know for sure?

A minute later, someone knocked lightly on my bedroom door. My hand rested on the dagger.

"Ruby?" Loch said from the other side. "Can I come in? I'd like to finish what we started."

My heart kicked against my ribs like a dog scratching an itch. What exactly did he want to finish?

I pulled my hand away from my weapon just as the door cracked open and he peered inside. "Are you okay?" Concern washed over his face.

I stepped backward, running into the corner of the bed, but I caught myself before I fell.

"What's wrong? Your heart's racing and you smell scared."

Until that moment, I hadn't been aware that fear really had a smell. But if it did, I was wearing it.

Loch's glacial eyes narrowed as he stood in front of the only exit. He slid his hands in his pockets as if he could feel my fear and he was trying to deescalate it. "Talk to me, Ruby."

My pulse raced. I didn't know what to say. I didn't know what to do. Whatever I said needed to be believable. Otherwise, he might kill me. There was no way I could win a real fight against him—he knew all my weaknesses.

"Ruby, what's going on? You're scaring me?" His eyes darted to the dagger at my waist.

*Tell me about it.*

"Hello?" He waved a hand in the air.

"Yeah, I'm sorry. I just . . . well . . . you know," I stuttered incoherently. "I . . . uh . . ." The corner of my eye started twitching. I rubbed the palms of my hands over my face, desperately trying to buy myself time to think. Though my instincts screamed not to turn my back on the enemy, I did it anyway and walked toward the window. Jumping out of it wasn't an option. A sheer cliff with a five-hundred-foot drop awaited me. I stood a better chance against Loch.

I crossed my arms over my heart, clasping my hands on my shoulders. "I don't want to sleep with you." It was the only other thing I could think of that frightened me at this particular juncture.

"Oh." He sounded disappointed. "Any reason why?"

"Because every time I look at you, I think of him," I whispered. Sticking to the truth was the best way to lie.

I jumped as a pair of warm hands rested heavily on my shoulders. A powerful burst of cool air mixed with rain, earth, and smoke caught in my throat right before a gust of wind slammed the bedroom door shut. We both jumped and spun around. The solid wood had a hairline fracture right down the middle.

"That's weird. Why do the doors keep slamming shut around here?" he said, though it didn't sound like a question. He cocked his head and stared at me for a few long seconds, looking as if he wanted to say something. "Did you do that?"

"Do what? Slam the door? I'm standing right here. Must be a ghost. Do you have those?"

He shook his head. "Hmmm. Anyway, are you sure that's all that's wrong?"

I shrugged. "I don't know. I feel overwhelmed. I think it's really getting to me. I haven't seen my family, my dog, I'm pretty sure my best friend hates me, the guy I'm in love with can only be with me if he kills his cousin, I'm not cut out to be anyone's queen, and to top it off, Liz and Grant are still missing. There's probably more if you give me a second," I rambled. I allowed the tears building up to spill over. I needed to sell my fear, even if he was purchasing the wrong one.

"Well, I can help you with the last one. That's why I left earlier. One of my friends landed in the valley to tell me Liz and Grant have been found. They're both alive."

"That's a relief," I said, though I already knew that. "Are they okay? Did they say what happened?"

"I don't know yet. All I know is that they're alive."

"Who told you? What did they say?"

"A friend. You've not met her. She said they'd been found but didn't know the details."

He knew I'd met Vanessa. His lying didn't bode well, but I wasn't about to push the issue.

I turned back toward the window. "When will they get here?"

"I don't know. Later today or tomorrow sometime." He rested his hands on my shoulders, his thumbs rubbing gently on my exposed skin. Goosebumps prickled down my spine. "I know you're not ready to do this yet, but you leave tomorrow. I'd understand if you'd rather sleep with Kai instead of me. But I want you to know, given enough time, I think we'd be happy together. I'm not going to lie, I'm surprised I actually like you. I thought you'd be uninteresting, boring, basic. The last generation of humans were so shallow, I figured you'd be no different. I was wrong."

Thirty seconds of silence passed between us.

He didn't stop rubbing my shoulders until he said, "Should I go make us some lunch, then?"

I reached up and grabbed his hand. "No."

I could do this. I had to. Tee was already angry at me for leaving her behind. If I slept with her boyfriend, our relationship might not survive. Sure, Tee would understand. If she knew what I was going through—being forced to sleep with someone who might want to kill me or sleep with her boyfriend—she'd tell me to sleep with Kai. *I knew she would.* But that would alter our relationship, probably break it. And even though broken things could be fixed, they'd never be the same.

"Stay," I said.

L och slid his hand down my arm and linked our fingers together. Though I didn't want to, I pulled the dagger from my waistband and set it on my bed. If I brought it with me, he was going to know something else was worrying me.

My eyes lingered on the weapon as he gently guided me out the door and up the hall to his room.

"Man, I've never felt you this nervous or scared. I can attack you, hold you down, threaten you with loogies," he said, trying to calm me with humor, "but I want to have sex with you, and you freak out. My ego is feeling the pain."

"What?" I stopped.

"You're making me feel bad. Seriously, if you don't want to—"

"No! Not that. Before—you said you could feel me?"

He hesitated. "Yeah."

"What does that mean?"

He cocked his head and an eyebrow. "Giants have better senses than humans? Hasn't anyone told you that?"

"Yes, but I didn't think they meant it like that."

"Well, some of us are better at it than others. I've spent a week with you, so it makes it easier to differentiate your emotions by the speed of your heart and the smell of your skin. Right now, you're mad. Earlier, you were terrified. Though I'm still not sure why." He stopped us in front of his door but didn't attempt to open it.

"Why didn't someone tell me?" I rocked back on my heels. It was like they possessed a built-in lie detector. They couldn't read my face, but they could literally read my body.

"Probably just fell through the cracks. Sometimes I forget all the things you don't know. You've only been here for four weeks or so. Give yourself a break. All your friends were given classes on giants. You skipped that part and dove right off the deep end."

*Not by choice.*

"So when I'm mad or scared, I smell weird?" I wanted to lift my arm and sniff my pits, but I resisted.

"Not exactly. When your emotions are heightened, you smell even better than normal. And normally, you smell *really* good."

Fire blazed from my chest to my cheeks.

"It's nothing to be embarrassed by. I think that's part of the reason giants have always been so attracted to humans. 'Fee, fie, foe, fum, I smell the blood—'"

"Yeah, yeah, yeah," I rapid-fired, holding up my free hand to stop him. He still had my other hand intertwined with his and didn't seem keen on letting it go.

"Well, not all of us want to *eat* you. At least not that way." He bumped my shoulder.

I brought my hands to my face, hoping to cool down my

blazing skin. "So why didn't giants come to Earth and kidnap humans before now?"

He looked as if I'd insulted his honor.

"Okay, I'm sure you could find plenty of people that would go with you willingly," I rephrased.

He nodded once upon my acknowledgement. "Because until you entered our gate, that electric shock killed humans. My cousin said something about you, in particular, disables the system for around an hour."

"Really?"

"I didn't believe it before, but Ruby, you're our salvation. I believe it now."

"Why?"

He turned his head away like he didn't want to answer. "Because if someone would've told me a week ago that I would want to marry you for more than the title, I would've told them they were crazy."

"So you're not just interested in the title?"

"Not anymore." He twisted the doorknob to his bedroom, gently swinging the door open. Light spilled in from glass-paneled doors. Cream curtains framed a suspended deck with wire railings that jutted out over the cliffside.

"Aren't you afraid you'll miss your chance at true love?" As I stepped over the threshold into his bedroom, my heart picked up the pace. I willed it to slow down.

He followed me but didn't close the door as he wandered across the room and stared outside. "You mean possession? I know every person in my Fiefdom. Unless she isn't born yet—which is a level of creepiness I'm not willing to accept—then she isn't out there. And except for the fact that I feel a responsibility toward my people, I love and respect them, I have more feelings *like that* for you than any of them." His breath fogged up the glass.

"Really?"

He turned and looked at me, his hand lifting with the question. "Why is that so hard to believe?"

"It's only been a week."

"And it took you only a week to fall in love with my cousin. Do you have any feelings whatsoever for me?" He crossed his arms as if protecting himself from my answer.

If Loch wasn't a psycho mastermind killer, then maybe. My heart, intent on doing acrobatics inside my chest, flipped and flopped through my confusion.

"Yes. No. Maybe. I don't know. Why couldn't one of you just make it easy for me?" I reached up and tightened my drooping ponytail.

Loch chuckled. "Kai did."

That was the truth. And now I was going to have to make sure he and Tee didn't pay the price for my screw up. Frustration and ridiculousness for the entire fucked-up situation simmered inside. An hour ago, this would have been a lot easier.

I was calmer now, about seventy percent sure Loch wasn't the mastermind behind the attempts on my life. I was fifty percent sure he didn't know who was coordinating them, and fifty percent sure he'd just found out that Vanessa was one of them. But my judgment wasn't always the sharpest.

He stepped closer.

I could do this, I convinced myself. If he wanted to kill me, he would've done it already. Or he could have let Vanessa do his dirty work.

He undid his ponytail and scrubbed both of his hands

through his hair before pushing it away from his face. "I'm going to take a shower. If you're here when I'm done, okay. If not . . ." his eyes darted away momentarily. "I'll understand."

I sort of smiled and nodded.

He yanked his T-shirt off. He was sculpted from his pecs down his rippled abs to the V-shaped muscles disappearing under his athletic pants. He balled it up and threw it on the floor right next to the laundry basket before he walked to the bathroom and closed the door.

The cream carpet was plush under my feet as I explored his room. A huge canvas of a wolf drawn with charcoal hung on the wall opposite a four-poster bed. Two end tables, with matching ivory lamps, were on either side. I twisted a strand of hair around my finger and sat down on the edge of the haphazardly made bed as I stared out the window. Floating particles glinted in the hazy afternoon light shining through the glass. Nervous energy bounced in my leg while I reassured myself for endless minutes that I was doing the right thing.

Sturdy iron rings hung from each corner of the bed. I was curious as to what those were for, but I didn't get a chance to ponder that thought long. The bathroom door opened, letting out a puff of steam, followed by Loch with a white towel wrapped around his waist. His dark hair was slicked away from his face and a real smile crept from his lips to his beautiful blue eyes when he saw me.

*If he wanted to kill me, I'd already be dead,* I placated myself again.

My heart raced and sweat warmed under the weight of my hair. I appreciated that he didn't point it out. I hoped he couldn't tell the difference between excitement and fear. I wasn't sure I could.

He stopped in front of me and placed a finger under my chin, gently forcing me to look up. "Since you're still here, I'm going to assume . . ." His voice trailed away.

I picked at my thumb cuticle and nodded.

"Would you like a drink? Something so we can relax?"

As much as I wanted to scream, *Yes! Please!* I shook my head. What if I was wrong and he *did* plan to kill me? Now, when I was in a vulnerable state, would be the time to do it.

"Suit yourself, but if you don't mind, I'm going to get one." He opened an armoire door and slid out a shelf with a decanter of alcohol and etched crystal glasses.

Judgment must've flashed across my face, unless judgment had a smell too.

"What?" He shrugged. "I like a glass before I go to bed some nights."

"And the kitchen's too far away?" I teased.

Despite the fact that I'd declined, he handed me a drink anyway.

"If you don't drink it, I will." He folded open the glass doors to the deck and beckoned for me to go first.

"You planning on putting on some clothes?" I sat down on one of the outdoor chairs separated by an iron table. I rested my drink on the table and stared at the rocky cliffs and green valleys.

"Why bother?" He sat down next to me, the split in his towel precariously high, showing off his thick, muscled thigh. He reached over and took my free hand. Invisible sparks raced up my arm, down my sternum, and settled into my core.

I was going to need that drink after all. If he wanted me

dead, it wasn't going to matter if I was drunk or sober. I took a sip. It burned my throat and warmed my stomach. Memories of my dad enjoying his nightly splash of Macallan flashed in my brain. It surprised me when I realized my parents would actually like Loch, though I was pretty sure they'd like Adam and Raiden as well. Trent—they might like him, but I didn't think they would respect him. I was pretty sure I'd have had their approval on any of the other three—so long as Loch wasn't planning my demise or knew who the actual ringleader was. It wasn't Vanessa, that I was sure of. She had too much trouble controlling her temper to be the mastermind.

We sipped in silence as the sun set below the mountains, painting the sky in layers of rose, lavender, and periwinkle.

I let out a deep breath, releasing some of the day's stress.

"I hear ya," Loch whispered. "It's a lot to shoulder sometimes. I spend a fair amount of time out here unwinding." He caressed the back of my hand with his thumb.

"I can see why."

"So if we were to marry, would you want to live in the capital or here?"

The question startled me. "Um, I don't know what the capital's like, but I'm starting to think you may have a hard time getting me to vacate this spot. My bed could go right here—" I pointed to the decking, "—where I can sleep under the stars." I wasn't sure if I was lying so he thought he had a chance at the title and didn't kill me, or if I was dead serious. Loch was a good fit and he *wanted* to rule. If I could trust him, logically, he'd be my first choice. The thought shocked me.

"*Our* bed can go right there if that's what you want, and

*we* can sleep under the stars." He downed the last of his drink, set it on the table, and stood. He dragged his fingers through his damp hair. "This is weird. I'm pretty confident when it comes to women. With you, no offense, a sure thing, I'm struggling."

I drank the last of my whisky and choked, not sure if it was because I was laughing at his comment or because it burned. "None taken. Because honestly, I'm not usually the girl who is a sure thing. I was heartbroken and I screwed up. And I regret it. But not because I have to sleep with you, but because I'm disappointed with my actions."

"So let's analyze this," he said.

"That's very Loch of you." I stood up and tapped his bare chest, his skin hot and smooth.

Quiet laughter shook his stomach as he grinned wide enough to expose his long, white, very sharp fangs. A thrill ran up my spine.

He tipped my chin up with two fingers, forcing my eyes to lock with his. "If we'd spent this week together and there was no Raiden, no contract, no title, would we be here right now?"

My gaze swept from his dark hair, falling over impossibly blue eyes, to his strong jawline, down his etched chest and stomach, to the top of his towel. If there was no Raiden? *Hell, yeah.* But there *was* a Raiden—*damn him.*

I swallowed my guilt and nodded. "Yes, I think we'd be here."

Relief flooded his face as a shy smile crept forth. He glided a hand behind my neck and wove his fingers deep into my hair. His eyes swayed with blue flames while he studied my face as if deciding on his next move.

A breeze carrying the scent of fresh air, soap, mint, and

man tickled my nose, and I made the decision for him. I grabbed his waist and pulled him closer, sliding my hand under the towel, encouraging the material to fall from his hips.

He cocked a brow as if I'd issued a challenge. Maybe I had.

In one sure move, his lips met mine. No question. No hesitation. He held on to the back of my head and lifted the hem of my shirt with his free hand. I ducked out of it with barely a breath between kisses. In a practiced maneuver, he unclipped my bra before I could help. The loose straps slid from my shoulders, but I reached up to keep it from falling.

Loch backed away from our kiss and gently peeled my fingers loose. The lacy black material drifted to the floor, stark against the pale decking.

I went to shield my nakedness, but he shook his head. "You're beautiful. No need to be shy."

He certainly wasn't. Shy, I mean. Beautiful wasn't a strong enough description.

Without taking his eyes off of mine, he reached for my pants. Seconds later, I stepped out of them, along with my socks.

I gasped as he lifted me up and carried me inside. He pulled the curtains shut, leaving us in almost complete darkness. He set me down on the mattress and rummaged around in the ottoman at the end of the bed. I could hear him better than I could see him. Flames arose from two candles he'd placed on each side table.

He stood up, dangling a pair of handcuffs from one finger and a black mask in the other. My heart, nervous a moment ago, tripped before it picked up the pace.

"Okay, I can see you're not ready for that level of trust."

He tossed the cuffs to the side, where they clinked on the hardwood floor, echoing loudly in the silence. He held up the blindfold. "Too much?"

Of all the giants to be kinky, why did it have to be him? I was already scared, but now it was worse. Honestly, how bad could it be? I could take it off at any time.

"I'm okay with that." I tipped my head at the blindfold.

"You sure?"

With my lower lip pinched between my teeth, I nodded. It would probably help if I couldn't look at him. Because every time I did, I was painfully reminded of who he wasn't. *Was that the point?*

He stepped in front of me, his magnificent body not hiding what his brain was thinking, and slipped the satin material over my head. One of my senses was left in utter darkness. It was weird but exhilarating knowing I couldn't see anything but he could.

The smell of vanilla and tobacco with a hint of smoke drifted into the room—sweet and sexy, yet masculine. Music began to play quietly at first. I strained to listen to the tune as it got louder and louder, until it was the only thing I could hear, taking away another one of my senses. Shivers peppered my arms just from the singer's voice. I'd never heard this version of "Billie Jean" by Michael Jackson, but I'd heard the original enough to know every word. Jackson was one of Tee's favorite artists, giving me a quick reminder why I was doing this.

Loch pulled my hair from my ponytail and slowly let the strands loose, tickling my back and shoulders. My breath hitched.

He slipped his arms behind my legs, hoisted me onto the

bed, and rested my head on his silk pillow. The feeling that I had no control, I couldn't see, couldn't hear, was terrifying yet exquisite.

The bed sagged. A finger traced the line above my black panties. Heat flashed in my groin. My pulse thumped erratically. He pushed a hand under the small of my back and lifted me like I weighed nothing as he shimmied my panties off. My foot twitched as something light tickled my heel, around my ankle, and up my calf. Whatever it was skimmed between my thighs. I arched my back and a small gasp escaped my lips. It twirled over my stomach, under my breasts, my nipples puckered in anticipation. Sadly, I was disappointed. He was taunting me.

Searing lips burned the sensitive skin along the crook of my neck. I stretched away so he had easier access, and a set of teeth nipped my earlobe. I flinched but remembered to hold still as visions of pearly white fangs appeared. He cupped my cheek and kissed along my jaw, finally moving to my mouth. The sharp tang of whisky changed my mind about not liking it. I reached behind his head to deepen the kiss, throwing caution to the wind. My brain short-circuited under the fire running the length of my skin.

His tongue danced with mine, his lips slow and deliberate, driving me wild. I gripped his shoulder with no fear of hurting him. A fang caught my lower lip as he kissed me harder. A growl rumbled from his throat before his lips drifted down my neck and over my collarbone. I stopped breathing, predicting his path. I twined my fingers into the sheets and held tight as his mouth, hot and wet, began to suck and pull on my pulsating nipple. He trailed a hand down my stomach, stopping inches away from the thumping between my legs. Frustratingly slowly, millimeter by millimeter, he swirled a finger through the hair there until finally it landed on my throbbing clit. I bucked but he held me in place with his arm, his mouth still devouring my breast.

His finger massaged up, down, and around, before he slid it inside me. He continued to rub my clit with his palm until his finger found the spot. I moaned as he worked it harder, until my body fought for release. Seconds before I climaxed, he pulled his finger out, leaving me unsatisfied yet anticipative.

"You taste as good as you smell," he whispered in my ear.

His weight shifted until I could feel his body straddle mine. His long, hard shaft glided easily through the wetness already between my legs. I lifted my hips, encouraging him. His breath drifted along my neck in a heated caress as he ran a hand up my arm and gathered both of my hands in his. He lifted them above my head and held them captive with one hand while the other traveled over my cheek, to my neck, fire following the path until he flicked my nipple, hard.

A startled yelp left my chest as he thrust his length all the way inside. A measure of pain and surprise immediately turned to desire as he plunged again, hard and deep. Stifled screams and moans tore from my throat. Just as I was about to tumble over the edge of oblivion, he let go of my hands and slowed his rhythm, extending my pleasure—or hindering it.

I dug my nails into his back and wrapped my legs around him. "Please," I whimpered between hot kisses.

I didn't hear him laugh over the deafening music, but I could feel humor rumble in his chest as he continued with his long, slow, deep thrusts, keeping me on the brink of climax but not allowing me to finish. I teetered on the precipice, that constant moment between pleasure and pain, until I could take no more.

"Please, are you trying to kill me?" I said as his chest rubbed against my tight nipples. Heat built like an inferno, threatening to combust if only he would capitulate.

He nuzzled into my neck and whispered, "Exactly the opposite. I'm trying to give you a reason to stay."

He picked up the pace, just enough to propel me to orgasm. It worked its way from my core and spread through my body like a shock wave, lasting far longer than I was accustomed to. My muscles slumped with satisfaction and relief.

But he didn't stop. He captured my hands above my head and pumped until I begged him not to stop again. This time, I cried out in satisfaction along with him.

He collapsed on my chest, breathing fast, and kissed the delicate skin beneath my ear. He lifted his finger and the blaring music softened. "Sorry, I was hoping to make that last longer. But damn."

*Longer?* I'd barely survived as it was. "That was incredible," I said, thinking there was no way he should be apologizing. My body tingled with the aftereffects.

"Oh, once you trust me, I have plans. So many plans." He kissed my fingertips before he lifted the blindfold off my face, his eye color flickering like live flames under the yellow candlelight. His expression was open and unguarded, making him appear younger and not as confident as he portrayed all the time. His beauty took my breath away. I'd bet my life that not many people had ever seen him like this.

"I could do this for a lifetime," he said.

417

Before I could reply, he covered my mouth with a finger, like he didn't want to hear whatever it was I was about to say.

418

# CHAPTER 41

# ISLE NOIR - THE CAPITAL

Dense clouds rolled under the pegasus's black hooves like we were galloping through a fog of dry ice, obscuring my view of the ground. Benji and I were flying to Isle Noir, the capital of the Fiefdom, on the final leg of my journey. Soon, all my weeks would converge with one decision.

"So Liz and Grant are okay?" I asked Benji. His wife, Ramona, flew next to us.

"Yes. They're both safe. We're pretty hard to kill." He patted the back of my hand.

The knot in my stomach loosened, knowing they were safe. I hated that I was the reason they'd been hurt in the first place.

"What did they say happened?"

"Vanessa shot their mounts with thornberry-infused arrows on their way back to the Fie. I think to make sure you didn't have any protection while there."

My grip on the saddle horn tightened. Somewhere along the way, I'd underestimated Vanessa.

"I apparently didn't need any guards while there," I said, still slightly suspicious of Loch's motives.

"Loch had Vanessa imprisoned right before we left," Benji said.

I straightened my back. "He did?" That made me feel better.

"Yup, but she refuses to talk," he grumbled. "I don't understand how Liz and she were ever best friends."

"Small pool of applicants?"

Benji chuckled. "I suppose."

"Can't her parents make her tell the truth?"

"No, that only works with the First Families."

Desperate to know if I could trust Loch or not, disappointment settled in my shoulders as I compiled a list of the reasons why Loch was innocent versus guilty. In the end, the scales were even. Though finding out he had imprisoned Vanessa tipped the balance. But, if a smart person wanted to look innocent, that was exactly how they'd behave.

Breaking through the cloud cover, we drifted over a tall waterfall. Thunder roared below, creating a billowing mist. Hazy sunlight, like fractured fingers, shone through the broken clouds and soft rainbows shimmered in the air.

At the base, the water split into two large rivers, widening around an island. In the middle was a monstrous black palace. Shiny obsidian spires reached for the heavens. Massive cathedral windows broke up the monolith of midnight. It was hauntingly beautiful yet seemed diminished, sad, lonely, though I couldn't explain where the feeling came from.

As we circled closer, a multitude of dead gardens and courtyards came into view.

Benji guided our mount lower until the horse's hooves

clattered on the cobblestone as we landed in a lope before slowing to a stop. A giant burst out of a barn, his curly red hair flying chaotically around his face. Horses hung their long noses over the side of Dutch doors and whinnied at the new arrivals.

The giant greeted Benji with a hearty slap on the back. "Once you're done here—" his blue eyes lingered on me for a second before continuing, "—come on over." He pointed to the barn with a calloused finger. "Vera's excited to see you guys."

"Sure thing." Benji patted him on the shoulder before escorting me toward the entrance of the palace.

"He has blue eyes and red hair," I whispered.

"Yeah, a lot of the giants that work here in the palace have dual affiliations. Rack and Vera are part Fum and Fie."

"Wait, I thought..."

"There are still a hundred or so giants left that have more than one bloodline. Some managed to survive, though the youngest is probably thirtyish."

Two trees with gnarled limbs stood like skeletal sentries on either side of the arched, yet pointed, doors. Brown ivy and lifeless rose vines with six-inch thorns crawled up the black stone walls and around the ornate window frames.

"Why is everything dead?"

"When Queen Dru-Noir died, all the flora on the island died with her. For a thousand years, this place has been barren."

Even the grass was yellow and dry. Before asking another question, the imposing entrance parted. Standing between the two white-oak panels was a giant with dark skin, golden hair pulled back in a severe bun, and muddy-green eyes. She was attractive but in an understated manner.

"Benji, Ramona," she said. Fondness curved her pink lips.

"Poppy!" They all hugged as we entered.

Stepping over the threshold, a tickle of electricity floated in the air, and a shiver wove up my spine as the weight of energy found refuge inside my chest. The strange sensation of coming home almost overwhelmed me. I pressed a hand on my heart, trying to contain the strange emotion because I didn't recognize my surroundings. Nothing about the place seemed familiar—not the marble floors veined with gold, nor the vaulted ceilings trimmed with decorative beams, the walls that were so absolute-black that they absorbed the light from the chandelier hanging stories above our heads, or the weapons and works of art cast throughout the room.

"This is Ruby," Ramona introduced me, disrupting my train of thought.

Poppy gave my hand a firm shake. She wore wide gold bands on each finger. "Ruby, it's a pleasure to meet you. I'm Poppy, one of the resident caretakers of the palace. I'm here to assist you in any capacity you need."

"Bea, please. And it's nice to meet you, Poppy." I said. I rubbed my chest, but the feeling refused to dissipate.

I held on to the gilded banister as we walked up the grand staircase. It was narrow at the base and wider at the top, curling around like a trilobite fossil.

The castle was massive from the outside and even bigger and more intimidating inside. After walking up dozens of staircases, though none as impressive as the first, and down long hallways, we made it to what Poppy referred to as the queen's tower. Sweat dampened under the collar of my shirt. I yanked it away from my neck and swallowed the bile creeping up my throat. Imposter syndrome weighed heavy on my head.

I paused in front of a window and surveyed the surroundings. The Eiffel Tower looked like a toy from this height. My feet tripped over one another and I stumbled backward.

A big hand clamped onto my shoulder, saving me the humiliation of falling flat on my butt. "Bea," Benji said. "We have to go. There are guards posted at the bottom of the queen's tower. There's only one way in and one way out, so you're safe here."

I brought my gaze to his. *Sure.* I had the dagger strapped snugly under my arm just in case.

"Well, as safe as you can be. I'll send Liz and Grant over at once. That is, if you still want them as your personal guards. It's understandable if you'd rather choose others."

"No!" I snapped rudely. I adjusted my tone. "I trust them. So long as they're willing." Though I couldn't imagine why they would want to keep the job. Someone had tried to kill them just for keeping me safe. What a thankless position.

Poppy's forehead creased but she didn't say anything as she brushed invisible lint off her long black skirt and straightened the cuffs of her starched white shirt.

Once Benji and Ramona had left, Poppy opened the door to the queen's bedroom. Beacons of sunlight poured from the considerable windows and fanned over the marble floors and black stone.

Again, the feeling of being home almost knocked me off my feet. I rested my hand on the doorframe to steady myself and swallowed back panic—because the surroundings were not familiar. There was no reason to feel at home here. Not even a hint of déjà vu. Just a warmth in my chest that said I belonged, even if the space wasn't my taste with its fussy antique furniture and Persian carpets. I walked to the fireplace, tall enough for me to stand inside without ducking, and studied the painting above the marble mantle.

"That's the queen before she ascended to the throne," Poppy said.

Her skin was dark like Poppy's, but her sleek hair was the shade of a shiny copper penny. Full lips were turned up, showing off white teeth and fangs. But the most unusual thing about her was her eyes. She had heterochromia—one was bright blue, the other golden brown. Under her portrait was a plaque with the title *Princess Dru-Noir IV*.

"Was she the fourth princess?"

"No. She was an only child. But she carried all four bloodlines. Unfortunately, because of that, she was barren. After she died without an heir, things quickly declined."

"And?" I asked.

Poppy clasped her hands behind her back, straightening her spine. "We were left without a leader and only a prophecy. So we went to war. After we realized the only thing we were accomplishing was the extinction of our race, the First Families settled into talks." She paused. "We've waited for you for so long, some of us had begun to think you didn't really exist." It sounded like an accusation.

"Welcome to the club," I muttered, shifting uncomfortably.

"You don't think you're our salvation?"

"I don't know. The prophecy is vague, yet it fits. As for your salvation, I feel more like a broodmare. You guys can't produce children." I motioned to my ovaries. "We can.

Humans are so good at it, it's part of the reason why we destroyed our own planet." I chuckled jadedly.

Poppy blinked a few times as if she didn't know how to react to my confession.

"Look, I'm nothing special, except for the fact that I already have giant DNA which gave me access to the Fiefdom. There's nothing about me that is exceptional. *Nothing*," I emphasized.

"I don't know." She quietly pondered something for a few moments. "I think you may be wrong. First, you got here in the first place." She held up one finger. "Second, third, fourth, and fifth—" she added more fingers, "—you endured a volcano, bested our oceans, survived thornberry poison, and killed a giant. And you're still alive. Then to top it off, just like us, you have no natural abilities. Or do you?"

"Not that I know of, but I've always been pretty good with fire."

"Can you conjure it out of thin air?"

"Not yet. And by the way, how *does* that work? I've been meaning to ask someone. Is there some kind of giant school of magic?"

"No. Their powers come naturally. So your kinship with fire could very well be from your Fum ancestry. Because with that color . . ."

I couldn't argue with her—my hair was a dead giveaway. "But earlier, what do you mean *just like you*?"

"Those of us with more than one bloodline can't harness the elements. The only thing we can harness is our own electrical field. We're known as Duels. D-U-E-L, as in our bloodlines fight. Giants with pure blood are known as Soles. We're looked upon as less than. Please forgive me when I say we're only slightly above humans in the eyes of many giants."

"What about her?" I gestured with my chin toward the portrait.

"She controlled all four elements. Back then, everyone had control of their affiliations. Over time, Duels lost theirs and Soles grew stronger. The opposite of what was normal."

"Do you mind if I ask which factions your bloodline comes from? Nobody really tells me anything around here. They skirt over my questions if they can."

"My father is Fee, and my mother is Foe. For some reason, giants are extremely drawn to other factions. That whole opposites-attract thing. But, for the last thirty years, all the children conceived by two different domes have either died or were destroyed shortly after birth. At thirty-one, I'm the youngest child of different factions in the fiefdom. The First-Born sons are the youngest children of single factions."

"Oh." I nodded, finally understanding.

"As soon as I was born, I was dropped off at the orphanage here on Isle Noir." She laughed at my reaction. "No, it was better that way. It was a delightful place to grow up surrounded by other outcasts. At least here, I'm one of many. Once we realized mixing bloodlines often went awry, most of the giants separated. But since we weren't willing to let the capital—especially the palace—fall to ruins, it was decided Duels would preserve it until you arrived. We've maintained it for the last nine hundred years. But there are fewer of us now."

"What about Duels? Can you guys have kids?"

She tilted her chin up and shook her head.

"Hmm," I said, embarrassed, thinking maybe I had overstepped propriety. I circled my finger around the room. "So you take care of all of this?"

"And other places. A few Soles live here also, but mostly to keep track of us. Though in the last month, more Fee, Fie, Foe, and Fum have arrived in preparation for your coronation."

"What does that mean for you and the rest of the Duels?"

"It means they'll probably replace us with Soles. They'll want to be closer to you."

"Over my dead body," I retorted.

Her eyes rounded.

My finger stabbed at the ground. "You were raised here. You work here. This is your home. I'll be damned if I allow them to sweep all of you under the rug." I held up my hands. "Of course, unless you'd rather do something else." Abandoning them wasn't an option.

She clamped her lips together while her chin trembled. She sniffed before she said, "Thank you. Most of us here enjoy our work." She paused and smoothed the sleeves of her shirt. Her eyes never left my face, as if she was searching for something. "You were wrong earlier when you said you're not exceptional. Never in a million years did I expect a *human* like you."

I rubbed the bottom of my nose. "I could say the same. But I'm going to need all the help I can get." My track record was consistent—assassination attempts every week so far.

She bowed her head. "Ruby Rose Walker, our future queen, the Duels are at your service."

Before another word passed over my lips, the doors slammed open with a bang and Tee ran through, her braids slapping her back. Sid sped around her and launched himself into my arms.

I toppled back onto the gold velvet sofa, holding on to one hundred and fifty-plus pounds. Wet kisses slobbered all over my face. Tee hugged my head from behind before she smacked me, her hand thumping hard off my skull. I had to admit, I was surprised she'd hugged me first.

"I left your schedule on the table by the door," Poppy said loudly. "First thing tomorrow morning, there's a private breakfast for you and your friends. If you have any questions, there's a call button with my name on it. Never hesitate if you need anything."

"Poppy, thank you," I yelled over Sid's whines. "Okay, buddy, I'm here. I won't leave you behind again."

The bind constricting my lungs released a notch, seeing with my own eyes that both Tee and Sid were safe—and appeared to be thriving. For the first time in Sid's life, I couldn't feel every rib under his flesh.

"That better include me," Tee said, propping her hands on her hips. She too had gained some much-needed weight. Her silhouette now had a few curves instead of only angles and bones.

Though I was thankful I had left them both safely behind, I didn't dare admit it to Tee. And if anyone tried to harm them now—

I.

Would.

Burn.

Them.

Alive.

"Come on, Tee," I said. "Let's get this over with." I motioned for her to go through the bedroom door, well

428

aware a verbal butt-whooping was waiting on the other side. I ran toward the four-poster bed draped with gold curtains and carved posts. Jumping into the middle, I slid over the red comforter, hitting the headboard. Sid and Tee piled into me.

Leaning up against the mountain of pillows with Sid lounging on my legs, I waited patiently for Tee to finish her lecture.

I took a deep breath and addressed her first complaint, the one where she'd been left behind with Kai. "I understand, but I couldn't knowingly put you in harm's way."

"That wasn't your choice!" She slapped the bed, anger burning like coal embers in her eyes.

I pressed my eyelids with the pads of my fingers and rubbed. She was mad. I would've been too.

"As for the other mess," I said, referring to the fact that I had to sleep with her boyfriend, "I got us out of that one too."

A tiny smile of hope rounded her cheeks. Then she smacked my arm again after I explained how we'd work around that one. "You shouldn't have slept with Loch. What if he wants to kill you? I would rather you had slept with Kai than die. You're so stupid sometimes." Her Southern accent somehow softened the insults. Though I rubbed my arm where she'd hit me.

I wasn't about to disagree with her. "Are we done?"

She pursed her lips. "For now."

"So where is Kevin?" I kind of expected him to pop his head inside the door at any second.

Tee's lips pulled away from her teeth like she didn't want to tell me something.

"What? Where is he? Is he okay?" I sat forward.

"Yes, he's fine. But he left a couple of weeks ago with Raiden. They refused to tell me where they were going or what they were doing. I couldn't even get the information out of Kai. And believe me, I tried. But he promised me they'd be okay."

I cocked an eyebrow.

"What? What should I have done?"

"Pftt," I blew a raspberry. "Nothing." It wasn't like Kevin listened to me. Nor did Raiden. At least Tee, Sid, and the rest of my friends were here and safe.

Moving on, we talked late into the night, with me recapping my adventures, not daring to leave out any details. Tee would know if I was lying or abridging the story.

"Good Lord," she said quietly. "You're lucky to still be alive. But they caught Vanessa, so you should be okay, right?"

I stuffed another pillow behind my head, really wanting to adjust my position. My legs were asleep, but I couldn't bring myself to disturb Sid. I stroked his shiny dark fur and grinned at his tiny snores.

"I don't know if she's the boss or not. And on more than one occasion, she's had help." I yawned. The heat from the fire was making me sleepy and it had been a long day. Hell, it'd been a long month.

"But once you're queen, it'll all be good," she said with finality.

I shrugged and moved on to more fun topics—like sex. She and Kai had decided to wait. Tee was not only a romantic but religious as well.

"You gonna make it that long?" I harassed her. I couldn't have resisted Raiden. The others, if my choices had been smart to begin with, I'd have been fine passing over. Fueling sorrow and anger with copious amounts of alcohol were at the top of the list of my many mistakes.

She fiddled with the edge of the blanket. "Well, we're planning on getting married as soon as we can." The apples of her cheeks reddened.

"I bet." Smugness curled my lips. I already knew what kind of fun she was missing.

"So, who are you leaning toward?" she asked, deliberately shifting the focus.

"I don't know," I groaned. "I've narrowed it down to two. It's not that I don't like Trent—I do—but he has no desire to help run a kingdom. Plus, his idea of fun and mine don't mesh well. And as hot as he is, it isn't enough. At first, I was sure I'd pick Adam, but after a week with Loch, I'm even more confused. It's like they each have something specific that I want or need. Adam, well, I can see a life with him. And given enough time . . ." I squeezed my eyes to ward off the impending stab of pain. "Maybe, I could love him. I adore his family, and his lifestyle is something I enjoy. He makes me feel comfortable, like I'm enough. And Loch, God, where do I start? He challenges me, doesn't back down to me. I'm not going to lie, there's something very attractive about his confidence. If only he didn't—"

"Look exactly like Raiden," Tee finished for me.

"Yeah. But I'm still not sure if he's behind the assassination attempts."

Tee pursed her lips to the side. "Hmm. I think too many people have tried to kill you lately and you're paranoid."

"Ya think?"

She held her hand up. "Rightly so. But from what Kai has said, I don't think Loch is behind it. He's not come out and said it outright, but the feeling I get is that the First-Born sons are bound to protect you. Besides, Loch has nothing to gain with you dead. Everyone knows you're not going to pick Trent, so it's either Adam, who doesn't necessarily want the job, or Loch, who does. He's got a fifty-fifty shot at this point. And honestly, if he wanted you dead, you'd be dead."

"That's what I thought too, but I'm still not ruling it out. What I don't understand is how all of them developed feelings for me in a week." Or how I did the same—not that I would admit it out loud. "That's just crazy."

"Is it?" she said like she didn't agree. "You're the gorgeous new girl. You're a bit challenging in the best possible way, and their dating pool is limited, so if they want kids you're their best shot." She tried to quirk an eyebrow without success. "And soon, you'll have the ultimate position of power. Girl, that's an intoxicating combination."

I snarled a lip.

"Plus, if you think about it, you're here to help the Fiefdoms unite. What better way than if all the future lords have a certain amount of loyalty to you? Maybe all of this was fate."

My eyes slivered at her word choice. Tee believed in destiny, fate, soulmates, and the rest of that mumbo jumbo. I shrugged, not ready to agree with her, but not having a valid argument to rebut. "I guess. Poppy did say something about the factions being irrationally attracted to other groups. I definitely belong to the *other* category. Who would you pick?"

"Raiden," she said without hesitation.

My breath caught in my throat and a razor blade sliced

my heart. I grabbed my chest to keep it together. "That's not fair, Tee," I snapped.

"I know. But a girl can still hold out hope."

I glared. "There is no hope."

"Haven't you learned anything? There's *always* hope."

"Seriously? You sound like a sappy romance movie. Hope has caused me nothing but pain." I'd spent years *hoping* my parents were alive, *hoping* they would come home. Now I was hoping that once I was crowned queen, I could find them. Or find out what had happened to them. I didn't have room to hold on to the hope that somehow Raiden would find a way for us to be together. I needed to be a realist and decide which man was the best fit for the job.

"Why is your glass still half full?" It amazed me, after all that she'd been through in life, how she was still an optimist.

"Because I realized at a young age that pain is the price of love. And I'd rather pay that price than never love. You— you closed your heart off the minute your parents disappeared."

"That's not true. I love *you*."

"I didn't give you a choice. You complete me." She patted her heart.

We busted out laughing at the same time my eyes filled with tears. She was right. We were the opposite sides of the same coin. Though not bound by blood, we were family.

# CHAPTER
# FORTY-TWO

I straightened the hem of my shirt and brushed the wrinkles from my pants. The outfit was a compromise between me and Poppy. She expected me to wear a dress. I told her I didn't like to do what was expected of me.

Something akin to approval flashed on her face.

Nerves prickled my stomach as I stepped into the dining room for breakfast with my friends the next morning. I was excited to see everyone yet afraid of answering all their questions.

Frederica was the first to run up and hug me, Frank right behind her.

"Oh, Bea! We're so glad to see you!" Frederica said. "Are you okay? How has it been? Who are you choosing? They're all so handsome." She snapped her hands to her mouth as if she hadn't meant to say that, but then continued bombarding me with so many questions I didn't have time to answer. Sid raced around the room, dodging in and out of people as he sniffed for dropped food.

My eyes scanned the room for Kevin, even though he

wasn't there. I was angry that he'd left without telling me about it. At least he was with Raiden, so I knew he was safe.

The thought of Raiden made my joy drain away. I closed my eyes and pushed away the memory of his face—his deep-set silver eyes, the perfectly formed peaks and swell of his lips. I was far from over him, but it didn't matter. I had to marry someone else and I still hadn't decided who. Just when I thought my mind was made up, I'd second-guessed myself.

The dining table was piled high with an array of food. I grabbed some kind of fancy china with gold filigree and loaded it up. I tossed a sausage to Sid, though he no longer needed it. None of them did. They all looked fantastic.

My spirits swelled.

Someone tapped me on the shoulder. "Hey," Noah said. He stuffed his hands into his hoodie pouch.

I controlled the urge to snarl my lip.

"When you have a second, do you think I could get a minute of your time alone?"

Stepping back, I glared at him. "Seriously?"

"No, no, nothing like that." He looked horrified, as if reading my thoughts of our past encounters.

My wariness subsided.

"I owe you an apology." He glanced around. "And I'd like to do it in private. If you don't mind?"

"Sure," I said. I guess I could save him the embarrassment of having to do it in front of friends. "Now?" I gestured at the door.

"Uh, yeah, that'd be great." He rubbed his hands together and signaled for me to go first.

Sid started to follow, but I told him to stay. It wasn't like

Noah was dangerous. Though I did regret having left my dagger in the queen's quarters.

I hesitated for a millisecond before I shut the door softly behind us and we meandered down the hall. A collection of eclectic art lined the black walls.

I waited a full minute before looking at him. This was going to be difficult for a man with that big of an ego, but jeez, he needed to get on with it. My stomach was rumbling.

Right after we passed a dark hallway, he said, "You always acted like you were too good for us."

My brows puckered.

"But you're just a hoity-toity bitch, and you're going to get what you deserve."

My fists clenched. I was positive that was the worst apology ever. I began to turn around, contemplating kicking his ass, but afraid that if I started, I might not quit.

Movement in my periphery startled me, but before I had time to react, a jolt of electricity spasmed through my head and out the tips of my fingers and toes. I shot back ten feet and landed with a smack on the polished floor before I passed out.

---

I GRABBED the back of my pounding head, not sure where I was and why my mouth tasted as if I'd gargled copper pennies. The faint smell of dirt and mold tickled my nose.

Upon remembering what had happened, the urge to scream was almost unbearable. *Fuckity, fuck, fuck.* Hammering my fists on the floor, I thought, *How did I end up like this again?* I sat up and leaned against the wall.

As my eyes adjusted to the darkness, a set of iron bars

imprisoning me came into focus. Up the passageway, candlelight flickered over the ebony walls. Hundreds of ivory skulls with dagger-like fangs sat like trophies on shelves carved into the stone. I averted my gaze.

Voices floated down the hall.

"Thanks," Noah said cheerfully. "I didn't think it would be that easy, but she's not very smart. I feel for you guys, I really do. I can't imagine having *her* as my queen. It was bad enough that Kevin and Bea Walker *walked* all over us on Earth," he said, thinking he was witty by using my last name.

Hate boiled inside. It was official. When I got out of here, I was going to kill him.

A woman chimed in. "What I don't get is how all the First-Born sons have fallen all over themselves to get with her. And Raiden too. She's not even that pretty."

Hate turned to surprise, then to shame. I recognized that voice. How could I have been so easily fooled? Sure, she had never been particularly friendly, but I'd chalked it up to shyness. Bile surged up my throat, but I slapped my hand over my mouth and concentrated on not screaming obscenities.

"She was a decent fuck, but I've had better," Noah said. "And she's nowhere as near as hot as you are."

Liz, my *former* bodyguard, giggled.

A female whose voice I didn't know admonished them. "Enough, you two. Do you think Grant suspects you?" Her voice was more mature than the others and had a slight island accent. I didn't know who she was, but I could guess where she came from. Foe.

"I don't think so. Especially after you almost killed me." Liz sounded angry.

437

"Well, we needed to make it believable," another guy said.

I cocked my head, thinking I'd heard that voice before too. My brain frantically searched the database but came up empty. Over the last four weeks, I'd been introduced to so many giants.

"We need to decide what to do with her," the Foe woman said.

The man didn't hesitate. "Kill her now."

"I don't know," Liz replied. "Don't you think it would be better just to keep her down here and let the signed contract play out? If she doesn't choose someone at the ball with the First Families there to witness her choice, she's going to die anyway. That way, none of us actually has to kill her. And if we get caught, we'll only be banished, not executed."

"But then you have to keep her down here and make sure no one finds her," Noah said.

I knew Noah didn't like me, but his actions stung. *Seriously?*

"No one ever comes down here. Finding this section of the dungeon is almost impossible. During the queen's reign, the most notorious criminals were held here. In order to get through, you must account for each bloodline." The guy schooling Noah seemed to know a lot about the castle.

"Yeah, but I think Poppy's getting suspicious. And if she finds out what we're doing, she'll turn us in," Liz said.

"Were you able to entice any of the Duels over to our side?" the Foe woman asked.

"No. But it's not like we could come out and ask them without giving ourselves away. Besides, we don't need them anymore. After she's gone, things can go back to normal.

And we can exterminate the rest of them," the guy said, like humans were nothing but rats.

"Except for Noah," Liz said.

"Yeah. Sure," the guy half-assed a confirmation.

The woman sounded impatient when she said, "And that's why we need some Duels on our side. If *we* kill her, the First Families will hunt us down and kill us. They're bound in blood to do so. The Duels, as far as I'm concerned, are expendable."

"And that's why we need to wait!" Liz insisted.

"You're probably right." The woman who seemed to be in charge conceded.

"What does Vanessa think?" the guy asked.

"If she were here, Bea would already be dead. She said Loch's under her spell too," Liz answered.

"Yes, but Vanessa is hotheaded and willing to do anything to marry Loch. And if not him, she'd settle for Raiden," the woman scoffed.

"Ugh," Liz huffed.

The guy answered. "Well, she would and you know it . . . Wait. Did you ladies make some kind of girl pact?" the guy asked like he was mocking her. "If you help her, she gets to marry Loch and you get Raiden?" His laughter echoed down the hall. "You're a fucking idiot, Liz. He's never felt that way about you any more than Loch wants Vanessa. Everyone knows it . . . Did you do this just to get into Raiden's pants? You don't even care that the First Families agreed to put a *human* on the throne, do you?"

It sounded like someone kicked the wall.

"Does it matter, Leonardo? I got the job done, which is more than I can say for you," Liz snapped.

My fists clenched. I knew I recognized that voice.

Leonardo was Adam's older half-brother. At our dinner with Adam's family, Leonardo had said that he worked at the capital. No wonder he knew so much about the castle.

"Hey, it's not my fault Raiden keeps finding her. Which is why we need to kill her *now!*" Leonardo said.

"No," the Foe woman chimed in, the only voice I didn't recognize yet. "He's not even here. Rumor has it, he and Kevin are searching for Raiden's parents. That's why Raiden was on Earth when he came upon Ruby."

Realization dawned on me. Now it made sense why Raiden was mad when he'd found me in the stairwell. He'd been searching for his family, and I'd interrupted him. I wondered why he'd never told me that.

"So for now, she lives," the woman ordered.

A sigh of relief quietly escaped my mouth.

"Do you need someone to guard her?" Noah offered.

"No. She can't escape." Leonardo's tone was berating. Noah didn't realize it, but the minute I was dead, they'd kill him too. Worry for the rest of my people constricted my ribcage, making it hard to breathe.

Footsteps faded down the hall and the candlelight extinguished, leaving me in utter blackness. The smell of wax and smoke floated in the air.

I reached up and held the necklace Raiden had given me, hoping it would lead him to me in time.

Pins and needles zapped along my calves as I stood up and stretched my legs and arms, holding on to the wall so I didn't topple over.

Hearing a squeak from the corner of my cell, I quickly forgot about the discomfort. My nerve endings flared and my brain conjured the image of a deadly creature. I readied

440

my stance and wished with every ounce of will that they would've left the torch lit.

Somehow, the flame roared to life.

A shadow of a rodent with an elongated nose and tail darkened the outside wall. I crept toward the bars, but the coward, smaller than its shadow suggested, scuttled away down the passage.

Goosebumps prickled my skin and the hairs on the back of my neck rose as my gaze landed on the skulls. Firelight danced over the white bone. It felt like they were watching me, judging me and my shitty choices with their empty eye sockets.

A sound between a scream and a growl rumbled from my chest, a breeze whipped by me. One of the heads tumbled to the floor and shattered on the ground. I scrambled away.

*What the fuck?* My heart raced. My palms perspired. First the flames, now this. I thought back to what Raiden had said and what Adam had reiterated when they'd questioned my ability, as a human, to survive a volcano, the ocean, thornberry poison, and Josha's assassination attempt. I started to question it all. Though nothing spectacular had happened down in the heart of the volcano, I had managed to take a shower on the deserted island even though there was no showerhead. At the time, I'd chalked it up to a hallucination, but maybe it wasn't. And I had survived a toxin known to kill even giants. Then there were the vines that had wrapped around Josha's legs and the heaved roots which may have tripped him, allowing me a fighting chance. And while with Loch, when I'd gotten scared, all the doors had slammed shut. Maybe *I* was the ghost?

Feeling a bit foolish, I gnawed on the inside of my cheek

and concentrated on extinguishing the torch outside the iron walls. Immediately, dense blackness ensued. I inhaled sharply, my pulse pounding loudly between my ears. But Poppy did say that a giant's affiliation with the elements came naturally. If I counted correctly, that would mean I carried all four bloodlines.

Not wanting to lose momentum, I focused on building heat behind my eyes like a fever, or at least what I thought one should feel like, since I'd never been sick. Pride swelled inside as an orange flame danced along the ebony walls. A tentative smile curled on my lips. It was like being given a gift you didn't know you wanted.

I tilted my head downward and stared at the creepy skulls, focusing on the air around me and what I wanted it to do. Sweat rolled down my spine despite the cool temperature. The first skull rocked back and forth before it finally rolled and crashed to the floor. I pumped my fist in victory.

After an hour of practicing, I was satisfied that the rudimentary skills were within my grasp. Now, if I could just figure out how to escape. I needed to get to Poppy. Apparently, she was, for certain, on the Bea Team.

# CHAPTER
# FORTY-THREE

S liding down the smooth wall, my trembling legs collapsed underneath me into a sitting position, allowing me to catch my breath. Magic-ing was hard work. I tapped the back of my head on the cold stone, trying to figure out a way to escape and get to Poppy. She'd know what to do. Desperation sat like the anxiety elephant on my chest. The scent of earth, smoke, fresh air, and rain drifted past my nose. Suddenly, my body fell backward as if the wall holding me up had disappeared, leaving me to fall.

My arms flailed, catching only air. "Whoa!" I hollered before my head hit the floor with a solid crack.

Poppy screamed as she dropped the gown she was hanging inside a closet. Her green eyes widened with fear.

I was sure mine mirrored hers as I scrambled off the floor with my fists raised and body weight forward on the balls of my feet. "What just happened?"

"How did you get here?" Poppy stepped back, mimicking the panic in my tone.

"I don't know. I was in the dungeons and now I'm here?

Where's here?" My voice rose with each sentence as my eyes darted around the room. Colorful clothes hung neatly on hangers and reflected in a freestanding mirror.

A strange look passed over Poppy's face. "Wait, where have you been!? We've been searching for hours. And why were you in the dungeons?"

"Because people want me dead." I tossed my arms into the air.

She folded her hands together and patiently listened to my tale of woe from beginning to end—even the part where Noah had outsmarted me.

"And right before you got here—" she tapped the floor with her foot, "—what exactly were you thinking about?"

"You."

Her complexion paled. "Well, if I didn't believe you were the heir to the throne before, I do now."

"Why?"

"Because the last person with enough power to control obsidian died a thousand years ago. The core of our world consists of this stone and our abilities are tied to it. So long as we have enough of it around, we thrive. But only Queen Dru-Noir had the power to mold it. Nobody knows why, but it's been speculated that it was because she carried all four bloodlines."

"But how did I get from down there—" I said, pointing to the floor, "—to up here?" My hand flailed in the air, encompassing the room.

"Well, from the few things I've read about it, the queen used the obsidian crystals as a vortex, like a wormhole. She could harness the power of the stone to step from point A to point B or Z—basically, anywhere she wished so long as obsidian was present. Whereas the rest of us cannot."

No wonder her quarters were located on the top floor with no elevator access. She hadn't needed it. And that left me wondering if that was why all the Fiefdoms had so much of the stone in their houses. The queen would've had a direct line to all of her subjects.

"Yeah, about that . . . I might have control over other elements too." I inhaled and concentrated on the particles in the air. Tiny shimmers of light, flowing like a lazy river, danced before my eyes. Next, I commanded the air like a mental whip thrown around the room. Clothes flew off the racks and dropped to the floor. "Do you think this means I have all four bloodlines too?" I wanted confirmation from someone else.

"I'd bet my life on it. It would also explain why you've connected so genuinely with each one of the First-Born sons. And why the strongest of those sons captured your heart." Before I could protest or inquire further as to which First-Born son she was referring to as the strongest, she waved her hand and kept talking. "Because Queen Dru-Noir had all four bloodlines, the loyalty in every Dome ran deep."

To hide how flustered I was by her revelations, I reached down and gathered the clothes from the floor. Things were starting to become clearer—especially as to why the castle felt like home and why I'd developed some feelings for Trent, Adam, Loch, and even Kai, though those feelings were more akin to what I felt for Kevin.

"So what now?" I asked, hanging the clothes back on the bar.

"Who else do you trust besides me?" she asked.

WITHIN THE HOUR, Poppy had Grant, Kai, and Tee gathered in my quarters. Though the remaining First-Born sons were en route to the capital, I wasn't positive I could trust them. So for the interim, I'd decided to keep them in the dark as to what was going on. I wished Raiden and Kevin were amongst my trusted four, but no one knew exactly where they were. And though I trusted Benji, he was Liz's father. I wasn't sure where his loyalty would land.

Grant placed his elbows on the table and rested his forehead in his palms. "How did I not see it?"

"I didn't either," I said.

His yellow gaze met mine as he fiddled with the beads braided in his beard. "But now, looking back, so much seems suspicious. The only thing I question is—why did they really try to kill us?"

"How important is Liz to their operation? They said they needed to make it look real, making me think she's expendable."

"Fair point," Grant conceded.

"So what are we going to do about this situation?" Kai asked, twirling one of his massive rings.

"There had to be four of them down there with you, Ruby," Poppy said. "Because the only way giants can enter that part of the dungeon is with each bloodline represented. Are you sure you only recognized Liz and Leonardo? That covers the Fee and the Fie. There had to be two more."

"The woman had an island accent, so she must be Foe, but whoever else was with them never uttered a word. Any ideas?" My question was directed toward Kai and Grant.

Both sighed and shook their heads.

"It's got to be the same guy who helped Vanessa throw you into the volcano," Kai said. "My people are known for being very human friendly. Why do you think Vikings are such large people and so many have red or blond hair?" He winked.

It made sense. Scandinavians were known for their size. "I'm not sure how to find out who they are, but I have a few ideas. I feel like we'll have a better shot if they think they've won," I said.

We spent the afternoon hatching a plan.

It all started with me and Sid heading back to the dungeon cell to wait for the enemy to check on me.

Luckily, Sid was able to pass through the barrier by my side. Unfortunately, the others couldn't. If they wanted to get into the dungeon, they were going to have to find a Fee, Fie, and Foe they could trust. With the way things were going, that seemed uncertain.

After only an hour of waiting, a faint whistling echoed down the stone corridor. Sid got off my lap and hunkered in the corner of the cell to hide, his fur blending seamlessly with the darkness.

The tune was easily recognizable—it was Noah's favorite song, "Friends in Low Places" by Garth Brooks. How fitting.

He stopped in front of the cell and pushed his hands into the pouch of his hoodie. Torchlight flickered behind him.

"How did you get down here alone?"

"Uh, they opened the door for me," he said like it should be obvious.

I backed away from the bars and crossed my arms. "Why? Why would you do this?" I asked.

"They made me a deal that if I helped them, they would allow me to stay."

"That doesn't even make sense. We *all* get to stay."

447

Noah shrugged. "Nope. They have plans to kill everyone else once you're dead. This way, I don't die."

"Wow. So what? You're just going to wait for me to die down here? Then slaughter everyone else?"

He didn't bat an eyelash. "Yeah. That's the plan. It's going to make for a spectacular ball."

"What about your parents?"

"I'll get them home."

"You know you can't do that without me, right? Humans can't get through the electrical barrier protecting the stairwells without dying. Only I can disarm it."

He crossed his arms. "Desperation doesn't suit you," he said calmly, but I could tell he was rattled by the information.

"So who's all in on this? I mean, I feel like it's only fair to know before I die."

"Don't know. Don't care." He leaned against the wall, the fallen skulls crunched under his feet. He looked down but didn't say anything.

I laughed. "Obviously, they don't respect you whatsoever if they aren't willing to share who's in charge." Noah was big on respect.

"I know more than you do," he snapped. "I know Liz was right under your nose the whole time and you didn't suspect a thing."

He was right. I hadn't. And if I was smart, I would have. Conveniently, she hadn't been around when the Fum threw me into the volcano, had seen me disappear with Trent, and was bested by Josha, not to mention all the times she acted strangely when Raiden got too close to me. I could now see it was jealousy. But I'd dismissed all of it. And then she'd almost died—so any suspicions I might have had vanished.

448

"And what about Leonardo? What's his reason for hating me? Is it because I'm human?" I said snidely before I goaded Noah further. "He sure doesn't think you're very smart."

"Well, he's a fucking idiot. He pretends that it's because he hates humans, but secretly, he hates his brother. It's bad enough that he's the First-Born son, and if Adam marries you, he'll become king."

I suspected as much. It seemed as if most of the giants who wanted me dead had ulterior motives. Liz and Vanessa wanted Raiden and Loch. Josha wanted Trent, and Leonardo didn't want his brother to become king. Someone had to want me dead just because I was human. *Seriously.*

"And the woman from the Foe?"

"Bali. She actually hates humans. So does Thur."

Strangled laughter yelped from my throat. Thur was a good name for the strong silent type. And Bali seemed familiar, but I couldn't conjure a face to go with the name.

Now having pieced together the rest of our enemies, I was no longer in the mood to talk further. I strode to the back of the cell. The sooner he left, the sooner I could tell the others what I'd discovered.

"I'll see you tomorrow," Noah said chipperly.

"Why bother?"

"If I'm being honest, seeing you like this turns me on."

I disengaged. He was a monster. I was starting to think I had a very poor people-picker. Not that I'd ever really liked him, but I'd never imagined he was a psychopath.

His footsteps echoed down the hall, then I heard the door squeak open and close. I grabbed Sid's collar and concentrated on the closet in the queen's quarters. We magically disappeared, only to reappear a second later.

449

"Alright," I said, stepping out of the dressing room. "I know who the four giants are."

—————

FOR THE NEXT THREE DAYS, Sid and I spent much of our time in the cell block waiting for Noah to harass me. I'd tried to leave my dog behind, but he adamantly refused. The ruckus he'd caused was far worse than the suspicion of him missing. Besides, having him near me kept me calm. And together we had ample time to debate the *husband* dilemma. Though he was no more help than Tee. Every time I spoke Raiden's name, he wagged his tail. At the mention of the others, he growled.

Above, Tee said the castle was in an uproar. Their future queen was still missing. Grant, Kai, and Poppy were watching everyone to see if they could figure out who was leading the cult of human haters.

The lords and ladies were not on that list. According to Poppy and her infinite knowledge of Fiefdom, they were bound by blood to protect me. Though I had an inkling that Lady Sylvia, while she might not actively be hurting me, wouldn't prevent my death either. Her proximity to Vanessa left me with an uneasy feeling. But I was positive Adam was innocent. And almost positive Trent was safe. As for Loch, his guilt had yet to be determined.

As I weighed their attributes, Raiden's handsome face flashed in my mind. I pinched the bridge of my nose. I wanted him. I loved him. But what I wanted and what I could have . . .

Silver lining—I'd narrowed it down to two.

I reached up and fiddled with my necklace, spending the

rest of my time wondering where Raiden and Kevin were. And if they were safe.

I stroked Sid's head in an attempt to distract myself from the hopelessness swirling inside me. His ears twitched as my long exhale ruffled his fur. His tail thumped on the floor.

The door at the end of the hallway clicked. Sid backed into the corner with a snap of my fingers.

"We've come to say goodbye," Liz said. I could hear her footsteps strolling down the passageway.

"You mean gloat?" I replied.

A tall man with blond hair—Thur, I assumed—stood behind her, Leonardo on one side, and Bali on the other. Her turquoise eyes and waist-length spiral hair triggered a memory, and blood rushed to my face.

"Oh, she does smell good enough to eat," Bali said. "I see you recognize me."

She was the only woman I'd ever kissed. Humiliation burned. I felt my body start to sink into the wall. Panicking, I jumped away from the stone. All four giants leapt back as if they were frightened of me.

"So, how many human haters are in your little bitch club?" I spat.

Bali frowned. "Enough."

I laughed. Giants were easy to bait, especially the ones who didn't like me.

"Uh-huh," I dismissed. "I'm guessing there aren't many."

Thur crossed his bulging arms. "There are plenty of us." He sounded as if he'd been gargling nails.

"No one down here is the mastermind behind all of this. None of you are alphas." I pointed to Bali. "Beta." I pointed to Leonardo and shrugged my shoulders. "Beta?" Thur was passed over. "I don't know you." Then to Liz and Noah. "Omega and human." I packed as much repulsion as I could into those final words.

"Well then, it's a good thing Penelope is an alpha," Liz snapped.

Lady Sylvia's attorney whose written contract had gotten me into this mess in the first place. *Bingo.*

# FORTY-FOUR

S tanding inside the closet in front of a full-length mirror, my reflection stared back at me. My eyes looked different in this light. The color blended away from my pupil—brown to yellow to green to blue in a starburst pattern.

Tee had outdone herself. When she'd heard there was going to be a ball at the end of my bachelorettehood, she'd designed our outfits *and* planned our makeup.

The red dress matched my hair and hugged every curve, leaving little to the imagination. The sparkling material covered everything but my hands and face. I reached under the long slit and adjusted the dagger inside my matching knee-high boots. Then I patted my trusty 9mm with magic-infused bullets in my tiny glittering purse. Kai had had the ammo made by a friend who worked at the metallurgy in Fum. Though it was illegal, he was doing his best to stack the deck in our favor.

I double-checked that the diamond tiara was firmly in place over my slicked-back bun. Tee said she didn't want my hair overpowering her creation. She had a point, but I felt naked without my blanket of curls.

My long diamond earrings swung as I turned my head. "You ready?"

Sid barked and jumped. His nails, which Tee had painted a brilliant red, clicked on the floor. His ruby-studded collar glinted in the light pouring through the window. I sighed, glad one of us was ready.

A healthy rose vine grew along the outside windowsill. After my arrival, the barren court had turned into a garden of splendor. My fingers feathered over the cool glass. The pink bud, the size of my head, bloomed toward me as if I were the sun. A thrilled smile coiled on my face. During the last few days, I'd been practicing with fire and water and manipulating air and plants. I didn't know why I was surprised that all the elements bent to my will. When I'd mentioned my disbelief to Poppy, she'd said I was being silly. Lots of humans were born with amazing talents. Then she listed examples of athletes, performers, and geniuses before reminding me that I did have all four bloodlines. But color me crazy, it didn't seem real.

You would think with the guest of honor missing, the lords and ladies would've postponed the ball, but apparently, because it was written in the contract that I'd signed in blood, they couldn't.

Before chickening out, I closed my eyes, placed my hand on the top of Sid's head, and focused on the back corner of the ballroom. Earlier, Tee had sketched the layout to show me where to land. So long as my destination was clear, or I knew who I wanted to see, the vortex of obsidian took me directly there.

We apparated through the wall and stepped onto a

black-and-white-checkered floor patterned like a chess-board. I laughed silently. *How apropos.*

A full quartet played on either side of the ornate staircase. Originally, I was supposed to enter from the second-story balcony and walk down those stairs so everyone could pay tribute. Instead, Sid and I concealed ourselves behind the crimson curtains. We'd matched my dress to the drapes for the explicit purpose of me blending until I was ready to make my appearance.

Green vines slowly crept along the outside of the windows as if they were trying to find a way inside. Crystal chandeliers illuminated priceless paintings. It was kind of hard not to recognize the *Mona Lisa* and *The Last Supper*, but I didn't have time to gawk.

The Fee and Fie, the pinnacle of sophistication, shimmered in silk and satin, dripping in diamonds and pearls. It was easy to distinguish the Foe, who were dressed in an array of bright colors, over-the-top designs, gems meant to impress, and equally creative makeup. The Fum had embellished their post-apocalyptic gear with corseted gowns, gold chainmail, and oversized metal jewelry.

In the corner, not mingling with the giants, stood most of my people. They were all dressed beautifully, but their postures were rigid as they shifted uncomfortably. For safety reasons, Tee had promised to keep them out of my way.

The ball was structured more like a human wedding than what I'd imagined a ball should be like. First, dinner was to be served at the stylish dining tables situated along the walls. Next, the dancing, then to me picking a groom. I pressed my hand to my stomach, trying to calm the wave of nerves.

In the center of the room, a half-moon-shaped waterfall poured out of the ceiling, cascading around the edges of an obsidian fountain. In the middle, on a raised platform, was a table set for five—Kai, Trent, Loch, Adam, and yours truly. I felt as if I should be holding a red rose to signify the end of the deadly dating game.

Duels, dressed all in white, sliced through the crowd, serving bubbling pink champagne.

Gathering courage, I stepped from the shadows and walked across the floor. One by one, the room hushed. By the time I reached my friends, the only sounds were my stiletto boots clicking on the tile, the crackling of the fire, and the falling water. Noah's face drained of color as he ducked behind his parents. But he couldn't go far.

I stopped and spun around, standing between Poppy and Tee. Grant and Kai fanned to the outside edges of the room.

"Oh my God, Bea!" Adam and Loch rushed to my side. Trent was only a heartbeat behind.

"Are you okay?" Loch grabbed my hand, his blue eyes filled with concern.

The rest of the giants started whispering at once. Hushed voices echoed eerily against the stone.

"I'm fine, I promise. Soon you'll understand."

My gaze darted between the two of them. My indecision needled me, but I had more pressing issues.

The three First-Born sons stepped aside.

Sid growled, and his hackles rose. His dark eyes were focused on Liz, who stood next to her dad. I didn't think Benji and Ramona had any idea what she'd done.

Her blue eyes snapped wide and she started backing toward one of the exits. In unison, the doors slammed shut from the outside. All the guests jumped. A champagne flute crashed to the floor. From the other side, you could hear the large wooden bars scraping over the doors as they settled into place, imprisoning all of us in the room.

Everyone exchanged confused glances.

Thur and Bali were surrounded by a group of giants now under suspicion by association. Neither of them moved, nor did they look particularly bothered by my appearance.

Lady Sylvia and Lord Issac stood next to Penelope. The attorney's knuckles whitened as she clutched her glass. Hatred burned in her eyes. I wasn't sure how I'd missed her contempt before, but I hadn't been looking either.

I was surprised to see relief sketched on both Lady Sylvia and Lord Issac's faces when they realized who I was.

Leonardo was conspicuously absent.

Clearing my throat, I strolled to the fireplace and stopped at the end of the room. Tee and Poppy stayed put. "I suppose most of you are wondering where I've been for the last three days." My gaze rested for a heartbeat on each of my captors-slash-attempted murderers. "It's a funny story. Liz, would you care to explain?"

Her face drained of what little color it had.

"No?" I said like I thought she was being shy. "Bali? Thur?"

Thur's face flushed angrily until the tips of his ears matched my dress.

I snapped my fingers, my blood-red polish flashing in the light as I pointed at Penelope. "Penelope? I bet you'd like to enlighten everyone."

Lady Sylvia and Lord Issac backed away from her.

"No? Well, then let's get this party started!" Having a reputation to maintain, I swiped a glass of alcohol off a platter and downed it like a shot of whisky. I threw my arms into the air and tossed the glass into the fireplace big enough to house a family of giants. After it shattered, I yelled, "Sláinte!"—the same toast my Scottish dad had used.

I snatched another drink and swaggered over to the fountain. All four First-Born sons rushed to my side. Adam, having been the closest, got there first, and helped me up the steps onto the fountain's clear glass platform. Kai, Trent, and Loch followed. Adam escorted me to the head of the table, then grabbed my hand and kissed the large ruby ring on my index finger. He held on for a few long beats as he pressed his lips together like he wanted to say something, but he shook his head and smiled instead. His dimples creased his cheeks.

Loch's eyes wandered from my face down my curves before he said, "You clean up well."

I laughed. "So do you." He wore a black tux with tails and a red vest under his jacket.

Trent ignored the formalities and clutched me in his arms with a beast of a hug. My feet lifted from the floor as he squeezed. "Love, I'm so glad you're alive. We've been so worried!" He put me down and stepped away, then gave me the stink eye. "Where have you been?!"

I snapped my fingers high in the air and a curtain of water encased the entrance of the fountain, effectively drowning out prying ears.

Adam, Loch, and Trent glanced at one another. Kai winked.

"Uh . . ." Trent said, pointing at the cascade.

A sly smile crept up my lips, then I outlined the previous

few days. The looks on their faces grew more murderous with every revelation.

"And they're still alive," Adam rumbled, the tendons along his throat tightening. "I'm going to kill Leonardo," he said.

I reached out and held on to the sleeve of his cream-colored tux. The hue complemented his olive skin and dark eyes.

"Not just yet. I need to draw out any others." That was the whole idea behind not actively accusing anyone just yet. Let panic simmer and brew.

"Vanessa and Liz?" Loch shook his head. "Vanessa's always been jealous of humans, but Liz?"

"Oh, they aren't in it because I'm human—they're in it because Vanessa's in love with you, and Liz is in love with Raiden."

Loch tilted his head back and laughed. "Vanessa is in love with my *position*. Liz," he said thoughtfully, "she's always been very protective of Raiden. I just thought she looked at him like a brother. We were all close growing up. But this?"

I snorted. Boys were stupid.

"And Bali?" I asked Trent.

"She hates humans, but after our party, I thought she'd decided to give you a chance." He yanked on the pearlescent-white shirt he wore underneath his blue velvet jacket. "She was probably who recruited Josha." The muscles of his cheek ticked with tension.

"So what's the plan?" Loch asked. "And once you have them, what are you going to do with them?"

Besides putting them in the dungeon, I was flying by the seat of my pants. I shrugged.

With a wave of my hand, the curtain of water in front of the stairs vanished. That was Poppy's signal to serve dinner.

I sat down at the table in the center of the fountain. Loch pushed in my chair before he sat next to Adam, opposite Kai and Trent. Poppy placed a glass of champagne in front of each of us. What everyone else didn't know was that my glass was filled with sparkling water and a dash of cherry juice. That lesson had been learned the hard way, though I was questioning the sanity behind it. If I'd ever needed liquid courage, now was the time.

Platters of food whirled through the ballroom, the smells, even though divine, making my stomach revolt. Poppy set a plate piled with decadence—meat, potatoes, greenery— in front of me with a sly wink. And though they were all my favorites, I pushed around the food, sneaking most of it to Sid, as I waited for the others to finish.

After dinner, Loch asked, "Do you want to dance?"

Adam's eyes slivered, and Trent crossed his arms.

"Yes."

He held out an elbow and led me to the middle of the floor. Every eye in the room tracked us.

"I've missed you." Loch wrapped his arms around me, holding me close as we swayed to the music.

I chewed on my bottom lip. "It's only been a week."

I hardly noticed as people began to join us on the dance floor, their colorful gowns and jewels flashing in my periphery.

"Yeah, well, that didn't stop me from dreaming about you every night. When I heard you'd disappeared, I rushed here as quickly as I could." He squeezed me tighter. "Ruby, please stop trying to die."

I swatted him on the back. "Please tell everyone to stop trying to kill me."

He leaned away slightly and looked down at me. "Once you're bound to one of us—hopefully me—they'll stop."

He was wrong. The faction that was after me were human haters. At least the leaders were. And though there was a fair amount of giant blood running through my veins, I believed they were past the point of caring. My enemies needed to be pulled out by the roots.

"Loch?" I rested my head on his shoulder. "Are you more interested in the title or me? Please be honest."

His hands dipped lower on my waist. Warmth pooled in my stomach. "At first, only the position, and then as I got to know you, I thought working with you could be enjoyable. And now, I'd marry you even if you weren't destined to be queen. I'm not kidding you when I said I've dreamt about you every night. Honestly, it bothers me how much I like you. It makes me feel vulnerable in a way I've never believed possible."

My heart rocketed and then plummeted. It was like being on a roller coaster. "And if I don't choose you?"

I felt him swallow. "Well, I suppose I learn what it's like to have a broken heart."

"Welcome to the club," I murmured into the side of his neck.

He shivered. "You still haven't decided, have you?"

I shook my head.

"Damn it, Ruby, nothing like waiting until the last minute. I'm assuming you've had plenty of time to think about it."

"It doesn't help."

"What will it take for you to choose me?" He slid one

hand up to the back of my neck and stroked the bare skin below my ear.

"I still don't know if I can trust you."

"Why?" He sounded surprised.

"I overheard you in the tunnel with Vanessa."

After a few seconds, laughter rumbled in his chest. "That answers some questions."

"Like what?"

"Why you acted so strange when I came back into the house. One minute, you seemed perfectly comfortable with me, almost as if you liked me, then you seemed scared."

"Why did you let Vanessa go?"

"Because it would've taken me too much time to arrest her." He leaned down and whispered in my ear sending chills down my spine. "You were in my bedroom waiting for me. I wanted you more than I've ever wanted anything. I still do. Besides, she wasn't going anywhere." He paused. "The real question is why would you sleep with me when you thought I might kill you?" He stopped and gently pushed me away so he could see me.

I shrugged.

His sharp brows creased. "Who the hell does something like that?"

"I didn't want to sleep with Kai."

He shook his head, shutting his eyes for a second. "Obviously. Seriously, Ruby, what's wrong with you?"

"What do you mean?"

He brought his fingers to my cheek. "You were willing to have sex with me even when you thought I might kill you."

"Yeah, well, family is worth the risk." I ground my teeth.

"And that is why I love you," he said, and kissed my forehead.

My lips parted then closed like a fish out of water. My heart fumbled.

Before I could respond, Loch said, "Come on. I have to get you back before Adam and Trent gang up on me."

Both were standing with their legs spread slightly apart and their arms crossed over their wide chests.

I held out my hand to Trent.

When we got to the dance floor, he wrapped his arms around my waist. "You're not choosing me, are you, love?" he said.

"It's not that I don't like you, but you have no desire to help run a kingdom. And Trent, I'm going to need all the help that I can get. My enemies are circling. They smell blood in the water."

"I know you're right, but it still stings. I've never felt this way about anyone. But on the bright side, at least now I know what it feels like and I won't be willing to settle for less."

"Still friends?" I chewed on my lower lip.

"Definitely. And if either of them gives you any flak—" he tipped his chin toward the other two, "—my door's always open." He twerked his brows.

A smile of relief bloomed at his attempt to lighten the awkwardness of our conversation.

"I mean it, love. Even if you're not mine, I don't want anyone to ever hurt you."

I sighed. "Thank you. Do you have any advice?" I glanced past him to Loch and Adam, who were standing a few feet apart staring at us.

"I don't know. Who's better in bed?"

A burst of air puffed between my lips. "It's a toss-up."

"And where do I fit in the lineup?"

463

"To be honest, I don't remember as much as I should."

"Well, that's disappointing. I'm not opposed to refreshing your memory."

I suppressed a grin. "You have a one-track mind."

His eyes swept down my frame. "It's hard not to."

"Whatever." I brushed off his humor with a roll of my eyes as we walked off the dance floor.

Adam didn't even wait for us to get back before he met me halfway and led me back out onto the floor. His arms pulled me in close. He didn't bother dancing, he just held me tight to his chest and breathed in my scent.

"You do realize you've yet to tell me if you're even willing to marry me," I said. A part of me wanted him to say no. He'd be making my choice easy. But the other half sat like the elephant on my ribs, making it hard to breathe, hard to think.

"I've spent so much time debating it. So much time thinking, what can I live without? And truthfully, I don't want to live without either you or my passion. But as I flew over Isle Noir, the palace gardens seemed to be springing to life. I could set up shop here and be happy. But a life without you, I don't want to imagine it. You and I, we fit."

He was right. We did. To spend my days outside amongst nature, with animals, rolling in the hay with the most beautiful man on the planet, was a dream. How could I go wrong? But I had to be honest with him. It was only fair.

"And the other issue?" I said, referring to Raiden.

Adam sighed. "Do you still . . ." He buried his face into the side of my neck and exhaled a warm breath over my skin.

I nodded. My feelings for Raiden were etched into my heart like a tattoo. I didn't think I'd ever be able to erase them. Just the thought of seeing his face made my heart stutter, the beasties in my stomach flutter wildly, and brought tears to my eyes, knowing the man I was obsessed with would never be mine. While a part of me could love Adam or Loch—probably already did a tiny bit—what I felt for Raiden was epic. Fated. Inevitable.

Adam pulled away and stared. His jaw flexed. "Do you think you could ever love me?"

I nodded.

His shoulders relaxed slightly. "And what about Loch? Do you have feelings for him too?"

"Yes."

"Ruby, how's that possible?" The pulse in his neck jumped.

"I don't know," I snapped. "It's like each of you has something I'm missing. He challenges me, makes me address problems within myself. He already runs his Fiefdom. What I feel for him is exhilarating. And you, you make me laugh. You make me feel comfortable with who I am, and who I'll become. What I feel for you is enlightening."

It was like each man had something I needed. Even Trent. He had spontaneity and the ability to have fun. Neither were in my possession.

But Raiden had it all.

I bit down on the inside of my cheek and forced that thought away.

"You still haven't decided, have you?"

"No."

"Wow." He shook his head.

*Tell me about it.*

"So Adam, are you going to make my choice easy for me or difficult?"

465

He slipped his hand to the back of my head, making shivers race down my spine. "Difficult."

He leaned in and kissed me. I guess he meant it. His lips burned against mine, coaxing them apart. His tongue explored my mouth as heat flared between my legs. Desire tightened low in my groin.

He pulled away. "I love you, Ruby. Don't break my heart." He turned and strolled away, leaving me standing alone on the dance floor.

*Fuck.*

# FORTY-FIVE

From behind me, a high-pitched scream pierced the air and echoed off the obsidian walls. I spun around.

Leonardo had Tee bound in his arms with a dagger pressed to her throat. Blood ran down her neck, staining the top of her chiffon gown. She looked like a tiny doll, dressed in pink and gilded in gold, dangling from his hands.

An actual growl rumbled from my chest.

"Leonardo!" Kai bellowed, his voice vibrating the air. His amber eyes glowed like molten metal.

"Anyone comes near me and I'll slit her throat." Leonardo leaned in tightly and sniffed her hair before he licked her cheek with his long tongue. "She tastes like a baby."

How did he know what a baby tasted like?

I reached inside my purse and pulled out my gun, then dropped the bag on the floor and aimed for Leonardo's head. "Put her down. I don't want to kill you." Though I kind of did.

Concern tightened his eyes but he shook his head, tossing his dark-blond hair from his forehead. "Bullets? Really?" he scoffed.

"Those bullets were made by the weapons specialist in Fum!" Kai yelled across the room. "They're infused with *my* energy. If she hits you in the right spot—You. Will. Die."

"I'll take my chances," Leonardo scoffed. "I don't think she's that good of a shot."

"Oh, she's that good," Tee confirmed, though her voice wobbled.

Leonardo shoved the knife further into her skin, and she whimpered.

I squeezed the trigger.

Nothing happened.

Fuck.

I racked the weapon again, and an unspent round flew through the air in slow motion, then clink, clink, clinked on the floor.

I squeezed again. Nothing.

Terror, like a geyser ready to blow, bubbled inside of me. *Not Tee.*

Leonardo tipped his head back and laughed, the sound echoing in the quiet room. "Maybe you're more giant than we originally gave you credit for. Guns don't work for us either," he sneered.

Out of the corner of my eye, I saw some giants back away. Kai stepped closer to Tee.

My nostrils flared. My hands trembled. The fireplace roared to life, flames flickering over the tall mantle. The precious painting above the hearth began to smolder.

Sid yelped.

I whirled around to see Noah yanking on his collar with

a gun pressed to the top of his head. Sid growled but didn't fight, knowing instinctively not to pull away.

"I'm human. Wanna see if this works for me?" Noah said, cocking the hammer.

My terror bled into an uncontrollable fury. Lightning flashed outside the windows, followed by a clap of thunder, rumbling the air with a low grumble. The floor shook. The crystal chandeliers tinkled violently. Vases of fresh flowers vibrated off the edges of the tables and hurtled to the floor.

Snakelike vines smashed through the windows and slithered over the shiny black walls.

Screams bounced around the room as some giants ran and hid behind the curtains. Others crawled under the tables, while some froze with their mouths agape.

My humans grouped together and slowly backed away, never averting their gaze from the danger—*me*. The violence inside of me was feeding off their fright, growing stronger with every scream and every whiff of their terror. I could smell their fear. And it smelled amazing.

Electricity sparked on my skin and flames rose behind my eyes. The humidity became heavy—almost stifling— and the air itself flowed like an angry river around the room.

The wind gusted, whipping the curtains like flags in a storm. Ladies' dresses and their hair flapped wildly. Shards of glass bounced across the floor, suspended briefly before they fell.

"What are you doing?" Noah's mom screamed. "Let Sid go!"

The fountain churned and the water level rose, spilling over the side. The swirling wind turned into a foggy mist as my fury whirled like a tornado until I mentally stepped into the eye of the storm. And with that brief pause came a sense of control and absolute clarity.

I inhaled slowly, calming my inner chaos, while allowing it to continue around the room. My powers built, notch by notch, stoking the hot coal fire I fueled with oxygen.

The vines hiding in the fog slid slowly over the floor—one toward Noah and the other toward Leonardo. The emerald-green ropes rose from the ground like cobras emerging from baskets. I directed one up the front of Tee's leg, on the outside of her dress, until it stopped between her breasts. The whites of her eyes widened and rolled like a terrified horse.

The other vine, I snuck behind Noah, draping a noose of twisted greenery and thorns above his head.

My nerve endings zapped as if lightning traveled under my skin. It bordered on pain—which just increased my focus, and in doing so, eased my ability to harness the elements.

I reached up and simultaneously commanded my plants to strike. One snapped around Leonardo's wrist and pulled the dagger away from Tee's throat. Kai, who'd been methodically pressing closer, dashed to her side at the same time Leonardo dropped her. The tentacles of the rose bush curled around Leonardo's throat like an anaconda. Blood spilled from the thorns.

The other vine simultaneously dropped its noose over Noah's neck and constricted so tightly his head detached from his body with a loud pop. A fine mist of crimson flashed over a Duel's white uniform and onto the wall, leaving behind a perfect giant-shaped outline. Noah's head tumbled to the floor and rolled to a stop with a trail of gore following in its wake.

Leonardo struggled with the plants. His eyeballs bulged inside his sockets and his veins plumped from the pressure. With his free hand, he slid it under the vine and pulled it away from his throat, gasping for breath. He ducked out of my noose and roared, his eyes burning a deep bronze.

I screamed, realizing my ineptitude—he was Fee and had a fair amount of control over the earth himself. My voice shattered any remaining glass as I whipped my hands at him, palms facing upward, and curled my fingers back, sucking the air from his chest and at the same time draining the moisture from his body.

He bared his teeth, his fangs glinting in the firelight, and dove at me.

Sweat ran down my face as I poured my everything into my powers, my muscles trembling.

As his powerful legs pumped closer, his body shrank, his cheeks hollowing, his skin wrinkling. I siphoned the oxygen from his body, collapsing his lungs until his ribs broke with a snap, crackle, and pop. A silent scream ripped over his face. But giants weren't easy to kill and I wasn't done. As he stumbled to the floor, smoke twisted from his hair and clothes before they burst into vicious flames. I fed the inferno with a soft breeze blowing from my lips.

His body crumbled to ash. Water, still trickling over the side of the fountain, carried him away in small gray rivulets over the checkered floor.

My legs failed as I crashed to my hands and knees. Sid ran to me and stuck his head under my chin. I buried my face into his fur and tried to hold back the building hysteria.

A maniacal laugh spilled from my mouth and echoed in the room. I still had to choose a husband. After what had just happened, would there be any willing participants left?

# CHAPTER
# FORTY-SIX

In the end, the weapons I'd brought with me, mostly for show, I hadn't even needed. My stomach soured as I thought, *I am the weapon.*

Noah's mom rushed to her son's contorted remains. Her wide eyes found mine, then looked at him. She fell to the floor in a puddle of blood and held his headless body in her lap. Wailing sobs, the only sound in an otherwise silent room, wracked her body.

I averted my gaze to keep myself from apologizing. I was *sort of* sorry he was dead. But it was his own fault. He'd struck first. Then he'd committed the gravest of sins—he'd tried to kill Sid. I wasn't sorry for what I'd done, but I was sorry for the pain it caused her.

Adam and his parents stood next to the mountain of ash that used to be his brother. The smell of seared flesh and smoke permeated the room. Adam's dark eyes landed on mine, his expression a blank canvas. I couldn't tell what he was thinking. Was he horrified? Surprised? Secretly pleased?

Still on the floor, kneeling in shards of glass, I looked

around the rest of the room. Everyone's attention was glued to me. A healthy dose of fear sat alongside the disbelief on their faces. Deep furrows creased between Loch's brows. Trent stood with his arms slack at his sides and his full lips parted. Kai held on to Tee, who blinked with shock, but to my relief, not horror.

"Are you okay?" I mouthed to her.

She nodded and said in sign language, "I love you."

Tears burned the back of my nose. My mom had always said, "Find the people your soul recognizes." Tee was my people. Sid was my people. Raiden was my people. If he were here, he'd be at my side. Sorrow hiccupped in my chest.

Using Sid's strong back to help me balance on my unsteady legs, I pushed myself up off the floor, then brushed the slivers of glass from my hands and knees, which tinkled on the marble. Tiny specks of blood peppered my palms.

A loud banging on the door interrupted the eerie silence in the ballroom.

"Ruby!" Raiden screamed through the thick wooden doors.

My heart leapt as if it were trying to break free of my ribcage. My legs stumbled forward toward his voice, my balance off kilter.

The doors burst open, shards of wood flying.

I paused for only a second before launching into his arms and burying my head into his muscled chest. The desire to cry was strong but I contained my feelings.

Raiden placed a finger under my chin, his other hand holding me up by my armpit. "Bea-bea, what happened here?"

I stared at his beautiful lips surrounded by a three-day shadow, then switched focus to his stormy gray eyes.

"Bea-bea? Come on. Tell me what happened," he gently coaxed.

"Me." My voice broke.

"You?" His voice raised a note.

I nodded.

"You did this?"

I nodded again.

A smile curled on his lips and mischief crinkled the corners of his eyes. He rubbed the side of my cheek with his calloused thumb. "That's my girl."

My forehead crinkled. I'd thought he was going to be angry or disgusted. I might have just destroyed precious works of art. Was it really the end for *The Last Supper*? Had *Mona Lisa* finally lost her smile? And to top it off, I'd killed two people. Even if they had deserved it.

Heat flashed behind his eyes, cutting off my ability to breathe. The muscles in his jaw flexed as he reached out and embraced me, stroking the back of my head. Relief and the feeling that being where I belonged flowed down my body like hot water from the showers I was so fond of.

"Ruby?" I heard a voice next to Raiden.

He tried pushing me back, but I gripped him tighter.

"Ruby-Baby?" the voice said, making it all one word.

I snapped my head to the side. "Momma?"

The tears I'd held back burst forth like a broken dam. A cry stuttered in my chest. I hiccupped, trying to catch my breath, then I blinked in an attempt to clear my vision to make sure she wasn't an illusion.

Her chin trembled while her mouth twisted into a radiant smile as if she couldn't believe I was real either.

Raiden steadied me so I didn't crash to the floor.

As she opened her arms, I fell into them. The last time we'd hugged, I was ten and fit perfectly in her embrace. This time, I towered above her—but somehow still fit.

"Momma," I whimper.

Someone else's hand rubbed my back, and I looked into her brown eyes as she ticked her head sideways. I turned and caught a glimpse of my dad's smile before he wrangled me into a bear hug of his own.

The emotions tearing through me were a concoction of contradictions but the sight of my parents, alive, overshadowed all the bad. How had they gotten here? Where had they been? But it didn't matter. They were alive.

"Where's Kevin?" My eyes frantically searched the room.

He stepped out from behind Raiden's wide body.

Relief sagged my shoulders. "What is . . . how? Uh . . ."

"Bea-bea," Raiden said. He bent over to look me directly in the eyes. "We only have a few minutes until midnight. Can you concentrate for me?"

I nodded.

Raiden stood to his full, formidable height. "Aunt Sylvia, Uncle Issac, come forth."

Lord Issac placed his hand on Lady Sylvia's waist as she lifted her chin and stepped toward Raiden.

"I believe you know who these two are." Raiden motioned to my parents.

Sylvia's icy-blue eyes squinted with anger.

"To everyone else, let me introduce you to Mr. and Mrs. Walker."

A hum of voices whispered in the air.

"I'm here to reclaim my title as First-Born son," Raiden addressed his aunt and uncle.

I placed a hand on Raiden's arm, my eyes darting to Loch.

Loch glanced at the floor and exhaled heavily before nodding and stepping forward as if he'd known this were a possibility.

"Raiden, no!" I said.

He looked down at me. "Bea-bea, trust me. Can you do that?"

I removed my hand.

"I have irrefutable evidence that Sylvia and Issac had my parents murdered." Raiden's lips pressed together in a straight line.

The cacophony of voices in the room increased.

"Lords and ladies." Raiden raised his hand, shushing them.

The First Families of the other houses strode forward.

"In light of this new evidence, I'm here to contest their appointment as lord and lady of the Fie. I am *still* the First-Born son."

Raiden removed something from his pocket and got down on one knee right in front of me. He flipped the box open, revealing a solitary pear-shaped diamond sparkling under the dull lighting from the dying fire. He grabbed my shaking hand. "If you'll still have me."

I blinked slowly. A sliver of hope blossomed and grew with every breath. My eyes flashed momentarily to Tee. Black streaks of mascara streamed down her smiling face. She'd known all along.

I glanced back at Raiden. "You mean . . . ?"

"Yes, Ruby." He cocked his head. "I'm eligible."

I placed my hands on either side of his face, and without

hesitation, I said, "I choose you." I bent over and rested my forehead gently next to his.

A tiny shiver vibrated over my heart and burned out with a sting.

Sylvia started to speak, but I raised my hand and pulled the oxygen from her chest, making her look as if she were dry heaving air.

My eyes darted to Issac next, daring him to try me.

I didn't need Raiden's *proof* that his aunt and uncle were guilty. The minute the energy over my heart had disappeared was irrefutable. If he wasn't a legitimate First-Born son, it would still be there. If only we would have known earlier, we could have saved everyone some heartache.

"Loch, can you come here?" I asked.

He looked genuinely hurt. I hoped he was, because the alternative was worse.

"Loch, did you know that your parents had your aunt and uncle killed in order to inherit their title?"

He hiked up the bottom of his tux jacket and stuck his hands in his pant pockets. "No. Not for certain. I had my suspicions, like everyone else, but no proof. I was hoping if I became king, I would have the freedom to dig deeper. Raiden's the only family I have left. If I had the ability to make his life easier by finding the truth, then I was going to do it. But now I don't have to."

"I believe you." I patted his arm. "That's why I must do this. So for once and for all, your name can be cleared." I turned and looked at his mother. "Lady Sylvia, invoke the parental promise. Ask your son for the truth."

"Go ahead, Mom, ask me." Loch puffed out his chest and clasped his arms behind his back.

Sylvia clamped her lips shut.

I looked to Loch. I was sure he was innocent. Why wouldn't his mom want him cleared? If I couldn't get them to speak, then everyone would think Loch knew all along that his parents were imposters.

"You failed," she spat at her son.

"Failed what, Mom? *Everything*? I've been doing your job now for the last five years while you and Dad fucked around doing who knows what. Ask me the damn question! It's the least you can do!"

She tilted her nose up in the air.

Issac pulled his arm from her grip.

"Don't you dare," she hissed. A gust of wind whipped through the room.

Isaac snarled at her before he said, "Loch, I invoke the parental promise. Did you know that we had your aunt and uncle killed?"

"No," Loch replied immediately.

Finally, I'd gotten one right. I turned and wrapped my arms around Loch's waist in gratitude.

A growl rumbled from behind us, and Loch pushed me away, sadness coloring his expression. "Thank you, Ruby."

Kevin had a tight hold on Raiden's shoulder.

I walked over to Raiden and lifted his hand. Turning it over, I planted a kiss on his palm. "I love you. Now calm down."

He glanced around the room. "You're one to talk," he grumbled.

"Loch," I said, turning back and stopping him as he walked away. I gave him a shaky smile. The last thing I wanted to do was break his heart. Too late. But there was something that could be done. "Since Raiden's no longer able to fill the position, will you please take your place as the lord of the Fie?"

The hurt behind his eyes softened. "Really?"

"Uh, yeah. Who else can I trust with the responsibility? Can I count on you?"

He clasped a hand over his heart. "Ruby, I'm not in a position to deny you anything. You know that."

A knot twisted in my throat as I realized he would have been the giant I chose.

Swallowing the lump, I pushed back tears. Even though Raiden was mine, a sliver of my heart would always belong to Loch, Adam, and even Trent. Though I was sure Trent and I would remain friends. He had the capability of separating what we could have had from what we did have.

I searched the room for Adam, but he was gone, as were his parents. The only person they'd left behind was a soggy pile of ashes.

Shoving down my exhaustion, I ordered Liz, Bali, Thur, and Penelope forward. When they were lined up in front of me, I looked at them one by one. "Any last words?" I asked.

Liz's blue eyes shot open. "You can't kill us! You can only banish us. You're still alive."

I turned to Benji and Ramona. Ramona's hands covered her face, chest quaking from crying. Benji shook his head slowly as if he couldn't believe what he was hearing. "Why? You were raised better. We're not a family of human haters," he said. His deep voice cracked.

Liz hung her head. "Because. She doesn't deserve him!"

Benji's eyes crinkled with confusion.

"She's in love with Raiden," I clarified.

Both Benji and Raiden exchanged a shocked glance.

"So all of this is because of your schoolgirl crush?" Ramona admonished.

"I *love* him," Liz screamed.

"I don't know if that's better or worse," Ramona said. She turned away from her daughter as Benji set a hand on her back and followed.

I pointed at the remaining three. "You three just hate humans?" I didn't wait for them to answer. "Good. That's so much less messy than emotions of the heart. Do you have anything to say?"

They all lifted their chins and stared past me.

"All right." I looked around the room at the remaining giants. "Here's the deal. If any of you come to me with names, I won't have you banished for treason. That goes for everyone in here, except for them."

"You can't have us killed. I know the law," Penelope said. "We can only be banished."

I smirked at Noah's pale body and what was left of Leonardo before focusing back on her. "I'm sure I can think of something. For now, Penelope, Thur, Bali, and Liz, you can enjoy the luxury accommodations in the dungeon. Sylvia and Issac, you'll join them until Raiden decides your punishment."

CHAPTER

# FORTY-SEVEN

My parents cozied up on the sofa next to the roaring fireplace in the queen's quarters as Kevin wandered around the room admiring the artwork. I sat on a cushy ottoman in front of them with one leg curled under me. They'd aged—silver streaked their hair now, and they had wrinkles around their eyes—but not like I had. I had been ten when they disappeared.

My mom stared at my face, wearing a silly little smile. "I always knew you'd be beautiful, but this was beyond my imagination," she said.

She had to say that—she was my mom.

"What happened?" I asked.

She wet her lips and took a deep breath. "The morning I left for work, your father—" she glanced both accusingly and lovingly at him, "—wouldn't let me go alone. The government was getting suspicious about my research, and I wanted him to stay behind to make sure you kids were safe. He refused. I'm still a little bit mad at him."

My dad grabbed her hand and kissed it. "I told you they'd be fine without us."

Not having an argument, Mom continued. "Anyway, when we got there, my boss had broken into my computer and ransacked my lab. Upon the commander's orders, we were *detained*," she said, using air quotes. "When we refused to tell them where you kids were, they arrested us and called my research biological terrorism. Soon after that, the world crumbled. The only thing that saved our sanity was knowing that we'd set you up for survival. And boy, did you ever survive. I'm so proud of both of you." Tears poured from her eyes, and even my dad had to wipe some away.

"And what about Raiden's parents? Did he ever find out what happened to them?"

Their expressions fell and they nodded. My mom couldn't even talk so my dad continued the conversation. "Lady Sinai and Lord Eyal. We actually became good friends." He smiled as he remembered. "After they were fed information about a young redheaded girl, they came to Earth searching for you. Sinai thought the prophecy of the Crimson Jewel pertained to a person and not an actual stone, so Sylvia used the rumors to lure them to Earth, but not because Sylvia believed the rumors or prophecy. She just wanted Sinai's title. Once Eyal and Sinai got there and learned that we were a quarter giant and that redheaded girl was our daughter, they realized you *were* the prophecy. And once they trusted us, we devised an escape. Let's just say it didn't go as planned. They were killed, and we were captured."

I could tell there was far more to the story. When—and if—they were ever ready, I'd be here to listen.

A strange pull of energy had me looking to the doorway.

I grinned when Raiden appeared seconds later. It was like I could feel his energy before I could see him. "You ready?" he asked.

I glanced at my folks. I was torn. I didn't want to leave them alone.

"That man," my mom said, referring to Raiden, "has been through hell. First to find us, then to get here in time before you committed to someone else. You need to go spend some time with him. Alone."

My face flamed all the way to the tips of my ears and nose. I did *not* want to talk about this with my parents.

She reached out and wrapped my hands in hers. "I promise we'll be here when you return. And I've been told giants keep their promises."

My dad nodded. "Go, kiddo. We aren't going anywhere."

---

Before Raiden and I left for our *alone time*, we placed Poppy and Tee in charge of the Fiefdom with Grant, Kai, and Kevin as their backups. The ladies and lords of each Dome, including Loch, assured us there would be no trouble while we were away.

"We'll be back in a couple of days," I said.

Grant pursed his lips, trying to control a smirk, and nodded his head like he didn't believe me. Kai avoided eye contact and instead stared at the ceiling. I didn't miss the amusement on his face.

My parents hugged me long and hard before pushing me into Raiden's arms. He pulled me effortlessly onto Arnold's back. Sid was tucked into his basket sack underneath. I hadn't even considered leaving him behind.

"Where are we going?" I asked Raiden once we made it into the air.

"I'm taking you home." His breath warmed my cheek as shivers fled down my spine and over my limbs. His arms clenched tighter around me and his chest burned hot on my back. The anticipation was killing me. The idea of sleeping with him terrified me as much as it excited me. He'd told me earlier that the first time we slept together, it wouldn't be sex, nor would it be love—it would be possession, us claiming our bond over one another. I was scared to ask what he meant, and he didn't seem keen on explaining it further. Though he was wrong about one thing—no matter what it looked like, I loved him.

"Bea-bea, get some rest. I'll wake you when we get there." He embraced me tighter.

I hadn't had a chance to sleep before we left. We'd been too busy catching up as a family. The only thing I'd managed to sneak in was a quick shower to wash off the blood.

Finally back in the embrace of the man I loved, I nodded off in the comfort of Raiden's strong arms.

---

I AWOKE to Arnold's slow descent. Below us, trees, twice as tall as California redwoods, some green, some blue, swayed in the breeze like an ocean current. The scent of pine mingled with the crisp air. I rolled my neck.

"Welcome back, sleeping beauty."

To think, the last time he'd called me that, I had tried to convince myself I hated him. Maybe at the time, it was true, but no longer. I reached down and squeezed his thigh. Every muscle in his body jerked.

485

Arnold snorted and tossed his nose in the air, his long mane catching the wind and slapping me in the face.

Raiden kissed the top of my head. Lava flowed over my shoulders, down my back, and pooled, hot, heavy, and aching, between my legs. A small, breathless moan escaped between my lips.

Raiden's breathing became stilted. His instant erection pressed hard into my lower back.

Arnold circled around the base of a mountain and landed in a dirt clearing. Before he came to a complete stop, Raiden hopped off and pulled me with him. Quickly, he unlatched Sid's basket, pulled off Arnold's bridle, and unbuckled the cinch on the saddle. It fell to the ground, but he left it there. Arnold crow-hopped away, bucking and kicking.

Humor rounded my cheeks—until I saw the look in Raiden's eyes. Gray flames flickered around dilated pupils. The evening sun backlit his black hair in flames of light. He looked like a god about to exact vengeance.

I stopped breathing for the space of a few heartbeats. My eyelids grew heavy, my mouth parted, and desire clambered between my thighs.

I caught only a flash of movement before he snatched me into his arms. A scream of surprise chirped from my throat as I threw my head back and laughed wildly.

With me cradled in his grasp, Raiden swept me up a long wooden staircase to a cabin built high in the canopy. He opened the front door, let Sid in, and slammed it behind us. Taking the stairs two at a time, he tossed me onto a massive bed in the middle of the loft. Outside the windows behind him was a crystal-clear lake at the base of the mountain. Though the view was spectacular, it wasn't nearly as fascinating—or intimidating—as the man standing in front of me.

Slowly, with his fists clenched, he backed away from the bed. He opened and closed them a few times before he yanked his shirt over his head and dropped it at his feet. The swells of his pecs and hard ridges of his stomach made my mouth water with the desire to kiss every square inch, but something instinctual warned me to stay perfectly still. My eyes wandered downward, past the V-shaped muscles to where his penis strained against the fabric of his pants. He placed his hand, shaking as if trying to maintain control over his actions, on the top snap. I bit down on my bottom lip, barely breathing. The energy radiating through the room was thick and dense like fog at twilight, frightening but alluring at the same time.

He unzipped his pants and dropped them before stepping out of them, followed by his plaid boxers.

I swallowed hard, my core clenching at the sight of his magnificent body. Holy mother of all that was—well, of all that was . . .

His nostrils flared and a low growl rumbled the air. The hollows under his cheekbones sharpened as light from the dying sun glistened over his wet fangs. My heart raced. If it were anyone else standing in front of me looking one hundred-percent predator, I might have vied for escape. I wasn't scared, exactly, but I wasn't stupid either. I'd assumed this expedition was going to be just the run-of-the-mill, hair-pulling, rough sex. Now, I wasn't sure. He seemed on the edge of losing control.

*Fee, fie, foe, fum. I smell the blood of an Englishman.*

My pulse thundered in my ears.

But this was Raiden. *My* Raiden.

And I was no longer breakable.

Once I had my panic under control, I stood up slowly, not making any sudden motions. The muscles in his jaw knotted, the tendons in his neck flexed, and the set of his shoulders stiffened, but he didn't move. With one foot, I pushed off my shoe, then the other, along with my socks. Without breaking eye contact, I shimmied out of my pants. Cold air swirled around my legs. I reached up for the buttons on my shirt and unhooked them one by one before pushing it off my shoulder. It floated like a white cloud to the pine floor. My arm snaked behind my back and I unlatched my bra but held it in place.

His eyelids drooped as he blinked slowly. He hadn't said a single word to me since we'd arrived.

Inhaling deeply, steadying my frayed nerves, I let it go. My bra swept down the front of me.

Unable to resist any longer, Raiden stepped forward. The air around him vibrated, making it look as if he had a fuzzy aura surrounding his body like a halo of sorts.

My thumb hooked into the top of my already-wet lace panties. His eyes, swirling like liquid silver, squeezed shut as he turned his head away. I waited until he looked back before sliding them down my legs and stepping out of them.

"Raiden," I said quietly. "You can't hurt me. You saw what I'm capable of." I moved toward him.

His Adam's apple bobbed.

"I love you with every ounce of my heart and soul," I whispered.

I didn't see him move, nor did I hear him. Without any preamble, he lifted me onto the bed and thrust himself deep inside me, threatening to tear me in half. A scream between pleasure, pain, and surprise caught in my throat. He tossed his head back and roared, thrusting harder, deeper. I dug my fingers into his back, blood running slick under my nails. His mouth crashed into mine, devouring every inch of the space with his tongue. Tiny pinpricks of electricity sparked along the hairs on my arms before they traveled to my shoulders, down my body, until they snaked their way through me. Every cell in my body began to vibrate as if they were alive. I met his every thrust with one of my own. I gripped his butt, pulling him in aggressively. The moans coming out of my chest heightened with every push.

He slid his hand into my hair and yanked my head back, exposing my neck. My eyes rounded with fear when I realized what was about to happen.

His fangs sliced into the delicate skin of my throat. Pain radiated but subsided as quickly as it was replaced with a ferocious need to finish what we'd started. The electricity sparking between the two of us grew until it was beyond my control. It snapped and crackled in the air, blue light dancing in the darkening room. He lifted his head away from my neck, his fangs and lips crimson. He reached up and violently scratched the side of his neck. Blood flooded from the wound as he brought my lips near and turned his head away. I inhaled an unsteady breath and swallowed hard. This must have been what they meant when they said a blood bond.

*Someone should have warned me.*

I chased the doubts out of my mind and latched my lips to his skin. Sparkles flashed behind my eyes, filling my head with delirium. A groan twisted from his throat as I pulled away. I licked the salty, metallic taste of him from my mouth.

I held on as he rode me with an unbridled frenzy. His

solid chest rubbed hard against my nipples. Blissful torture grew slowly, steadily, bit by bit, until I couldn't focus on anything except the intensity building in my core.

My insides quaked from the pulsing electricity as my cells tore themselves apart and then crashed together. Scorching fire spilled into my womb as wave upon wave of pleasure rocked my soul.

I threw my head back and screamed until my voice was raw.

Raiden dropped onto my chest, his breathing ragged and rough on my cheek.

I stroked the back of his buzz-cut hair. The short stubs felt nice on my palm.

When his breath steadied, he rose up on his elbows and looked down at me. He picked up a curl and wound it around a finger before he dropped it on my naked chest. He licked his lips and then wiped his mouth with his hand, seeming nervous. Though after what had just occurred, I wasn't sure why.

"I'm sorry." His eyes darted away. "That's not how I was hoping it would go. I wanted to have more control."

I leaned up and kissed him. "I love you."

A smile tried twitching at the corner of his lips. "Is that your way of saying the sex was awful?"

"No. My way of saying the sex was awful would be—the sex was awful."

Concern wrinkled his brow. "Was it?"

"*No*. It wasn't. But it wasn't what I'd imagined it to be either. I feel like someone should have warned me about the whole giants-like-to-bite thing."

"Nobody told you?" Horror flashed on his face.

"No."

"I figured..."

"Nope."

He turned his head away from me. "I thought I would have more control. I wanted to walk you through this slowly. But when I smelled your desire, I lost it. Instinct took over and well, I was rougher than I'd planned. I'm sorry."

With a finger to his chin, I turned his face back to mine. "Don't be silly. It was fantastic. That whole electrical jolt thing?" My heart picked up its pace, and my insides constricted at the mere thought. "That was mind-blowing." My lids drifted shut.

When I opened them, he was staring at my parted lips. He glanced at my naked chest and my nipples hardened in response.

He kissed the spot on my neck where he'd bitten earlier. I flinched. It was still sore, but I could tell the wound had already healed. He drifted down my collarbone to the swell of my breasts, his tongue flicking my nipple. My back arched in response. I gripped the comforter in my fists. His mouth surrounded my aching nub as his thumb pinched the other. If he kept it up, I would climax just from that alone.

He kissed down the side of my waist, my nerves flaring with every touch, and positioned himself between my legs.

I leaned my head back and bit the inside of my cheek. The palms of his hands slid up the insides of my thighs and pushed my legs as far apart as they would go. His fingers spread my throbbing flesh and a gust of icy-cold air touched my clit. I bucked.

He laughed and pulled me back into the position he wanted me in. "Hold still," he ordered.

He inserted two fingers inside of me, curled them slightly, and rested the pad of his thumb on my frantically aching nub. An electrical current started pulsing from his fingers and his thumb growing into a vibration, faster and faster, pushing me higher and higher, until moans and whimpers came out of me in stilted breaths. I orgasmed in a matter of seconds.

My body sagged with satisfaction as he crawled up, resting his weight on my chest and laughed.

"That was completely unfair," I said, smacking him on the back.

"No, that was completely necessary."

"You cheated."

"There is no such thing," he mumbled as he scooted in behind and wrapped his arms tightly around me.

# CHAPTER
# FORTY-EIGHT

The next morning, my muscles were still sore, so I utilized the scalding-hot shower, the steam soothing the ache. Once finished, I picked Raiden's shirt off the floor and pressed my face into the material. Instead of dressing in clean clothes, I pulled it over my head, reveling in his scent.

I wandered downstairs, leaving him quietly snoring in the loft. I gave Sid some food and opened the refrigerator. Inside was nothing helpful. The cupboards weren't much better. I found some granola and ate it dry as I stepped out onto the front porch overlooking the lake. The mountains reflected in the rippling surface.

A feeling of peace and contentment nestled in the hollow of my throat. I'd never felt that before, and it was as welcome as it was foreign. Sid ran down the stairs behind me, eager to pee on every vertical surface.

"Good morning," Raiden startled me from behind. He stretched his arms over his head, then ran his fingers through his hair. He wore only a pair of athletic shorts. God, he couldn't have been more beautiful if he'd tried.

I picked a nut out of the granola and tossed it at his face, but he caught it in his mouth. Someday, I would get used to his sneaking abilities.

"Sleep well?" His voice was rough.

"Never better." I padded over and pulled him down for a kiss. His lips were soft and warm.

"Truthfully?" he asked, his lips still touching mine.

"Yes." I'd slept like a baby in his arms. "Can we just stay here forever?" I strolled to the edge of the deck. The railing sat right below my breasts and was a good forty-foot drop to the forest floor.

"I wish. Maybe after things are settled in the capital, we can go on a honeymoon. Isn't that what you call them?"

"Yes. But most of the time you get married first." I kicked a football-sized pinecone off the edge with my foot. It bounced down tree branches.

"We're the equivalent of married now, you know that, right?" He sounded worried.

I'd gotten that impression.

"We don't have weddings like humans do," he contin- ued, "though if that's what you want, I'm sure it can be arranged."

"I don't want," I said. Being with the person I loved had always been a part of the dream, but getting married never was.

"What *do* you want?" He sat down on the outdoor couch and rested his arms along the length.

"I told you. I want to stay here forever." I wasn't kidding.

"So you don't want a honeymoon?"

"Yes, I want a honeymoon. Right here." I turned around

to find him smiling so widely that his fangs glinted in the morning sun. I was never going to get enough of him.

"So we're basically married?" I pointed quickly between us.

"Yup. So long as I'm alive, no other man will touch you and live through it."

"Well, that's a little extreme. So if I walk by some dude and his shoulder brushes mine or I hug Adam or Trent or Loch, you're going to kill them?"

Raiden's eyes narrowed. "I might think about it," he said with a pout.

I tapped my foot on the wooden planks.

"No. I mean if another man touches you like I did last night."

I walked over to him and leaned down to his neck, inhaling deeply—peppermint, fresh mountain air, pine needles, and something uniquely him. "You mean like this?" I nipped the side of his neck.

The muscles along his jaw twitched.

I ran my fingers down his lightly hairy chest, over the ripples of his stomach, memorizing the dips and valleys as if they were my favorite passage in a book. Which they were. "Or like this?" I quirked an eyebrow.

He spread his hands on my hips. Fire fanned from his touch.

With my free hand, I tugged his shirt over my head.

His eyes snapped wider. I didn't have anything underneath. He stood up and quickly yanked off his shorts before he grabbed me by the waist and set me on the edge of the outdoor couch. He knelt in front of me and spread my legs wide.

Never having been exposed like this in broad daylight, I

stopped breathing as a blush ran up my neck, settling in my cheeks. He didn't bother teasing me with kisses to my thighs as he dove straight to the aching source. His tongue swept through my flesh and landed on my clit. As his mouth feasted, he inserted a finger, then two, curling them as I arched my back and moaned. My unsureness faded away as I grabbed the back of his head and urged him on. Pleasure mounted, focusing directly at the source, and grew with every heave of breath until a kaleidoscope of colors flashed behind my closed eyes and shattered. My screams echoed off the mountains.

As I caught my breath, Raiden, still kneeling, chuckled. "I guess it's true what they say about redheads."

I wasn't sure what exactly he was referring to, but I could guess.

The ache inside of me, though tempered, wasn't yet satisfied. I stood up and guided him to my former position, intent on returning the favor.

"Later," he said as he pulled me down onto his lap. "I want inside of you. Now," he ordered.

I straddled him, lowering myself one inch at a time down his long shaft, until he filled me completely. I reformulated my plan to do this slowly, to take my time, but I wanted him so fucking bad I was having trouble controlling my actions.

Staring into his gray eyes, I addressed his earlier concerns. "No man will ever touch me again like this except for you. I promise. And if you touch another woman like this, I'll kill them. And then I'll kill you."

Instead of balking at my threat, he smiled, as if my possessiveness pleased him.

"I know you think my kind can be flaky and unfaithful. And I'm so sorry about what I did."

"Ruby, don't. Part of that was my fault as well."

"The hell it was. I take—"

"No. I left you without any explanation. I should've told you what I was doing. I just didn't want to give you false hope. So let's put the past in the past and look only toward the future."

"God, Raiden, all I've ever wanted was you. All I will ever want is *you*."

---

I LAID BACK with my head in his lap and stared at the baby-pink clouds skating across the periwinkle sky. "How did you figure out our parents had a connection?" I asked.

He handed me his T-shirt. "If you want to talk, you're going to have to put that on."

My cheeks flushed. I loved that the sight of my naked body was enough to distract him even though we'd just finished another round.

"You'll survive," I said. I enjoyed the sun and the cool breeze on my skin.

He chuckled. "You told me your parents went missing approximately twelve years ago. I found it curious that my parents disappeared a couple of years after yours. I'd already known that the last time my parents were seen alive was near the stairway I found you in. Plus, my mom's dire wolf was with them and he went missing too. Sid reminds me so much of Navarre that I just knew they had to be related somehow. And the timeline fit. Then, when Kevin told me you guys were part giant, what your mom did for a living, and where she worked, well, there were too many coincidences to ignore. That, on top of my suspicions about my aunt, led me to ask your brother if he was interested in investigating further."

"How did you get them out?"

He sighed. "It wasn't easy, but the military has become a bit lax in the last few years. It's not like anyone has challenged them lately. Their perceived superiority was their mistake."

I smiled. I could relate.

"We also enlisted Bach's help with the promise of turning over the location of your parents' stash."

"Is he . . . ?" I didn't care for Tee's dad, but he was still her father.

"Yeah, he's okay."

"I'm sorry about your parents." I reached up and touched his chin, running my fingers over his scruff.

"Me too. But knowing helps. Did you know they became friends? Our parents."

I nodded and waited for him to expand, but he seemed lost in the memory. I figured eventually, he'd tell me the whole story. We had our whole lives ahead of us for him to tell me.

# FORTY-NINE

A couple mornings later, back at the palace, I paced the floor of the library as I scanned everyone's faces. Raiden sat at the head of the table next to my empty chair. Tee and Poppy were on either side of me, next to Kai and Grant. I'd debated inviting Loch, Adam, and Trent, but it was just too soon for any of us.

I had sent word that I'd like them to be on my board of advisors after I was officially crowned Queen of the Fiefdom. Since my acquired powers had come to light, the current lords and ladies had agreed the ceremony was just a formality.

Apparently, when they'd inherited their titles from their parents, or married into the family, they'd all signed a blood oath similar to the one I'd signed. They vowed they would not take possession of the Crimson Jewel. That the jewel itself would choose its destiny and, in doing so, would save the Fiefdom. And if they broke the vow, they would die.

It explained why I'd received so little help from them and why Lady Sylvia came close, but never actually got her hands dirty. Though I suspected she'd walked a fine line. I had to give her manipulation skills credit, I'd almost picked Loch. And though he wasn't in on his mom's plan, she'd almost won. But instead of the crown, she was going to get a one-way ticket to earth, compliments of her new queen.

I'd never asked for it—still didn't want it. My mom had always said we had to live with our choices, and I'd made mine the minute I'd traded my freedom for the safety of my people.

*My people.*

Over the last month, the classification of who *my people* were had expanded. And I would do my best to protect all of them, except for the ones sitting in prison for attempted murder.

WHILE WE'D BEEN GONE, a few more giants had come forward with names of those who wanted my life. They'd been willing to talk in return for amnesty. I was relieved that no other humans were involved. The giants that were already imprisoned in the dungeons had kept their silence.

"So how long can we keep them locked up?" I asked Poppy. She was an expert on Fiefdom history and had broad knowledge of their rules.

"Indefinitely," she said. "But the longest example I can find is a year."

"That gives us time," Raiden said. He tapped his coffee cup with his long fingers.

My face blushed as I thought of what those fingers were capable of. His gray eyes flashed to mine. His nostrils flared and he pressed his lips together while pretending to study the open book before him.

"I think you should exile them," Tee said. "If you kill them as your first act as queen . . ."

"But if you don't," Kai added, "it may be perceived as a weakness, and you don't want to look weak."

From anyone else, that might've sounded like disrespect, but I'd been very adamant from the beginning of this administration, for lack of a better word, that we'd face obstacles with complete honesty and transparency.

"Agreed," I said. "But not following your laws may also backfire. It clearly states that the punishment for *attempted* murder—" though having been through it, I wasn't sure I could see a difference, "—is exile. And *murder* is execution. I think the law is clear."

Raiden placed a hand on my shoulder. "Even though banishing them separates them from their magic, they'll find a way. Though they don't know where the gates are located, I can see this biting us in the ass someday."

Poppy nodded. "They'll want revenge. Plus, their lifespans will be drastically shortened on Earth, so they'll be in a hurry to rectify their situation. And you."

"I'm sure, but I'm prepared to deal with that when the time comes. We'll keep them locked up for a year, that way we can discuss it further, but for now, I'm comfortable with exiling them on Earth. Each one to a different area. Are you with me?" My fingers were crossed that if we kept them separated, they wouldn't cause as many problems. I wasn't sure if I was making the right choice, but everyone agreed.

"Once I'm crowned queen, I'll announce our decision." Now that we'd finished with business, my eyes landed on my best friend. "Are you ready?"

She jumped out of her chair, kissed Kai on the cheek and bolted from the room, with me tailing.

Come evening, she was getting married. She'd begged me to have a double wedding with her. I'd politely declined. She'd insisted. I'd refused. For once, I won.

It usually took months to plan a wedding, but Tee had spent hours, long before Kai was in the picture, planning hers. And though giants couldn't create ideas on their own, they excelled at putting Tee's vision together in less than a week. I wasn't surprised when she admitted that she'd brought her wedding binder from Alaska.

I held my hand out to Raiden. We planned to stay in the capital for the summer and the fall, then if circumstances allowed it, we were going home for the winter. *Home.*

Most of my friends had jobs in the capital now. I was relieved to have them near, in case anything went wrong. Frederica had set up a small medical clinic in the castle. Frank, in the office next door, had started a consulting company to help all the Domes with any engineering problems they encountered. Tee, after the wedding and honeymoon were over, had her sights on a design business offering event planning and new clothing concepts. She'd already promised jobs to a few of the girls from Alaska.

Poppy already had Kevin hard at work. I wasn't sure what his job title was, but it didn't matter. The perplexed smile on his face told me he was happy and that was all that mattered. Poppy had asked if it was okay if she set him up in a room in the castle. I'd told her it was fine, and she didn't need my permission to run the day-to-day operations. She'd said *that* was fine, but she was going to run things by me regardless.

Once we got to Tee's room, Raiden kissed me long and hard, probably trying to tempt me back to the queen's quarters with him. He was hard to resist but I wanted to spend every second with Tee. After this, she was going to live with Kai. A small pain stabbed my heart—but not because I was afraid for her. Kai was all the protection she could ever need. It was pure selfishness on my part—I was going to miss her.

A bottle of champagne and fresh orange juice sat on her dresser. I popped the cork and poured us a mimosa.

She burst out of the bathroom wearing a towel on her head and one wrapped around her chest, ready to spend the next five hours getting herself ready for her wedding.

———

WHILE RAIDEN and I'd been gone, outside the many gardens had continued to bloom with life. Plots of colorful flowers fragranced the air. Huge willows with draping limbs and Japanese cherry trees blanketed in pink blossoms shaded the path to the altar. The mist from the majestic waterfall billowed. Rainbows shimmered in the air.

I almost expected a unicorn to walk out of the trees and poop glitter everywhere. Nothing could surprise me at that point.

As a harpist began to play, I looked down at Tee. Fear and excitement shined in her brown eyes. She looked like a princess on top of a cake, adorned in real diamonds and a puffy white dress with a laced corset bodice. Her curly hair was piled on top of her head with tight spirals dangling around her face and down her back. She was breathtaking as she clutched her bouquet of magenta roses.

With my spray of baby-pink roses in one hand, I held out my free elbow.

My tiny best friend, larger than life, grabbed it. "I love you."

"Ditto," I answered.

Sid, wearing a collar decorated in pink crystals with his toenails painted to match, led the way. Clasped arm in arm, we walked to where Kai waited patiently in front of a trellis coiled with greenery and draping strawberries.

Tears stung my eyes, but I sniffed, trying to keep them from falling.

Tee jabbed me hard with her sharp elbow. "Don't ruin my wedding," she said under her breath.

I wouldn't dare.

"So, you pregnant yet?" she asked.

"What? No!" I whispered. "Are you *trying* to tick me off?" I jabbed her back while laughing quietly.

She glanced up and blinked innocently. "You think I'm scared of you?"

"I'm pretty sure you're the only one who's not," I mumbled as I looked at the seated crowd and remembered the expressions on their faces the other night.

Her grin spread, crinkling her round brown eyes until they almost disappeared. "That's right. And don't forget it. So no crying. Got it?"

I heard her sniff when she finally saw her groom. His red hair, shaved on the sides, was pulled back off his handsome face. He was dressed in a tux with a chainmail vest and a golden tie that matched his eyes. If he was at all uncomfortable during our human tradition, it didn't show.

The mixture of humans and giants as guests made my heart hopeful. It was a start.

I stepped up next to Kai and presented his bride. There was no need for me to tell him to take care of her—he'd promised.

Leaning down, I hugged the best person I'd ever known.

She smelled like sugar, sunshine, and happiness. "Be nice to him."

"Don't worry, I'll keep him in line," she said as she stepped up next to Kai. Between the extra five inches her hair gave her and the four-inch heels, she was still almost a foot and a half shorter than him.

A lump formed in my throat as I took my place next to her, with Raiden standing next to Kai. For fear of what Tee would do to me if I sullied her moment, I had to bite the inside of my cheek hard enough to taste blood to keep from bawling.

After the ceremony, she made all the single ladies line up for the bouquet toss. Thankfully, I got to sit that one out.

She turned around and wound up her throw. Kevin, holding a plate piled with food, walked behind the group.

Tee tossed the flowers with every ounce of muscle she had.

The bouquet arched high in the air, pink petals flying in its wake. My brother dropped his plate of food just in time to catch whatever was diving at his head.

His eyes burst open with shock, horror, and surprise as every eligible woman turned and stared at him. Embarrassment, the color of the flowers he'd been holding, flushed up his neck to his face and the tips of his ears.

I caught my parents' eyes as I bent over laughing, Raiden holding me steady so I wouldn't fall.

Poppy walked over and took the flowers out of Kevin's hands. "Thank you," she said, before she kissed his cheek.

Was there another wedding in our future? I couldn't have picked someone better for him.

I swallowed hard, having a difficult time containing all of the emotions swirling inside of me. At one time, I'd believed tears to be a weakness, but now I realized those emotions I'd tried most of my life to deny were actually strength.

Everything I'd been through had been worth it in the end. Something, perhaps more encompassing than just love, filled my chest. The notion that we might all live happily ever after finally seemed possible.

THE END!!!

THANK you for reading *Crimson Jewel*. If you enjoyed it, please leave a review. You have no idea how much authors appreciate it!!!

# ALEX GORDON
## FOLLOW ME ON SOCIAL MEDIA

Alexgordonauthor.com

TikTok—@alexgordonauthor

Instagram—@alexgordonauthor

Facebook—Alex Gordon

Goodreads—A. Gordon

Amazon—A. Gordon

# ACKNOWLEDGMENTS

First, thank you to my friends and family. You have no idea how much I appreciate your support. I'm blessed that not only do you buy my books, but you tell other people about them. Word of mouth is powerful marketing, and I love that you guys are loud.

Thank you to my Alpha/Beta readers (here's where I admit that most of them are my friends and family): Kara, Geri, Shannon, Alisha, Michaela, Melani, Loni, Megan, Heather, Bob, Laurie, Lacey, Tyler, Jeanie, Deb, and Dave. I know, I know—never use people who are close to you—tell me that *after* you get to know some of them. They're readers, they're brutal, and I love them for it!

And to my life-line (aka my critique partners) in this publishing chaos, Sherri, Christa, Lo, and Liz, thank you. Holy cow, we're an eclectic crew, but somehow we magically fit.

A big shout-out to Rachel Throp and Susan Marie Graham for the developmental edits. I hope I fixed all of the issues and controlled my strange fascination with eyebrows, stomping, and flaring nostrils. I can't help that I like a well-placed eyebrow.

Thank you to my editor Jessica McKelden—you're a beast. I mean the best. Seriously, you're both! I knew you were the one when you didn't go easy on my sample edit.

The only way to grow is to face the pain, and I learned so much from you that I can't wait to go back for more.

To my cover designer, Ivy, thank you for a cover that made me cry. I love, love, love it.

To Leraynne S., the incredible artist I found on Fiverr, you should know, I'm obsessed with all the character art you created, but Sid will always be my favorite. Thank you.

Thank you to my husband, Dave, for never doubting my abilities even when I do. You're a waving green flag of support and comfort—except when I'm driving. But what did I expect when I married a New Yorker?!

And finally, to all the readers willing to give a new author a shot, thank you. Your TBR is long and your time is precious, **thank you, thank you, thank you** for spending it with Bea, Sid, and the First-Born Sons.